ROWLEY FARMS

POTATOES, VODKA, ALMOND EXTRACT.

The
Reason
I Married
Him

USA TODAY BESTSELLING AUTHOR
MEGHAN QUINN

Prologue

WYATT

"You smell."

I glance up from the couch where I've left a permanent imprint of myself after claiming squatter's rights in my best friend's house for the past three weeks. Yup, three weeks, I have no shame. "No, I don't."

"Yes . . . you do." Laurel immaturely holds her shirt over her nose. "Really bad."

"Fuck off. I smell fine."

"Do you?" she asks. "You're nose blind, completely oblivious to the smell surrounding you."

"That's not a thing."

"Yes, it is," she says as she holds her phone out to me, flashing the screen of a recent Google search. "It's also known as olfactory fatigue, where you get used to your own odor. It decreases the perception of scents around you, leading to you being perfectly peachy in your musk while the people allowing you to stay on their couch choke to death."

I lift up on my elbow and stare at my one true best friend I've known since grade school. "You're being rude during my time of sorrow."

"For God's sake," she says, tossing her arms up in defeat. "Wyatt, you know I feel bad for you. Cadance leaving you the night before your wedding will leave a permanent scar on your heart, and I've told you time and time again to please stay with me as long as you want. But, dude, you have to fucking shower. You have to scrub the armpits." She mimics scrubbing her underarms. "And all the important hot spot crevices."

"Those crevices aren't in use at the moment," I say.

"Exactly my point. Which means they're festering."

I wince in disgust. "Don't say my crevices are festering. They're not festering."

"You have not bathed in a week. The festering has reached new levels of fester. Levels of mold growth and, once the mold can't fester anymore, it festers into new mold growth, which then starts to fester. It's a vicious cycle." She motions over my body. "There's so much festering that I'm truly afraid critters from the streets will think your crevices are holes they can start burrowing into as homes for winter."

My eyes narrow. "That's a little dramatic, don't you think?"

"Not one bit, not when I saw a raccoon sniffing around here the other day. What you think is dramatic will be a reality pretty soon if you don't shower. Now get up so I can remove your couch sheets, burn them, and add new ones while you shower. And you need to wash, rinse, and repeat at least three times to get the skunk off you."

"It's not fucking skunk," I say as I stand from the couch, feeling slightly weak from lack of nutrients and fresh air. Huh, maybe Laurel has a minor point. I won't tell her that, though.

"Dear God, the couch has an imprint," she says as she slips on a mask and rubber gloves.

"Is that necessary?" I ask her.

She nods. "If I had a hazmat suit, I'd be putting that on as well, but I'll work with what I have." She motions for me to go shower. "Everything is set up for you in the bathroom, even fresh clothes and a warm towel. Now go."

Grumbling, I move through her bungalow-style house made for one lady—and not her annoyingly heartbroken best friend— into the vintage bathroom with the salmon and powder-blue tiles. She claims the tiles are a part of history. I say they could easily be removed and replaced with a fresher design that doesn't make her seem like she's a grandma hanging on to her youth.

I push back the frilly white shower curtain and turn on the water since it takes at least two minutes to warm. Then I turn around and look at myself in the mirror.

Whoa. Yikes.

Grown-out beard. Dark circles under my eyes. And is that . . .

I lean closer to get a better look.

Yup.

That is a melted chocolate chip on my face. I rub my index finger over the mark and bring it to my nose for a sniff. Yep. A melted chocolate chip. After all the festering and mold talk, I was nervous there for a moment that I'd sprouted something of the fungal descent.

I reach behind my head and pull my shirt up and over, only to drop the fabric to the mini-square-tiled floor. When I look at my chest in the mirror, I cringe. Sure, I've been here for three weeks, but that's after spending three weeks alone in my apartment doing nothing but the bare minimum for my job—i.e., answering emails and casually making my way through some edits of a manuscript releasing next year. But the fact that I can already see my hard-earned workouts fading is an indication that maybe Laurel is right . . .

I lift my arm, and just for the hell of it, I give my armpit a sniff, only to be slapped in the face by a bag of moldy onions.

"Mother of . . . fuck," I say while I snort air out of my nose, attempting to reverse the smell I just inhaled.

Okay, yeah, Laurel was right. I needed to be sprung from that couch probably a few days ago. Thank God she had the courage to do it today. Who knows what two more days on the couch would have brought.

Possibly a mushing between the toes . . .

Now, there's something to brag about.

I strip the rest of the way then step into the slightly chilly water, but my body needs soap, and it needs soap now. As I move through the process of washing off the stink, I consider how I got into this position in the first place.

There's truly only one reason . . .

Cadance Clearwater, that's how.

Heiress to Clearwater Coffee—the brand that no one has ever heard of, but Cadance swears is the best coffee on the market. Just a little spoiler alert, it is not.

We met on a windy day in Silicon Valley. It was at a local coffee shop, no less, where she was attempting to sell Clearwater Coffee to the store manager. I was working on my latest thriller about a doctor who helped a husband and wife get pregnant only to use the cord blood of the baby to save the life of their current living but very sickly child—a bestseller, if you're wondering. I was brought out of the moment when I caught her fumbling with her bag of coffee.

She stumbled over her words.

Her bag fell out of her hands.

And the coffee beans spilled all over the floor.

It was cringe-worthy for everyone around.

The store manager was uninterested, and when he dismissed her, she pointed her shaky finger at him and told him he was making a big mistake.

I liked her tenacity.

I found it . . . endearing and ended up helping her pick up her spilled coffee beans.

She said it was love at first sight for her.

For me, I thought she was hot, but love wasn't even a distant thought.

Like, not even close.

But . . . because I thought she was hot, I asked her out on a date.

One date turned into two, then three . . . then four. And on the fourth date, she invited me into her apartment and seduced me. Yup. She was all over me.

She stripped me out of my clothes and had me right there on the floor of her kitchen. Shocked and pleasantly surprised, you could imagine that I was all for it.

The next morning—because obviously, I spent the night— she made me a cup of Clearwater Coffee and then sat naked on my lap. Everything about it was like living out a wet dream . . . well, not everything.

There she was, tits bouncing in my face, rocking over my erection as I brought the cup of coffee up to my mouth. The smell was . . . heinous.

But coffee can be sour sometimes, so I took a sip, and that was when the white light of death flashed before my eyes.

I felt the skin on my face peel back.

My teeth pushed forward, out of my mouth, like a horse reaching for a carrot.

And my armpit hairs twisted in a spiral, indicating the Grim Reaper was on his way, my name on a tombstone being carefully carried in his skeletal hands.

It was official. With one sip, Clearwater Coffee was the most disgusting coffee to ever pass my lips.

Some might classify it as sludge.

I put it under the umbrella of a way to poison your enemies, grow a mustache in under thirty minutes, and get rid of any sinus infection with one sniff.

A dangerous and hazardous artifact to society.

And you must be thinking, who put you in charge of ranking coffee? Let me tell you, being the avid coffee drinker and frequenter of small business coffee shops, I'm well versed in the multitude of coffee flavors. Clearwater Coffee is like roadkill in liquid form.

One sip was all it took for me to make my assessment. This

was not something I planned on drinking ever again. It was evident by the way I gagged, shoved her off my lap, and ran to the sink, where I directed my mouth under the faucet and rinsed it out, nearly drowning myself.

Even after that, it took exactly thirty-two hours and eleven minutes for my tongue to forgive me and allow me to taste other things again.

You can imagine how she took that response, though.

She didn't talk to me for a month.

What can I say? Clearwater Coffee is made from tar, and I'm not good at faking it.

I considered it a minor loss. I wasn't too hurt because, let's be honest, I got laid.

I went on with my daily life, writing, researching, and looking up creepy facts on the Internet that could borderline get me thrown in jail.

Until one day, at the same coffee shop I met Cadance before, she ran into me again. Thankfully, when she confronted me, I was drinking tea and told her I was sorry about the coffee gagging. I told her I wasn't much of a coffee drinker, so I wasn't used to such a rich coffee flavor. Lies . . . so many lies, but like I said, she was hot. And besides the coffee, I'd had a good night with her.

To my surprise, she giggled, flipped her hair over her shoulder, and said it was all right.

I invited her to sit with me.

And then from there, we dated.

Fell in love.

I proposed.

She said yes.

And we planned a wedding.

I was the happiest I had ever been, ready to make a life with this woman—coffee-free, which was a sacrifice I was willing to make—until the night before our wedding.

I know what you're wondering. Did she walk in on me drinking coffee, become thoroughly insulted, and call off the wedding? Hell, I wish. I think that would have made the blow much easier to accept.

Nope. Instead, she came up to me wearing her veil, tears streaming down her face and a wobbly lip holding back her sobs. At first, I thought something really wrong had happened, like one of her parents was sick.

Maybe the coffee wasn't delivered for the wedding guests who were attending—the poor guests had no idea what was coming for them.

But, no.

She was upset that she'd let our relationship go this long—*to the point of getting married*—because she didn't love me like she thought she should.

Yup.

She didn't love me.

That was it. Plain and simple. I had love in the tank for her, but she was running on empty for me.

Do I wish she had told me sooner? Yeah.

Do I wonder where I went wrong?

Every fucking minute of every day since she called off the wedding.

She offered no explanation, no reasoning why she fell out of love with me. She just did, and that was that. The wedding was called off, the food was donated to food banks, the wedding gifts were returned, and the flowers were given to local funeral homes for the recently deceased. It seemed fitting since my relationship was as dead as the people in the morgue.

I rinse the rest of my body, still feeling the stab I took to the heart that night. Why did she wait so long to tell me? Why couldn't she have said no when I proposed? At least if she said no to that, I could have squashed the hopes I had of starting a family.

But nooooooo, she had to wait until the night before the wedding.

Thank God we hadn't planned a honeymoon because she'd

had a big coffee conference to attend. We were going to decide on something after that.

Good luck at your conference, Cadance. Your coffee tastes like burnt tires that ran through a pile of fresh manure.

I turn off the shower and whip open the curtain. I grab my dusty-rose towel and quickly dry myself before I move in front of the mirror, only to stare at myself again.

Sad.

Pathetic.

Defeated.

That's all I see.

My penis is even sad. Look at it all drooped and depressed. I can't remember the last time his spirits were lifted—if you know what I mean. *Actually, I can. It was a week and a half before the wedding. Yup. She hadn't loved me, but she'd loved my dick. Yay.*

I drag my hand over my face.

The only good thing about any of this? I don't have a book due for a while because I decided to spend a few months off enjoying married life.

Now those few months off will be spent on my best friend's couch, where I'll wallow in pain.

I finish getting dressed, brush my teeth, and don't even bother with my hair before I walk out of the bathroom, smelling a whole lot better.

"Wow, you look like you scrubbed off a film of disgust." Laurel leans in and tentatively sniffs. "Oh, lovely, you used my soap. Much better."

"I was tempted to use your deodorant as well but opted for mine instead."

"The small miracles are really pulling this day together," she replies as I take a seat back on the couch.

"So . . ." She rocks on her heels. "You're just going to go back to sitting there?"

"Do you want me to do something else?" I look up at her. "Do you want me to leave?"

She shakes her head. The box braids she just had done look

incredible on her, and the deep violet adds nice dimension. "No, but I do have to talk to you about a few things and thought that a change of scenery might be nice, like the back patio."

"Are you saying I need some fresh air?"

"Yes . . . yes, I am."

I sigh heavily but follow my friend out to the patio where she has two glasses of lemonade set up as well as a plate of chocolate chip cookies.

"You spoil me," I say as I take a seat and pop one whole cookie in my mouth.

Her eyes watch my puffed-out cheeks handle the large cookie before she takes a seat. "Maybe next time, eat it in bites."

"Where's the fun in that?" I say around a mouthful of cookie.

"The fun is in not choking." She sips her lemonade. "Now, like I said, I want to talk to you about a few important things."

"Okay," I drag out. "Why does it seem like you're about to deliver bad news?"

"Just listen."

Oh boy, that can't be good.

I grab another cookie, but I take a bite like she asked.

"First things first. I have a date tonight."

"You do?" I ask, looking surprised. I didn't think Laurel was into dating at the moment. Then again, she said that about four weeks ago when I asked her why she wasn't bringing a date to the wedding. Things could have changed since then.

"Yes, I actually met her at the bookstore when I was inquiring about your books and why they didn't have them in stock."

That's Laurel for you. She's my number one fan and will travel up and down the Pacific Coast Highway, making sure every bookstore keeps my books in stock.

"Did she tell you why?"

Laurel smirks. "Because you're far too popular to keep on the shelves." That brings a smug smile to my face. "We bonded over *Baby for a Baby*, and when she told me she liked my tattoo while leaning in close and touching it, I knew I was good to ask her out."

"The wrist tattoo?" I ask. She got the tattoo several years ago after she came out to her family. She had a few birds tattooed on her wrist where she used to cut herself during her darkest times of depression. The scars were covered up with freedom.

She nods. "Yes. I told her I got it when I came out to my family, and that's when she smiled and moved her finger over it. Anyway, she's really pretty and super smart. I'm excited, but I don't want you to think I'm leaving you in your time of need."

I shake my head. "Live your life, Laurel. And if you need me to leave, I can leave."

"That's not necessary. I have zero plans to bring her back to my place or do anything like that. Just getting to know her is all, but I didn't want you to think I'm rubbing it in your face."

"Nah, I'm happy for you." I take another bite of my cookie. "Don't let my shit love life distract you from living yours."

"Cool." She sets her glass down. "Now that we got the easy part over, I have something more serious to talk to you about."

"What?" I ask.

"Well, when I was running errands earlier today, I went to pick up your mail for you, and this came in." She pulls an envelope out of nowhere and hands it to me.

"What is it?" I ask, staring down at it.

"I think it's the title to that farm your brother left you."

"Oh." My brows crease together. "Yeah, I completely forgot about this. Cassidy passed away a few months ago. I wonder why this is arriving all of a sudden. Not that I really care about it."

"Probably took the family lawyer some time to wrap everything up."

I scratch the back of my neck, looking down at the envelope. "I still don't know why Clarke made me a beneficiary should his wife pass away. What the fuck am I supposed to do with half a farm? Can't I just give it over to Cassidy's family?"

Laurel, who is currently a lawyer—a good friend to have—says, "You could give it to them. You could make them purchase it from you. It's really up to you as to what you want to do with it."

"I'm not going to make them purchase it. I doubt they have the money. I don't need their money, and I don't need their farm. The whole thing really is an inconvenience."

"Do you know who owns the other half?" Laurel asks.

"There's Ryland, Aubree, and Hattie. Those were Cassidy's siblings. I met them around Clarke and Cassidy's wedding. My guess is that one of them is taking care of it. I'm pretty sure, from what my parents told me, that Ryland is taking care of MacKenzie, my niece. So that leaves Aubree and Hattie." Sadly, I didn't spend much time with MacKenzie, so even though she's my niece, she's almost a stranger. As are Cassidy's siblings. I'm not particularly proud of that, but our lives never naturally intersected, and it was harder to initiate contact once we lost Clarke. The more time passed without me contacting Cassidy, the worse I felt.

Laurel twists her lips to the side, thinking.

"Why do you have that contemplative look on your face?"

She lets out a heavy sigh and turns toward me. "Because I also ran into someone at the store when I got your mail. Someone you can't stand."

"Was it Cadance?" I ask, feeling my heart twist in my chest. "Had her roots grown out?" One can only hope for the petty things in life.

Laurel shakes her head. "No . . . worse. I ran into Wallace."

I feel my entire body go cold.

Not fucking Wallace.

Wallace is my cousin. He's the bane of my existence. A fucking asshole who doesn't know anything about loyalty and family. Then again, do I? My brother died, and I didn't do much to help Cassidy, but we're not going to get into that right now.

This is about Wallace. And Wallace is the type of guy that when you look him in the eyes, you wonder if his irises are actually yellow or if they're playing a trick on you.

He's vile.

He's calculated.

He's a non-fiction descendant of Scott Farkus from *The Christmas Story.*

He has hated me ever since we were teenagers when I grew a foot in middle school, and he didn't.

"What the fuck did he want?" I ask.

"Nothing, but he did make a comment that made my skin crawl."

"What was it?" I ask. "Did he say something gross about girl-on-girl action? I have no problem throwing a log at him next time I see him. Lord knows he wouldn't be able to lift it off himself."

She sets her hand on the table and carefully looks me in the eyes. "He mentioned how he's closer than you at claiming the cabin now."

Fuck.

Not . . . not the cabin.

I sit taller in my seat as anger races through my body. "He fucking said that to you?"

"He did."

And Farkus . . . I mean Wallace just crossed a line.

"That's fucking poor taste, not to mention no one's business outside of the family. And sure, I know I've told you everything because I wanted you to look at Grandfather's will, but Jesus fuck, why would he say that to you?"

"Probably because he knew I would tell you."

I squeeze my lips together, anger bristling inside me as I consider the idea of Wallace taking possession of the family cabin.

The sacred, beautiful A-frame cabin that was the sole basis of happiness during my childhood. He'd renovate it until it resembled nothing of what it's like now. He'd erase all of the memories we created there. I know this because he's said it. He never got along with Grandfather, nor did Wallace appreciate the outdoors or the community where the cabin is located. His parents rarely took him up there, and when they did, Wallace would complain the entire time about the ponderosa pines blocking the sun and the weird, kitschy town not having good food.

Unfortunately, when Grandfather passed last year, he stated in his will that the first to get married among the grandkids would take possession. Since I was engaged, I knew that would be me. And now with Cadance gone, Wallace is the only other grandchild in a relationship . . . meaning, if he's already thinking about the cabin, there's no doubt in my mind he'll propose out of spite.

"Fuck," I say while pulling on the back of my neck. "He's going to take it, isn't he?"

"Seems like it," Laurel says. "Unless . . ."

"Unless what?" I ask.

"You get married."

I sardonically chuckle. "Think we missed the boat on that one."

"I was thinking more like a business transaction."

I raise one brow as I glance in her direction. "Are you saying I marry you? Because you know I would in a heartbeat. The only problem is you don't like the penis, and everyone knows that. Pretty sure Wallace would call fraud on us and claim the cabin."

"Not talking about me. I was thinking maybe . . . maybe one of Cassidy's sisters."

I blink.

I stare.

Laughter bubbles up out of me. "You can't be serious."

"I'm very serious," she says. "It would work out perfectly. You can make a trade, the farmland for their hand in marriage."

"Laurel." I reach across the table and take her hand in mine. "You are my favorite person in the world, and we promised each other to always be honest, especially when one is showing signs of insanity. Well, this is one of those moments. You're insane."

"Am I, though?" she asks. "I was going over the will, and you technically only have to be married for a year. You strike up an agreement with one of the sisters—pending one of them is single —offer them the farmland for free in exchange for one year of marriage so you can secure the cabin in your name, make sure all of the paperwork has gone through, and then divorce. What's a year of someone's time, really?"

"Uh, a fucking year. Twelve months. Three hundred—"

"I'm well aware of how many days are in a year," Laurel says. "Think about it, Wyatt. You don't care about that land, and something tells me they do. And I'm going to guess they'll care a whole lot more if you show up and try to take control of the portion that's yours."

"Wow." I cross my arms over my chest. "Law school has truly made you diabolical."

She chuckles. "It's part of my job to look at every angle, and this is your best bet. You said you want that cabin. You even told me once that you weren't sure if you loved Cadance or the cabin more. Are you really going to give it up to Wallace?" She leans in closer and says, "He flicked his rat tail at me."

I feel my nostrils flare. "Fucking disgusting."

"I wanted to snip it right off."

"I've spent many hours awake at night envisioning how it would feel to cut it myself."

"So are you going to let him take the cabin and destroy the thing that matters the most to you? Or will you continue to sleep on my couch and wallow about the love you lost?"

"When you put it like that . . ."

She brings her glass of lemonade to her lips. "Want me to help you pack? Possibly plan out the wedding? Write up a prenup? When you divorce, she takes all of the land and you take the cabin? I'm at your disposal. You just tell me what you need."

"This is insane," I say. "I have to think about it."

"Don't think about it too long. Wallace is one ring purchase away from taking the cabin right from your grasp."

Chapter One

AUBREE

"No, stop. Stop hitting him. Please, Dad. Please stop hitting him," I cry out, catching the grateful look on Ryland's face when our dad pauses for a moment and then slowly turns his head toward me.

"Do you want me to hit you instead?" The evil in his eyes should scare me at this point, but it doesn't. It just reminds me of how dead I am inside.

"Don't touch her," Ryland shouts and charges toward my dad, but he's smacked down before he can even get close.

Ryland lies on the floor. *Is he unconscious?* As Dad walks toward me, I move back toward the corner of the house, my legs quaking under me. With every step, where he draws closer and closer, my stomach churns.

Where's Cassidy?

She would end this.

She always ends this.

When I bump into the wall, I squeeze my eyes shut, ready for his hand. When I don't feel it, I look up at his maniacal smile.

"You're a worthless bitch. You offer nothing to this family

other than another mouth to feed." He shakes his head. "Maybe I should just end you. No one will *ever* want you." His muttered words of, "Ugly bitch," finish his tirade. *His standard.*

And then with that, he turns back to Ryland, raises his fist and Ryland's ear-piercing scream echoes through the house . . .

I shoot up from where my head is resting on my desk and look around my small office on the farm.

Sweat coats the back of my neck.

My heart beats wildly in my chest.

And tears are on the precipice of falling over as my throat grows tight from the memory still reverberating through me. *It feels so real.*

Like it was yesterday.

I pat down my face, taking a few deep breaths to calm myself from the terrible nightmare.

How did I even fall asleep?

Oh, I know. From stressing over the fate of the farm.

Of Cassidy's farm.

Clearing my throat, I sit taller and wake up my computer. It lights up and brings me back into the mess that is the Excel sheet in in front of me.

"What is going on?" I mutter as I stare at my computer, trying to figure out why income is down when we've had the best tourist season to date.

I lean back in my chair and rub my hand over my forehead after staring at my computer for over an hour with no solution in sight. I've gone over production—we made nearly twice the number of bottles of almond vodka and almond extract than ever. We've increased our harvesting. We've even added bees to the farm for honey production so we can start infusing almonds with honey.

Yet here we are, not pulling in as much as we were last year.

Nothing has changed . . . other than I'm the one in charge now. And *that* does nothing for my self-confidence.

Needing to get out of the tiny office at the edge of the farm, I stand from the chair, shut the computer, and stretch my hands above my head just as Parson, my head harvester, walks into the office.

He removes his grungy, sweat-soaked hat and smiles at me. "Hey, Aubree, how are you?"

Clarke hired Parson. They knew each other through the volunteering they used to do throughout college. Parson majored in horticulture and has been a valuable asset to the farm. A hard worker, lover of model trains, and very much keeps to himself, never to be seen with a significant other.

"Doing okay," I say, not wanting to lay down my frustration with him or talk about the dream I just had. "What's going on? Are you done for the day?"

"Yes, I was coming in to let you know everything is looking good on our end and was wondering if I could take Friday off. There's a convention over in San Francisco that I've been tinkering with going to. Since there isn't much going on for the rest of the week, I thought it could be an opportunity."

"Of course," I say. "Take a long weekend. Enjoy yourself. Let the ladies know as well."

The ladies, as in Aggie and Esther. Sisters with a work ethic stronger than anyone I've ever met. They are operations managers. Aggie takes care of the vodka, and Esther takes care of the extract. They are a godsend, and the reason I was able to take care of the farm and The Almond Store at the same time.

The Almond Store is our flagship retailer in the middle of town, where we sell our products and everything you could think of, including Cassidy's famous almond cherry cookies. When Cassidy passed, she left me responsible for the shop and the farm. While I was busy in the shop, Aggie and Esther were there for me, aiding me with everything I needed. Now that Hattie has taken over The Almond Store, I can focus solely on the farm.

"Great. Thank you. Doubt they'll take the time off."

"Tell them it's a requirement," I say with a wink. "Have fun at your convention, Parson." Smirking, I ask, "Does it have anything to do with model trains?"

He smiles back. "Perhaps."

"Are you going to take Rodney with you?" Rodney is the owner of the model railroad museum in town.

"Was thinking about it," he says. "Rodney talks a lot, though, and sometimes I like to enjoy the calm and peace away from the ladies." He sticks his hands in his pockets. "Don't tell them I said that."

I chuckle. "Your secret is safe with me." I offer him a smile. "Well, have fun."

But he doesn't move. Instead, he studies me. The crinkles in the corner of his eyes deepen while the smile lines around his face fade. "You know, you've been acting strange the last couple of days. You haven't been out in the fields like normal. Is everything okay?"

"Yup." I try to smile brighter, even though it feels so incredibly fake.

"Are you sure? Because if something is wrong, we can help you."

"I appreciate that, Parson, but everything is great. Go enjoy your long weekend. And stop by The Almond Store on your way out of town. Tell Hattie I sent you to grab some cookies for your trip."

"That's awfully kind of you, Aubree. Thank you. Maybe those will keep Rodney quiet, at least for a little bit."

I wiggle my eyebrows. "That's the plan." I offer him a wave, and he steps out of the small shed—my office.

I recently made it feel homier by painting every inch of it white, including covering the mismatched floors with a washable rug—we're on a dusty farm after all. I also added a few black-and-white pictures of the farm—one including a family picture of Cassidy, Clarke, and MacKenzie—as well as a few plants. Not to mention, two chairs for any employees who need a second from the fields. With the in-window AC unit, it's pretty cool in here and offers a good break from the heat. One of the many upgrades I've made since taking over.

When I first realized I could shift all my focus to the farm, I sat down with the employees and asked them what changes they would like to see. Parson wanted an air-conditioned place to eat his lunch since he was eating in his car. Apparently, his niece yelled at him one day for idling his truck and causing unnecessary gas emissions. I chuckled because I feel like Mac would say that when she's older. She's headstrong.

Esther and Aggie wanted some updated equipment. It wasn't anything too expensive, just a few things like a new cart to drive around in and some updated iPads. That was an easy fix.

We also talked about what we could do to help bring in more income, and that was when we decided to go all in on the honeybees, which of course required a new hire. That new hire is Echo Alaska. She's a small-town girl from Texas who spent her whole life living on a honey farm. Recently, she decided to venture out and see what was outside her small town. Well . . . she found another small town. She's our beekeeper, and when she's not on our farm, she's driving around to different locations in the state to help with honeybee infestations. She collects the bees and brings them to the farm to increase our honey production. It's a smart business plan, and I hope it adds a new level to the farm.

And I hope it helps with the finances.

I just don't get it. We sold more but made less.

How?

I let out a shaky breath. Just thinking about it makes me feel nauseated, which means I need to get out of here before I lose my mind.

Before I start spiraling down a slippery slope of hatred and lies.

Lies my father burned into me growing up.

Not smart enough.

Will never amount to a thing.

Worthless.

Ugly bitch.

Not beautiful like my sisters . . .

No, not going there.

I pack my bag, slip it over my shoulder, and head out of the office. I lock up and turn toward the electric four-by-four I was able to find for a great deal and slide in just as I see Echo approach. As always, she's wearing her short overalls with a tank top and a straw hat. She's adorable.

"Are you leaving?" she asks.

"I was going to head back to my place. Why? Do you need something?"

"Uh, I just thought I'd have a conversation with you, but if you're on your way home, I won't bother you."

"You're never bothering me." I pat the seat next to me. "Take a seat, and I can drive you back to your car or wherever you need to go."

"Yeah, that would be great." She takes a seat and sets her backpack on her lap.

"So what's going on?"

"Well, this is sort of embarrassing and doesn't have anything to do with work, but I spoke to my mom last night, and she told me that I need to come back to Texas."

"Oh," I say. How does that not have to do with work? That completely disturbs my future business plans. "Is everything okay?"

"Yes. She's just, uh, a bit controlling." Echo swallows nervously. "I don't want to go back home. I like it here."

"Well, I'm glad. We like having you here, Echo."

She nods, and I drive down the dirt path toward the parking lot behind the barn.

"Thank you. One of my mom's arguments was that I don't have a life here. She said I have no friends, and all I do is talk to my bees."

"How would she know that?"

"I stupidly told her," Echo says as I round the bend and slow down as the barn comes closer. "Anyway, I told her that I did have friends, and that although the bees are my friends, I don't always hang out with them. I hang out with other people, and that's when I said I hang out with you and Hattie. Well, she's coming out here to visit, and I was hoping that maybe you could, I don't know, act like we're friends or something while she's here so she doesn't try to manipulate me to go back to Texas. I really don't want to go back there, Aubree. I have a bad history there, and I like it here in Almond Bay. It's new and fresh, and the people are nice. I know that's asking a lot, but do you think you could pretend when she's here?"

I pull up to her light blue Jeep Wrangler and put the four-by-four in park before turning toward her.

"How about this? We actually hang out, and then we don't have to pretend?"

Her brow creases. "You would do that? But you're my boss."

I chuckle. "That's okay. We're allowed to be friends, Echo. There's no rule when it comes to stuff like this. As long as we keep business separate, then we're fine."

"Okay." She nods. "Then, yeah, I would like that."

"I can invite Hattie too. I'm sure she would love to have some more friends in town other than her boyfriend and me."

Echo's smile grows wider. "Hattie is so sweet. I would love to get to know her better."

"Perfect. I'll set something up with her."

"Awesome. Thank you." She steps out onto the dirt and smiles at me. "Have a good night, Aubree."

"You too, Echo."

She takes off, and I continue toward my place, where I know I have a family dinner tonight with Ryland, Hattie, Hayes, and Mac. I believe it's Hattie's turn to cook, which means Hayes is probably cooking since Hattie has been known to disappoint in the kitchen.

I drive down the dirt road, taking in the beautiful sunset of bright orange, and let out a deep breath. Cassidy loved sunsets, especially out here on the farm. It was one of her favorite things. She would sit out back on a rocking chair, just staring at the colors and enjoying the wonders that nature can create. I've started to associate these sunsets with her, almost as if they're a sign from her, letting me know that even though she's no longer here, she's still with us. God, I miss her. Every day. Desperately.

I park behind my quaint guest house and grab my backpack.

21

Since I spent zero time out on the farm and in the fields today—something I love doing—I don't need a shower, so I head straight to the farmhouse.

When Cassidy was dying from breast cancer a few months ago, she told our brother, Ryland, that she wanted him to take guardianship of MacKenzie—Mac—her four-year-old daughter. Mac came with the very small two-bedroom, one-bath farmhouse, and they live there together. The guest house, located right next to the farmhouse, is where I live so I can help Ryland. Cassidy asked if I would be his support system, and I promised her I would. So even though my living conditions are not ideal, I would never complain, because there's a four-year-old girl in there who lost her mom and her dad and needs all the love she can get.

And then there's Hattie, the youngest. She was finishing school when Cassidy passed, but now that she's returned to Almond Bay and taken over The Almond Store, we've been able to spend more time together—necessary given the strain on our relationship during Cassidy's passing.

Now that everything seems to be at peace with my siblings, business is now at the top of my mind. *And not flourishing.*

It will be fine.

I'll figure it out.

Hayes's Rivian is in the driveway, meaning they're already here, probably cooking, so I jog up the front porch steps and open the squeaky screen door.

"Aunt Aubree!" Mac shouts as she comes barreling toward me as if she didn't see me this morning and coaxed half of my donut away.

"Hey, kiddo," I say as I hug her. "How was your day?"

"Neighhhhh!" she says as she pretends her favorite item on this earth, Chewy Charles the horse stuffy, licks my leg. "He's licking you. Isn't that funny?"

I smile down at Mac and her bouncy curls and round face—a face that resembles Cassidy so much that sometimes it's hard to look her in the eyes. "That is funny. Does he think I'm a salt lick or something?"

"Why would Chewy Charles need a salt lick, Aunt Aubree?" she asks, hands on her hips. "He's not a horse."

Uh, that's news to me.

"He's not?" I ask. "What's with the long neck, tail, and mane?"

"That's his disguise. He's actually a skunk dressed like a horse, so don't make him mad. He will skunk you."

I hold up my hands in surrender. "I'm sorry. I don't want to be skunked. Lick away, Chewy Charles."

"No, he doesn't think you taste good." She bolts away, only to jump into the air and fling her body onto the couch without any care as to whether she will break her back on the arm of the couch.

Ahh, to be that young.

She also does this thing that makes Ryland nearly throw up. She likes to jump up in the air and land on her knees as if her legs have no bones. It makes Ryland shiver every time.

It makes me laugh. I love my older brother, but as a middle child, sometimes it's nice to see your siblings squirm.

I head into the kitchen, where Hattie sits on the counter in the corner. Hayes is nowhere to be found, and Ryland leans against the fridge with a beer in his hand. He will only have a drink if there are other grown-ups present. Something I noticed a while ago. He's very protective of Mac and makes sure that she's taken care of at all times. Meaning if he's alone with her, he won't have a drink just in case he needs to drive.

"Hey," I say to them as I move toward the cup cabinet and grab one to fill it with water. "How's it going?"

"Good," Hattie says.

"Where's Hayes?" I ask.

"Out back grilling some kebabs."

God bless Hayes.

The funny thing is, a few months ago, there is no way in hell I ever would have said that. Hayes Farrow, world-renowned musician and America's heartthrob, was Ryland's best friend growing up, along with Abel. They were inseparable until their relationship fell apart one day. I won't get into it, but they stopped talking for years . . . I mean, years. It wasn't until a few months ago, when Hayes returned to Almond Bay around the same time Hattie did, that he came back into our lives. Long story short, they fell in love, and the anger and resentment was resolved. Now, we're one big, happy family.

Hayes has stepped up and takes his role in the family very seriously. He's great for Hattie, is there for Ryland whenever he needs it, and is quite the chef. Plus, Mac loves him. He truly completes our family.

"Is there pineapple on them?" I ask.

Hattie slowly nods. "Yup. Steak, pineapple, and green peppers."

My stomach growls at the thought of that.

"He's also roasting corn, and he brought cut-up watermelon," Ryland says before lifting his beer to his lips.

"How did we get so lucky?" I ask.

Hattie raises her hand. "Me, that's how. And you're welcome. I accept gifts if you want to show me your gratitude."

"I'm pretty sure Hayes is your gift. Be happy with that," I say.

"I am," Hattie says with a blush to her cheeks.

Are you wondering if I'm jealous that my little sister has found love and beams with happiness?

The answer would be no . . . and yes.

Maybe a little more yes than no.

Like . . . eighty percent yes, twenty percent no.

I had a serious relationship a few years ago. His name was Matt—and no, not the same Matt who Hattie dated, who turned out to be the biggest douche in the world. Well, this Matt—we will call him Original Matt—did turn out to be a douche, but in a different way. Secondary Matt—Hattie's Matt—told her she was boring and broke up with her. Original Matt, well, he didn't want to live in Almond Bay and told me I wouldn't be living my life if I stayed in one place. We broke up because I was invested in helping Cassidy, and he didn't want to be with someone who farmed potatoes.

Simple as that.

I wasn't good enough for him to stay in a small town. His dreams were bigger than mine. *I just can't see myself ever feeling settled in a place with so little upward trajectory, Aubree. You're farming potatoes, for God's sake. Small-town life just isn't enough for me.*

I try not to think about it too much—I'm barely hanging on as it is.

Ever since that relationship went up in flames, it's been pretty . . . dry here.

Very dry.

Like years.

Hence the eighty percent jealousy. I'm jealous of the way Hayes can walk in the room and make Hattie's cheeks blush. That blush says everything.

But the twenty percent that's not jealous? Well, that's because I don't think I could handle anything or anyone other than myself and the responsibilities that fall under my command right now.

"So is he going to propose soon?" Ryland asks. "Because he hasn't asked me for permission yet."

Hattie's cheeks turn a deeper shade of red. "I think we're just, you know, content with where we are right now."

Why don't I believe that?

Maybe because I've seen my sister in a relationship before, and she was never this infatuated. If you look up the definition of head over heels in love, Hattie's picture would come up. From the googly eyes to the absentmindedness to the giddy behavior— she's a fool in love, and it's great to see.

I take a seat at the table right next to the kitchen. "Do you want to get married?"

"Yes," she answers. "I love him, and no one will ever come close to stealing my heart like he has, but I don't want to scare him either."

"Why would you think getting married would scare him?"

I ask.

Anyone on the outside looking in wouldn't think Hayes could be scared. He's solid and set in his ways. He looks at Hattie as if she's part of every aspect of his future.

"I don't know." Hattie shrugs. "Sometimes it seems too good to be true, and I don't want to . . . I don't know, mess it up."

I can feel that. Things were good with Original Matt . . . until they weren't.

"He won't be scared," Ryland says. "He's very much infatuated. Also, if he's scared, he deals with me."

And there it is, our overprotective brother. He's been like that ever since I can remember.

Our mom died of breast cancer when we were young. Our dad was left with four kids, and well, he wasn't happy about it. He spent most of his nights drinking in front of the television while Ryland and Cassidy tried to hold the household together. Cassidy was mainly in charge because Ryland played baseball most of the time. But he protected his three younger sisters when he wasn't playing baseball.

"I don't think you're going to have to put your big brother foot down," Hattie says just as Hayes walks into the house holding two plates, one full of roasted corn and the other stacked with kebabs.

When we fall silent, he glances around us and asks, "Were you talking about me?"

"No," Hattie says as both Ryland and I say, "Yes."

He brings the plates to the table, and my mouth waters as I take in the charred kebabs. Seriously, this man.

Where can I find a Hayes Farrow? Not that I'm looking, but if one happened to fall into my lap, I wouldn't be mad about it.

"Glad to see my girlfriend is the one lying to me."

"Hey, how do you know I'm lying? They could be lying." Hattie points at me and Ryland.

"Are they?" Hayes lifts an eyebrow, and Hattie cowers.

"No, but I was trying to spare your feelings."

"Uh-huh, and what were you talking about?"

"Nothing," Hattie says quickly while attempting to give us a subtle evil eye.

"About marriage," Mac says, bouncing into the kitchen. "Are you going to marry Aunt Hattie?"

Well, leave it to the four-year-old to tell it like it is.

I glance over at Hattie, who is now bright red.

Hayes scoops up Mac and says, "Probably."

"Probably? Why just probably?" Mac asks.

"Well, you see, she does this thing that I'm not sure that I like yet, and I need to figure out if I want to spend the rest of my life dealing with this thing that she does."

"What does she do?" Mac asks in almost a whisper.

I lean in, as do Hattie and Ryland, wanting to hear the answer.

"I don't think I should tell you. It's kind of gross."

"What gross thing do I do?" Hattie asks, offended.

A subtle grin spreads over Hayes's lips as he says, "She drinks pickle juice straight from the jar."

"Ewwwwww," Mac says as she looks over at Hattie. "Why don't you use a cup?"

That makes us all laugh because I'm pretty sure that's not the offense Hayes was talking about. Then again, Mac loves pickles as well, so drinking pickle juice wouldn't faze her.

"Go to the bathroom and wash your hands, Mac," Ryland says. "Dinner is on the table."

"Okay," Mac says. Hayes releases her, and she takes off toward the bathroom.

That's when Hayes eyes all of us. "Marriage, that's what you're talking about?"

Hattie points at both me and Ryland and says, "They were, not me. I was just sitting here telling them that I love you."

Hayes smirks and walks over to Hattie. He places his hand on her thigh and lightly kisses her. "Nothing is going to happen until I talk to your brother."

"You know, some might say that's a misogynistic, old-school conversation that takes the power out of the woman's hands.

Why does she need her brother's permission to get married?" I ask, folding my arms across my chest.

"Glad to see you're your typical curmudgeon self today, Aubree," Hayes says before walking over to the fridge and pulling out the watermelon.

"I wouldn't say that's being a curmudgeon. I would say it's sticking up for all women. We can make our own decisions."

"You can," Hayes counters. "Just because her brother says yes doesn't mean Hattie will say yes."

Hattie sticks her finger in the air and says, "Uh, for the record, I would say yes."

Hayes glances over his shoulder. "Good to know."

"Well, don't you think you should talk to both me and Ryland?" I ask. "He might be the older brother, but I'm the cranky witch of a sister who can make your life a living hell if I don't approve."

Hayes chuckles. "Noted to include you . . . if that conversation ever comes up."

Mac runs into the room and shouts, "Uncle Ry Ry, watch this." She leaps into the air and lands on her knees before doing a tuck and roll right into one of the dining room chairs.

"Jesus Christ," Ryland says as he walks over to her. "Are you okay?"

"Wasn't that cool?" Mac asks, tangled in one of the chair legs.

"Yup, the coolest," Ryland replies, his voice full of sarcasm. "Now, let's sit down and get you a plate of food."

Together, we move around, getting drinks for everyone and making sure Mac is situated with food. When everything is set, the grown-ups take a seat and start digging in.

"Getting ready for the school year?" Hayes asks Ryland. Ryland is a math teacher at the local high school, where he's also the varsity baseball coach. Last season, their team took second in the league, and he wasn't happy about it. He blamed himself because he hadn't found a balance yet between his responsibilities of being a math teacher, the head varsity baseball coach, and taking care of Mac. I think he'll get the hang of it soon, though.

Right now, Mac still goes to "school"—more like day care for half the day—during the summer, but with the new school year approaching, she'll be going to preschool, which I know will help Ryland out a lot more.

"I mean, not much to prepare," he says.

"Are you telling me you don't decorate your classroom?" Hayes asks.

Ryland raises a brow. "Does it look like I'm the type of guy who decorates a classroom? I slept on a couch for months. Pretty sure I'm not about to put up bulletin boards in my classroom."

I felt bad when he was sleeping on the couch, but he refused to sleep in Cassidy's room. That was until Hattie thoughtfully cleared it out and redecorated for him.

"Maybe you should," Hattie says. "Might make math more fun."

"I don't need decorations in my classroom to make math fun. Math is fun on its own."

"To whom?" Hattie asks with a comical look of disgust on her face.

"People," Ryland replies, knowing none of us at this table find math fun besides him.

"Well, if you need anything for the classroom, let me know," Hayes says. "I can grab you anything you need."

"Oooo," I say while I sprinkle cotija cheese on my corn. "Maybe we should go into his classroom and give it a makeover."

"No," Ryland says. "My students will think I've lost my mind. They like the jail-like feel of it."

"Pretty sure they don't," Hattie says while Mac dances her fingers over the table, pretending they're spiders.

"Look, the spiders are eating the plate," Mac says, laughing to herself.

"No spiders at the table, Mac," Ryland says. "We talked about this."

She drops her hands to her lap as her shoulders droop. Poor girl . . . the spiders just wanted to eat her plate.

"Um, some weird news for you. Do you know who came into The Almond Store today?" Hattie says. I could sense some reluctance in Hattie's voice.

"Who?" Ryland asks.

"Amanda."

My head lifts from where I'm biting into my corn. "Amanda . . . as in . . ."

Hattie nods. "Amanda Berteaux."

"What is *she* doing here?" My skin crawls from the mention of her name.

Amanda was my closest friend growing up. We had some of the best times together until she moved away, and we lost touch. I figured that was what happened when you grew up. Until I started hearing that she was talking shit behind my back, using the same rhetoric as Matt—I was stuck in a small town and going nowhere. When Cassidy was dying, I never heard from her, and when I was left with a farm and a store to take care of, as well as help my brother with a four-year-old, I didn't receive one message, one note. It solidified the notion in my head that she wasn't the friend I thought she was.

But that doesn't stop the spiral in my head from happening. Because why is she here?

"She actually moved back to town," Hattie says.

"What?" I drop my corn on my plate and pick up my napkin. "Why would she move back here? She hates small towns."

Hattie winces. "The only reason I'm going to tell you this is because I don't want you to be caught off guard, just in case you run into them."

"Them?" I ask. "Who's them?"

"Amanda . . . and Matt," Hattie replies.

I feel all the blood from my face drain as I sit back in my chair, completely knocked out from the news.

Amanda, the horrible, and Original Matt. How?

My eyes meet Hattie's as I say, "Don't tell me they're a couple."

"They're . . . married," Hattie says. "And expecting. They moved back to Almond Bay because they thought it would be the perfect place to raise their child."

"You've got to be fucking kidding me," I say. The fucking irony. *Small towns are not for me, Aubree. I'm destined for so much more.* He treated this town like a disease, wanting to sprint away from here as fast as he could when, in reality, he knows this is the best place to be.

"Hey . . . language." Ryland nods toward Mac, who is drinking her milk with two hands on the cup.

"Sorry. But . . . are you fucking serious?"

"Aubree," Ryland warns again.

Mac sets her drink down and wipes the back of her hand over her mouth before saying, "Uncle Ry Ry, you say fuck all the time."

"Mac, don't say the F-word," he says.

"I didn't. I just told you that you say fuck. That's a bad word."

"Yes, I realize that," Ryland says. "So don't say it."

"I didn't," Mac defends. "You said fuck."

Ryland pinches the bridge of his nose. "Just say the F-word."

"You want me to say fuck?" she asks, confused.

If I wasn't so dumbfounded and sick to my stomach at the moment, I'd laugh at the hilarity that is Ryland trying to teach Mac what to say and what not to say.

"I think he means use the term F-word instead of saying fuck," Hattie says softly.

"Only if you guys say it," Mac says, a lift to her chin.

Oooh boy, good luck, Ryland.

"We will do better," Ryland says, staring me down.

"Yes, sorry." I turn toward Hattie and ask, "They seriously moved here?"

"Yes. Not sure where in town, but they came in for cookies

and some almond-scented candles. Said they wanted their new place to smell amazing."

"I'm sure she does," I say as I push my watermelon around with my fork.

I doubt she really wanted the candles at The Almond Store. She probably wanted to rub it in my face that she's married to my ex and expecting a child. What did they bond over? Their hatred for me? The reason they left Almond Bay? Only to come back and live here. Did they gleefully chuckle over the idea of shoving their relationship in my face? Talk about a whole bunch of insecurities racing through my mind.

Both left me for the same reason.

Both caused me heartache.

Both made me question who I am and what I want in life.

And now they're together.

It settles horribly in the pit of my stomach.

"You okay?" Ryland asks.

I look up at him and plaster on a smile. "Of course. Why wouldn't I be?"

"Because your former best friend is married to your ex. They left you because they didn't want to live in a small town, and now, they're back. That has to sting," Ryland says. Wow, is he good at pointing out the obvious. No sugarcoating it either.

I tilt my head to the side and stare at my brother. "Thanks for the recap, but I'm good. They can live their life the way they want."

Verbally, I'm taking the high road. Internally, I hope their new house breaks a main valve and floods.

"Okay, but it seems like you're . . . I don't know, irritated."

When am I not irritated is the question.

The constant badgering on this subject when I'm clearly trying to move on isn't helping.

It's actually making it worse.

Way worse.

"I'm fine," I answer. "If they want to contradict themselves, move back here, and raise a child, that's up to them. Who am I

32

to say what they can and cannot do? It's not like they went on and on and on about how they thought Almond Bay was the kind of place that you get stuck in forever and have no chance of growing as a person. And sure, I might not like doing all of the town activities, hate them actually, but that doesn't mean I think Almond Bay is a bad place to live. I like it here. I've always liked it here, and if they realize they're wrong in what they said, then sure, they're just growing as people. And shouldn't we accept them for the idiots they once were but note their growth?"

"You said idiots, Aunt Aubree. That's not nice," Mac says.

I turn to her, and in a sweet voice, I say, "Well, they're being idiots. It's fact. Wouldn't you rather me tell the truth than lie?"

"Aubree," Ryland says in a terse voice.

"Then Oliver and Landon are idiots," Mac says.

"Mac, we don't call our friends at school idiots."

"She can if they're acting like them," I say, tapping the end of my fork on the table. Continuing my rant, I say, "And isn't it just fitting that they would somehow find each other? They must have so much in common, even though Amanda said many times that she thought Matt was not my type and predicted that he'd leave me. Which she was right, but where was her concern with that comment when jumping into his bed? And not to mention, Matt once told me that Amanda had the resting face of a platypus. But you know, people evolve. They change." I toss my hands in the air. "They move on. Their blinders can be lifted. If anything, I'm happy for them. Really happy. So happy that I should send them a gift. A bouquet of contradiction. Something that really says I'm happy that you were able to see the light and change. Because I'm happy. So fucking happy for them," I roar just as I get out of my seat and push my chair in, taking off toward my guest house.

"She said fuck," Mac says right before I shut the screen door to the farmhouse.

Yes, I'm fine.

Totally *fucking* fine.

Chapter Two

WYATT

"That's a beautiful blouse," I say as the owner of the Five Six Seven Eight Inn smiles back at me.

"Why, thank you. You know, this was part of the wardrobe I wore thirty years ago during the *Annie Get Your Gun* production. I still fit in it."

"And it still looks amazing. I remember my brother telling me all about this inn when he was around and how the owner was a beautiful singer and dancer. Please tell me you still put on some shows."

Ethel clamps her hand over her chest in pride. "Occasionally, I might tap my toes and sing a few songs during town events."

"Any coming up?" I ask. "Please say yes."

She nods. "The End of Summer Jubilee is right around the corner. I might be performing *Summer Loving* from *Grease*."

"Well, count me in."

"Will you be staying long?" Ethel asks as she hands me a key to my suite. I booked the biggest room she has. "Your booking says for only a week."

"Well, I have no problem extending my stay, especially if

things start going my way."

Okay, I know what you must be thinking . . . are you really in Almond Bay about to propose to a woman who you barely know in exchange for some land?

The answer would be yes.

And before you judge me, hear me out. The other night, I was lying awake on Laurel's couch, thinking about what I should do. Initially, I thought her whole plan was insane. Not only am I not in a position to even think about marrying someone else—still questioning if I'm even fucking loveable from how Cadance treated me—but I also thought the idea was absurd.

That was until I received a text from Wallace that night.

A picture of him and his girlfriend—for the life of me, I can't remember her name, something like Banana. Anyway, he and Banana were smiling brightly, holding up her hand, showing off a diamond ring. Nothing in my life has ever made my balls shrivel up as fast as that picture did.

He's engaged.

Which means he's soon to be married.

You can imagine, desperation hit at 10:05 that night. I considered the plan, committed, backed out, looked at the picture of Wallace and Banana one more time, and then made the executive decision that I would make my way out to Almond Bay and strike a deal.

But being the author that I am, I know it won't be that easy. I can't just waltz into a small town and offer a woman I barely know a proposal of marriage in exchange for land. This isn't a Hallmark Christmas movie.

This is real life.

Any good plotter worth their salt would understand that an abrupt and cold demand would come off brash, insulting, and very alpha male-esque, which some people enjoy. But what little I know about Aubree is that she's ornery, so it's not something she'll jump on board with. Not sure an alpha hero strongarming her into submission will work.

So . . . I thought it over. I wrote down notes, and I made a plan of attack.

Step one is to immerse myself in this town.

I need to make sure that everyone around me likes me so when I do make the proposition, she has no choice but to say yes. It will be hard for her to walk around town and not hear my name. People will ask, "Oh, have you spoken to Wyatt? He's a great guy."

And, "I was having some car troubles, and out of the blue, Wyatt helped me. He's magnificent."

And let's not forget, "My brittle bones struggled with walking across the street by myself, but Wyatt, he carried me with his herculean strength. He's dreamy."

Okay, sure, those examples might be far-fetched—*and sound a lot more like Laurel than me*—but you get what I'm after.

Win them over, win her over.

See how that works? The likable guy is hard to say no to.

So last night, before I drove out here, I pulled out one of my empty notebooks and started plotting. I recalled everything Clarke ever told me about Almond Bay. One of the most significant things was the Peach Society—aka, the ladies who run the town. I recall Ethel being the ringleader, and I remember that because I was incredibly fascinated with the name of her inn—Five Six Seven Eight. I thought it was clever and funny and fit her perfectly.

She's target number one.

Because she talks. She talks a lot. If she goes around town telling everyone that I'm the best guy she's ever met, it will help me in the long run. Plant the seed and let it grow.

"Remind me, Wyatt, who is your brother?" Ethel asks.

"Clarke," I answer. "Cassidy Rowley's husband."

An expression of sympathy passes over her face as she reaches across the check-in desk and takes my hand in hers. "Oh, I'm so sorry. When I heard about Clarke, I was devastated for Cassidy, and then when she passed . . . that poor little girl." She touches her chest and shakes her head. "The kind of loss she has suffered. Are you here to help out?"

"I'm here to reconnect."

If you're wondering if I'm ashamed to say that, the answer would be yes. I know I've been out of the picture in MacKenzie's life, but I'm hoping I can make genuine amends.

"Oh, that's wonderful to hear. Will you be taking a vacation, or are you able to work while you're here?" She releases my hand, and I stuff it in my pocket.

"I'm actually an author. Maybe you've heard of me. My pen name is W.J. Preston."

Ethel's eyes widen. "W.J. Preston? You can't be serious."

I nod. "Yup, that would be me."

"Oh my goodness," she says as she moves around the check-in desk and closes the space between us. "I love your books. I have them right over here." She brings me to a seating area in the inn with a fireplace and bookshelves lining the wall. She points at the section, and sure enough, there are my books.

"That's so cool," I say.

"Well, we need to have a book signing while you're here. Don't worry, I'll set it up with Judy over at Pieces and Pages. Depending on how fast we can get your books in, it can be part of the End of Summer Jubilee." She presses her hands together. "We can have a booth for you. Oh please, I hope you stay longer. This would be so special for the town."

"Well, if everything goes well with the Rowleys, I plan on staying much longer."

She smiles brightly, pressing her hand on my shoulder. "Don't worry, I'll be sure to help you in any way."

And that is how it's done.

I thought it might take a bit more, but I have no shame in throwing my author name around to gain what I need.

"Thank you, Ethel, I really appreciate it. And hey, can't wait to see you singing on stage. It will be a highlight for sure."

She clears her throat and stands an inch taller. "Well, now that I know we'll have another celebrity in the crowd, I best up my practicing schedule."

"Doubt you would need to practice at all. I bet you sing just as beautifully without a warmed-up voice."

"You are such a sweetheart." She taps my shoulder, and we move back to reception, where I gather my things. "One day, while you're here, I would like you to sign some of my books, but I won't bother you now. I'm sure you want to get settled."

"Yeah, I'm a bit tired from traveling, but I promise I won't leave without signing your collection."

"Thank you." She winks. "Good luck with the Rowleys. I'll be sure to put in a good word for you."

"Thanks, Ethel."

Key in hand, I walk over to the stairs, hoisting my large suitcase up the steps while my overstuffed backpack hangs on my shoulders.

Yup, really feeling out of shape.

Job number one while being here—execute my plan.

Job number two—get back into shape because, Christ, I shouldn't be out of breath carrying my suitcase up the stairs. Luckily for me, the inn has a gym. Ethel told me all about it. She says no one is ever in there, but she made sure to have one so she didn't get any negative online reviews. She then gave me a smooth once-over and said she was sure I would be using it.

It might look like I have muscles, but they're pretty much for show right now.

Once I get to the top of the stairs, I wheel my luggage down the wooden floors padded by a red-and-gold runner to the end of the hall where I'll be staying in the corner suite.

When I open the door, I'm pleasantly surprised by the large space and beautiful view of the coast. *Okay, Ethel, you're not fucking around.*

The room is large enough for a four-poster king-sized bed, a sitting area near the window, a desk and chair, and an accompanying bathroom decked out in tile and brass fixtures. The bedroom walls are a soft taupe, while the bedding and curtains are a vibrant red with gold and greens sewn throughout the fabric. On either nightstand are bedside lamps and, to my surprise, outlets to charge your phone. That's one of my biggest pet peeves when staying in hotels—there's nowhere to charge your phone.

The floors are original hardwood—at least that's what it looks like—but a large taupe area rug spans nearly the whole surface, giving you that cozy feel. And of course, the scattered pictures of Almond Bay on the walls give guests a sense of community. I didn't know what to expect when I booked a stay here at Five Six Seven Eight. Small-town inns can sometimes be questionable, but this is really nice.

I roll my bag over to the dresser and set my backpack on the desk. I can unpack later. Right now, I have one thing to do, and that's make myself known to the Rowleys. Yes, I have an agenda and don't want them finding out through the grapevine that I'm here. But I'm actually keen to see my former sister-in-law and brother's home. Their beautiful little girl. It's been a few years since we lost him, and there are still grief-stricken days when I go to call him, even if just to shoot the shit. *And then I feel his loss all over again.* To think that the Rowleys lost not only Clarke but also Cassidy breaks my heart.

I want to show up unannounced, though, to win them over and give them my condolences. Cassidy was an amazing woman.

Fingers crossed, they welcome me with open arms.

But with my luck, they won't be too happy to see me. *Plans have more than one strategy, of course.*

I open my suitcase and pull out the gifts I brought with me.

If anything, I'll kill them with kindness.

⊏━⊐

"MAKE A RIGHT ON FARMHOUSE LANE," the GPS says.

"Thank you, Lady Navigation," I say as I turn down Farmhouse Lane and spot the white farmhouse in the distance. I've been here no more than a handful of times when Clarke was alive. And from what I can see, nothing has changed.

The quaint two-bedroom, two-story house is located right on

the edge of the farm with a guest house off to the side and the towering barns and silos directly behind. I remember when Clarke and Cassidy purchased the farm. I thought it was insane. Neither of them had any farm experience, but they had a dream —a vision—and I had to appreciate that. Because when I first started writing, I had zero experience with what I was doing, but I did have a dream of what I wanted to achieve. So I worked with that and have created something—a solid readership, strong writing ability, and thick plots that keep you guessing until the very last page.

Same as my brother and Cassidy.

I'm just sad they couldn't see the fruits of their labor.

I slow down as I drive over the dirt road, not wanting to kick up too much dust as I approach the house. There are a few cars out front, one of them being a Rivian—nice—so I pull in next to that and put the car in park.

Well, here goes nothing.

I grab my gifts from the passenger side, hop out of my car, and head up the front steps of the porch. I'm about to knock when I hear, "Can I help you?"

I look over to my right, and sure enough, Aubree Rowley stands next to the guest house, arms crossed with an irritated look on her face. Clearly, she wasn't expecting a visitor.

"Hey, Aubree," I say. It takes her a second, but I witness the moment she recognizes me—her jaw goes slack, her eyes widen slightly, and her arms drop to her side.

"Wyatt?" she asks.

"Yeah, it's been a bit, huh?"

Just then, the screen door opens, and Ryland stands in the doorframe. Tall, broad, and nearly half a decade older, Ryland looks completely different with the fine laugh lines near his eyes and a more mature, carved face. When he notices me, he says, "Wyatt, holy shit."

And then, like the nice guy he's always been, he greets me with a firm handshake. "How are you doing, man?"

"Who is at the door?" I hear MacKenzie ask as she charges

out to the porch. Her big eyes look up at me, and her button nose wrinkles as she asks, "Who are you?"

Yeah, I knew that would happen. When you're MIA from your niece's life, they tend not to know who you are. I plan on fixing that.

I squat down to her level and say, "I'm your uncle, Wyatt." I hold out the present I brought her, a stuffed horse that I know will match the one she already has since she received one when she was born. "This is for you."

She takes the present but then says, "I don't have an Uncle Wyatt."

Ryland bends down as well and says, "Mac, Uncle Wyatt is your dad's brother."

Her eyes lift to mine in confusion. "But I've never seen you before."

"You have," I say, "but only when you were a baby. I've been pretty busy lately, but I wanted to come say hi."

"Oh." She glances down at the present and then smiles back up at me. "Thanks, Uncle Wyatt." Then she charges back into the house, the screen door shutting behind her.

Okay, great connection. One for the memory books.

Ryland and I stand, and I hand him the box of baked goods. "Just some cookies and stuff from my town. Wanted to bring you something as a peace offering in case there was resentment for me showing up unannounced and a few months too late."

"Why would there be resentment?" Ryland's brow pulls together. "It's good to see you. Come in." He holds the door open for me, and I'm pleasantly surprised.

I walk into the house, and wow. Absolutely nothing has changed since the last time I was here. *Nothing.* Same pictures on the wall, same dilapidated couch off to the right, and same curtains that I remember helping Cassidy hang when they first moved into the farmhouse.

It feels like that happened only yesterday. Clarke asked me if I would supply some of the muscle they needed to move their stuff, and of course I said yes on one condition . . . they provided me with all the pizza I desired from By the Slice, easily the best pizza place I've ever been to. They filled me up with crispy crust and gooey cheese while I worked hard for them. It was a fun weekend. I got to know the Rowleys better, Ryland and I bonded, and I witnessed pregnant Cassidy run around the house, trying to get it ready for when MacKenzie arrived.

"Who was out front?" Hattie asks from the kitchen. She turns around just in time for me to notice just how much older she's gotten. Significantly younger than her siblings, she didn't do much during the move except bake cookies in the kitchen. She said she had to help Cassidy break in the kitchen so that it was ready for all of the baking they would do in the future. No one blinked an eye because she was so young . . . and because Cassidy had such a soft spot for Hattie.

"Hey, Hattie." I wave and then stick my hand in my pocket.

She squints for a second and then surprisingly says, "Wyatt?"

"Yup." I chuckle. "I know, a surprise."

She comes over to me, and just like Cassidy would, she pulls me into a tight hug. "Oh my goodness, it's been so long. How are you?"

The screen door opens and shuts, a slam of wood slightly startling the group. We all turn to watch Aubree slink into the house. She's clearly not as keen to see me, which doesn't really surprise me. She recently lost her sister and has probably had so much on her shoulders. How I hope she won't stay in battle mode once I talk to her.

Plotting gods, please help me.

Turning back to Hattie—I am a little fearful of Aubree's anger—I answer, "I'm pretty good. How are you?"

"Good, great actually," Hattie replies, all smiles, the complete antithesis of the woman behind me. A man comes up to Hattie's side and puts his arm around her waist. When I focus on the man's face, I'm floored.

Holy shit.

"Uh . . . dude, I know I'm just meeting you for the first time, but Jesus, you look a lot like Hayes Farrow."

He chuckles and holds his hand out. "I get that a lot. George, it's nice to meet you."

"Stop that," Hattie says, batting our hands apart. "He is Hayes Farrow."

"No shit, really?" I ask, stunned.

Hayes shrugs. "That's what it says on my birth certificate."

I take a second and look at Ryland, then back at Hayes. Motioning my finger between them, I ask, "Wait, if my memory serves me right . . . weren't you guys in a heated hate campaign between each other?"

"Ooo, I like the way you put that," Hattie says. "A heated hate campaign."

"Neighhhhhhh," MacKenzie says as she pretends to gallop her new horse between us. "Chewy Chonda coming through."

Chewy Chonda, now there's a name for you.

"He's chasing the spiders." MacKenzie dances her fingers across the table, then Chewy Chonda stomps over them. "Die. Die."

"Uh, hey, Mac. Let's not say 'die, die,' okay?" Ryland says.

"That's what Aunt Aubree says when she kills ants in the house."

Ryland looks over at Aubree, who just shrugs her shoulders. "They need to die."

"Aubree, come on," Ryland scolds, but she's unfazed.

MacKenzie bounces away and flings her body on the couch before rolling off it and onto the floor, where Chewy Chonda stomps all over her other horse. Man, I can only imagine how full Ryland's hands are with her.

Bringing the conversation back to the adults, Hayes says, "We've recently solved our differences."

"We did," Ryland says, taking his eyes off MacKenzie. "Kind of forced to when Hattie fell for the enemy."

"The peacemaker, huh?" I ask Hattie, who chuckles.

"You know, no one has called me that yet, but I will accept it." She then turns to Hayes and presses her hand to his chest as she says, "This is Wyatt, Clarke's brother."

"Oh wow, hey," Hayes says, offering me a handshake. "What brought you out here?"

"That's what I was wondering," Aubree says with a growl from the side. When I glance over at her, all I can think is . . . Yikes!

There she is, everyone, my blushing bride.

Let's face it, I knew Aubree was going to be a challenge, but from the sneer and annoyance pulling on her shoulders, I'm guessing she'll be a lot more of a challenge than I initially expected.

Staying calm and remembering the plan, I clasp my hands together and say, "I wanted to come visit. It was long overdue. I should have been here when Cassidy was passing, and I wasn't. I want to apologize for my absence and see if there is anything that I can do to help."

"A few months late," Aubree says, that scowl having the ability to scare the hair off grown men. Me included.

"Hey." Ryland glances over at her. "Don't be rude."

"Don't be rude?" Aubree asks, looking shocked. "Uh, earth to Ryland, he hasn't been around for a long time, and then all of a sudden he shows up?" I have this unnerving feeling that she can see right through me.

"I know how it looks," I say. "But I do want to spend some time with MacKenzie and, I don't know, maybe revisit the town that my brother loved so much. There were things about it that he loved, so I figured I could soak them in."

"Do you have a place to stay?" Hattie asks. "Hayes and I have plenty of room. And I know Ryland would offer up the couch if you're into lumpy slumbers."

I chuckle and shake my head. "Thanks for the offer, but I really don't want to impose. I have a suite over at the inn."

"The inn is beautiful, isn't it? Did you know that Ethel has your books on her shelves?" Hattie asks.

"Yup," I answer. "She showed them to me. She actually wants to set up a book signing while I'm here. I told her I was up for anything."

"God, she must have been fumbling all over you," Ryland says. I can't help but inwardly chuckle at how Aubree's siblings bypassed her crankiness and kept up with the good-natured conversation. "We never told her who you were out of fear that she might maul you. How was it . . . did she try to bury her body against yours?"

"Nah." I smile. "She was really respectful. Fun conversation with her actually."

"Good," Hattie says. "So do you have an itinerary while you're here?"

"Not really. Don't have any books that need to be written. On a bit of a lull at the moment." To avoid weakening my image, I decide it's best not to discuss my recent loss. *The broken groom.* Not the greatest life moment. Perhaps I should write Cadance into one of my books. *As the assailant.* "Figured I would just help out where it's needed, especially with the farm, and hang out around town."

Aubree grows closer. "Why did you say especially with the farm? The farm is doing great. We don't need your help."

If I didn't know any better, I would have sworn she grew Wolverine-length claws as she said that, ready to strike at any time.

I offer her a reassuring smile. "I'm not saying it's not doing well, but you know, I'm here to help in whatever capacity needed."

"The farm doesn't need your help."

"Hey, Aubree, why don't you chill out," Ryland says.

On a huff, she rolls her eyes and heads out the screen door, letting it slap against the doorframe to announce her exit.

Ryland lets out a heavy sigh. "Sorry about that. She got some news today that she wasn't expecting, and I think she's reacting from that."

Doubt it, but I'll run with the storyline.

"Not a problem," I say.

Ryland holds up the cookies and says, "Shall we have some dessert and catch up?"

"Would love that," I answer. "Can I wash up first?"

———

"THAT'S AMAZING," Hattie says. "A freaking movie. Please tell me when your agent got the call that a producer was picking up your book for adaptation that you peed in your pants just a little."

I laugh before sipping the soda Ryland brought me when we sat at the dining room table. "I wouldn't say I peed, but there were definite tears in my eyes."

"Aw, that's so amazing. Do you know when they'll start filming?"

"Well, right now, they're in the casting phase, which can sometimes take forever. There's a script, which was job number one, but when they send it to certain actors we want to cast, they have exclusive reading rights for three weeks. If they pass, we have to offer it to someone else for another three weeks, so it takes some time."

"Oh, that's annoying."

"It's how the business works," I say. "But hopefully, we'll have something soon."

"Maybe Hayes can write an original score for you," Ryland says with a goofy grin on his face.

"Ooo, that would be amazing," Hattie says. "Then we could go to the Oscars."

"Jumping the gun there, babe," Hayes says.

"No, have you heard your stuff? It's Oscar-worthy," Hattie says.

"I'm always up for collaborating," I say. Pretty sure having Hayes Farrow write and perform an original score for my movie will only help me, given his popularity and talent.

"Thanks," Hayes says. "I'll have to give it some thought."

Hattie turns toward me, a huge smile on her face as she says, "That would be a yes from us. Thank you." She has the same spirit as Cassidy. Almost feels like she's sitting across from me right now.

"Are you working on anything new?" I ask Hayes.

"Some things here and there. Nothing too serious, though. I recently finished a year-long tour, so I'm taking a break before I start back up. Plus, I enjoy helping Hattie with The Almond Store."

"Is that what you've been running?" I ask her.

She nods with a giant smile. Seriously, this girl's energy is electric. I remember her being bubbly, but this is a whole new level. I wonder how much of it has to do with her being in the right place in her life? Probably all of it. Great job. Great family. Great partner in life. I remember when I was close to that, and now . . . this is rock bottom, getting ready to beg a woman who can't be in the same room as me to be my wife.

"I took possession of it a few weeks ago, and it's been amazing. Aubree's working on the farm, and Ryland, well, he has the toughest job of all." Hattie nods toward MacKenzie, who half hangs off the couch, sleeping with her horses, one in each arm.

"Oh Jesus," Ryland says when he spots her. "I should get her up to bed."

"And I should probably get going," I say. "I've overstayed my welcome."

"Not at all," Ryland says. "You're always welcome here, man."

"Thanks," I reply as I stand and offer him another handshake. As he picks up MacKenzie and carries her up the stairs, I turn toward Hattie and ask, "Is he doing okay?"

Hattie nods. "Much better than when Cassidy initially passed away. I think a lot was riding on him, and now that I moved back here and Hayes is here, there's more help than just Aubree."

"Aubree was helping too?" I ask.

Hattie nods. "She lives in the guest house so she can help Ryland whenever he needs it. At first, she took care of the farm and the store, which was a lot on her, but now that I have the store, she can focus on the farm. She loves it."

"Seems like she was right. I was a few months shy of being able to help."

Hattie waves her hand dismissively. "Don't listen to her. She's grumpy because her ex-best friend and ex-boyfriend are back in town . . . and married. To each other. Granted, they both treated her like shit, so she's a little sensitive to that, but she'll come around."

Interesting. Good information to have. Don't make friends with those people.

"Oh shit, that's awful. Who is it?" I ask.

"Amanda and Matt. I think they just bought the yellow house on Nutshell Drive. Anyway, she'll be better. I promise. I'm sure if you stop by here tomorrow, she can show you around the farm. You own half of it, after all."

"That would be awesome," I say, surprised Hattie knew about my ownership. Then again, the Rowleys are a tight-knit group. They probably know everything about each other. "Any suggestion on what to wear?"

"Anything that you don't mind getting dirty. It's dusty out there, so leave your nice clothes at home."

"Noted. Thanks, Hattie, and thank you for being so welcoming. I was pretty damn nervous driving over here. Wasn't sure how I'd be received."

"Listen," Hattie says, walking up to me now. "You're family. We're all bonded by MacKenzie, and the more people she has in her life who love her, the better. I'm just glad you came to visit."

"Thank you."

She hugs me, and Hayes follows up with a handshake.

I thank them one more time and step out of the screen door, not letting it slam in case that wakes MacKenzie. As I work my way down the porch steps, I glance at the guest house and spot Aubree sitting outside, rocking on one of the rocking chairs out front.

Why does my scrotum shiver the moment I see her?

Maybe because she's already put this fear in me with her crossed arms and snappy tone.

"Going home?" she asks.

Since she initiated the conversation, I decide to walk up to her and engage.

As I approach, I take in her soft features illuminated by the glow of the light coming from the guest house. Her hair is pulled back into two French braids while her face is completely devoid of makeup. Since her hair looks wet, I'll guess she took a shower while we enjoyed the cookies. She's also wearing a hoodie and a pair of cotton shorts. A simple outfit that says she's done for the day and searching out comfort.

What I wouldn't give to get out of these jeans right about now.

"Home as in the inn? Or home as in back to the Silicon Valley?"

"I would prefer it was back to the Silicon Valley, but I'm guessing I won't be that lucky."

"Unfortunately, you're not," I say as I grin at her.

She looks away, clearly annoyed with me. "Great. So how long are you going to be here?"

"Not sure. I'm booked for a week at the inn, but Ethel really wants me to stay for the End of Summer Jubilee."

"That long?" she asks, her expression in total disbelief.

I shrug. "We'll see. I want to accomplish some things while I'm here, so it just depends on how long that takes."

Her eyes narrow. "And what exactly are those things?"

"Nothing you need to worry about at the moment."

"Um . . . I'm worried," she says.

"Why?" I ask.

"I think we both know why I'm worried."

"I don't," I say, even though I could make a solid guess.

She rocks back and forth, her eyes remaining on me. "Just tell me why you're really here, Wyatt."

"I'm here because I'm trying to reconnect."

"You're such a liar." She stands and closes the space between us. "Why won't you admit you're here because you own half of the farm and want to try to take it away from me?"

Whoa, okay. I can see that this is a hot-button issue for her. *Tread lightly, man.*

"Aubree," I say carefully. "I'm not here to take your farm away. Why would I do that?"

"Uh, I don't know, Wyatt. Why would you?" She places her hands on her hips and stares up at me, fire in her eyes, steam ready to blow.

"I wouldn't. I don't know how to run a farm."

"Says the guy who likes to research for his books. Wait, is that what this is? You're writing some thriller novel about a deadly farm, so you came here to get some real-life experience? News flash, Wyatt. We farm potatoes here. Nothing extravagant, nothing that will give you the plot twist you're probably looking for."

"I'm not here for book research, although a killer, mutated potato does intrigue me."

She purses her lips, clearly not amused. "Just stay away from the farm, okay? We don't need you here."

I wince. "Oh, I know you don't need me, but I hate to say it, half this farm is mine, so you can't really keep me from coming here."

"I knew it," she says, pointing her finger at me. "You're here to try to mess with it. What are you going to do? See where you can make improvements and then sell your half to some developer who'll put apartments right in the middle of the potatoes?"

"Do I seem like that kind of person?" I ask.

"I wouldn't know, Wyatt, you haven't been around."

Got to hand it to her—good comeback.

She seems to be a bit stabby, though, so before this gets more out of hand, I decide it's best I back away. "Well, I'm here now, so . . . I guess I'll see you tomorrow."

"Don't bother," she says, moving toward the door of her guest house. "I'll be too busy." And then she leaves me alone in the dark night with crickets chirping in the background.

Well . . . that went well.

I can practically hear the wedding bells.

Chapter Three

AUBREE

"It's going to be a better day," I mutter as I pour my coffee into my to-go cup, leaving just enough room for creamer. Hattie believes if you add the creamer first, you don't have to stir the coffee because it stirs itself. She's a liar. I know this because I tried it once and nearly grew hair on my chest from the gulp of black coffee I drank.

Never again.

I pour creamer into the cup and then give it a good stir before putting my spoon in my bathroom sink—because that's the kind of life I live. No kitchen, just a dual-purpose sink.

I cap off my coffee, set it on my nightstand, then reach for my boots to slip them on. I chose a pair of khaki shorts for today, a bright red tank top, and my worn-out baseball cap that I pulled my hair through the back and made a messy bun. I also applied a good layer of sunscreen on my body because I plan to be in the sun today.

I adjust my taupe tube socks, making sure they have the perfect ruffle, and put on my shoes. I have one hell of a tan from my high socks, but they're necessary when I'm traipsing through the farm. Dirt and weeds and everything you can imagine get stuck in my shoes. I learned pretty quickly to wear work boots and high socks to protect my ankles.

Once dressed for the day, I stick my phone in my back pocket, grab my coffee, and then head out my door.

The morning has a crispness to it now that summer is ending, and a light amount of dew is on the ground from the night before. The sun barely peeks past the horizon, and I'm not sure Mac is even awake yet, so I quietly hop into my four-by-four and ride it around the backside of the guest house, taking the long way to the barn.

Sometimes I enjoy this route to check out the land, take in the mountains in the distance, and see how far this parcel has come since it was first purchased.

I'm pretty sure everyone thought Cassidy and Clarke had lost their minds when they said they were buying a farm since they hadn't shown any interest in farming. But then Cassidy laid out her plan, and I found it fascinating that they could devise a plan and see it through. It's why I've sworn to keep this farm afloat.

I just wish I could pinpoint the financial problem. I'm going to try to tackle it later this week. I think I need to be immersed in the day-to-day grind to clear my head and then look at the numbers with a fresh mind.

I wind through a gathering of trees where we promised Mac we'd build her a tree house, something we haven't gotten to just yet, and then round the corner toward the barn, where I see a strange car parked in front. Huh, that's weird.

Maybe it's one of Esther's or Aggie's friends—they visit occasionally when they're working. It's cute. They'll go around helping with certain chores and treat the work as something to do rather than a job. That's what happens when you're retired— they told me—they just want to be useful in some way. I'm not complaining.

I'll take all the help I can get. *Except Wyatt Preston's.*

I park next to the right side of the barn, where we've been slowly building a large chicken coop. It's another new venture we decided to take on, something that wouldn't create too much work but would also provide another source of income. We wanted to offer enough space so the chickens had grass and some free range to walk around, so we chose the right side of the barn. We made a feeding hole through the barn as well as a door next to the beds where they will be laying eggs so we don't have to step over them to retrieve the eggs. We can just open the door and collect. It was well-thought-out, but because of that, it's taken us longer to put it together.

We're not in a rush, though. I'd rather it be right than have to make changes later. We plan on selling the eggs at The Almond Store. We'll add a cooler to the store to sell the eggs, some honey, and possibly frozen cookie dough so people can slice it up and bake it themselves. Just some small ideas we've thought about to expand the business.

Coffee in hand, I hop out of my four-by-four and head into the barn, where I hear some voices in the distance.

"Good morning," I call out.

"Morning," Parson says.

"You in the back?" I ask.

"Yup," he calls out.

I make my way through the barn and toward the back doors, only to find Parson sitting on the tractor and a man helping him load some tools onto the trailer.

"Oh, hello," I say.

The man stands tall, and my face immediately turns into a sneer. *Wyatt.*

The moment I saw him last night, I knew exactly why he was here. Not to see Mac. Not to reconnect with the family. Nope, he was here for business. "Morning," he says with such an annoying grin that it makes me want to chuck my coffee at him. The man is deadly attractive, an in-your-face kind of handsome that makes people feel weak in the knees, with the slight curl in his hair, captivating eyes, and sharp jawline. "Parson and I are headed out to the fields to see if any potatoes need to be covered. I had no idea you had to make sure there was dirt on them at all times."

"They grow underground. What else would you expect?" I ask, my voice full of snark.

He stands taller and wipes his hand over his forehead. "I can see you haven't had your full cup of coffee just yet."

"That's an asshole thing to say." The minute the words slip from my mouth, I realize that I'm standing in front of Parson as well. He has no idea how much animosity I feel toward Wyatt, so I'm just coming off as a total bitch.

Tacking on a smile, I turn to Parson and say, "Would you mind heading out to the field so I can have a conversation with Wyatt?"

"Not a problem at all," Parson says. I'm sure he wants nothing more than to escape this interaction.

He backs up the tractor and takes off, heading down the side road that leads to the fields.

When he's out of earshot, I turn toward Wyatt and grip my cup tightly as I say, "You don't belong here."

"Oof, I think the deed to half of this land I hold in my possession tells a different story."

I blow out a deep breath, trying not to get overly angry about this because we knew it would happen. The moment I found out Wyatt owned half of the farm, I had this bad feeling he'd try to claim it somehow, take over, or do something to mess up the plan I've laid out for myself.

The plan Cassidy had for this property.

That's why I was talking to my lawyer. I wanted to see if we could do anything on our end, but there was nothing. Wyatt is the rightful owner, and the worst part of it is that he owns most of the farmland. This means he is the main owner of the potatoes. The potatoes that our entire business plan relies on. If he takes charge of his land, then everything, and I mean everything, is thrown off.

Wyatt's arrival *is* the worst-case scenario.

One that puts me on edge.

Because I don't want to lose this. I don't want to lose

Cassidy's memory. I don't want to lose the one thing that makes me feel . . . semi-worthy.

"Wyatt, why are you here?" I ask, just wanting to get to the bottom of this.

"I told you."

"I want the truth," I say. "You haven't had any interest in being here, being a part owner, so why now?"

"Isn't it obvious?" he asks. "Going through a midlife crisis. I need something new in my life, something to keep me occupied. And I like potatoes."

"You barely look younger than my brother, so that's not midlife. And don't you have book deadlines to keep you busy?"

He leans against the barn door and crosses his arms. "Actually, I don't have any deadlines at the moment, so I have some time off. Which makes it the perfect time for me to be here."

"But the problem is, Wyatt, I don't want you here."

He nods and toes the ground. "That's been quite obvious, but that won't make me leave." He pushes off the wall and walks over to where the tools hang. He picks up a pair of gloves and a shovel. "Now, if you don't mind, I think I'll tend to my dirt."

He attempts to walk by me, but I stop him by standing in front of him. "Wyatt, do not mess with my flow. Everything is under control. I don't need you digging around in the dirt to fulfill some fantasy you have built up in your head. Your little keyboard fingers won't be able to handle the real work we do out here."

"Umm, that's insulting. And maybe instead of being rude, you can actually offer to show me around. Tell me about the farm and inform me of what's been going on."

"Why?" I ask. "Why do you want to know?"

"Because . . . I own part of this land, and I should know what's going on."

Growing very frustrated because I know it can't be the real reason he's here, I place my hand on my hip and stare back at him. "But why? Why do you want to know what's going on? And don't say because you own the land. You've owned it for a while.

Something must have changed recently that's brought you here, and I want to know what it is."

"Don't you think that's a little personal?" he asks.

"No."

"You barely know me. Why don't you offer to take me out to dinner before you start digging around in my personal life?"

"I'm not asking you out to dinner."

He scratches the side of his jaw. "Might be good for you to get to know the owner of the other half of the farm. Maybe we can come to an agreement of sorts."

"What kind of agreement?" I ask, feeling the hairs on the back of my neck start to rise.

"The kind of agreement where we can mutually agree on how to run the farm."

"Uh, the farm is running just fine, thank you."

"Is it, though? You're growing potatoes."

My protective walls are firmly in place as I stare him down. "We grow potatoes to make vodka. With that vodka, we produce almond vodka and almond extract for The Almond Store. We also started harvesting honey and will soon sell eggs as well."

He slowly nods his head. "And this is for The Almond Store . . . but you grow potatoes."

"Yes," I say, exasperated with this conversation. "What don't you understand?"

"I don't get why you don't grow almonds. Isn't that the main part of your business?"

"It is," I say through clenched teeth. "But if you were part of the farming industry, you'd understand that the best place to grow almonds is inland, not along the coast, which is where we're located. Therefore, we purchase the almonds and grow the potatoes."

"Interesting." He pauses for a moment and looks around. "Have you tried growing almonds?"

"I can't with this," I say as I walk away. "You have no idea what you're doing, and I'm not about to waste my time attempting to educate you."

"That doesn't seem very friendly," he says, following me.

"What made you think I was friendly?"

"Great point," he says. "Don't know what I was thinking." I hop into my four-by-four, and before I can even get it started, he hops in as well.

"What the hell do you think you're doing?" I ask him.

"Going for a ride." He grins at me.

"No, you're not."

"I think I am." He buckles himself in, and my irritation hits an all-time high.

I grip the steering wheel and take a few deep breaths. Arguing with him doesn't seem to be doing anything. Maybe I need to take a different approach.

What would Echo say?

You can catch more bees with honey.

So with a deep breath, I say, "Wyatt, I think we got off on the wrong foot."

"I could not agree more. Let's push everything leading up until now behind us and move forward. Why don't you give me a tour of the farm, and we can see where I can make corrections?"

Corrections? Oh, the freaking arrogance.

Don't punch him, Aubree.

It won't do you any good.

It will only make things worse.

Maybe if you just show him the farm, he'll see that everything is fine, that no one needs his suggestions, and he can go back to life with his keyboard and creepy stories.

Tacking on a smile that both of us know is fake, I say, "Sounds lovely." I start the engine and press my foot to the gas pedal, shooting him back in his seat and causing him to fumble to find something to grab onto.

"Jesus, warn a guy." He straightens up and adjusts himself.

That was worth it.

Hiding my smile, I bring him around the barn and to an abrupt stop in front of the future chicken coop. He flies forward and back against his seat again, looking like a floppy noodle rather than a man with working muscles. "This is where we're going to house our chickens. It's an addition we planned for this year. It will bring in some income and—"

"Are you afraid your chickens will die?"

I turn toward him. "Why would you say something like that?"

"Aren't you aware that potatoes are toxic to chickens?"

Uh . . . no.

I was not aware of that, but to hell if I'm going to admit such a thing to him.

"Yes, quite aware," I say, lying right through my teeth.

He glances around the ground in front of us, noticing all the scattered potatoes dropped during transport. "Well, there are a lot of potatoes around. Chickens will try to eat them, and then boom, your egg layers are dead. Not only would that be sad but also a huge waste of money."

"First of all, the chickens won't be fed potatoes. If you want, we can put up a sign that says no potatoes. And second of all, the chickens will be in the coop. Therefore, they won't be exposed to the potatoes."

"You're not going to let them roam?" he asks. "Free range organic is all the rage."

"So are coyotes, and they like chickens. We're not about to let the chickens run free so they can gnaw on some potatoes and drop dead only to be scooped up by a coyote."

"Seems like a death wish, yes, but have you thought about how the chickens might feel about being trapped in a coop day in and day out?"

"Uh, it's a giant coop," I say. Once again, my irritation is clear through my tone. "There will be plenty of room for them to run around. There will be grass and beds and things for them to climb. It will be the mansion of all chicken coops."

"Oh, if that's the case. Great idea." He smiles.

My nostrils flare.

He picks up my coffee cup.

I stare at him as if he's lost his mind.

He brings the cup to his lips.

Before I can stop myself, I punch the cup right out of his hand, sending it to the ground on the other side of the four-by-four.

Quietly, he looks down at what I can only assume is spilled coffee and then back up at me.

After a few silent seconds, he asks, "Was that necessary?"

"More than you know." I press the pedal again, sending him flying in his seat.

⸻

"BEES?" he asks, looking at the stacks of bee boxes from afar. Since we're not suited up, we don't want to get too close, although the thought of driving close enough to the bees only to make a quick turn in hopes that Wyatt would fall out of the four-by-four is appealing.

"Yes, bees. Like I said, we're harvesting honey and plan on adding jars to The Almond Store by offering almond and wild-flower-infused honey as well as honey butter, but that is further down the road. And of course, just regular honey."

He slowly nods, taking in all the bee boxes Echo has lined up. "Will you be adding to the bakery side of the store?"

"What do you mean?" I ask.

"Well, given you're creating more room for things on the farm like honey and eggs, those could be used toward other forms of income like breads and baked goods that specialize in the flavors you're creating around your brand. For instance, if you do the honey butter—which, in my opinion, investing in some cows on the property to make the butter would be wise—then you can sell loaves of crispy artesian bread with the butter and upcharge for the combo. You could also add in things like cherry almond baklava. You incorporate your brand flavors, use the honey, but then also create another signature piece for the bakery section that will bring in tourists from all around."

I hate him.

I really, really hate him.

Because dammit, that's a good idea. Cherry almond baklava? Good God, where can I get that now? My mouth waters just thinking about it. *But who would bake it?*

"And then of course the cow manure can help fertilize, not that you would have enough cows to fertilize all of the potatoes, but let me ask you this. Do you ever have leftover potatoes from harvest?"

My nostrils flare because I feel like I know where this is going. "Yes."

He nods. "You're unable to produce vodka with all the potatoes?"

"No, we do sell them to local restaurants, though."

"At what cost? Probably something cheap because you're all small businesses trying to make a penny in a small town, so you pat their back, they pat yours. Although, how are they truly giving back to you as a restaurant? Sure, they can say if you want dessert, try the one dessert item The Almond Store offers, which is a cookie. But customers could be in the mood for ice cream, so they'll go to the ice cream store instead, which makes me wonder, should you be offering some ice cream at The Almond Store? With the cows coming in, they can help provide milk for the butter and ice cream, and once again, you take your signature flavors of almond, cherry, and honey, use the eggs you have of course, and create an ice cream palate of unique flavors, driving more people into the store, which of course will spur them on to buy more."

How?

How is he seeing all of this?

How can he just sit here casually and ramble on about how to improve the farm by just looking at bee boxes and make sense of it all? It's infuriating.

"Not to mention, if you cut down on the potato fields, maybe down to half because you could probably lose half the fields and produce just as many potatoes that you need to process the vodka and the almond extract, you could use the extra space for the cows. Also, the farm next to yours is a dairy farm. You could possibly form a connection with them, offer some of your land for rent to expand their cows, and then take some of their milk. I'm just spit-balling here, but the possibilities are endless."

How did we go from bees to this?

Is this what writers are like?

They just ramble on forever, drawing up new images and ideas in their head, making you feel inferior in the field you've been training?

I clear my throat. "Well, that was a tangent." A helpful one, but a tangent.

"Yeah, but with a lot of potential. Shall we move on?"

I'm afraid to.

What will he say when we reach the potatoes?

⸺

"IT SMELLS like rotten potatoes in here," Wyatt says as he looks at the silos. We had just finished visiting the fields, and lucky for me, he didn't have much to say other than if I switched to drip irrigation rather than a sprinkler system, we'd save fifty percent on water.

I countered that a sprinkler system reduces the chance of frost.

Then he questioned how much frost we were getting.

I then pretended to act like Parson was calling me, and I took off without looking back.

Now that we're in the silo section of the farm, I know he'll tell me we don't need such large storage systems, especially ones that aren't kept up as well.

"Well, potatoes sometimes get stuck in the silo, leading them to rot."

"That's very unappealing," he says as he looks up into the cylinder tower. "Why do you need so much space? This seems like a lot. Have you ever thought about ways you can distribute the potatoes around town other than for the vodka?" He looks at me. "How many potatoes do you have to compost a year?"

"More than what you probably want to hear."

"Exactly," he says. "You need to figure out another way to get these potatoes off your hands. I mean, if you have an overproduction of a crop that is not your main source of income, then you need to change it up."

"But it is the main source of income," I counter.

He shakes his head. "The vodka and almond extract are. The potatoes just provide a way to make that. You shouldn't have an overproduction of potatoes. That's wasting time, farmland, and money. Either you need to cut down on the fields you're using for potatoes and distribute that to something else like the cows, or you need to find a new way to use the potatoes rather than just selling them to local restaurants."

I fold my arms and say, "Okay, then what would your suggestion be if you're so smart?"

"I'm glad you asked." He smiles and faces me, sticking his hands in his front pockets, looking like the arrogant man he is. "There is a plant just outside of Silicon Valley that specializes in making biodegradable plastics by using potato starch. I know the CEO and have actually toured the factory. It's impressive, and they're always looking to buy potatoes despite having their own fields. They're at a deficit at the moment." Is that why he knows so much about freaking potatoes? Here I was thinking he went and researched potatoes for a week straight before he came here. "So your potato surplus could help him out, and you're helping the environment by creating a biodegradable plastic."

"Well, that's . . . interesting," I say even though I don't want to.

"And if you went that way, then I'd keep the fields, but then strike up a bargain with the dairy farmers behind you for the milk so you can make the ice cream and butter. But if you're still thinking about cutting down on the potato fields to make room for more cows, then you could also turn over your potatoes to make potato flour. A farm about half an hour from here makes all kinds of flours, potato being one of them. And of course, with that potato flour, not only could you add it as a retail item in The Almond Store—part of the brand—but you could take that flour and make another specialized bakery item unique to the store." He twirls his finger in the air. "A full circle moment."

God, do I want to kick him so badly. Right in the nuts. I want to make him keel over in pain because just yesterday, I was going over the books and trying to figure out why we were coming up short on growing the farm and the business. Then he comes waltzing in, wearing a pair of new boots that now look like they've been through the trenches of a war field, acting like he is the mighty potato czar.

And even though I hate to admit it, a little part of me believes it. I mean, his ideas were unlike anything I would have thought of. How could he look at a situation, quickly assess, and find a solution or a way to expand? He looked at the resources, reused them, and put them back into the product, the farm.

Hell, I wouldn't be surprised if he tells me we should have a few cherry trees to "go with the brand." I'd buy it. I would probably, in my mind—not out loud, of course—think wow, what a genius.

"I can see you're thinking." He leans in with a grin. "Are you thinking about how clever I am?"

A wave of his fresh, earthy cologne comes barreling into my space as I say, "No." Even though I'm thinking, yes.

He is clever.

Annoyingly charming.

And has a knack for comebacks that make me stutter over my words.

I've intentionally resisted reacting, resisted adding to the banter, because the last thing I want is for him to think he can make me laugh.

"Come on, surely you thought that one of my ideas was smart. I was throwing out some good ones."

"They're ideas, Wyatt. They're not action plans. There's a

difference." And they all require upfront capital that we don't really have.

"Want me to draw something up for you? Like I said, I'm available right now. I can talk to the cow neighbors and my friend down at the biodegradable plastic plant to see if we can negotiate a deal. Then we can write up a plan of action, a step-by-step process, and maybe throw out some projections. I would need to look at the books, but that won't be too hard. I could have something on your desk in the next few days."

Why is he like this?

I thought he wrote thrillers. He's acting like a billionaire trying to monopolize the potato industry. Who does he think he is? Huxley Cane?

Lord knows he probably knows who Huxley Cane is. They're probably best friends.

"Uh, are you going to answer me?" he asks.

I focus my eyes on him and tilt my head to the side. "Do you happen to know Huxley Cane?"

"I don't, but I did serve on a board with his brother, Breaker. Great guy. Why? Do you need me to ask them something? I bet I could set up a meeting with Breaker and Huxley."

Dear Jesus.

I shake my head and move past him toward the four-by-four.

"Is that a no?"

"Tour's over," I say from over my shoulder. "Find something else to do. Hint: annoying me is not an option."

And then I drive away, leaving him alone in the silos. I can't deal with him, not right now. Not when he makes me feel far too inferior.

"THERE YOU ARE," Echo says as she approaches with a bagged lunch.

I'm resting under one of our large oak trees, my back up

against the trunk with my water bottle in one hand and an egg salad sandwich in the other.

"Hey, Echo," I say. "How's your day?"

"Great," she says as she adjusts her straw hat and takes a seat next to me. "Can I join you?"

"Of course. Want to lean against some of the tree trunk?"

She shakes her head. "No, that's okay." She lets out a deep breath and says, "Gosh, I don't know if you've met him yet, but Wyatt, he's something else."

Finally, someone to bemoan with.

"Oh yes," I say as I set my water down and pick up a piece of my apple that I cut up. "I've met him. He really is something else." My voice is full of sarcasm.

But Echo doesn't seem to pick up on it as she says, "I don't think I've ever met anyone as smart as he is."

Great!

He got to Echo.

Last night, it started with Ethel, then he made his way here, captivated Mac with a present, and then charmed Ryland, Hattie, and even Hayes. This morning, he won over Parson and now he's won over Echo. He's probably already made the rounds to Esther and Aggie. They're going to love him more than they love me. Because how can you not like the charming, smell-good guy over the curmudgeon wench in a pair of khaki shorts with a terrible sock tan?

At this point, I'm sure if my life were one of his novels, everyone would be cheering on Wyatt while they complained about how annoying I am, wishing I was the one the villain captured only to have my body parts sold on the black market. Isn't that how it always goes, though? The man gets the praise, while the woman gets the blame?

Will that happen here on the farm? They're all going to love him, and I'm going to fall to the wayside, so much so that they'll form a mutiny. Then I'll be asked to step down from my role while Wyatt takes over. And then what? I don't ensure my sister's dreams come true, while Wyatt turns the farm into a fully high-functioning modern farm with cows and milkers and creamers and God knows what, with the most beautiful cherry trees George Washington's ghost has ever seen. People from miles away will visit the farm to look at the cherry trees.

News reporters will flock to Almond Bay to interview the man-wonder who turned around a potato farm that saved the planet with a thing as simple as starch.

He'll receive awards.

The president will call and name a day in honor of him where everyone gets off work. Wyatt Day. But I won't get it off because I'll be working a retail job somewhere open on Wyatt Day because that's the day that everyone buys a potato, tosses and kisses it, thanking Wyatt for his contribution to society.

"Uh, you okay, Aubree?" Echo asks, probably stunned by my silence. If only she knew what was going on in my head.

"Oh yeah, sorry. Just blanked there for a second."

"That's okay. You must be tired. Running a farm is not easy."

Apparently not for Wyatt.

"Yeah, just busy, and you know, I gave Wyatt a tour this morning, so I'm trying to catch up from that."

"Parson was telling me Wyatt owns half of the land. Is that true?"

Ugh, Parson. I love him, but sometimes he can't keep anything to himself . . . just like the rest of the town.

"That is correct. Wyatt is Clarke's brother, and it was part of the will that when Cassidy passed, some of the land stayed within his family, so yes, he owns a portion of it."

"Makes sense. Well, he's done an amazing job on the chicken coop."

"Yeah, the chicken—wait, what?" I ask, looking over at Echo.

"Oh yeah, I just assumed you assigned him that task. I went over there to grab wood for more bee boxes, and he was working on the coop. I was shocked with the progress he'd made."

No.

There is no freaking way.

"You look angry," she says.

I try.

I try to change my face into something neutral, but my eyebrows won't work with me, nor will the frown I can feel pulling on my lips. This girl might explode.

"Just . . . annoyed," I say, unable to hold it back.

I know I shouldn't talk to an employee about this, but for the love of God, I know if I said something to Hattie or Ryland, they'd tell me he has the right to help around the farm. This is his property too.

But they don't get it. This is supposed to be my project. I'm the one supposed to continue Cassidy's legacy, not some thriller author who picked up a hammer for the first time today.

To be fair, I don't know if that's the case, but this man with his worldly views and talents . . . and connections. It's frustrating.

And if you think I feel inferior and that makes me sound insecure, you're correct.

Put yourself in my shoes. My courageous sister leaves me her farm, and I'm struggling to make sense of it all. My father told me when I was young that I would never do anything productive with my life. I want to prove him wrong. I want to make Cassidy proud, and then Wyatt walks in, not a stress on his shoulder or a worry in his chest, and he's solving what feels like the Great Potato Famine of the 1840s.

"Why are you annoyed?" Echo asks. "If you don't mind me asking."

I let out a deep sigh and stare down at my sandwich. "I wasn't expecting Wyatt to visit. He sort of showed up out of nowhere last night, and I'm just . . . taken aback."

"Ahh, I see." Echo nods. "I think I know where you're coming from. When I was working on my parents' bee farm, I had a distant relative come into town. My parents knew about it, but I didn't, and she was this bright light of ideas. Everyone fawned over her, and it was irritating because I had been making some of the same suggestions for months. Honestly, it was one of the reasons I decided to leave. Because if they could value her opinion, why didn't they appreciate mine?"

"That would be infuriating."

She nods. "Is it like that with Wyatt?"

"Sort of." I pause, and my teeth pull on the corner of my lip.

She must notice my hesitation because she says, "You know, if you want to take a time-out from being my boss and just talk for a second, I'd be more than happy to listen. I won't hold anything you say against you. I promise. I had my family do that to me time and time again. I wouldn't do that to someone else."

"I appreciate that," I say and then let out a deep breath. I could really use the chance to get this bubbling anxiety off my chest, at least to calm my nervous system before I spiral into insanity. "I don't know why he's here, Echo. He's shown no interest in our family, in the farm, nothing. I thought he'd own part of the farm but never really care about it. He's a very popular author. He doesn't *need* the farm. But then, out of nowhere, he decides to come into town and turn everything upside down. I know there's a reason behind it, but I can't figure it out. And do you know the worst part of all of this?"

"What?" she asks.

"And don't think this is directed toward you in a mean way, but he's so freaking charming and nice that everyone likes him. I seem to be the only one who thinks he's being calculating and looking for something else."

"I mean, he was really nice to me, took interest in who I was, and asked me a bunch of questions. He made eye contact and was very thoughtful when he spoke. So yeah, I get why he's likable."

"So do I," I say. "When I gave him a tour, he had great ideas, was able to solve problems without me asking, and even cracked a few jokes. I, of course, didn't give him the satisfaction of laughing because I want him to know that I'm not buying what he's trying to sell to everyone."

"And what do you think that is?" she asks as she opens her bag and pulls out a ham and cheese sandwich.

"I think he's trying to be charming and likable because he

wants something, and when he asks for it, everyone will say yes because it would be hard to say no to the nice guy. Make sense?"

"Do you think he'd be that crafty?"

"Yes," I say. "I do. The man plots storylines for a living. Why wouldn't he plot a way to get what he wants?"

"I guess that makes sense." She leans back on one hand as she takes a bite of her sandwich. "But I wonder what he wants."

"That's what I'm trying to figure out, and it's driving me crazy."

"I know," Echo says with a smile. "Why don't you get him drunk and then ask? He'd be bound to slip up."

I chuckle. "Great idea. The only problem with that is I'd have to spend time with him to get him drunk willingly, and I bet he'd see right through me."

"True. Maybe you should befriend him then. If he feels like you're friendly, he might be willing to share his diabolical plans."

"That seems far too painful. I've already spent enough time around him. I don't want to befriend him."

"He might see right through that as well," Echo says. She takes another bite of her sandwich as she thinks. "Oh, I know," she says. "Find out where he's staying, then in the middle of the night, sneak into his room, capture him, and then torture it out of him. I've heard men are very protective of their junk."

I snort so hard that I feel a few drops of snot fly out of my nose. I wipe my nose with my napkin before I say, "Echo Alaska." She just chuckles and shrugs. "You know, I think I might have to keep you close. I don't think it's smart to piss you off."

"You would be right about that," she says with a devilish grin.

Yeah . . . very close.

Although I'm not opposed to the torture thing. I might have to think about that.

Chapter Four

WYATT

I wrap my towel around me and slip out of the bathroom into the main part of my bedroom and sit on the edge of my bed.

What a fucking day.

I would never admit this to Aubree, because I think she'd find too much joy in it, but fuck am I exhausted.

And sore.

Holy shit, am I sore.

Here I am, thinking I work out and can lift all the weights, but the moment I dabble in some manual labor, I'm humbled very quickly.

I even got a blister today from wielding a hammer.

I think the last time I got a blister was when I was doing some work for a local marina, hauling in rope from the harbor as research. Another brutal day out on the job.

Just goes to show that the pads of my fingers might be tough from typing all day, but the rest of my hands and body are not prepared for manual labor.

"I'm going to need ibuprofen," I mutter as I drape my hand over my head just as my phone dings with a text message.

These days, that can only really be one person. It seems that when Cadance fell out of love with me, she decided she no longer wanted anything to do with me. Fuck, that has stung. From preparing for life till death parts us, professing love and faithfulness, to walking away with no further contact. *Man, did I read her wrong.* Definitely in the *I refuse to grieve her any longer* stage.

Even if that doesn't completely dissolve the hurt.

I take a look at my screen.

Laurel: *How was your first day?*

I sit up on my bed and text her back.

Wyatt: *Last night was superior. The Rowleys welcomed me, and we all shared some cookies while we caught up. Hattie is dating Hayes Farrow, which I was surprised to see. MacKenzie was cuter than ever and loved the horse we picked out. And Aubree . . . well, she was less than thrilled to see me.*

I position my pillow against the headboard and get comfortable as Laurel texts me back.

Laurel: *But we kind of knew that was going to happen, right? She's the most jaded.*

Wyatt: *I don't even think jaded is the right term. She was something else.*

Laurel: *What do you mean?*

Wyatt: *For one, she was not happy to see me. I'm pretty sure she growled and sneered at me when she recognized who I was. Like a feral animal ready to attack its prey.*

Laurel: *Aw, your future wife.*

Wyatt: *Yeah, if I'm fucking lucky—or unlucky. Not sure which one it would be.*

Laurel: *Have you done anything to her in the past that would make her so angry with you?*

Wyatt: *No, we've barely interacted. I've been to a few of the family gatherings and helped Cassidy and Clarke move into their farmhouse, but I've never done anything that would have made her mad at me. She's younger than me, and I never thought to interact.*

Laurel: *Huh, so if it's not something you did in the past, what would make her so angry?*

Wyatt: *She's incredibly protective of the farm. She was calling me out for being there today. Asking why I would show up when I had no interest before. Honestly, she's smart. She can see right through me. I tried to act like I cared. She gave me a tour, and I was spouting off shit, acting like I knew what I was talking about.*

Laurel: *Did she buy it?*

Wyatt: *I think she did. I mean, I knew some things, but I mainly talked out of my ass, hoping for the best. I was surprised with some of the things I came up with. They made sense.*

Laurel: *The author brain is a scary place.*

Wyatt: *I never believed that until today. Because while talking about cherry almond baklava, I was thinking to myself, how are you coming up with this? Where did cherry almond baklava even come from? It was impressive. Then when she ditched me because she'd had enough, I walked back to the half-finished chicken coop, looked at the plans, and started building. I got a blister.*

Laurel: *Aw, look at you getting your hands dirty. How cute for you.*

Wyatt: *I only wish I had a tool belt. It would have completed the outfit.*

Laurel: *I would have given anything to have a picture of you in a tool belt building a chicken coop.*

Wyatt: *Maybe I can muster something up for you tomorrow. Oh . . . hey, how did the second date go?*

Laurel: **blushes* Good.*

Wyatt: *Yeah? Like . . . really good?*

Laurel: *Let's just say she's really good at kissing.*

Wyatt: *I assume there will be a third date?*

Laurel: *She told me she's already planning it.*

Wyatt: *That's awesome. I'm happy for you. Do I get to meet her?*

Laurel: *Maybe when you're done building chicken coops something I never thought I'd say.*

Wyatt: *LOL. Me neither.*

Laurel: *So everyone else likes you besides the one person supposed to like you. How do you plan on fixing that?*

Wyatt: *Well, as far as I see it, I have two options: I can kill her with kindness until she wants to murder me, and that's when I strike up the deal.*

Or I can annoy the shit out of her until she wants to murder me, and that's when I strike up the deal. The latter seems more fun.

Laurel: *The latter seems like it could end in slow, deadly torture for you.*

Wyatt: *It would be worth it.*

SO I'VE SPENT my fair share of time in small towns because the best thriller novels take place in towns just like Almond Bay, where it seems like everything is pristine and perfect. In fact, there are deep, dark secrets no one knows about. But Almond Bay hits differently than any other small town I've visited.

The buildings are a mixture of old Victorian style and Western. Instead of concrete sidewalks, they're planks of wood. A sign for every business extends from the roof and hangs in front of the entry. Iron streetlights line the boardwalk while potted plants hang from them, brightening the walkways with an abundance of color. Not to mention, since it's a coastal town, you have the subtle sound of waves in the background as well as the smell of the sea wafting through the air when the wind picks up.

It's clean and brilliantly coordinated, offering the quaint feel any tourist looks for when visiting that cute little Gilmore Girl-esque town. I can only imagine what it looks like in the fall and the winter.

I hate to admit it, but I like it here.

"Hello," a man says with a nod.

"Good evening," I reply.

And the people are friendly. If I walked around my hometown, I doubt anyone would say hello. But here, it's hello after hello.

Do you know what Almond Bay actually reminds me of?

Canoodle, California. It's a small town in the San Jacinto mountains just outside Palm Springs, where the family cabin is. A cat runs the town at the moment—yes, you read that right, a cat —and it's quirky and perfect with its diner decorated with trolls and its rustic cabins that blend in with the tall ponderosa pines and boulders that flank the mountain. But whereas Canoodle is in the mountains, Almond Bay is right next to the ocean, just tweaking the atmosphere ever so slightly.

Same vibe, though.

Same quirky characters.

Same cute shops.

And this is why small towns are the best.

You feel a sense of community.

A sense of belonging, even if you're from out of town.

The streets aren't bustling, the weather is a comfortable sixty-six, and a light breeze kicks up from the ocean. The sun sets along the horizon, and the streetlamps flicker as they turn on. From a few speakers strategically planted along the planked sidewalks, quiet instrumental music plays. It sets the mood but doesn't block out conversation.

If this were a thriller, I'd mention the music but make it eerie. The kind of music that makes everyone believe that this scene is just a little too perfect—like something is about to happen.

Someone is about to pop out and—

"Do you like trains?" an old man asks, coming out of nowhere and nearly making me whiz myself.

"Jesus fuck," I mutter as I grip my chest and stare at the wrinkly old man.

With a horseshoe of gray hair around his head and a shiny dome on top, he's sporting large brown tortoiseshell spectacles, a brown vest with a cream button-up short-sleeved shirt, and brown tweed pants. His shaky hand holds up a model train, and a quizzical pull props his brow up at an impossible height. Have you ever watched that Pixar short where the old man with the giant nose and huge eyes plays chess? That's what this man looks like.

"Well, do you?" he asks again, leaning in closer.

And see, this is the quirkiness of the town. He's not a threat, but I'm not sure you'd find an old man wandering the streets asking people if they like trains anywhere else.

"Uh, they're pretty cool," I say. "Why, do you like trains?"

He straightens up, giving us some space between each other now. "I love them."

"Yeah?" I ask. "What's your favorite train engine?"

He crosses his arms and frowns at me. "How could I possibly pick a favorite? That's like picking your favorite child."

"Very true, my mistake." I hold up my hands. "Is that, uh . . . N gauge?" My grandpa used to build model train sets and work with N gauge. That's as far as my knowledge goes.

"HO," he replies. "Do you like N?"

"My grandpa used to have a large ten-by-ten model train setup, all N scale."

"Really?" The man's eyes light up.

"Yup. He took my grandma to Vermont one year for their anniversary, and they fell in love with the town of Stowe. So he modeled his town off Stowe in the fall. It was really beautiful. I occasionally helped him work on the town. I think it's been taken down since he's passed, but we have many pictures of it."

"Can I see?" he asks, his eyes looking like they're going to pop out of his head out of pure excitement.

"I don't have any on me at the moment. I can dig them up on my drive on my computer, though."

"Where do you live? I'll go with you."

Oh boy.

I chuckle. "Well, I'm visiting at the moment, and I have to hit up the general store for some supplies, but I'm guessing you have something to do with that model train museum over there?" I thumb across the street where a tiny shop is squeezed between two large ones. It's not as pristine as the other businesses surrounding it, but it seems like it meets the town's standards, which I'm sure is good enough for him.

"Yes, I'm Rodney."

"Rodney," I say, holding out my hand. "I'm Wyatt. It's so nice to meet you. How about I stop by tomorrow or the next day with those pictures? You can show me around your store. Does that work?"

He nods. "Yes, that will do."

"Great, I'll see you . . ." He walks away before I can finish talking.

Okay, I guess that's it.

I head toward the general store when someone says, "William. William."

I turn around to see Rodney holding his hand up, trying to get my attention. I walk back toward him. "It's Wyatt, actually."

He dismissively waves his hand. "I'm leaving for a convention this weekend. So you'll have to come to the museum on Monday."

"Okay, I can do that. Are you going to a train convention?"

He nods. "With my good friend, Parson. Would you like to come?"

"Oh, I would, but I have some things to take care of here." *Also, I don't know you, man. You look like a cute old grandpa, but that doesn't mean you don't have skeletons buried in your backyard from people you've killed over the years.*

"Shame. I'll grab you a hat." He pats my shoulder and walks away.

Huh . . . okay. I mean, I'll wear the hat. Not to mention, thanks for the book inspiration, man. There will definitely be a creepy old train man in my next book. Maybe make him seem like the murderer when it's his arthritis making him a cranky old coot.

I make a mental note to stop by the railroad museum on Monday and then head toward the edge of town to the general store.

Almond Bay really has it all. Tourist shops like The Almond Store, Almond Outpost, and Ambrosial, which is a soap place. Then there are plenty of places to choose from to eat, like Provisions, The Cliffs, By the Slice—my favorite—a Cantina on the other side of town, and The Hot Pickle, which serves sandwiches. They top it off with The Sweet Lab and Sozzled Saloon for any nightcaps. Seriously, whoever planned this town had everything in mind.

I cross the street and pass by Pieces and Pages. I consider going inside for a moment but then think better of it. I really need some ibuprofen and hopefully Icy Hot if they have it. Not to mention, I'll need some food as well.

The general store has this Pacific Northwest feel with the gooseneck lights and weathered roof shingles that add to the ambiance rather than make it seem unkempt. I open the front door and smile when the bell rings above me.

Immediately, I'm transported to the general store in *Gilmore Girls*, which is organized and quaint with everything you might need. The wooden plank floors look like they were stripped from an old barn, while the shelves are fully stocked, nicely labeled, and organized in a way that makes sense but also seems slightly chaotic.

I grab a green basket from the stack near the door and head straight for the medicine section, but it's so small I'm actually disappointed. What the hell?

"Looking for something?" a familiar voice says.

I look to my right, where Hayes stands with a jar of pickles. "Oh hey, man," I say. "Uh, yeah, I was looking for some ibuprofen and possibly Icy Hot."

"You'll want to check out the pharmacy for anything medical."

"Oh shit, I didn't even think about that."

"Small-town living," he says. "Every business in town has a claim on a specific market. Abel, the doctor in town and a good friend, opened a pharmacy next to his practice, selling everything you might need regarding pain and illness. Coleman's barely carries anything, and I think what you're looking at there is what they have left in stock, and fuck knows how old it is."

I chuckle. "Makes sense."

"I heard she's expanding the wine section to take over this part of the store, but it will take some time."

"Wine probably brings in more income than ibuprofen."

"Sold together, and you have a winning combo." He smirks.

"Fuck, you're right." I nod at his pickles. "A fan?"

"Hattie is." He holds up the jar. "I don't know if you remember, but Cassidy and Hattie used to eat these pickles together all the time."

"That's right," I say, remembering catching Cassidy hovering over a pickle jar at the farm once. I assumed it was because she was pregnant and had weird-ass cravings.

"These are Hattie's favorites, and she ran out last night, so I thought I'd stop by and grab some for her."

"That's a good boyfriend."

He scratches the side of his head. "Some might call me that." He then nods at me and asks, "Do you have a girlfriend?"

A fiancée and she left me at the altar, but that's neither here nor there.

"Nope," I say.

A slow grin spreads across Hayes's lips. "Ever think about chasing Aubree?"

If only he knew.

But this is the perfect opportunity to lay a foundation for my plan.

"You know, not when I first met her. Never really spoke to her, but I have to admit, I realized just how beautiful she is last night when I saw her again."

"It's in the Rowley genes," Hayes says as we move around the store together. I grab a few things while we speak.

"Not sure she's too fond of me, though. I tried to talk to her this morning, and I'm positive I made her hate me even more."

"Probably," Hayes says, not even sugarcoating it. "Aubree's always been a touch on the serious side, but you have to realize where she's coming from."

I grab a bag of trail mix—one of my favorite things to snack on when I'm writing. This bag has cashews in it, which is a total score. "Where is she coming from?"

"Well, they didn't have the greatest childhood, you know that. Their father was an absolute dick. A drunk. Treated them terribly. Ryland and Cassidy were in charge most of the time, and because Hattie was so young, they focused a lot on her. Aubree was the assistant, if that makes sense."

I pause in front of the fruit and grab a bag of apples. Turning toward Hayes, I ask, "So what you're saying is, Hattie got the motherly attention from Cassidy that she needed while Aubree was there to help dole out motherly attention when she was too young to do so?"

"Yeah. She was just old enough to help but still young enough to need that reassurance of love. Having some of that attention would have benefited her. I'm not criticizing Cassidy because she never should have been put in that position, but yeah, it was all pretty fucked up, and Aubree was sort of left behind."

"That makes sense." I move over to the cucumbers and grab a few. "But why would she be so closed off?"

"I think she's just trying to prove herself, you know? Make something of herself because she was lost for so long." Hayes shrugs. "I could be way off base here, but she is very different from Cassidy or Hattie. Colder. I think there's warmth inside her, I'm just not sure she will ever let it out. I mean, I see it on occasion with Mac and sometimes with Hattie, but she's very guarded."

"Interesting."

"Which means . . ." Hayes turns toward me, and in a serious voice, he says, "Don't fuck with her. If you want to take her out on a date, make your intentions clear."

"What makes you think I want to take her out?"

"You mentioned she's beautiful, and she's half owner of the farm. I'm not sure exactly why you're here. You said reconnecting, but I think there's more to it than that. Just be careful, cautious. She's been hurt, man. Her father . . . he was cruel, and Aubree bore the brunt of that cruelty more than the others. Verbally, anyway. Don't hurt her more. She's bendable, but at some point she will break."

"I don't plan on hurting her," I say.

"Good." He nods at me. "Why are you limping?"

"I'm not limping," I say. "Just . . . uncomfortable walking at the moment."

He chuckles. "Get your hands dirty today?"

"Probably too dirty." I shuffle toward the front of the store, where I grab a bag of Red Vines and then set my basket on the conveyor belt.

"Hey, Dee Dee," Hayes says to the cashier.

"Farrow, are you treating our girl kindly?"

"Grabbing her favorite pickles."

Dee Dee smiles. "Good man."

Hayes gestures toward me. "This is Wyatt Preston, Hattie's brother-in-law and Clarke's brother."

Dee Dee's face registers with shock. "Wyatt, it's nice to meet you. Are you visiting?"

"I am," I say. "Not sure how long. Hard not to fall in love with such a beautiful small town."

"It is, isn't it? I believe Ethel was telling me something about a famous author visiting who is related to the Rowleys in some way. Does that happen to be you?"

See how the grapevine works in this town?

Let's just hope it continues to work in my favor.

"That would be me." I lean in and whisper, "But I'm trying to keep the author part on the down-low."

"Shouldn't have told Ethel then." She laughs as she finishes ringing me up, and I pay with one tap of my card to the credit machine.

I laugh. "She's a great lady. Love her inn also. Clean and comfortable, beautiful setting. Amazing breakfast. She's making it hard for me to move on. I might stay there forever."

"I bet she'd love that," Dee Dee says as she rings up Hayes's pickles.

He pays with cash and tells her to keep the change.

I pick up my one paper bag, and Hayes skips the bag, opting instead to hold his jar.

"It was nice meeting you, Dee Dee. I'm sure I'll see you around."

"Yes, you will," she says with a wave before she helps the next customer.

"Want me to walk you down to the pharmacy? If Abel is in, I can introduce you as well."

"That would be awesome," I say.

"It's right across from Five Six Seven Eight, so you'll be headed in the right direction."

"Perfect."

Together, we move down the boardwalk, passing Pieces and Pages once again as well as The Sweet Lab. I look through the window to see what they have. Seems like a lot of pie. Yup, I'll be going in there.

"So what did you do today that made you require ibuprofen and Icy Hot?"

"Well, took a tour from Aubree at first. I think I made her mad by offering different, what I thought were helpful suggestions at the time, but probably came off as a know-it-all."

"Ooo, yeah, she undoubtedly hated that."

"It was clear as day. So to make it up to her, I started working on the chicken coop. The plans were out in the open, no one was working on it, and I felt like I could be useful, so I was. I got all the framing done for the outdoor part, and tomorrow, I plan on setting up the fencing."

"Did she see you working on it?"

"Yeah. She didn't look happy."

"I wouldn't think that she would." We pass The Hot Pickle, and I consider grabbing a sub for dinner after I'm done at the pharmacy. It smells amazing like they make their own fresh bread. No doubt that they do. Almond Bay isn't just any regular small town. They seem to be more on the upscale side. Like what small town has a soap store?

"Won't stop me from working on it tomorrow."

"That's if she didn't finish it tonight," Hayes says as we cross Nutshell Drive and run right into a sizable white-and-purple building with a Pharmacy sign. Farther down the building is another sign that says Doctor. It makes me chuckle.

"Wait." I pause as his words register. "Do you really think she would finish it tonight?"

"Out of spite, yes," Hayes says and opens the door to the pharmacy for me.

Clean, white, orderly, this place screams drugstore. A cooler along the wall holds a variety of drinks, while the aisles contain shelves with everything you might need when it comes to being sick, ranging from medications to crutches to tissues. There's even a chicken soup aisle, electrolytes, and soft foods. Smart.

"Hey, Abel," Hayes says as we walk by a tall man in a pair of khaki pants and a rolled-up, checkered button-up.

"Hey, man," Abel says as he glances over at me. "Wait, is this the infamous Wyatt, aka W.J. Preston, who Ethel is nearly fainting about every chance she gets?"

"She got to you too?" I ask.

Abel nods. "Dude, she has visited everyone on Main Street at this point." He holds his hand out. "I'm Abel, it's nice to meet you."

"You too," I say, liking how easygoing he is. A doctor who just goes by his first name is rare where I'm from. *I certainly see why Hayes has settled here.*

"Did you come in for something specific?"

Hayes places his hand on my shoulder and says, "Someone went a little hard out on the farm and is now starting to hurt from it."

Abel chuckles. "I understand that completely. Let me hook you up." He moves through the aisles, bringing us to the pain relief section.

"So are you the pharmacist in town as well?" I ask him.

"Ehh, just doctor, but I own the pharmacy. Our pharmacist is out for the night, and I cover on occasion. I was about to leave, though. You caught me at the right time." He reaches for a gel cap ibuprofen bottle, then he moves around to the other side of the aisle. We follow him. He pulls a roll-on bottle off the shelf and hands it to me. "This is a form of Icy Hot but has CBD oil in it, which will be way better for those aching muscles."

"So do I just bathe in this when I return to my room?"

He laughs. "That sore, huh?"

"The fact that my back is already tensing up tells me things won't be good in the morning."

"Maybe we need to get you some electrolytes as well. Do you have a water bottle?"

"I do."

He walks us over to the drink section and asks, "Do you like lemon lime?"

"Love it."

"Then this is for you." He pulls out three tubes of Nuun Hydration electrolytes in the lemon-lime flavor. "Have a couple of these a day. Just fill up your water bottle and drop one in. It will help, and if you really want to soak the sore muscles, I can grab you some Epsom salts so you can take a bath."

"Ehhh, sitting in a bath, just staring at my dick doesn't do much for me."

Both of the men laugh. "Dude, look at your phone or something," Hayes says.

"When I tried that, I dropped my phone in the water. I have butterfingers. Not a good idea."

"Well, if you want to sit in water and stare at your dick, just let me know. I would be more than happy to direct you toward the Epsom salts."

"If I see you tomorrow, you'll know I'm desperate."

We head toward the register, and I set the items down. Abel checks me out and slips the items in my brown paper bag.

When I pay with my card, he says, "How is Aubree taking to the help?"

"What do you think?" Hayes says before I can even open my mouth.

"My guess is, not well." Then Abel looks me in the eyes and says, "You here to take over the farm?"

"What?" I ask, brows creased. "No, why would you think that?"

"When they found out that you owned part of the land, they

weren't too happy about it. I know Aubree even saw a lawyer to see what could be done."

"Really?" I ask.

Hayes nods. "Yeah, she's terrified that she might lose it to you."

I shake my head. "Nah, I don't want to take anything from her. I'm honestly really impressed with what she's accomplished. I just figured I owe it to my brother to be a part of it in some way."

Okay, I know that's a lie. You don't have to point it out. And sure, do I feel bad lying to these guys? Of course I do, but like I said, it's all part of the plan. Aubree will get her farm. I just need to weasel my way in first to get what I need. Don't fucking judge me.

"Have you told her that?"

"Uhh, maybe?" I ask. "Honestly, today is pretty murky, but I'll be sure to tell her tomorrow."

"Probably a good idea. I know it's something they were all worried about. When I heard that you were in town, I texted Ryland, and he said you came over last night and had a great visit."

"Ryland is a hell of a guy. They didn't have to welcome me in like they did. The only one who wasn't welcoming was Aubree, but I can understand why. I'll work on that."

"Smart man," Abel says. "All right, I'm heading out. See you around, Wyatt."

"Yeah, maybe tomorrow." I smirk. "You know, for the dick staring."

"Weird way to put it, man," Abel says, shaking his head and laughing.

Hayes and I walk out of the pharmacy together and head toward The Hot Pickle. "The inn is that way," Hayes says.

"Going to grab a sub for dinner."

He nods. "Okay, then I'll part ways with you."

"Thanks for the chat and helping me around town."

"Anytime," he says.

"Oh hey." I step closer and say, "What do you think about that Rodney guy? Safe to be around?"

Hayes grins. "Did he ask you if you liked trains?"

"Approached me right on the street, nearly made me wet myself."

Hayes lets out a boisterous laugh. "Rodney is an awesome guy. Eccentric, slightly deranged at times, but in a fun, *I'm old and crotchety* way. But he's harmless, just really invested in trains."

"Seemed like it. And what about Ethel? This morning, she left a note under my door telling me how excited she was that I was staying at her inn."

"Also a great lady. Will spread gossip like it's her job and has no problem poking her nose into your business. Careful what you say around her. She'll never repeat it wrong, but she will repeat it."

"Good to know. Anything or anyone else I need to worry about?"

Hayes shakes his head. "Other than Aubree, I think you're good."

"Think she's my biggest hurdle?"

"Mountain, man. She's your biggest mountain."

And with that, he takes off, heading back toward the general store, pickles in hand.

Yeah, I think he's right. To get what I want, I'll have to climb a mountain.

———

FUCK ME, why do my inner thighs hurt so much?

It's not like I did a set of lunges with extra weight that would turn my legs into noodles today, but here I am.

I brought some muffins from The Sweet Lab for everyone to share this morning, hoping to gain some favorable points for my side, but the moment I pulled up to the barn and parked my car, I realized that there really isn't anyone else here, besides Aubree's four-by-four.

Maybe it's a late start day or something.

I walk—and I mean slowly tip tap across the dirt driveway because, Jesus Christ, my legs—and stop when the chicken coop comes into view.

Hayes was right.

The wiring has been installed and a ramp from inside the barn to the outside portion has been built as well.

Did she stay up late and work on it, or wake up early this morning? Maybe a little of both.

Either way, she'll give me a run for my money. I didn't think winning over Aubree would be easy, but if this is what I'm dealing with, I'm in a lot of trouble.

Unsure of where she is, I head toward the barn with the muffins—and my electrolytes—just as she appears from the dark side of the barn, holding a pair of wire cutters.

And I know that I said Aubree was beautiful in front of Hayes, but fuck . . . I meant it. She has a natural, earthy beauty that you don't see very often. Today, she's wearing short overalls and a red tube top so her curvy sides are showing. Her hair is styled into two French braids, and she has scrunched socks and work boots on her feet. But what sends me over the edge is the rolled-up bandanna in her hair and the coat of mascara framing her breathtaking eyes.

"What are you doing here?" she asks as her morning greeting. It could have been worse. She could have told me to go to hell.

Or she could have taken my box of muffins from my hand and chucked them against the barn wall, so I should be happy with this.

"Good morning to you as well."

"It was good until you showed up."

Ooo, is she ripe today.

I kind of like it.

"Clever," I say and then hold out the box of muffins. "Stopped by The Sweet Lab. I asked Debbie behind the counter what kind of muffin Miss Aubree Rowley enjoys, and she told me you like the maple apple muffin, so I got you some."

She stares at the box but doesn't move.

"I know you want one. She told me you love them so much that she sees you buying one at least once a week."

"She's lying."

"Is she?" I ask with a raise of my brow.

"Yes," she says, snatching the box from me and setting it on the tractor wheel. She flips open the lid, takes one, and bites into the top without even removing the wrapper.

Okay . . . maybe we're getting somewhere. Maple apple muffins are the way to her heart.

Well, the way to her not spitting venom.

I walk up to the tire to grab one, but she swats at my hand. "What do you think you're doing?" she asks.

"Uh, enjoying breakfast with you?"

"These are my muffins. You got them for me, no?"

"I did," I reply.

"Then that means they're mine, and I'm going to tell you right now that I'm not good at sharing."

"If I don't have a muffin, I'll starve."

"That sounds awfully dramatic, don't you think?" she asks.

"Yes, but I'm an author. I'm supposed to be dramatic."

She takes another bite, and the scent of maple and apple wafts toward me, causing my stomach to growl. "Is that a requirement?"

"With the writer's guild, yes."

"Well, not a fan, so take your drama somewhere else. Maybe take it back into town where you can get breakfast—hey!"

She shouts when I snatch the muffin out of her hand.

"Give me that!" she shouts just as I lick the top of the muffin, claiming it as mine. "Ew, what is wrong with you?"

"I told you I was hungry."

"Do you really think I won't eat that even though you licked it?"

"I'd be impressed if you did." I hold the muffin out to her.

"Go ahead and take it. The bread is probably moist from my saliva."

She huffs and goes back to the bakery box. "You're disgusting."

"You made me be disgusting. If you'd just shared, I wouldn't have had to lick your muffin . . ." I think about it for a second, my words registering, and a smile crosses my lips.

She points her finger at me. "See, disgusting."

"Hey, you thought of it too."

"Only because you grinned like an immature teenager." She unwraps her muffin this time and takes a bite of the crunchy bottom.

"You don't have to say disgusting, by the way. Nothing disgusting is involved when . . . I lick a muffin."

"Doubtful," she says. "You probably breathe too hard, lose focus, and waste time."

"The perception you have of me is entirely too flattering. You'll give me such a big ego that I won't fit through these barn doors."

"Don't worry, I have no problem popping it so you fizzle right through them."

"I have no doubt about that." I motion to the chicken coop. "Looks like you couldn't stand the fact that I framed out the coop yesterday. Had to show me up, did you?"

"No. I just didn't want you to have the joy of completing a project on the farm."

I stare at her. "That's a little psychotic."

"Are you really calling a woman psychotic?"

"Uh . . . no?"

"You better not. If I were a man and I decided to finish the chicken coop that a lady started the day before, it would look as if I was chivalrous. Like I was a kind man, not making the lady do all the work, but because you're the man starting the project and I'm the one finishing it, I'm coming off as a bitch, aren't I?"

"Well, I wouldn't use the word bitch. Probably strong-willed.

And it's not about you completing the project but more so your attitude."

"What if the roles were reversed? Wouldn't you be seen as the grumpy man, the Luke Danes who everyone loves, while I'm the crotchety Emily Gilmore?"

"Nice references," I say. "And I don't see you that way."

"You're just saying that," she says as she toes the ground. "Trust me when I say I know what everyone in this town thinks of me."

"Oh yeah? What do they think of you?" I ask.

"That I'm stubborn, mean, rude, jaded."

"Is that how you feel?"

Her eyes meet mine, and she pauses for a moment, making me believe she actually might talk to me . . . until she says, "I wasn't looking for a therapy session this morning, Wyatt."

"Wasn't offering one."

She takes a bite of her muffin, and with a full mouth, she asks, "What are you doing here? All I heard yesterday from Ryland is how the town is falling in love with you. You've been here for one day. What are you trying to do? Win them over so you can steal my farm out from under me? I'm going to tell you right now—"

"I don't want the farm," I say, causing her to pause midsentence in shock.

She swallows her bite. "Wait, what?"

I let out a sigh, wishing I didn't have to have this conversation now, but if I don't, I think she'll keep trying to get rid of me, and we'll just go around in circles. If I have the conversation now, maybe she can warm up to the idea or even say yes. Maybe she'll be relieved, who knows.

"I think this conversation would be best if we go sit down somewhere."

I can sense her hesitation, but with her muffin in hand, she walks out of the barn, and I follow her, thinking that's what she wants.

She brings me to a small white building, which she opens up to reveal a quaint office. Where was this on the tour?

Probably didn't want me to see it in case I started snooping. I wouldn't put it past her.

She sits at the desk while I sit in one of the chairs across from her.

I manspread while she crosses one leg over the other.

"You want to have a conversation." She motions her hand toward me. "Converse."

I guess, here we go.

"I don't want the farm, Aubree. I actually don't want anything to do with it. I'm willing to hand over my rights, free of charge. You just take everything."

She sits taller, her muffin ignored now.

"Why would you do that? Unless . . . is there a catch?"

"Yes," I answer, not wanting to hide it.

"Of course." She leans back in her chair. "There's always a catch. I knew you were here for a reason. You came in here, acting like you wanted to get close to your niece—"

"I do," I say quickly. "I do want to spend time with MacKenzie. I think that's important."

"But not the main reason you're here."

I shake my head. "It's not."

"What's the real reason? Maybe this time you'll be honest with me."

Here it goes.

"I want to marry you," I say.

The words fly out of my mouth and float between us, creating an awkward tension. I know she heard them because she's having a hard time blinking as she stares blankly at me.

Consider her shocked.

Stunned.

Probably wondering what sort of fifth dimension she just walked into.

"Uh . . . what?" she finally asks when she finds her voice.

"I want to marry you."

"Yeah." She nods. "Heard that part. But why?"

"Because I'm in love with you."

That makes her face fall flat. "You know, if you're not going to be serious about this, Wyatt, then you're wasting my time. You either tell me the real reason you're here or just freaking leave."

"I want to marry you."

She stands from her chair on a huff, grabs her muffin, and heads toward the door. I pop out of my chair just as quickly, and before she can exit, I grab her by the wrist and pull her back into the middle of the office.

Her eyes flash down to where I'm gripping her and then back up to me. "Do not touch me."

"Don't walk away," I say, matching her tone, growing more serious so she knows I'm talking business.

Her chest rises and falls as her eyes match mine. "I'm not staying here if you're not being serious."

"I'm being serious. I'm asking you to marry me."

"Stop it," she says, attempting to pull away.

"I need you to marry me," I say this time, which causes her to pause.

She wets her lips before she says, "What do you mean, you *need* me to marry you?"

"If you sit down, maybe we can talk about it."

"No, tell me here, now."

Knowing I won't win with this woman, I say, "My family owns a cabin that is supposed to go to the first grandchild who marries. My cousin, who I absolutely hate and who cares nothing about the cabin, is now engaged and rubbing it in my face. I need to get married before he can take possession of the cabin."

"You're serious?"

"Never been more serious," I say.

"Then why not ask some random girl on the street? Maybe a friend? You don't even know me."

"My one friend I could ask is gay, and my cousin knows that. I need someone who would make sense. You would make sense."

"Uh, no, I wouldn't. We've barely spent any time together. And also . . . I'm not marrying you."

"We have a connection," I say, my heart racing as I lay out my plan, seeing it's already starting to fail from the look of disbelief in her eyes. "The farm."

"What do you mean by that?"

"Can we please sit down? I can tell you everything."

She purses her lips, and I can see her debating what to do.

"Please," I say, practically resorting to begging here.

She lets out an irritated sigh and then moves past me, bumping my shoulder in the process, and sits in one of the chairs in front of her desk. Grateful, I take the seat next to her. She crosses her legs, pulling them both up on the chair, and stares at me expectantly.

Okay, you have her attention. Let it all out.

"Like I said, there's a family cabin that means a lot to me. Consider how much this farm means to you, and that's how I feel about the cabin. When my grandfather passed, I just assumed, given our close relationship, he'd leave it to me. However, per his will, the first grandchild to get married takes possession. I'm not sure if he did this to make sure the lineage is carried on. Either way, it put a wrench in my plans. My cousin Wallace is engaged now. He didn't have the same relationship with my grandfather. He hated the cabin, and I know if he takes ownership, he'll bulldoze it and build something more modern. I can't stomach that. So my friend Laurel helped me come up with this plan."

"And what is the plan exactly?" she asks, folding her arms over her chest.

"You marry me for a year—"

"A year? That's insane."

"It wouldn't be that long in the grand scheme of things."

"A year is a year. And why would I even consider doing this for you?"

"Because," I say, taking a deep breath. "If you marry me for a year, then I'll give you the rights to my half of the farm when we divorce. It's all yours, no questions asked."

Her eyes narrow at me. *She's not a fan of the plan.*

"That's blackmail."

"Uhh, not really," I say. "It's called making a deal."

"A deal is like I'll give you an apple for this orange. You're asking me to marry you!"

"Well, if you think of the apple as the marriage and the orange as the land, then it could resemble the deal you're talking about."

"You have lost your mind." She shakes her head. "Wyatt, marriage is serious. And what am I supposed to do, marry you and then say peace out, see you in a year?"

I cringe, knowing she's really not going to like this part. "Uh, actually, we would have to pretend we're married."

Jaw clenched, she asks, "What do you mean, pretend?"

I clear my throat. "You know, uh, live together, that sort of thing."

"No fucking way." She stands from her chair and moves out of the office before I can even stand.

I chase her and say, "It won't require intimacy if that's what you're worried about."

She turns on her heel and faces me. "Anything that involves having to live with you is intimate. It's bad enough I have you following me around this farm. The last thing I need is to come home to my *guest house*, and see you there, with your feet propped up on my pillow, typing away on your computer."

"I'll have you know, I'm the kind of husband who'd never prop his feet up on your pillow."

"Jesus," she mutters before she continues walking.

"We could make it work, Aubree. We could get a house in town or something."

"With what money?" she asks. "Also, I like being near the farm. I like being near Ryland to help him out. I'm not going to move just to accommodate your asinine idea."

"Not to sound like a total douche, but I have a lot of money. We could build a tiny home to live in, something larger than what you have."

She walks up to me and presses her finger to my chest. "Why don't you take that money and buy yourself a mail-order bride?"

And with that, she takes off toward the chicken coop, where I hear her slam some wood around.

Wow, that went way worse than I thought it would.

WYATT: *I proposed to Aubree.*

Laurel: OMG! Did you get down on one knee? Did she kick you to get up? Did she say yes?

Wyatt: She told me to find a mail-order bride. Makes me wonder if getting down on one knee would have convinced her that I'm the husband she needs.

Laurel: From what you've told me, doubtful. What are you going to do now?

Wyatt: I'm not giving up. I'm here for at least five more days. She gave her employees a long weekend, meaning I can drive her nuts without them knowing.

Laurel: Your action plan is to continue to poke the bear? Do you really think that's a good idea?

Wyatt: Sometimes you have to keep poking until the bear cracks. I have no problem doing that. Although, I wonder if the general store carries protective cups for men. I might need one from the anger in that one.

Laurel: Look into overnighting one.

Wyatt: Might have to. But in all honesty, I think I saw a small sliver of interest in her eyes when I laid out the plans. She lost her mind a bit when I told her we'd have to pretend to like each other for a year and live together.

Laurel: Doesn't she know that you're great at sleeping on couches and being a slug? Do you need me to write a letter of recommendation on your behalf, stating just that?

Wyatt: Is this your attempt to be the helpful best friend?

Laurel: Am I not doing a good job?

Wyatt: Normally, you exceed expectations, right now . . . no.

Laurel: How am I supposed to help you when you think poking the bear is the way to go?

Wyatt: *I'd like to know that when I get my balls chopped off, you'll be there to nurse me back to health.*

Laurel: *Are you going to want to be nursed back to health if your balls are chopped off? You're not a starfish. They won't grow back.*

Wyatt: *You don't know my body's abilities.*

Laurel: *Aw, you started a fresh state of denial. It's good to see you growing.*

Wyatt: *Right before your very eyes.*

Laurel: *Well, good luck with the poking because it seems like you'll need it.*

"WHAT THE HELL ARE YOU DOING?" Aubree asks as she comes up behind me. I have a landscape wheel in one hand and marking pins in the other.

"What does it look like I'm doing?" I ask.

After she stormed out and I spoke to Laurel, I decided to get some lunch and make a list of things I can do to push Aubree to her limit. *I know what you're thinking. Wyatt, that's a dick thing to do.*

And yes, you'd be correct. And before you sneer at that, please note that I asked her nicely several times and even offered up a tiny home, something I certainly thought she'd like. So I tried. She said no, and now we're here.

Will this backfire on me? The likelihood is very high, but it's a risk I'm willing to take.

Also, if I didn't notice just a hint of interest, I'd probably go on my sad, lonely way. But I saw it in her eyes—it's there. I just have to make her see what a fantastic idea it is.

"It looks like you're trying to piss me off."

Can't get anything past her.

"Why on earth would I want to piss off my future bride?"

I swear, hand to heart, I see steam come out of her ears as she says, "*Don't* call me that."

I haven't seen Aubree in a violent state, so she might be all bark and no bite. Even with that knowledge tucked away, seeing her snarl at me doesn't stop my testicles from shivering with fear. They're knocking together in horror.

"Is it not true?" I ask her.

"It's not. I didn't accept your ridiculous proposal."

"Was it because I didn't get down on one knee? Because I can."

I start to kneel, but she swats at me. "Get up. Good God, you're ridiculous."

"So it wasn't the knee thing. Well, if it comes down to jewelry, I can get you the ring of your dreams or something very modest. Maybe a promise necklace . . ." When her face sours, I add, "Or perhaps a promise key chain."

"It wasn't the proposal. It's you. You're the problem. Your personality. Your idea of being married. That's why I said no."

"Hmm, seems a bit harsh," I say. "Maybe if you got to know me better, you'd say yes."

"I'm not saying yes. I don't want to get married. I don't want to be tied to anyone. And I especially don't want to get married to you, because that means you'll stick around here. The last thing I want is you walking around the farm with stakes and a freaking landscaping wheel."

"Shame. I'd be a good husband." I turn away from her and keep walking out toward the field. *Although, if you ask Cadance, I wouldn't have been that.*

"Where are you going?" she asks while trailing after me.

"To the fields."

"Why?" she asks.

"Given that you're not my wife or bride-to-be, I don't think I have to answer that question."

She rushes in front of me and says, "Given that I'm part owner of this farm, I have the right to know."

"Not when it's my piece of land."

Let the poking begin.

"Do not go out there and start messing things up," she says.

"Why would I mess things up? It's not like I'm going to destroy your business out of spite because you rejected my proposal of marriage." I grin at her, and her eyes fall flat with fury.

"Wyatt Preston, I suggest—"

"Wyatt Joseph Preston, in case you wanted to use my middle name in your tirade."

Her lips purse.

Her eyes narrow even farther.

And her hands twitch at her side.

"Wyatt Joseph Preston"—ahh, she used my full name—"I suggest you tell me what you're going to do, or I'm going to attach myself to you."

"Perfect, that's just what I want. Maybe you'll get used to me then."

I move past her and head out toward the field, and to my surprise, I hear her feet pad against the solid dirt ground, and then she nearly pulls me backward as she hops up onto my back and loops her legs around my waist, clutching onto me in a piggyback.

It takes me a second to gain my balance, but I playfully nuzzle my head against hers when I do.

"What are you doing? Stop that." She lifts to avoid me while still staying attached.

"Just cuddling with my missus. This is what you'd get with marriage, all the cuddles."

"That's not a selling point," she deadpans.

Enjoying the free ride she's taking—because it means she's next to me, and I can keep needling at her until she says yes—I ask, "Do you not like to be touched, Aubree?"

"Not by strange men I don't know."

"You know me enough. Your sister hugged me. That means something."

"My sister would hug a lamp post if it glittered under the sun in just the right way. That means nothing to me."

"Mac hugged me."

"She's a child, and you gave her a present."

"Solid point. But . . . your brother hugged me."

"No, he didn't."

"How do you know?" I ask as I carry her across the farm, not really fazed by the extra weight on my back. I'm sure I'll be crying about it tomorrow, though. Might have to pick up those Epsom salts. "You were scowling in the corner, so you could have missed the fact that he gently caressed my back as a hello."

"That's not what Ryland does."

"Either way, you know enough about me that if I were to flip you over my head, onto this ground, and then hover above you to offer you a hug of apology, you'd accept the touch."

"I'd knee you in the junk and get up myself."

"Technically, that would be touching me, so I win." I smile to myself.

"What exactly are you winning?"

"You, of course. What a prize too. A little bit of ornery, a lot of sass, and a bunch of growling. What a lovely bride you'll make."

"I don't growl."

"I saw you growl at a rabbit yesterday. Its poor legs gave out on it, and it scrambled away, army-crawl style, into the bushes, and then you sat there, pointed, and laughed."

"What the actual hell?" she says. "Is that what your author brain does all day, make up scenarios in your head that are not true?"

"Yes," I answer. "It's how I create scenes and dialogue. Do you not give in to your thoughts during the day?"

"I sure as hell don't think about a nice lady scaring off a bunny army-crawl style."

"I like that you slipped nice in there as a description for yourself. Not something I'd have chosen, but then again, I wouldn't have chosen you as my own personal koala either, but here we are."

"If you only told me what you were doing, I wouldn't have to ride you," she replies.

"This wouldn't be my definition of riding me," I say. "I have a completely different image in my head."

"Ew," she says. "I would never."

"Don't knock it until you've tried it."

In an annoyed tone, she says, "I've tried it several times. I just mean I wouldn't do it with you."

"Now that's not fair. I'm a good-looking man with strong fingers from typing all day. You have no idea the kind of pleasure I could bring."

"Good thing I have no desire to find out either."

"Your loss." I shrug. "My acupuncturist told me I have the strongest thumb muscles she's ever seen."

"Am I supposed to be impressed with that? What are you even going to do with thumb muscles?"

I pause and say, "Uh . . . a lot, Aubree. A whole fucking lot."

"Forget I even asked."

"No, let's dive into that. I think a little education would be nice on our jaunt, don't you?"

"Not if it involves you talking about your thumbs and sticking them places."

You know, despite her grouchy attitude and irritated disposition, she's really quick-witted and, perhaps, a touch humorous? I know that might be a bit of a stretch, but her responses have made me smile.

"If we're going to be married, we should discuss these things."

"We're not getting married," she says, exhausted.

Hmm, maybe if I say it enough, I'll wear her down. Add that to the list of things to poke her with.

"So you think, but mark my words, five days from now, you'll be saying I do!"

"In your author dreams."

———

"PUT THAT BACK," I yell at Aubree, who has removed yet another one of my wire stakes.

"No." She has them all gripped in her hands, definitely pleased with herself.

"I'm doing hard work here, and you're ruining it."

"Just like you're ruining my day?" she asks. "I could be finishing that coop. Instead, I'm out here in the hot sun, helicoptering over you as if you're a toddler running wild in a potato field."

"That was your choice. I didn't force you to come out here. You're the one who climbed me like a tree . . . so . . ." I wiggle my eyebrows.

"Stop being disgusting," she says with an unamused glare.

"Seriously, put the stake back."

"Not until you tell me what you're doing."

Rolling my eyes, I say, "What does it look like I'm doing? I'm marking my side of the land. I have some people coming Monday who are going to tear up the fields to make room for my cows."

Her mouth falls open, and her body goes slack.

"Excuse me?" she says.

"You heard me. I truly believe you have too much potato waste, and we could be using this space for something more substantial, like cows."

"You know nothing about farming. Do you know how expensive the start-up will be for that?"

"Well, thank God I'm a single man with an expendable income that I can fuck around with. Moooooo-ve over . . . the cows are coming, baby."

I guide the landscaping wheel down the field while using an app on my phone that shows me the land's topography. When I hit a corner, I put down a stake, only for her to snatch it again.

I turn toward her and say, "You're making this very counterproductive for the both of us."

"You are not tearing out my fields."

"My fields." I boop her on the nose, and she swats me away. "But they could be yours if you become Mrs. Wyatt J. Preston." I look up at the sky dreamily. "Aubree Falooloo Preston. Has a beautiful ring to it, doesn't it?"

"You're deranged. Now stop this nonsense. I have things I need to do, and I can't babysit you this whole time."

"I never asked you to babysit me. Feel free to leave anytime you want. I'm just going to keep working."

"You realize if I leave and you still stake, I'll come out here tonight with a flashlight and remove all the stakes, erasing your unnecessary work."

"You're going to be that spiteful?"

"You have no idea how spiteful I can be."

"Well, Mrs. Preston, it seems you have met your match," I say, grinning at her.

Oh, I can tell . . . this is going to be fun.

Chapter Five

AUBREE

I rub some aloe vera over my shoulders as I stare at myself in the bathroom mirror. I wasn't expecting to be out in the field without sunscreen during the hottest part of the day, but that happens when Wyatt Preston thinks he's some funny guy attempting to make a statement.

Guess who won?

Me.

He ran out of stakes, and when he tried to take them away from me, I ran away, sprinting across the fields in boots and leaving him in my dust. He left after that, and I have never felt more satisfied. Well, besides when he saw me working on the chicken coop he'd been determined to build. I proved to him that I'm fine without his help or opinion.

Or the offer for his hand in marriage.

Honestly, I still can't get over the audacity. He doesn't care about this farm. He said it himself that he would hand over the land freely. The only reason he's holding on is because he wants something from me, and that something is the most ridiculous thing I've ever heard.

Marriage.

He wants to marry me . . . out of convenience, to save some family cabin.

Don't get me wrong, I can understand the desperation to save something close to you, hence why I've been battling with him over this farm. But he needs other options because I'm not one of them.

I slip into a tank top with a built-in bra and slide into cotton shorts. I'm just having dinner with Ryland and Mac. It's not like I need to dress up. With my hair wet and down, I slip on my sandals and start toward the farmhouse when my eyes connect with the stupid SUV that keeps popping up on the farm.

"You have got to be kidding me," I mutter as I stomp toward the house and up the porch steps. When I open the creaky screen door and see Wyatt on the ground, dressed up like a ninja and rolling around in mock pain from Mac's zappy hands, I inwardly groan.

Whyyyyyy?

Why is he here?

Can I not have a peaceful moment without him tagging along?

"Aunt Aubree!" Mac says as she charges toward me. She sees me every day but still acts like I'm visiting for the first time in months. *She is the absolute best balm for the end of any and every day.*

"Hey, Mac, how was your day?"

"Great. I'm zapping Uncle Wyatt until he turns into dust."

"Need help? Because I'd love nothing more than for that to happen."

Wyatt looks up from the floor. "I'm sure you would," he says.

Ryland jogs down the stairs, freshly showered and wearing comfy clothes just like me. "Oh hey, pizza is in the oven. Should be done soon."

"Great, need me to do anything?" I ask.

"No, I'm good. Just going to set the table. Hey Mac, go upstairs, go potty, and wash your hands."

"But I don't need to go potty," she whines.

"I understand you don't need to go potty, but I bet there's pee inside you that needs to come out."

"No, no pee." She shakes her head defiantly. What I've heard from people around town when I talk about Mac is that four is one of the worst years to parent because they really like to hold on to that independence and defiance. Not a bad thing, but boy oh boy when you try to get them to do something, it's really hard.

"Okay," Ryland says. "Then don't go potty. That's your choice. I just hope the pee goblin doesn't get you."

What the hell is the pee goblin?

"If it does, I'll zap him with my zappers," she says, holding out her hands and curling her fingers.

"Pee goblin is immune to zaps."

"He is?" Mac asks, looking almost stunned at that new information.

Ryland nods. "Yup. He'll come for you no matter what."

She sighs. "Fine, I'll go potty."

And then with her head turned down, she drags herself up the stairs to go to the bathroom.

"What the hell is the pee goblin?" I ask.

Ryland places his hand on the counter as he leans against it and says, "Don't judge me, but it was something she came up with when she said she peed her pants one day at school, that the pee goblin came to get her. And well, I ran with it." He shakes his head. "I'm not perfect, just trying to get the girl to go pee so she doesn't get an infection. Jesus Christ, she's a camel. She holds that pee in longer than anyone I know."

"I like the pee goblin," Wyatt says as he removes his ninja mask and looks me up and down. "You look nice, Aubree."

Uh . . . what is he doing?

I stand there, stunned and confused because why would he say that in front of my brother? Unless . . . this is part of his scheme.

"Aren't you going to say thank you?" Ryland smirks.

"No," I say as I move toward the kitchen and grab the napkins to help set the table.

"Let me get that for you," Wyatt says, coming right up behind me and taking the napkins. "You had a hard day on the farm. Just look at that sunburn. Do you need me to get you any lotion for it?"

Wow, and the Oscar goes to . . .

"I just put some on, and I don't need you—"

"Uncle Ry Ry, I'm pooooooping!" Mac shouts from upstairs.

"Great," Ryland mumbles as he moves past us. "Can you finish setting the table? I have to tend to my niece, who likes company when she poops."

At times like these, I thank Cassidy for not listing me as Mac's legal guardian.

Once Ryland is up the stairs, Wyatt walks up to me and says, "Want my help?"

I turn toward him and reply, "What I want you to do is to leave this house and never return."

"Is that how you should be talking to your husband?"

Through clenched teeth, I drag out, "You are *not* my husband."

"Not yet." He tilts my chin up with his finger. I go to push him away, but he captures my wrists in his hands.

"What are you doing?"

"Just letting you know . . ." He leans in until his mouth is right next to my ear. The minute he starts talking, chills spread down my legs. "You are not to tell anyone about my proposal, not a single soul, and if you do, I'm selling my half of the land."

A gasp falls past my lips as he pulls away. "You wouldn't."

"I would, Mrs. Preston." Then he moves past me, grabs the plates from the cabinet, and starts setting the table.

"You know, this is not going to work," I say, seeing through his whole act. "You think you're going to change my mind in the next four or five days before you leave, but what you don't know about me is that I'm as stubborn as the cows you want to purchase. I'm not budging."

"You've clearly underestimated me," he says with an arrogant confidence that drives me nuts. Then his eyes scan me before he says, "Your nipples are hard. Did I do that?"

"Oh my God!" I nearly shout, covering my breasts as I walk into the kitchen.

And yes . . . yes, he did do that.

But not because I think he's an attractive man or find the way his hair falls over his forehead intriguing. It's because when I get angered, my body reacts, and unfortunately, that includes my nipples.

I'm facing away from him when I feel his heated body behind me. His hand lands on my waist, and I'm so insulted by his presumption that I turn around to face him.

Bad idea, because he's so close that he presses me up against the counter.

"It's okay to admit that I get you revved up."

"Can you not be so obnoxious?" I ask, still covering my chest with one hand, hoping to calm them down. "It's chilly in here, and I'm not wearing a bra. My nipples have nothing to do with you. Also, that kind of talk is completely inappropriate."

"Not when you're my future wife."

"Oh my God, Wyatt. You realize you have a serious problem, right?"

"The only problem I see is standing right in front of me." He grips my waist a touch tighter, just to remind me he's holding me, possessing me in a way he has no right doing.

Yet why am I not pushing his hand away?

"Just admit it, Aubree," he says, talking closer to me. "You want the land, and I want the cabin. It's the perfect opportunity to help each other out."

"But what about the fact that I don't want to help *you* out?" I ask. "At this point, the last thing I want to do is help you make your dreams come true."

"Sometimes your words can hurt, Aubree."

"Please, you don't have feelings," I say. "All you have is your self-importance. I suggest you don't waste your time with me and try to find someone else."

"Uh-huh, and what happens when I do and then use my half of the land for something else? Like . . . oh, I don't know, sell it off for commercial space."

"You wouldn't do that," I say even though a slight panic enters my heart. He was right about earlier. I don't know him that well, and I have no clue what kind of integrity and loyalty this man possesses.

Other than the love he has for his cabin.

But from his proposal, it seems like he has no problem stepping over people to get his own way.

"I very much would and would enjoy every second of it."

Just then, Mac and Ryland come down the stairs, and I see the moment Ryland notices us in the kitchen, in an intimate position, because his eyebrow raises in question.

Thankfully, Wyatt pulls away and continues setting the table, but that doesn't stop Ryland from staring me down, a slew of questions rolling around in his head.

I ignore him, though, and get everyone drinks. The last thing I need is for Wyatt to do something brash, like sell off the land. So I keep my mouth shut and move around the kitchen, pretending to be helpful.

⸻

"THAT WAS GREAT, THANK YOU," Wyatt says as he pats his stomach after dropping off his empty plate of food. "Was that homemade crust?"

"Dude, does it look like I have time to make homemade pizza crust?"

Wyatt laughs as I finish loading the dishwasher for Ryland. "No, but I wanted to be polite and not assume."

"I appreciate it, but assume away with any shortcuts. The easier, the better for me."

"Good to know."

I wipe my hands on the kitchen towel. "Is there anything else you need help with? Want me to give Mac her shower?"

Ryland shakes his head. "Nah, I can handle it. You can head home. Thanks for doing the dishes."

"Anytime," I say.

"Here, I can walk you home," Wyatt says as he comes up to me.

"Uh, I think I can make it," I say, highly annoyed with him. Not just because of everything he did today but because he was so freaking charming during dinner.

He had Ryland rolling with laughter and Mac sitting on his lap at one point, playing with his cheeks. The entire dinner was consumed by him. And the worst thing? He sat next to me at the table and draped his arm over the back of my chair several times, making it seem like something was happening between us.

A budding relationship if you will.

It was subtle but significant, enough for Ryland to piggyback off catching us in the kitchen together. I can only imagine what's going on in my brother's mind at the moment.

"Nah, I'll make sure you get home safely," Wyatt says with a knowing smile. "Have a good night, Ryland."

Ryland smirks as he shakes Wyatt's hand. "Have a good night, Wyatt."

And then with his hand on my lower back, Wyatt guides me toward the front door as if he's my escort and I have no idea where I'm going.

When we reach the porch and head down the stairs, I spin away from him and whisper, "Stop that. I know where my house is, and I don't need you acting like we're a couple in front of my brother."

"Why not?" he asks. "When you say yes to my proposal, it won't come off as a big surprise."

"Uh, getting engaged after being around someone for a week will be a big surprise no matter how many times you place your hand on my lower back."

"Well, it will soften the blow. Trust me, I know about this kind of stuff."

"You know about fake marriages?" I ask. "Please, tell me how?"

"Uh . . . it's called being an author," he says as he follows me to my guest house. I open the door, ready to slam it shut on him, but to my horror, he helps himself in. "I wrote a book with a marriage of convenience as part of the plot, so I'm well-versed. I know all the ins and outs of what to do and what not to do. When I say giving subtle hints to the people around you about a possible romance is key, I'm not lying. It played off beautifully in my book."

"That's fiction," I counter. "This is real life. It's completely different."

"Some might say fiction is just research for real life."

I stare at him, deadpanned. "Absolutely no one says that."

"Some might."

"No one," I reply. "Also, what the hell do you think you're doing, coming into my house? I didn't invite you in."

"Husbands don't need invitations," he says as he kicks off his shoes and looks around.

I point at his shoes. "Put those back on. You're not staying."

"Don't worry, I'll leave before you go to bed, but I just want to get a good look at where I'll be living." He moves to my closet and opens the door. "Hmm, we'll need to make some room for my stuff."

I shut the door and block him from it with my body. "You're not staying here. Therefore, we don't need to make room."

"Oh, you want to go for the tiny house situation? Not a problem. We can also do a small barndominium, and once we get divorced, you can turn it into an Airbnb. You're welcome for the idea."

"I didn't say thank you."

"You will when you start seeing the extra income." He flops back on my bed, arms extended. "Ooo, comfier than I thought it would be. This will do."

"You have lost your freaking mind if you think I'll share a bed with you."

"Where else would I sleep?"

"On the floor," I reply as I grab my toothbrush and start brushing my teeth.

"Aha," he says, lifting and pointing at me. "You're thinking about it. I'm wearing you down."

Crap, that got past me.

"I meant, on the floor outside because you wouldn't be my husband." I spit into the sink and rinse my toothbrush.

"Nice try," he says, flopping back on the bed. "You know, the Airbnb wouldn't be such a bad idea. Think about all the branding you could incorporate into the space. Offer up a gift basket of all things from The Almond Store and fresh eggs for breakfast."

"Can you stop it with your ideas? They're getting annoying."

Because they're actually pretty damn good. An Airbnb would do very well here, especially since the inn is one of the few spaces available to book with all the amenities. Apart from the RV park outside of town, there's a camping ground about three miles up the coast.

"Sad that you're not thinking of them? It's okay, babe. We can think up some ideas you can develop."

"That's so condescending," I say as I sit on my bed because my legs are sore, and I have nowhere else to sit. That's how small this room is.

He turns to face me and props his head on his hand. His five o'clock shadow is coming in very dark, making it look like he almost has a full beard. Not that I care to admit it, but it looks nice on him.

"Trust me when I say I won't be condescending when we're married."

"Oh great, so you're just condescending when you try to court me?" I scoot down on my bed, freaking exhausted from the day. When I sink into the pillow, my eyes start to droop.

"So you think that we're courting? Good to know. Is this like a . . . I bring you flowers every day kind of thing? Because I know how to woo."

"How about you try leaving me alone? That'll score you some points."

"Thank you for the suggestion. I'm afraid I can't take it because I'm rather attached to you already."

"You like to be tortured with sarcasm and sass?" I ask as I sink deeper into my pillow and cross my legs at my ankles.

"Call it my guilty pleasure," he replies as I slowly shut my eyes. "Are you falling asleep on me?"

"I am," I say, not bothering to open my eyes. "And if I find you here, in my bed, in the morning, you will face a serious problem."

"Shouldn't you want to get used to sleeping with me?"

"No," I answer. "Because I'm not marrying you, so there's no need to get used to sleeping with you. Simple as that."

"You say that now, but I'll wear you down."

"I wish you luck in your endeavor because you'll need it. I know how stubborn I can be. You're in for a real uphill climb." I curl into my pillow.

"Good thing I like a challenge." He stands from the bed and moves toward the door. "Sweet dreams, Mrs. Preston."

The audacity.

How I wish I could wake up tomorrow and this all be a horrible nightmare.

I will never be Mrs. Preston.

No matter his threats.

LAST NIGHT, I easily got the best night of sleep I've had in a very long time. Not certain why. I know it has nothing to do with Wyatt, that's for damn sure, but it was amazing. I feel refreshed and ready to start my day.

I might have slept in just a touch, but that's okay because it's the weekend, and I have the day off if I want to take it, but I don't. I want to finish up that chicken coop before Wyatt can get his hands on it. If anything, I want to show him that I don't need his help.

So with a fresh travel mug of coffee in my hand, I head out of my house and hop into the four-by-four. It will be hot today, so I slathered on the sunscreen and put on a pair of worn jean shorts with paint spots all over them and a green tank top that says Save the Trees. I tossed my hair into a bun and tied a rolled-up bandanna around my head to help keep the stray hairs out of my eyes.

I plan to finish up some last-minute framing of the chicken coop and then paint all day. While the paint dries, I want to build some flower boxes to place around the chicken coop to make it more visually appealing. That was something Cassidy really believed in when she was creating this farm. We might use old barnwood, but a flower plant will be next to it. Which reminds me, I need to water them all today.

I drive down the path toward the barn. When I round the corner and Wyatt's SUV comes into view, I inwardly groan.

No.

No way he's here. It's eight in the morning. Doesn't the man know how to sleep?

Why is this happening, and what did I do in life to deserve this?

Growing irritated immediately and losing all the joy that my great night of sleep brought me, I park and hop out just as Wyatt comes into view wearing a pair of cargo khakis with a hammer hanging onto one of the belt loops. His black T-shirt is tight around his biceps while it falls over his narrow hips. And today, he's wearing a backward hat that seems like it's seen its fair share of hard workdays.

"Morning, babe," he says when he spots me.

"Can you not call me that? I'm not your babe."

"You will be." He winks. "Your favorite muffins are in the barn as well as some fresh fruit and coffee." His eyes land on the mug in my hand. "But I see you already have some. Either way, it's there for a refill."

It's bad enough that he keeps showing up here every day. What's even worse is that he knows my favorite muffins are my absolute crutch, and even though I can't stand the man, I find myself moving into the barn, where I can already smell the maple apple waiting for me. Damn him.

I take a seat on the tractor and bite into a muffin. The delicious flavors marinate over my taste buds as I consider what my life has come to.

I have a man following me around my farm, calling me Mrs. Preston, proposing marriage like a lovesick fiend, and bringing me muffins that I can't even muster up the strength to say no to. If you told me last week this is where I'd be, I wouldn't have believed you. Not even a little.

"I have to admit, you're good at picking out muffins," he says as he picks one up and takes a large bite of the top. I eat them the same way. None of this working around the sides. Nope, just dive right into the top. "This is my second one this morning."

"You act as if that's an accomplishment," I say. "I've had six in a day."

His brow rises. "Six?"

"Not even ashamed. Just be happy I'm not stabbing you with that pitchfork over there because you've had two from this box."

He glances behind him at the pitchfork and back at me. "You know, I truly believe you'd do that."

"Good, the more unhinged you believe I am, the better."

"Doesn't scare me, though." He leans in close and says, "I like my women a little on the crazy side."

"If that's the case, maybe you can find a bride on Craigslist. I think the majority of people on there offering human services such as marriage are unhinged."

"Nah, why look around when I have the perfect specimen sitting right in front of me?"

"You have serious issues." I shake my head. "Also, why are you here?"

"Do you really have to ask?" He pours himself some coffee. "My future bride is here, and I want to spend as much time with her as I can. Would I prefer to do it somewhere besides a chicken coop or dusty potato fields? Of course, but she has this stubborn streak that I have to work around."

"Have you ever taken the hint that maybe I don't want you around?"

"Babe, I was able to read your distaste for me the minute I walked into the farmhouse the first night I was here. Trust me, I'm well aware of your feelings, but you need to understand I have every right to be here on the land, and I plan on being here for as long as I want. Might even extend my stay. I know Ethel has been waiting on confirmation for me to do so. I have nothing better to do, and I have goals to meet. So stop fighting it. I'm here to stay."

"You are not here to stay," I say as I take another bite of my muffin. "You'll be here until you get bored with the monotony of farm life or a new book idea pops into your head."

"Honestly, I like it here." He leans against the tractor wheel, looking up at me. "I like the town, the people, the atmosphere. Ethel told me last night that I could write anywhere in the inn that I wanted to, so I'm taking that as an open invitation. I was looking at real estate last night, and there are quite a few places I'm interested in."

"Stop," I say, lowering my muffin. "No, you're not."

"I think it would be good to be closer to Mac. Help out Ryland. I know Clarke would have appreciated that."

"Ryland has all the help he needs."

"Wait," he says, turning toward me. "Is that . . . is that panic I see in your eyes?"

"No," I answer even though I feel panicked.

"I think it is." He smirks. "Why would you panic about me moving here? Worried that you might have to see me every day on the farm, attempting to stake out my side of the property?"

"There's no panic."

"There is," he says as he comes up to me now, standing right in front of me so his chest touches my knees. "Afraid you might fall for me?"

"Oh my God." I roll my eyes. "No, not even a little."

"Then why the panic?"

"There is no panic," I try to say as casually as possible. "If you want to move here, move here. If you want to spend your days on this farm, by all means, spend your days here. That is your choice, but there will be rules about who works on what project, and right now, this chicken coop is my project, so you can figure out something else to do."

"Ooo." He winces. "I actually worked really hard on the framing, and if it weren't for me, you wouldn't be as far as you are on this project, so . . . technically, it's mine too." He places his hand on my leg and says, "But we can work on it together."

"Over my dead body." I hop off the tractor, ready to move toward the coop, when he pins me in place, using his large body to keep me from moving.

One hand on the tractor, the other on my hip, he leans forward and says, "Come on, Aubree, it'll be fun."

"Your definition of fun is much different from mine."

His hand grips my hip tighter, just like last night, and if my head were on straight, I'd push him away. I'd kick him in the shin. I'd do anything to free myself of his imposing self.

Yet I stay here, grounded by him. *Which is so strange as I never felt grounded by Matt.*

"Maybe we can talk about what we find fun," he says, his thumb rubbing along my hipbone.

"If you really think you're going to win me over by attempting to turn me on, you're interacting with the wrong woman." The words fly out of my mouth, but I don't think I necessarily believe them.

"Turn you on?" he asks. "I'm just trying to get you to look at me without creasing your brow in disdain."

"Your chances of that happening are slim to none," I answer.

He sighs and leans forward as he says softly, "Why do you hate me, Aubree?"

His deep brown eyes with a hint of green around the outer edge stare back at me, looking for answers I don't have.

Because I don't know if I can pinpoint what annoys me about him.

Maybe it's because he came out of nowhere and started claiming the land he shouldn't have in his possession.

Maybe it's because he waltzed into town looking like a hero and sweeping everyone off their feet.

Maybe it's because he has this likable charm, and I've nearly been caught up in it.

Maybe it's because he is annoyingly and stupidly attractive, and no man should ever be that good-looking, but he is. Or that he has more muscles than a man who sits at a keyboard all day every day should have.

But it's probably because I fear he'll find the deficiencies of this farm, know how to fix it, and become a better fit for the job than I am . . .

"Still thinking, are you?" he asks, his voice deep and sultry as his thumb rubs across my hipbone again. "It's okay to admit that you don't actually hate me, and this is all a front. That you find me extremely attractive, and the only way you can keep yourself away is by pretending to hate me. I get it. I've written about it before in a book, but just like in fiction, you'll give in at some point."

"Can you not compare me to your books? This is reality, Wyatt."

"And my books are so popular because I bring reality into them. I bring real thoughts, real dreams, real heartache. They might be thrillers, but the emotions and people are real." He studies me for a second. "The feelings you're storing away, keeping hidden, those are real, and it will help the both of us if you just let them out." Nope.

Not. Happening. Ever.

"I have nothing to share with you," I say as I knock his hand down and move past him. Mentioning feelings and "opening up" to me? That's the minute I check out. That's a big no for me.

Sure, he can rub his thumb over my hipbone.

He can pin me against the tractor.

He can call me babe and Mrs. Preston and put his hand on my lower back.

But the moment he asks me about feelings is the moment I'm out. That's my hard line.

I head toward the chicken coop, where I notice he has finished the construction portion. Everything is almost done from the roof to the ramp, to even a few flower boxes and laying stalls. I turn toward him in disbelief. "What time did you get here this morning?"

He comes up next to me, his chest against my back, his presence so freaking overwhelming that I can feel my knees knock together. *It's from my irritation pulsing through me and not from the idea that this strong, attractive man standing behind me wants to marry me.*

Jesus, Aubree, it's not even for love. It's for convenience.

But still, it's been a long time for me to even have a male presence other than my brother around. I've forgotten what it's like to have a man look me in the eyes, grip me by the hip, and tell me what he wants—even if it's make-believe.

If Cassidy were still alive, she'd be screaming at me to get this man off the farm. She'd be fuming that I deserve way more than a marriage of convenience. *She would know.* She married for the wrong reason, and even though she loved Clarke, I know she loved someone else more, someone she never got to be with. She wouldn't want Hattie, Ryland, or me to make the same mistake she made. *She was all about feelings and true love.*

We were so, so different.

"I came in around five thirty. Organized and tried to keep quiet, then got some work done."

I look over my shoulder at him. "Five thirty? Why on earth would you do that?"

"Wanted to beat you to the coop."

I shake my head. "That," I say. "That will never gain my trust." Not that I want him to gain my trust.

He's deliberately trying to anger me. That's what he's doing. *Don't let him.*

I walk over to the paint cans where I picked out the color Iron Ore for the coop and the fencing.

"Want me to grab the rollers?" he asks.

"No, I want you to leave."

He walks up to me, and to my surprise, he places his finger under my chin, forcing me to look him dead in the eyes. "Aubree, I'm not going anywhere. Please, stop fighting it," he says softly. "I'm here to stay for a while, so put me to good use. If you don't, I'll just do what I think needs to be done, and I'm sure you don't want that."

He's right, I don't want that at all. I don't need him waltzing around the farm, trying to see what he can help with, especially when nothing needs his help. So even though I don't want to spend my morning painting with Wyatt as he pesters me with his ridiculous terms of endearment, I settle with the idea that it's the better choice than letting him go off on his own.

"Fine, grab the rollers."

He grins at me, his thumb under my chin. "Such a good Mrs. Preston."

I swat his hand, making him laugh. "Don't call me that."

He moves over to the rollers and sets them up while I open the paint, stir it, and then pour it into paint pans. Would it be easier to use a paint sprayer to get the job done? Yes, but I don't have one, so we're going with this. We work in silence together, prepping the area. The whole time, I ignore the glaring realization that we can accomplish a task together without talking. We somehow know what the other person will do and move around each other to prep.

Once we're set, he hands me a roller, and I hand him a paint pan. "You start on that side. Paint everything, including the wire fencing."

"You want me to paint the wire fencing?" he asks, looking confused. If he wasn't so annoying, I'd think the crinkle of confusion in his nose was cute.

But it's not.

"Yes, it will make it easier to see inside the coop. Trust me."

"You're the boss," he says as he rolls his roller in the paint and starts painting, the sound of wet paint being spread out on wood and wire filling the silence between us.

It's peaceful.

And for a moment, I almost forget he's here as I get into the motion of painting, rolling up and down, dipping back into the paint, only to repeat the process, but then . . . he speaks.

"What's your favorite part about the farm?" he asks.

I dip my roller into more paint. "You know, we don't have to talk."

"How am I supposed to get to know my future wife, then?" he asks.

This motherfucker.

I swear I've never met someone as persistent as he is. He's nonstop. It's actually—I hate to admit it—*slightly* impressive because he gives zero fucks. He just puts it out there, and if you don't like it, he really doesn't care. He just keeps moving forward. To live your life that way . . .

Ignoring his last comment, I say, "Why do you want to know? Besides your stupid future wife crap that's not going to happen."

He chuckles. "Well, because after being here for a few days, I think I have a place I like. It's probably my favorite."

"If you say your favorite place is being in my presence, I'll honestly throw up on you."

He laughs wholeheartedly. "Although a close second, it's not that."

"Then what is it?" I ask.

"I asked you first."

"How do I know that you're not going to say the same place as mine when I answer just so you can go on some tirade about how we're so meant to be and our marriage is made for the ages?"

"I like the way you think," he says as he wiggles his eyebrows.

"Be serious."

"Fine," he says as he pulls a pencil out of his pocket and writes something on the post in front of him. He then faces me and says, "My answer is on the post behind me. Tell me your favorite place, and we can see if it's mine."

This is a very risky situation because if our places match by some chance, then I'd be wary of the universe trying to tell me something. And even though there is no way I'd ever say yes to his proposal, matching common favorite places would at least make me think deeper about my circumstances.

I set my roller down and brush off my hands before reaching for my mug of coffee and taking a sip. After a few seconds, I say, "The big oak tree out past the silos."

The moment the words fall out of my mouth, I watch as a slow, knowing grin falls over his lips.

No freaking way.

He steps aside and smirks, gesturing to his answer. I don't have to get close to know what it is.

It's clear as day.

Giant oak behind the barn.

The son of a bitch.

He has to be a mentalist. This can't be real. There is no way this man, who I can't stand having around, has the same freaking favorite spot as me. He's been here for two seconds, and he doesn't even know the significance of it.

I shake my head and turn around to get back to painting—ignore, ignore, ignore.

After a few seconds, he says, "Well, I know where I'm going to propose now when you're ready."

"Don't even think about it." I grip my roller tighter as I continue, "That tree is sacred, and I don't want you messing up my memories of it with some asinine, fake proposal that'll mean nothing."

He pauses, and I can feel him turn toward me, but I keep my back facing him. "Sacred?" he asks, his voice softening. "What kind of memories do you have under that tree?"

"Nothing I want to share with you," I answer.

"Are they with Cassidy?" he presses.

I sigh. "I said I don't want to share them with you, Wyatt."

He's silent for a moment—*but I can* hear *him thinking*—and then he says, "Fair enough, Aubree. I am truly sorry you lost your sister. Cancer is fucked."

He turns back and starts painting again.

Cancer is fucked.

God, he is so right. But as I allow more silence to continue, because I have no idea how to answer that comment, I begin to feel the weight of the oak tree between us. He doesn't need to know why it means so much to me. He doesn't need to know that I hate emotional tension, either. Or dealing with emotions. But he showed true sympathy just then. *Which I appreciate and also hate.* But I'm not good at them.

When Matt left me, that had been one of his complaints. *"You need to learn to express your feelings, Aubree. No one likes being with someone who is so closed off. So . . . unavailable."*

That's me.

Thanks for that, Matt. I'm sure Amanda is all about her emotions and feelings and all that other shit I just don't deal with.

I do it if it's necessary. Like when Hayes and Hattie split up, I was there for my sister. And the night that Ryland realized he was going to be Mac's legal guardian and the weight of that hit him, I was there for him as well. But other than that, I just wish to keep my emotions to myself.

When we both end up on the same side, painting, Wyatt finally breaks the silence when he says, "I wrote a Halloween thriller once, a short story for my publisher about killer chickens."

I glance up at him. "And you said your books were based in reality."

He grins. "That one might have been a bit far-fetched."

"Maybe a little," I say as I keep rolling, grateful he broke the tension.

"Think you'll have any killer chickens?"

"I can only hope because then I'd direct them toward you."

He grips his chest over his heart. "The things you say to me, wife, they truly are a blessing."

IT'S SO HOT TODAY.

Hotter than I want it to be.

Normally, if it were this hot on a Saturday, I'd call it a day and go back to my guest house, where I'd shower and then binge-watch some show I wanted to catch up on. Maybe take Mac to town to grab some ice cream or even to the beach to dip our toes in the water.

But there is no way in hell I'm calling it a day when Wyatt is still here working.

Currently, he's on top of the chicken coop, installing shingles. How does he know how to do that? I have no idea. My guess is he spent last night watching YouTube videos over and over again, hoping he could apply the knowledge today.

While he continues to bang away on the roof, I finish the paint touch-ups.

Because it's so hot, the paint dries quickly, making the project easy but also miserable at the same time. All we have to do is install the flower boxes, and we're ready for the chickens. Not that I care to admit it, but I don't think we would have gotten this done as fast as we did if Wyatt hadn't helped me. Because Parson, his men, and Echo are busy with their daily tasks. Esther and Aggie are doing their own thing, and then I pick up projects around the farm as well as take care of the business, so this was one of those projects I wanted to do but just didn't get to it . . . until Wyatt put his hands on it.

"Fucking fuck, it's hot," Wyatt says from the roof. "Aubree, I know you want me to shrivel up and die under the sun while I'm up here, but can you please hand me my water?"

The temptation to let him shrivel up is heavy, but I also need to give credit where credit is due. He helped me with this project, so I should give him some water as a thank-you.

I set my roller down and walk over to where his water bottle rests in the shade of the barn. Just as I bring it out to the chicken coop, a piece of fabric plops on the ground. Confused, I look up to find Wyatt standing on the roof, shirtless and glistening under the bright sun.

Mother of God.

For someone who writes books all day long, the man sure does have a body.

And we're talking an incredibly fit, toned body.

I mean . . . who truly has abs like that? Two well-defined rows, divided down the middle and horizontally, meeting up with a delicious deep V at his hips.

And now that he's removed his shirt, there's a reason his pants barely hang on to his narrow waist. An enticing dark patch of hair leads from his belly button to the waistband of his briefs. Call me sun sick, but it fascinates me . . . makes my mouth water, makes me wonder what is just below the zipper.

"Uh, my water," Wyatt says as my eyes lift to his chest where they focus on his thick, flat pecs that expand all the way out to his shoulders, defining him in a way that I'm not privileged to see when he's wearing clothes. "Can you hand it to me, Aubree?"

"What? Oh yes," I say as I lift on my toes to hand it to him. But I'm not tall enough, so to my surprise, he hops off the roof, landing right in front of me with an earth-shaking plop.

Dear God, that was . . . umm . . . well, some might say hot, but I'm not going to say that. I'm just going to keep my mouth shut.

"Here," I say, handing him his water.

He slides his fingers over mine, and in a husky tone, he says, "Thanks, wife."

I steal my hand away and take a step back as a smile crosses his face.

Annoyed with his arrogance once again, I say, "Why did you need me to get your drink if you were going to hop off the roof anyway?"

"Last-minute choice," he says. "Thought you might want a closer look since you can't seem to stop staring."

"Oh, get over yourself. I was not staring." Oh God, he caught me staring. My cheeks flame with embarrassment.

"Uh . . . you were, this was you." He tilts his head, parts his mouth, and stares at my chest.

I attempt to push him away, but he captures my wrist and holds me close, his sweaty skin inches from mine.

"I'm totally open to you checking out what I have to offer, but just let me know next time so I can flex for you."

I straighten my back and look him dead in the eyes. "You, Wyatt, are an idiot."

He chuckles and releases my wrist. "Denial looks pretty good on you, Aubree."

God, he's insufferable. Just when I was starting to think that it was nice to have him help me with the chicken coop, he changes my mind.

"Since it's noon, do you want to grab something to eat?" he asks.

"No, I'm good."

"Come on," he says. "I know you're hungry. I can see it in your withering eyes. My treat. I can take you to The Hot Pickle, or we can grab some pizza . . ."

"This is just you trying to get me to go out with you," I say.

He shakes his head. "This is me trying to get food in my stomach so I don't turn into a raving man beast with fangs, looking for his next meal. Which could very much be you." He nods toward his SUV. "Come on."

My stomach growls right on cue, and it's loud enough to block out the sound of the wind whispering past the barn.

Wyatt chuckles. "Looks like your stomach has spoken."

"Fine," I say. "But we're grabbing food and then coming back here. We're not sitting at some table, eating food together while you try to stare longingly into my eyes."

"It's such a shame when you take the romance out of things."

"Put your shirt on, I'm driving."

"I WOULDN'T HAVE PEGGED you as a truck girl," Wyatt says as we bounce down the driveway's dirt road toward town.

"I have to have a truck if I live on a farm," I answer.

"But this truck is different. Very, uh . . . not comfortable."

I roll my eyes as I pull out onto the back country road, which is paved. "Is your precious author ass getting bruised?"

"It is," he says. "Will you rub it for me later?"

I shake my head. "Should have seen that coming."

"You seem to have something against me being an author because you've made quite a few backhanded comments about it."

"I have nothing against it. I could never write a book, but I just find it annoying that you come on this farm, thinking you know everything when your knowledge comes from Google and mine comes from real-life experience."

"Understandable," he says. "I can see how that would be annoying. Thank you for sharing your feelings with me."

"Are you treating me like a child?" I ask.

"I sure as hell hope I'm not treating you like a child." He laughs.

"No, I mean when you validated my feelings and told me you understood. That's a technique we use with Mac when she gets upset."

"That's called empathy, Aubree. Are you not familiar?"

Such a smart-ass.

"Not so much," I say as I make a left at the stop sign, pastures of cows on both sides of the road as we make the short jaunt into town.

"Are you not familiar because you weren't shown empathy growing up or because you don't like the acknowledgment of other people's feelings?"

"Both," I answer. "I don't like emotions, and I don't like feelings. I avoid them at all costs, and if you think this is a gateway to diving deeper into that mindset, you would be wrong."

"Noted," he says. "So if I were to, I don't know, break my leg while finishing the chicken coop roof, would you feel bad for me?"

"I'd be grateful that you'd be out of commission and unable to bother me around the farm anymore."

That makes him laugh. "Wow, okay. That's some real sociopath kind of thinking, yet"—he glances in my direction—"I'm still intrigued."

"What does that say about you?" I ask.

"That I like hardworking women who don't take any shit from anyone. Hence why I want you to be my wife."

"You want me to be your wife because of a cabin, not because of my personality."

"Your personality is real and authentic. It might be a bit harsh at times, and sure, am I afraid that if we slept in the same bed, I might wake up with one testicle missing? Of course. But at least I'd know that the one testicle removed then stored in a jar on her nightstand was kept by a woman with character and ambition."

"You are something else," I say with a shake of my head and a slight smirk.

"Doesn't hurt that you're a smokeshow either," he says.

I stop at a stop sign and glance in his direction. He's grinning like a fool.

"Stop that."

"Stop what?" he asks as he reaches over to my side of the truck and attempts to place his hand in mine. I quickly retreat.

"Stop trying to flatter me. I don't need your inflated opinion of my looks to get me to say yes to your foolish idea. I'm comfortable with how I am and what I see in the mirror."

"Inflated opinion?" he says, his voice changing from easygoing to serious. "That's not an inflated opinion, that's facts. You're hot, Aubree. I have no problem saying that."

"Please, Wyatt—"

"Please, what? Tell you more? Okay," he continues. "You have these very intense green eyes that suck me in immediately because I have to know if they're real or not. It's difficult not to stare, not get captured. Then there are your freckles, barely visible to the naked eye, but they darken when you've been outside longer. I've never been a hair man, but something about those braids you like to wear flips my stomach upside down. And not that I should mention your body, but fuck, Aubree, it's curvy but muscular, soft but strong. You can hold your own, but you also look like someone I'd like to hold. And last, those lips, like two flower petals, waiting to be explored."

I pull into one of the town community parking lots and turn off the truck, only to turn toward him. *What the hell is he on to say such crap?* Even if some of that was nice to hear. "Are you feverish?"

"Nope," he says.

"Flower petal lips? Really? Is that how you describe your characters' lips in your books?"

He shakes his head. "Nah, never really focus on that shit." He turns toward me, his large body eating up all the space in the truck's cab. "You know, some people who just received as many compliments as you would say thank you, maybe blush, possibly even act a little shy while repaying the favor."

"Why would I thank you when I don't believe a word you said?"

"Why wouldn't you believe it?" he asks, looking insulted.

"Because you're sarcastic. You run around the farm calling me Mrs. Preston and telling me that I'm a good wife. Why the hell would I believe that you actually think I'm pretty or hot or whatever you said?"

"Good point," he says. "But I wouldn't lie to you about something as personal as looks. That wasn't out of sarcasm or to boost my appeal. Those were cold, hard facts. I thought you were hot the day I helped Clarke and Cassidy move into their house, and I still think you're hot. Simple as that. Feel free not to repay the compliment. I don't need any validation."

And because I grew up in a hostile environment where no one told me I was pretty until my sophomore year in high school when I went to the homecoming game in Cassidy's brown floral dress, I can't quite process what he just said to me. My mind can't wrap itself around the compliments. Instead, I brush them off, not wanting to focus on them.

Not wanting to get caught up in them.

I revert to what I know best—being argumentative. If my dad taught me one thing, it's that you argue until you get your way.

"Of course you don't, because you think you're the hottest man alive, don't you?" I hop out of the truck, and so does he.

"No, that would be Chris Evans."

I pause and wait for him to catch up. "You think Chris Evans is the hottest guy in the world?"

"Yeah. He has it all. The slight hint of a Boston accent, good looks, great body, a sense of humor. How could you not?"

"Easy, the hottest guy in the world is Michael B. Jordan."

"Oooo." Wyatt nods. "Great choice. He is quite the looker. I might have to change my answer."

"He's mine. You keep your Chris Evans, while Michael and I—"

"Hey, what are you guys doing?" Hattie says.

Startled, I stop right on the spot, which causes Wyatt to run into my shoulder.

"Shit, sorry, babe," he says, causing the hairs on the back of my neck to stand straight.

My eyes connect with Hattie's inquisitive expression as she looks between us, a slight smirk on her lips.

I know that look. I've seen it many times before.

She thinks she sees something, knows something.

And there's no doubt in my mind that Ryland has said something to her about last night, how Wyatt draped his arm over my chair possessively, or how he caught us in the kitchen close to each other.

"Uh, hey . . . there," I say awkwardly.

Hattie smiles even brighter as she looks between us. "Hey." She beams. "So . . . what are you two doing?"

Clearly making a huge mistake by being out and about in

town together. Sometimes when I'm hungry, I don't think things through. This is one of those times.

"Grabbing sandwiches," Wyatt says while bumping my shoulder with his. "We finished the chicken coop just as Aubree's stomach barked at us."

Hattie chuckles. "I've heard it bark before, quite a terrifying thing."

"Very terrifying," he says. "What about you?" I hate how casual he is. How he's able to chat it up without a worry in the world. While I'm over here sweating, my skin prickling, my stomach flipping, and every anxious bone in my body sending out warning signs that this was a bad idea.

"Heading up to By the Slice for some pizza with Hayes. After, we're going to drive up the coast for a hike. Just got done with a few things at the store. Marlene is closing, so we thought we'd have a fun afternoon."

"I tried to get this girl to have a fun afternoon with me, but you know how she is, work, work, work." He nudges me, and I feel my mouth go dry as Hattie looks at me gleefully. When I don't say anything, Wyatt nudges me again. "Tell them, Aubree. Tell them how much you denied me fun today."

"You were the one who got up at five thirty this morning."

"You, uh . . . you know what time he woke up?" Hattie asks, implying that I was there when he woke up.

"Oh my God, no."

"You know what time I woke up," Wyatt says, not making any of this better. "Don't lie."

God, I could kick him in the shin right now. He knows exactly what he's doing.

Trying to gather myself, I add, "I mean, yes, I know what time he woke up, but only because he told me, not because I was there in person to see him rise from his bed. I wasn't there. I was in my house, and he was at the inn. There was no knowledge of wake-up times other than what has been communicated between us, not from . . . firsthand experience."

Wyatt drapes his arm over my shoulders and says, "What

your sister so eloquently is trying to say is that we didn't sleep together."

Hattie chuckles. "Good to know." She then eyes me suspiciously like I have something to say to her that I'm not saying, and I really don't. All I'm hiding is the fact that he asked me to be his wife and I said no.

And for the briefest moments, when he offered me the land, I considered taking him up on the deal. It was so brief, though, it was not even worth mentioning.

Also, if I have to admit to it, Wyatt is an attractive man.

But like I said, not things she needs to know.

"Are you blushing, Aubree?" she asks.

"No," I say, covering my cheeks with my hands. "Why would I be blushing? There's nothing to blush about. Not a single thing."

"Probably sunburn," Wyatt says as he continues to hang his arm wrapped around me, which is not helping the situation. "I told her to put some sunscreen on her face, but she wouldn't listen to me."

Hattie folds her arms against her chest. "She can be stubborn, can't she?"

"So stubborn, but it's one of the things we love about her, isn't it?" Wyatt asks.

"Yes . . ." Hattie says in a knowing tone. "One of the many things we *love* about her."

Her emphasis on love doesn't slip by me, nor does the way she keeps looking between me and Wyatt. I can only imagine the narrative going on in her head.

"Well, I'll let you two get your food so there is no more barking from Aubree's stomach," Hattie says with a grin. "Wouldn't want to unleash the beast."

I shake Wyatt's arm off me as he says, "To be honest, I'm slightly curious as to what the beast would do."

"It's not pretty," Hattie says.

"Yet, she's pretty herself. Would love to see that contradiction, but I don't think I'm brave enough to tempt it . . . at least not yet."

Hattie chuckles. "Probably smart. Okay, well, catch you two later. Have fun." She winks knowingly and takes off.

When she's out of earshot, I say, "What is wrong with you?"

"Probably a lot of things," he answers. "Can you be more specific?"

I turn toward him, hand on my hip as I speak quietly *and* tersely. "You realize that between last night and right now, my brother and sister will assume something is going on between us."

"Perfect," he says, pressing his hand on my lower back and moving us toward the sub shop. "Then I'm doing my job."

I stop and turn toward him. "No, you're putting on a show that I didn't—"

"Aubree?"

Oh God, I know that voice.

And not in a good way.

This is the only reason I hate small towns.

Because you bump into people you never want to see.

Turning around, I come face to face with my ex-best friend.

"Amanda," I say while adjusting the bandanna on my head. What's the use? I look like I've been rolling around in dirt all day long and she looks pristine and put together like she just walked off a photo shoot. "I, uh, I didn't know you were in town," I lie, because what else am I supposed to say?

"Oh really? I thought your sister would tell you that Matt and I went into The Almond Store." Of course she did, but the last thing Amanda needs is the knowledge that people were talking about her presence.

"Must have slipped her mind," I say.

"Probably, now that she's with Hayes Farrow. Seems like she is completely occupied. I get that, though. When you fall in love, it's hard not to be distracted. Which speaking of, the light of my life."

The light of her life? Oh my God, could she be any cheesier?

And then to my horror, my ex-boyfriend walks through the open door of The Hot Pickle and joins Amanda as he places his hand on her back. There's no doubt in my mind that she does this for show because the evil wench places her hand on his chest and kisses him very . . . provocatively. Like, there's tongue action going on. We're on a sidewalk in front of a sandwich shop. Reserve the tongue for the home and the drive-in movie theater.

When she pulls away, she wipes her thumb over his lip. "Oh, sorry about that, my handsome man, I got lipstick all over you."

"Never going to complain," he says as he looks up at me. "Oh hey, Aubree. Wow, it's been a while."

Yes, it has. *Last time I saw you, you told me that small towns were for losers and that you wanted to grow and would never be caught dead living in one.*

"Yes, it has," I say and then gesture to the both of them. "I'm assuming you're together."

Amanda rubs her stomach. "And expecting. I hope that's not weird for you." She winces. "I've heard through the grapevine that finding love has been difficult for you."

What.

A.

Bitch . . .

"I wouldn't say hard, just been preoccupied, you know, since my sister died and left behind a farm, a business, and a four-year-old daughter," I say, the bitterness in my voice unmistakable.

"Oh yes, I'm so sorry to hear about that. I can't imagine what your family must be going through. I can only imagine how much easier it would have been if you had someone by your side to help you through it all. Like I have Matt." She snuggles in close to him and smiles, the look on her face basically saying I won the prize . . . and you didn't.

Well, guess what, Amanda? Matt had a very hard time finding the G-spot, and when he did, he congratulated himself with a personal, one-on-one handshake. So who really is winning?

"But yup, we're having a little baby girl, and we're so excited. Just moved into town where we can raise our baby in a beautiful, peaceful environment. And of course, Matt was just promoted and granted access to work remotely. Isn't that great? He can be the father he's always wanted to be and still provide for us financially."

Is she trying to write her annual Christmas card right here on the spot? Because that's what it sounds like. Next thing I know, she'll start saying how they're volunteering at the soup kitchen this year while also adopting a rescue dog from the shelter who will be named Mitzy. And isn't that just adorable?

I'm stunned if I'm honest. How is this the same person I used to call my best friend? *How can someone who I used to believe had my back—loved me unconditionally—be so callous and cruel now?*

"Oh, and we just adopted the cutest little furball." What are the odds? "A kitten named Whiskers. Isn't that the sweetest name? Matt named him. And he told me he'll be in charge of all the cat litter so I never have to worry about it."

"What a hero," I say with a thumbs-up.

"He truly is. Boy, do I wish you had a man in your life like him. I think it would really make you less grumpy and happier. I hope that's not offensive." It's really offensive. "I've just been asking around about you, you know, wanting to see how you've been since we've had our falling out, and the word around the street is that you're the grump of Almond Bay."

Uh . . . pardon me?

That's news.

"The grump?" I ask, falling for it of course.

"Yes. Apparently, a lot of the locals were happy when Hattie took over The Almond Store because she's much warmer like Cassidy was." I feel Wyatt place his hand on my back while stepping in closer, reminding me that I'm not alone in this conversation. His embrace is kind, but I feel utterly humiliated that he is witnessing this. "Although, Cassidy and Hattie were always so close, and you *were* the outcast in the family."

Thanks for the reminder.

For digging your dagger right where you know it belongs.

That's what happens when you know someone so well for so

long—they understand your trigger points. And she nailed this one.

"Well, it was great seeing you," I say with the fakest smile I can muster, desperately wanting to cut this short before she takes that dagger and goes after my other trigger points.

"So great seeing you. Maybe one day, you'll find the kind of love that Matt and I have found."

Jesus Christ.

When she came to Almond Bay, did she make it her mission to find me one day and just drive it home that I'm single and she's not?

That she is with my ex-boyfriend?

That I seem like some grumpy loser with nothing going for me other than the dirt on my knees and the paint under my fingernails?

I hate that she's making me feel inferior. I have different goals in my life.

I hate that she's making me second-guess myself even though I'm confident in my choices.

And I hate that she's put a sense of panic in my heart to prove to her that I'm not the kind of person she thinks I am.

A panic so strong . . . so overwhelming that before I can stop myself, I lean back into Wyatt and say, "Already found it, with this guy." I rap my knuckles on his thick chest.

Both Matt's and Amanda's eyes move up as they take in the tall, broad-shouldered Wyatt standing directly behind me.

"Oh," Amanda says, looking startled. "I just assumed he was one of your helpers out on the farm. He's so . . . large."

I look up at Wyatt's face and do not miss the scowl. But he replaces it with one of congeniality and lends out his hand to both Amanda and Matt, who shake it. "My name is Wyatt. Nice to meet you. I do help Aubree out on the farm, not that she needs it. She's so incredibly resourceful, strong, and independent. Talented. But my main job is writing books and making sure she's happy and satisfied." I look up at Wyatt just in time to see him wink.

Normally, I'd roll my eyes at the comment, but given the situation, I just go along with it as his hand on my waist grows tighter.

"Well." Amanda lets out what seems like a frustrated sigh. "I guess that's great. Good to see you're in a happy relationship."

"Very happy," I say as I scoot in even closer to Wyatt. He wraps both arms around me now and, to my utter shock, kisses my neck.

It's two parts thrilling and one part horrifying. I shouldn't like the feel of his lips on my skin, nor should I have chills running down my legs. My stomach shouldn't be bursting out in a cloud of unruly butterflies. But my body reacts a certain way. My mind begs it to stop, and I wonder if he will kiss my neck again.

"Good." Amanda awkwardly looks around. "Well, I guess we'll let you get to your lunch. It was great catching up. We'll see you around. Maybe we can schedule a lunch sometime."

"Maybe," I say, knowing full well that will never happen. I would rather sit on top of a bed of razors than share a meal with this woman, especially after this display of pettiness. I offer her a wave, and we go in different directions.

When we're in the shop, I do an A+ job of ignoring the rather large commitment I made to a man I barely know. I quietly stare at the menu—even though I always get the same thing.

But my blatant disregard for him and his presence doesn't stop the smarmy grin I can see from the corner of my eye.

Or the heavy drape of his arm over my shoulders.

Or the subtle bump of his hip against mine.

After a few moments of silence, he leans in close to my ear and says, "It was how I referred to your lips as flower petals that broke you, wasn't it?"

Grinding my teeth together, I say, "Shut up, Wyatt."

Chapter Six

THE SIBLINGS

Hattie: *Ryland! Guess who I ran into in town?*

Ryland: *That could be hundreds of different people.*

Hattie: *No, this was close to home.*

Ryland: *I don't know, Hattie. Who?*

Hattie: *Aubree and Wyatt! Together. Right there. Walking close together. Looking all chummy. OMG, do you think something is going on between them?*

Ryland: *Possibly. I didn't say anything last night because I was tired as shit and thought I was making something out of nothing, but I caught them talking in the kitchen. He draped his arm over her chair several times at dinner. At the end of the night, he said that he was going to walk her back to her place.*

Hattie: *STAHPP! Ryland, that is vital information. You should have told me immediately. What is wrong with you?*

Ryland: *I have a four-year-old to take care of who has a weird obsession with a horse named Chewy Charles. The storylines I have to keep straight about that horse, it's exhausting. And now there's Chewy Chonda too.*

Hattie: *LOL. Understandable, but oh my God, this is huge, Ryland. What if she likes him? Do you think she likes him? I thought she was angry* *that he owned the land. When would they have even talked to have formed a relationship? Is that what it is? A relationship?*

Ryland: *I see where Mac has been picking up on all of the incessant questions.*

Hattie: *I'm being serious. This could be great for Aubree. Wyatt seems fun and could bring Aubree out from her shell, you know?*

Ryland: *Yeah, I like Wyatt. He's a good guy. It would be good for her, but you never know with Aubree. She's a wild card.*

Hattie: *She is, but you should have seen them. Something was definitely there.*

Ryland: *Something was there last night too.*

Hattie: *Why don't you ask her?*

Ryland: *And put myself at risk of getting hurt by the snarly beast? No thanks. I have three sisters. I know when not to poke the bear. And I have a kid to watch over.*

Hattie: *Use the kid as a human shield.*

Ryland: *That's really great, Hattie. Throw your niece to the fanged monster.*

Hattie: *Not like an actual human shield. Use her as a way for Aubree not to freak out at you, meaning bring up Wyatt and her possible love connection when Mac is there. That way she can't hurt you.*

Ryland: *It will just be delayed hurt. I'm not willing to risk it.*

Hattie: *Are you really going to be a baby about this?*

Ryland: *Yes, yes, I am.*

Hattie: *You're going to make me ask, aren't you?*

Ryland: *You're the one who's more invested in her love life than I am. I'm just trying to make it day to day.*

Hattie: *Fine, I'll ask her.*

Ryland: *Tread carefully.*

Hattie: *I will. Just know, I'm doing this for the family.*

Ryland: *Don't try to act all cavalier about it. You and I both know this is for your own personal curiosity.*

Hattie: *Can't you let me have my moment?*

Ryland: *Fine, you're doing this for the family.*

Hattie: *Thank you.*

Chapter Seven

WYATT

"Soooo, are we not going to talk about what happened at The Hot Pickle?" I ask Aubree as we sit on the back of her truck parked in front of the barn.

She didn't say much after she ran into Amanda and Matt. She was quite silent actually, especially on the drive back, and I didn't push her to talk because I felt like she was probably still processing.

Processing running into Amanda.

Processing the horrible things she said to her.

And processing the relationship she claimed we have.

But now that we're eating our lunch, it has to be addressed . . . for obvious reasons.

"There's nothing to talk about."

That makes me chuckle. "Nothing to talk about? Uh, how about the fact that you called me your boyfriend in front of what I can only describe as an elevated version of Regina George."

"So?" she says with a shrug as she remains fixated on her sandwich and in full denial mode.

"So the town talks," I say.

"She won't."

"Uhh, I might be new to this town, but given she seemed to find out how you were doing, what's going to stop her from telling everyone that I'm your boyfriend?"

Aubree is mid-bite when she pauses. I can see her mind working, thinking over her mistake. That's right, it's going to be known around town very shortly that I'm her boyfriend. I have no doubt about the "telephone" that passes through this town, especially if the news gets to Ethel.

After some thought, she shakes her head. "She won't say anything to anyone." And then she takes a bite of her sandwich.

"Do you really believe that, or are you living in a state of denial?"

"Believe it."

"You are such a liar." I chuckle. "You know by tomorrow, the entire town will congratulate us on our newfound love."

She side-eyes me. "Just because I called you my boyfriend doesn't mean I love you."

"Ouch," I say, clutching my heart. "That stings, wife. You know, I love you. You're my moon and sky and everything in between. You are the light of my life. The apple of my eye. My one true love and the reason I can breathe on this planet. You give me—"

"Oh my God, shut up," she says, thoroughly annoyed with me.

I laugh some more. "I'm starting to think this relationship of ours is one-sided. I'm thinking . . . that I might, I don't know, like you more than you like me."

"That's one thing you're one hundred percent right about." She sets her sandwich down and picks up her drink. She lets her feet dangle off the back of the truck as she stares out at the field. I watch her cheeks hollow as she sips on her Powerade—the same drink I opted for. Who says we're not meant to be? After a few bouts of silence, she finally says, "She's going to tell everyone."

A slow smile spreads across my face. She might put up a fight at first, but she knows when to concede. I like that about her.

I decide to tread lightly because it almost feels like Aubree has fallen into a state of shock.

"Yeah, she is."

"People will think we're together." She stares blankly.

"Yup, that seems to be the consensus."

"But we're not together," she says in a monotone.

"Not at the moment, but we are linked by land, so at least we have that going for us."

She slowly turns her head to look at me. "But I don't like you, so why would I say you were my boyfriend? That was stupid." Uh-oh, this is what we call a spiral. "Like, who would believe that we're dating? We don't even know each other. This is like the fifth time I've seen you in person. I have no idea if you're some sort of sick serial killer like in your books——"

"Aw, you've read my books."

Her eyes narrow. "I'm being serious, Wyatt."

"Well, rest assured, I'm not a sick serial killer. I just know a lot about it from countless hours of research, not experience. Just in case I need to really make that clear."

She places her hand on her forehead. "I can't make a retraction on my statement. I mean . . . you kissed my neck in front of her."

"Nice touch, wasn't it? I'm quick on my feet. For future references, was the kiss too much pressure? Just want to gauge what you like."

"Do you really think that's what I want to worry about at the moment? The pressure of your kiss?"

"Seems like vital information. What if I do it again, and next time, you squirm away from me because it was a featherlight kiss that creeped you out? You think I want people thinking you're disgusted by my neck kisses?"

"Oh my God, Wyatt! There won't be a next time."

I scratch the back of my neck. "Color me confused, but I can't possibly see a scenario that doesn't end in embarrassment where there isn't a next time. What are you going to do? Spread a rumor about Regina George being slightly out of her mind and making things up?"

"Yes!" Aubree lights up, her eyes looking—dare I say it—a touch crazy. "That's what we'll say. Her pregnancy brain made up the whole thing."

"Hold up," I say as I hook her chin with my finger. "I might not know all of the womanly things, but I'm pretty sure that's an offensive thing to do. She's carrying a child. Let's not use pregnancy brain as a default for her. Also, her husband was there. He saw everything, so if you try to spread that rumor, he'll debunk it."

"We blame his inaccuracy in storytelling on man brain." Her eyes are still lit up. I'm going to need to dim those things down.

"You're not wrong about man brain, but I don't think we can tap into that scapegoat." I tap my chin, thinking about it, then shake my head. "No, it's going to be he said, she said, and right now, the points are not in your favor because your sister saw us together in the parking lot, Ryland saw us together last night, the people in The Hot Pickle saw us standing in line with my arm over your shoulders. All signs are leading to you being my special love dumpling."

"Ew, do not call me that."

"Not a fan? What about sugar plum?" Her nose curls. "Boobala? My aorta?" Her eyes focus in on me, making me nervous. "Snuggle bum? Moo Ma Me Ma?"

"What the hell is wrong with you? What is a moo ma me ma?"

I shrug. "No idea, but your staring made me nervous, and I just said what was on my mind."

"If that was on your mind, then you have some serious issues."

"Possibly, but it also makes me a great writer."

"Does it? Is moo ma me ma winning you all the bestseller titles?"

My lips turn up. "I'll include it in my next one and let you know."

"We're getting off track," she says as she leans back in the truck bed. "We need to come up with a plan, something that—"

Ding.

We both look toward her phone, which is between us. I see Hattie's name scroll across the screen so I say, "Uh, that's your sister. Do you think she knows?"

"Please, it doesn't happen that fast," Aubree scoffs while she sits up and snags her phone.

I watch as she unlocks the screen, opens the text message, and reads it. Her eyes scroll, and her lips turn into a frown.

Yup . . . Hattie knows.

Slowly, Aubree's eyes lift to mine, and she says, "Mother . . . fucker."

I try not to crack a smile.

I really do.

But . . . it's just so comical.

The news in this town travels faster than the truck we're sitting in.

"Let me guess." I lean back on one hand. "The news got to her already about me being your boyfriend?"

"Yes, and she's asking why I didn't say anything to her."

"Yeah, why didn't you? I can't imagine what it's like to find out your sister is dating your brother-in-law's brother . . . wait, would I be your brother-in-law?"

She pinches her nose, her frustration starting to boil. "Wyatt, this is not helping."

"Okay, then how can I help? Should I get down on one knee and propose? Make this official? Draw up a contract about our impending marriage? I have a lawyer who can create something tonight."

"I'm not marrying you, Wyatt."

"Uh . . . what do you mean? I thought you called me your boyfriend because you were heading in the direction of making a deal. Remember, your hand for my land?" I wiggle my eyebrows. "Catchy, isn't it?"

She pushes her hand over my eyebrows. "No, it's annoying. And I said you were my boyfriend because Amanda was making such a big deal about me being a lonely, old spinster. I just wanted to show her that I wasn't."

"Well, now everyone in town, including your siblings, thinks you're not a lonely, old spinster. The only question is, what are you going to do now? You know I'm open to hitching my wagon to your . . . truck. Is that the term? Either way, I'm here for you."

"You say that as if you're doing me a favor. I wouldn't be in this situation if you hadn't followed me around for the last couple of days, calling me Mrs. Preston and wife. You've slipped into my subconscious and now that has trickled out into the real world. Technically, this is all your fault."

I throw up my hands in surrender. "I'll take the blame. I know what I did. The question is, what are you going to do about it? Are you going to take back your words, or will you venture into the realm of a marriage of convenience and play along? You have a lot to gain."

"And a whole lot to lose," she answers while setting her phone down and lying back again. Her hands go to her face, and she groans.

"What would you really have to lose? Your first marriage? Sure, if you're the type of person who is stuck on only being married once, that might be a hit, but divorce is okay. Sometimes you're just with people for certain seasons in your life. You and I? We can be a one-year season. Not to mention, you'd get your land, I'd get my cabin, and I could always give you a parting gift on our divorce, like a new truck or something. You know, a little pat on the ass as a thank-you."

"I don't need your pity ass pat," she seethes.

"Either way, I promise to be a good husband. I'll be everything you need and more, and in the end, when we inevitably divorce, I won't make it painful. I'll be sure to make it as painless as possible and also cover all of the expenses. So really, it's like you get one of the best years of your life, attached to me, and then you walk away with your land."

She peeks through her hands to say, "You really think being married to you will be the best year of my life?"

"Guaranteed, babe."

She groans again, but this time, she sits up. "This is such a nightmare."

"Could be a dream if you let it."

Her eyes shoot over to mine, and even though they read like they're about to murder me, I can also see that she *might* be teetering in my direction. And when I say slight . . . I mean minuscule.

"How would it be a dream? You already irritate me."

"I'm only irritating right now because I'm trying to badger you into agreeing to this idea."

"Badgering a woman, wow, you put that on your Tinder profile?"

"I don't believe in dating apps." And given I was engaged to be married this time a month ago, that's not a lie. *I'd thought dating apps were a thing of the past for me.*

She rolls her eyes dramatically. "Seriously, how could I possibly deal with you for a year if I want to kick you out of this truck right now?"

"Is this where I sell myself to you?"

She folds her arms and nods. "Yes, this would be that moment."

I rub my hands together. "The moment I've been waiting for." On a deep breath, I start, "I've never had a cavity—"

"That's what you start with?"

I pause, seeming confused. I'm sorry, that's a solid accomplishment.

"I think it's a plus in my column. Shows I have good dental hygiene."

"There are people with good dental hygiene who still get cavities."

"Either way," I say, growing a little frustrated. "It's just something about me. Jesus." I clear my throat. "May I continue?" She gestures with her hand for me to continue, so I say, "I've never killed a plant—"

"Have you ever owned one?" She raises a brow.

"No, but that's by choice."

"Then how can you lead with you've never killed a plant when you've never even owned one?"

I casually drape my arm over the side of the truck. "It just shows my common sense."

She runs her hand over her forehead. "Shows that you twist the truth."

"Uh, no. I just thought it was an interesting fact."

"It's not." She shakes her head.

"Fine, how about this." I clear my throat again. "I know how to make a really delicious peanut butter and jelly sandwich." She snorts, but I continue. "I can give you an entire rundown on the history of *The Great British Bake-off*, who hosted what year, who judged, who won. I write bestselling novels that as you probably know are quite entertaining, and you'd get them for free. We're talking hours upon hours of entertainment. I clearly know how to build things, so if you need a nail driven into wood, I'm your man. And not to mention"—I tap the side of my head—"this noggin is full of brilliant ideas, so whenever you need assistance or a think tank, you can come right to me. Last, I smell nice, cut my toenails bi-weekly, never leave beard clippings around the sink, and know the importance of putting the seat down after I pee."

"Wow," she says while slowly clapping. "You are truly a prize to be won."

"That's what I've been telling you." I playfully nudge her with my foot even though her sarcasm is thick. "You can't get better than me when it comes to a marriage of convenience. I'm your man. I'm respectful, and encouraging, and funny, and I'm here to cheer you on while also letting you subtly know when you do something wrong. Because what's marriage without checks and balances?"

"It's not a real marriage."

"Technically, it is very real. Legal and all, but how we treat the marriage is up to us. All I ask is that we're not embarrassing each other by, you know . . . running around on each other. This will require you to be exclusive to me."

"Trust me, if I marry you, there's no way I could balance a side piece with everything else on my plate."

"Good to know." I lean in and say, "And you have my full discretion as well. I'll be as loyal as they come. I could even make a shirt that says Team Aubree if you want."

"Why would you do that?" she asks with a skeptical look.

"To show my loyalty."

She groans. "Will you be this annoying if we get married?"

"Can't be sure. Still trying to figure out everything that annoys you about me."

She motions her hand in front of me. "All of it."

"But are you annoyed . . . or are you possibly a touch intrigued and masking it with annoyance because you have too much pride that I might actually tickle your fancy?"

In the most deadpan tone I've ever heard, she says, "Annoyed."

"Well, we have time to change that." I smile brightly, and I'm met with her scowl, which, to be honest, I've sort of grown fond of.

I like the way her nose turns up.

The crinkle between her eyes.

The purse of her lips.

You know . . . the look might be better than her smile.

I nudge her with my foot again. "What do you say, Aubree?" I wiggle my eyebrows. "Your hand . . . for my land?"

She eyes me.

Her mind races.

Her breath picks up as she thinks.

It might . . . by God, it might become a reality.

This idea.

This planning.

This constant following her around and calling her my wife.

That look? She's leaning in my direction.

I can see it clear as day.

She's going to say yes.

After a few more silent moments, she looks away and mutters, "I don't want you living with me."

"What's that?" I lean my ear toward her.

"I said, I don't want you living with me . . . if we do this."

Jesus Christ, it's happening.

Tread carefully, man.

"I get where you're coming from. Privacy can be a big factor in decisions like this, but unfortunately, given that we'll have to put on a façade, I'll have to shack up with you to keep this falsity alive."

She grumbles and folds her arms. "Then . . . I don't want you touching me."

I cringe. "Afraid that's unavoidable. You're my wife, after all. I would have to show affection for it to be believable."

She hems and haws over that for a second and then says, "Fine, but I don't want you touching me when we're alone."

"Oh." I nod. "I see where your mind is racing off to. Don't worry, it will be purely platonic between us. Consider us friends without benefits."

"Friends?" She lifts a brow.

"Yeah. Do you really think we can pull this off with the rapport we have now? Our current conversations resemble complete meltdown. If we're going to make this believable, we'll have to ease up on each other. Which means"—I lean forward and press my finger on the wrinkle between her eyes, flattening it out—"you'll have to stop hating me."

"Then don't make it so easy," she replies, but then follows it up with a smirk. And that, right there, ladies and gentlemen, that little smirk, yup, that means I won her over.

I smile back. "I'll give it my best shot. So . . . what do you say?" I lend out my hand to her. "Your hand for my land?"

She stares down at my hand and then back up at me.

Her lips grow tight.

She groans in frustration.

And then . . . magically, her hand meets mine.

Success!

Holy shit, I did it.

"Really?" I ask her, shocked.

She pulls her hand away and buries her head in her palms. "God, I can't believe I'm saying this, but . . . yes." She looks up at me and points her finger. "But only because I can't stand the fact that Amanda and Matt pitied me. And because I really want the land, and from the looks of it, it doesn't seem like you're giving it up, which is a real dick move."

"It's not a dick move," I counter. "It's smart. Tit for tat."

"Yeah, but this is giving up a year of my life."

"Like I said . . . *wife* . . . it's going to be your best year."

"Doubtful."

⸻

"KNOCK, KNOCK, IT'S YOUR HUBBY," I say from outside her guest house.

After we finished eating, Aubree went into silent mode. I've never seen anything like it. It's as if she turned off her brain and just went to work. She didn't talk, didn't recognize me as the person working next to her, she just . . . worked. I chalked it up to her being inside her head and trying to come to terms with what she'd just agreed to.

I was fine with it, but once we finished with the chicken coop and cleaned up, she started to walk away without a word. That's when I grabbed her by the arm and asked her if she was in shock. She nodded, and I understood, so I told her that I'd be back later to go over things, but I gave her time to work through whatever was going on in her head.

And in all honesty, if she came up to me and said she couldn't go through with it, that it was too much for her to handle and she couldn't help me out, I'd leave it at that. I'd find another way to save the cabin, even if it meant buying out my cousin, which would be a tough pill to swallow. Especially since I think he'd either upcharge me or just keep that cabin out of spite, knowing I had all the means to make it mine but couldn't.

I don't trust Wallace as far as I can throw him. It's why I've been so adamant about this. Why I've wanted to marry Aubree. She wins. I win. And then we can move on with our lives.

Conventional, no.

But sometimes we have to think outside the box to get what we want.

After a few seconds of silence, I see Aubree walk up and open the door to her guest house.

Freshly showered, she's wearing a pair of plaid shorts and a white tank top. There's nothing fancy about her outfit, and I like that. I like that she can be comfortable around me and not care that her hair isn't done or that she isn't wearing makeup. Not that she needs to impress me.

"Feeling better?" I ask her.

"Barely," she says as I walk into the guest house that smells like fresh soap and whatever hair products she uses. She shuts the door behind me as I take a seat on her bed. I take note how the bed is made so that when I do live here, I know how to make it to her liking. "I dry-heaved a few times in case you need to know."

"You did?" I ask. "Why? Nerves?"

"Yes." She takes a seat on the bed as well. "I don't know how you can remain so calm about something like this, but this whole idea freaks me out. I understand that there are pluses to it, for you and me, but . . . what if, I don't know, Mac gets close to you, and then when we divorce, she's sad that you leave? She's already lost two parents. I feel like I can't do that to her again."

I turn toward her and say, "I will always be a part of her life. I know I've been missing for a bit, but now that I'm here, now that I'll be here for a year, I know the importance and commitment it will take to be here and be present with her. I'd definitely visit."

"You wouldn't stay here?" she asks. "When we divorced, you'd move away?"

"Attached already?" I ask with a smile.

But she doesn't find it funny. "I'm being serious, Wyatt."

I nod in understanding. "I wouldn't. The point of this deal is to acquire the cabin. Once I acquire that, then I'd move in. Stay in Canoodle. Make that my home. And then come up here to visit with Mac. The great thing about my job is I have freedom when it comes to my schedule. She won't be left behind."

She worries her lip. "And what about . . . you know, money and stuff? Will we sign a prenup? I don't want anything from you, just the land, and I don't, well . . . I don't want you taking the farm from me."

"Do you really think I'd do that?" I ask.

She shrugs. "I like to believe you wouldn't, but then again, I don't know you as well as I probably should, and knowing that side of you wouldn't be solved by asking twenty questions. That's the kind of thing you learn about a person as you get to know them through experience."

Looking her dead in the eye, I say, "I won't take this farm from you, Aubree. In fact, we'll make sure we have a legal and binding document that clarifies both parties' needs. I know what it means to feel sentimental toward property, hence this entire façade. My plan is simple: marry you, take ownership of the cabin, move on. I don't want anything else from you."

"Okay," she says, looking relieved. "And you would have to live here?"

"Yes. We have to make it seem real."

She glances around her small space. "Would we have to go on public dates?"

"I think so, just so people see us together. The only reason I say this is because I know Wallace will put up a fight when he finds out we got married. He won't be happy about it and will most likely contest the whole thing, so we have to make the marriage believable, especially with the town, because they'll back us up."

Understanding falls over her expression. "Do you think he'll come here?"

"I wouldn't be surprised if he did." I let out a deep sigh. "I know this is asking a lot of you, and if you want, I can tack on some other things to sweeten the deal, like any new farm equipment you might need, or if you want me to buy you some cows. You name it, it's yours."

"I don't need anything else from you, just the land."

"Okay, but if you change your mind, let me know. I'm an honest man, Aubree, and I keep my word. I promise you when this ends, you'll have your land, and I'll be out of your hair. The only time you'll see me is when I come to visit Mac."

She slowly nods and then lets out a deep breath just as an SUV comes screaming up the dirt road. Our eyes watch as it parks, and Hattie flies out of the front seat, rounding the back and charging toward the guest house.

"Oh God," Aubree says. "Prepare yourself because things are about to get real."

Hattie doesn't even bother knocking as she barges into the guest house and stands in the doorway, huffing with anger as she looks back and forth between the two of us.

Hands on her hips, she says, "Care to explain what's going on?"

Aubree glances at me, looking like she's about to panic, so I take the lead.

Clearing my throat, I speak very calmly as I say, "A few months ago, your sister contacted me when she found out that half of the land was given to me in Cassidy's will. She wanted to get on the same page where the farm was concerned. I was in Palm Springs at the time and asked her if she could meet me halfway so we could talk in person. She agreed to it."

"Why didn't you tell me you were meeting with him?" Hattie asks.

"Uh, because you were going through a lot." Aubree nervously clutches her hands together. "I didn't want to bother you with a small detail."

She's good. Look at her playing along. I'm proud already.

"When she arrived, I was caught off guard," I continue. "I forgot just how beautiful she is and well, instead of talking business and about the farm, I got distracted." I glance at Aubree who looks like she's gained a touch more confidence.

"Very distracted," she adds.

"And well, we started talking about everything else but the farm," I say. "By the end of the night, I asked her if I could keep in touch. It was one of the first times I had a true conversation with someone who I felt heard me. She said yes, so after that day, I started texting her."

"Very needy texts," Aubree says, making me smile.

"Needy because I was crushing hard," I add, loving this story already. "And then those texts turned into one phone call." Hattie looks between us, still confused. "And those phone calls turned into FaceTimes. And with every call, every moment I saw her face, I started to fall for her. For her kind heart under that rusty exterior. I fell for her snappy, witty comments and her ball-busting ways. And I fell for the sound of her voice that often calmed me before I went to bed. I quickly realized that . . . well, I loved her, and that's when I knew I had to come out here."

Hattie blinks a few times.

Her hands fall from her hips.

And then she rubs her palm over her forehead in distress.

"But . . . you were pissed when he came into town, Aubree. You clearly hated the man. And Hayes told me he spoke to you in the grocery store, and you seemed like you didn't know her at all."

"Because she wasn't ready to tell you guys. I lied in the grocery store, trying to make sure it seemed like we didn't know each other," I say, completely forgetting that conversation for a second. "She was afraid of how you might take the news, and with everything that's been going on, with you taking over the store and Ryland taking care of Mac, she didn't want to trouble you guys with this. Of course, I wasn't happy about it and took matters into my own hands. She was rightfully pissed at me."

"Let me get this straight," Hattie says. The expression on her face makes me believe this is far too painful for her to even take in. "You two have secretly been talking for months, and Wyatt decided to take a chance and come into town, and you, Aubree, were mad about it?"

"Because I didn't want to make a fuss about things," she says.

Hattie puts her hands back on her hips as she addresses her sister. "Do you really think Ryland and I would make a fuss about you having someone special in your life? This is . . ." Her eyes start to well up, and guilt immediately starts to swarm me because . . . yeah . . . lies. "This is amazing, Aubree."

Hattie swoops in and hugs Aubree, who awkwardly remains seated and stiff.

She gently pats her sister's back before Hattie pulls away and cups Aubree's cheeks. "Are you in love too?"

Ooo, bold question.

"Um, well," Aubree starts.

"She hasn't said it yet," I cut in, so Aubree doesn't have to finish that sentence. "And I'm not offended at all. I know it will come."

Hattie pulls away. "Why don't you love him?"

Okay, coming on a bit strong, Hattie.

"Hattie," I say gently. "We all move at different paces—"

"I love him," Aubree says, but rather than sounding as though she's in love, she sounds more annoyed, like she wants this over and done with.

And I'm not sure if Hattie doesn't recognize it, if that's how Aubree normally acts, or that Hattie is so gleeful that she surpasses Aubree's tone and scoops her up either way.

"Ahhh, you're in love. Oh my God." They fall back on the bed, and Hattie straddle-hugs her sister, clinging to her like a koala.

Aubree offers me an annoyed side-eye that makes me lightly chuckle. There is no way Aubree is enjoying any of this, but I find small delight in it. There's just something about an annoyed Aubree that amuses and comforts me at the same time. It's odd.

When Hattie rises, she straightens out her shirt and apologizes. "God, sorry, that's the first time Wyatt is probably hearing it, and you guys probably want to kiss or something . . ." Hattie squeezes her hands, looking back and forth between the two of us. Does she want us to kiss in front of her?

From Aubree's body language, I'll take a wild guess and say that won't happen.

"Can we, uh, get some privacy?" I ask Hattie, thinking that's probably the best choice for the situation.

Hattie's eyes widen. "Yes, of course. Sorry." She gleefully claps her hands. "I'm going to go tell Ryland. We were texting, and I wasn't sure what was happening between you two. Still, then I heard from Ethel, who heard from Dee Dee, who overheard Amanda talking about it. Well, I had to rush over here to confirm it because you know how sometimes the things the town talks about aren't true, and I didn't want to look like a fool when people asked me, and oh my God, I'm so excited. We can go on double dates, and you're going to be so happy, and you're in love and . . . ahhh!" She claps again and leaves the guest house, only to run over to the main house.

"Jesus," Aubree exhales as she leans back on the bed and drapes one hand over her face.

"So . . . you love me, huh?"

She lifts her arm, giving me that classic side-eye that makes me laugh. "Please, I can't handle any teasing from you at the moment."

"Fair enough." I smirk. "Glad that we're in love, though. It really solidifies this bond we have."

"Yup . . . soooo in love," she says with a heavy dose of sarcasm that makes me laugh.

"Looks like we're doing this. Now the question is . . . how am I going to propose?"

She lifts her arm and looks me dead in the eyes. "If you make a spectacle of it, I'll murder you."

Just the response I was looking for . . .

Chapter Eight

AUBREE

Dinner last night was eventful to say the least.

Wyatt thought it would be a good idea to head over and talk to Ryland, who just stood in the kitchen for the longest time, stunned. I don't blame him. If the roles were reversed, I'd be just as shocked, because I haven't been acting like someone falling in love. I haven't even mentioned one word. If anything, I've expressed my displeasure about Wyatt and his part ownership of the farm. I was mad about that. So for me to suddenly be in love is probably startling.

Of course, being the good big brother that he is, Ryland shook Wyatt's hand, and we sat down and ate dinner.

Wyatt was careful with being overtly affectionate—probably got the vibe that I wasn't into it in front of my family—and kept things minimal with just an arm draped over my chair.

After dinner, I helped Ryland with the dishes while Hattie, Wyatt, and Mac played *Space Escape* in the living room. I occasionally glanced in their direction to see how Wyatt interacted with Mac, and it was nice to see him playing with her . . . not because I'm thinking of future children or anything like that, but because it's nice for Mac to have another person in her life who she can love.

Once Mac started yawning, we said our goodbyes, and Wyatt walked me to the guest house, where he leaned in and whispered in my ear that he'd contact his lawyer to get a prenup drawn up.

I thanked him, and then when the coast was clear and Hattie was gone, I pulled away from him, slipped into my house, and stared up at the ceiling for an hour, wondering what the hell I was doing with my life.

And let me tell you, nothing came to mind.

I eventually fell asleep but woke up early this morning with bloodshot eyes, a heavy feeling on my chest, and the need to get out on the farm and do something with my hands.

So that's exactly what I'm doing.

I shut the door to the guest house and take a walk out back toward the barn, where I see Wyatt's SUV parked.

I let out a long exhale.

Yup, why would he be anywhere else?

Coffee in hand, I close the distance, and when I reach the barn, I find him sitting on the tractor with a bakery box next to him and wearing a bright smile.

How is this man happy all the time? Does he take uppers every morning?

He doesn't even have any coffee with him.

I don't get it.

"Morning," he says, hopping down and grabbing the box. "I was going to knock on your door this morning, but I wasn't sure if you were awake and didn't want to disturb you. I came here and did some touch-ups on the chicken coop, making sure we covered everything with paint."

I walk over to a bench in the barn and take a seat, crossing one leg over the other. "You could have knocked on my door. I was awake."

He follows me and takes a seat as well while popping open

the bakery box to reveal my favorite muffin again. It's a sweet gesture, one that I'll always accept. He might annoy me, but underneath it all, he's a nice guy.

"Let me guess, you didn't get much sleep last night."

"Barely any," I say.

"Me neither," he says. That surprises me. He seems so untouched by this entire scenario like he wasn't mentally affected by any of this.

"Really?" I ask. "That doesn't seem to bother you."

"Why do you say that?" he asks as he takes the paper wrapper off one of the muffins.

"Because you just seem so chill, like this isn't a big deal."

"I know what kind of sacrifice this is, Aubree," he says softly. "That doesn't escape me. I just tend to keep things positive if I can. But yesterday, when Hattie hugged you because she was so excited about you falling in love . . . I don't know . . ." He stares down at his muffin. "It made me feel guilty. I didn't think she was going to be that thrilled."

"I think it's one of those things where she's in love, so she wants everyone to be in love, you know?"

He nods in understanding. "Anyway, I just felt bad and started thinking about everything." He looks up at me, those deep brown eyes so sincere that it's almost hard to keep our gaze connected. "If you want to bow out, it's fine. I understand." He sighs while dragging his hand over his face. "I just feel like I went about this the wrong way, and now——"

"You're getting cold feet," I say.

"No," he replies. "I'd still do this. I just feel bad about the way I pressured you. We're not talking about being fake boyfriend and girlfriend; that would be way less of a stress for me. We're talking about getting married. And the guilt I feel about dragging you down this journey is consuming me. So . . ." He wets his lips and picks at his muffin. "You can just take the land, Aubree. I know I don't want it, and you do. I feel like a dick, forcing you to do something just so you can cherish a piece of your sister. It makes me feel like a total asshole, and I don't want to feel that way. So it's yours."

I am stunned.

Because that was the last thing I thought he'd say when I saw him in the barn with a bakery box.

I assumed he was here to talk logistics and to let me know when and where he'd propose. Maybe give me an update on the prenup.

But to just offer me the land . . .

"Wyatt, you don't—"

"I do," he says, his demeanor changing. "I laid awake all night thinking about it. Thinking about the way Hattie hugged you out of pure joy, and it just hit me that this isn't just our lives we're messing with. This is a lot of people's lives. And I don't want to ruin what you have going on here. You have a great support system and a great town. I'm just going to mess it up with this plan, so . . . yeah, you can have the land, and I'll figure something out when it comes to the cabin." His eyes meet mine. "I'm sorry I brought this stress on you."

He smiles softly and rises from the bench, stepping away from me. And at that moment, the weirdest thing happens to me. I'll probably never be able to describe it properly, but with that one step, that slight distance, it feels like something inside me is being pulled with him.

It's an odd feeling.

It's something unexpected that forces me to reach out as he passes and grab his wrist.

Surprised, he pauses and stares down at me, looking for answers.

But I have none. I'm just as stunned as he is.

Because this is what I wanted. I wanted the land, no strings attached. I wanted to be able to just focus on the farm, making it grow, and carrying on Cassidy's dreams of what this place could become.

But here I am, grabbing Wyatt's hand, preventing him from leaving.

And I have no idea why.

"Yes?" he asks after a few seconds of silence.

Nothing comes to mind.

Not a word.

Not a thought.

It's just all blank in my head.

"Aubree."

"Hmm?" I ask.

"You're holding my wrist."

I wet my lips. "I know."

"Why?"

I shake my head. "I don't know."

"Well, do you want to let it go?"

"No."

"Okay." His Adam's apple works up and down. "Do you want me to sit back down?"

I think about it for a moment and then nod. "Yes."

"Okay," he says as he moves back to the bench and sits down.

When our eyes connect, I feel that guilt he was talking about, but it's not guilt over deceiving people. It's guilt over what he's giving up.

Ever since he got here, I've been annoyed with his presence. Irritated that he thought he could waltz on in and act like everything was fine, like he owned this land, could help make choices, and no one would hold him accountable for it. I think I was so annoyed that I missed one important aspect of it all—he's grieving the loss of something that I've grieved as well.

I want the farmland just like he wants his family cabin.

I know the desperation he feels. I know what it means to hold something so close to your chest and want it as badly as he does, which is why I grabbed his hand.

Why I didn't ask him to leave.

And why I'm staring back at him, ready to say what I'm going to say.

"We can get married, Wyatt."

He shakes his head. "No, Aubree. I know you're just saying

that to be nice, and I really don't want to create something bigger than it should be. This is my problem, not yours."

"Let us get one thing straight," I say as I bring my feet up on the bench and my legs close to my chest. "There is one thing I never do, and that's 'be nice' just for the hell of it. I think anyone who knows me can attest to that. And I'm not going to just take the land for free. So you have two choices." I hold up my fingers. "We have someone come out to the farm, assess your part of the property, and tell us how much it's worth so I can attempt to find a way to buy it off you, even if that means I take out a loan. Or . . ." I pause for a moment and collect myself. When I meet his eyes again, I say, "We go through with the original plan and get married. That's it, those are your two choices. I'm not going to take the land just because you feel guilty. I don't take handouts or anyone else's pity."

He looks away as he grips the back of his neck. "Aubree——"

"Two options, that's it," I repeat, wanting to make it very clear that I won't listen to any other suggestions.

That's when he turns back to me and asks, "What's with the change of heart?"

"There's no change of heart," I say. "I went to bed last night with the knowledge in my head that I'd be marrying you. I woke up this morning expecting the same thing. You're the one with the change of heart, and just because you feel guilty doesn't mean I'll allow you to take pity on me."

His brow creases, and his head tilts ever so slightly. "I'm not taking pity on you, Aubree. I'm trying to do the right thing."

"The right thing isn't giving me the land for free. Clarke and Cassidy left that to you for a reason. I'm not sure why, but they did. That means it's your land, and if you're willing to sell it or trade it, then I'm willing to participate in such an exchange. But I won't accept it for free. I've worked for everything in my life. I'm not about to stop that now because you have feelings."

He chuckles. "Because I have feelings, huh? Nice way to put it." I just shrug. He blows out a heavy breath. "Okay, if you insist, then I guess we'll get married because there is no way I'll take your money."

"Great," I say. "I guess we're getting married, then." I glance away as my stomach turns upside down with nerves. I know that feeling distinctly, but I dare not show it. I don't want him to know how I feel about all of this.

I wasn't allowed to show emotions growing up, and I'm not about to show them now.

"Are you okay with that?" Wyatt asks.

"Yup." I smile at him, putting on that faithful mask of mine that got me through the nights of my dad screaming at Ryland. Of the mornings when Dad beat Ryland with a shoe because he hadn't put out the trash the night before. Of the days when I longed so desperately to be held by anyone . . . anyone who would comfort me like a mother or tell me that everything would be okay when I knew deep down it wasn't.

"Are you sure?" It's as if he can see right through me, and I don't like that.

So I roll my eyes at him. "Jesus, Wyatt, yes. Like you said, it's a year. It's not a big deal. We will get what we want and go our separate ways. Works out great. Does your lawyer need anything from me for the prenup and agreement?"

He eyes me.

Studies me.

Watches over me for a beat too long. *Please stop examining me. I don't think you'll like what you find.*

But finally he says, "I'll let you know if she does. Oh, and it might help if I actually have your information in my phone." He pulls it out from his pocket, unlocks it, and hands it to me.

I stare down at the wallpaper on his phone and back up at him. "What's this?" I flash the screen at him.

"My phone."

"Uh, no, the picture on your phone?"

He smirks. "That's you. It's my screensaver too. Pretty clever, huh?"

"When did you take this picture of me? I'm squatting over a paint tray like a chicken as if I'm ready to lay an egg."

He chuckles. "I know, I found it funny."

One year of tolerating his grating sense of humor. One. Year.

"You could have asked for a more flattering picture," I say.

"And stare at your pretty face all day?" He shakes his head. "Nah, I'm good."

My body goes still, a blush creeping over my cheeks.

Pretty face.

He really said pretty face. Just so casually, as if it's a natural thing to compliment your fake wife. Compliments were rarely handed out when I was growing up. Ryland rarely complimented us. Cassidy would, but it was few and far between as well. I don't think I've ever met anyone who just says what's on their mind, and that . . . that worries me. "I can see you're trying to process my comment." His smile is infuriating and also . . . comforting. How is that possible? "Do you not take compliments well?"

"They're . . . they're just not needed," I say, shaking my head.

"Well, it's true. You do have a pretty face."

"Stop that," I say as I plug my phone number into his phone. "You're making me uncomfortable."

"Fair enough," he says. I finish typing my info into his phone and hand it over to him as he says, "I'm here to help you, Aubree. I need you to know that. I'm not your enemy. I'm not here to harass you or to make you feel bad. I'm not here to treat you like shit or to dredge up any ill will. I'm on your side. I'm your support. I'd like to be your friend. I think the more we recognize that we're in this together, the easier our time as a married couple will be. Okay?" His brow crinkles with his question, and I find it kind of cute.

"Okay," I say. I figure I should give him a rundown of what he's working with. It's only fair. "But I need you to know that I don't trust a lot of people. I didn't have the best childhood, which I don't plan on discussing, so please don't ask. I hate dealing with emotions and feelings. I like to work and get things done. I have two goals in life: to make sure Mac is cared for and loved and to ensure this farm prospers for many years. Don't get in the way of those two things, and we can be friends."

"That seems simple enough," he answers.

"Good." I set my feet on the ground. "Then if this is all done, I think I'll get to work."

He stands at the same time I do. "How can I help?"

"Go back to your room at the inn and do whatever you need to do. I just need some time to myself."

His lips twist to the side as he studies me. "Normally, I wouldn't want you working alone, but I can understand the need to be in your own head. So I'll leave you alone, but tonight, I'm taking you out."

"Why?" I ask, confused.

"Because I think it would be good for you and so people can see us around town. I can make a reservation. I'll pick you up."

"I can just meet you in town, so there's no need to drive all the way out here for no reason."

"Aubree—"

I hold up my hand. "I can drive, Wyatt. I'll meet you at the inn, and we can walk to wherever from there."

"Fine," he says, capitulating, which is kind of funny because it appears very painful for him. "Be at the inn around six. Does that work?"

"Yes." And before he can leave, I ask, "You're not expecting me to dress all fancy for you, are you?"

That makes him grin. He leans in and cups my chin. "Wear whatever you want to wear . . . wife. I'll proudly walk with you on my arm." And then he takes off, an extra pep in his step.

Why do I fear that I just made a big mistake . . . but also, possibly a great decision?

━━━

BETWEEN YOU AND ME, it took me two hours to get ready.

I know what you're thinking. Why on earth are you taking two hours to get ready for a simple date? It's called overthinking. Every outfit I put on felt too conservative, too dressed up, or too revealing. Something was wrong with every article of clothing I owned, so much so that I almost contacted Hattie to ask her for something to wear, but then I realized how absurd that would be, so I skipped out on that idea.

I settled for a simple red sundress with sleeves and a pair of sandals.

When doing my hair, I went back and forth between curling it or letting the natural curls take over with a little help from mousse. I went with the natural style. Curling my hair would have made it seem like I was trying too hard, and I don't want him to think I was eager to impress him.

Because I'm not.

I put on some light makeup, a small dab of gloss on my lips, and then headed out the door so I wouldn't analyze myself any more than I needed to.

And now that I've parked my car and am walking up the front steps of the inn, I'm starting to second-guess everything about this arrangement. I don't do well with situations like this. The last time I was out on a date was with Matt, and I think we all know how that went. And even though this isn't really a date, we have to treat it like a date, and that makes me nauseous and nervous and all the things in between.

"Oh hello, dear, don't you look lovely," Ethel says, startling me out of my thoughts. Wearing one of her many kaftans, Ethel is perched in her rocking chair, iced tea in hand, and surveying the town.

"Hey, Ethel," I say.

"Are you here to pick up your man?"

Here we go . . .

"Yes," I answer. "We're going to dinner."

"How lovely." She sips her tea. "It's so nice to see you out and about, all gussied up." Not too gussied up, just not wearing dirt-dusted clothes.

"Well, figured I could kick the boots for some sandals

tonight," I say, feeling so freaking awkward, like I'm talking to the parent before the date.

"You did a lovely job, and from here, I can smell your beautiful perfume." I swear I only did two spritzes. "Is that gardenias?" She sniffs the air.

"Uh, not sure. I just liked the smell of it and bought it."

"I believe that's gardenias. Do you know what they symbolize?"

If she says it's some sort of sexed-up aphrodisiac, I'm rinsing myself in the bathroom.

"Not sure," I answer.

She sips her tea again and stares out at the quiet road. "Purity and gentleness."

Oh-kay.

"Huh, didn't—"

"Are you trying to present yourself as gentle and pure?"

How does one answer that question?

"You know," she continues, "given your hard exterior."

"Never really thought about it that way."

She nods and rocks. "Must have slipped into your subconscious while you were picking out the scent that will grace your bosom tonight."

Dear.

God.

"I just sprayed it in the air twice. I wasn't pointing it at my bosom," I say just as the screen door to the inn opens and Wyatt walks out.

He must have caught my last sentence because he greets me with a raised brow and a question in his expression.

"There he is," Ethel coos as she stands and walks up to him. She straightens the collar of his polo shirt and pats his shoulders. "Looking handsome as ever."

"Thank you," he says. "This color is quite beautiful on you, Ethel."

She waves her hand at him. "Oh, you flatter me too much."

"Not flattery when it's facts," he says and then directs his attention toward me. "Wow, Aubree, you look beautiful." And then, to my surprise, he leans in and presses a light kiss on my cheek.

It's a peck.

Just a featherlight touch from his lips.

But for some reason, I can feel it all the way down to my toes.

When he pulls away, he smiles at me, and I know it's my turn to say something about him. "I, uh . . . I like that your shorts don't have pleats."

His smile turns into a full-on grin just as Ethel scoffs next to us. "You're talking about his non-pleated pants? Goodness, Aubree, look at the man's chest and how his shirt is snug in all the right places, or the dark five o'clock shadow that accentuates his eyes, or the way his hair falls over his forehead deliciously. Focus on those things, not the pleats."

I don't want to focus on those things.

Focusing on them will make me more nervous because despite not wanting to admit it, Wyatt Preston is extremely attractive, has a soothing voice, and has turned out to be a very nice guy. I'd like not to focus on things that could change my opinion of him, which right now is just . . . regular.

Yup, a regular opinion.

If anyone even knows what that means.

"I'm sure she'll tell me how devastatingly handsome I am without an audience." Wyatt winks, and that seems to soothe Ethel.

She starts rocking again in her chair and says, "Well, you two have fun tonight. Treat her well, Wyatt. She's been through a lot."

"Don't worry, I will," he says as he places his hand on the small of my back and directs me down the stairs and to the boardwalk.

When we're out of earshot, Wyatt says, "Do you want to hold my hand?"

"Uh . . . I don't know," I answer, keeping my hands clasped to my purse.

"You don't have to," he says. "But the offer is there if you want to take it for the show of everything."

"Uh, thanks," I say.

"Not sure you want to hear this, but you're looking a little uncomfortable."

"That's because *I am* uncomfortable," I reply. "I haven't done this in a long time. I've never fake done this either."

"Long time?" he asks. "What does a long time entail?"

"Long enough that I don't know what to say or how to act."

"Want me to give you a quick rundown on what the dating world is like at the moment?"

"Even though I don't particularly care for a condescending conversation, I wouldn't be opposed to it."

He chuckles. "No condescension here. Just education." He drapes his arm over my shoulder as we walk past a couple holding hands. "Now, the dating world is the same as years ago. Two people agree to go on a date, they meet up for coffee or food or a mutual place, and during that time, they talk. Now, how these people meet up depends on the circumstances. Some are online, some are by friends and family, and others are from shared farmland. No matter where they come from, the date should always be the same. You ask questions, you get to know each other, you tell witty anecdotes about the picture on your phone and the girl who looked like she was laying an egg in a paint tray."

Strangely, I feel almost calmed by his charm and choice of words. I'm sure he'd know all about dating, looking like he does. *Will he miss that in our year together?*

"So nothing has changed."

"Nothing. Well, that's not true. There's a lot of catfishing, ghosting, and people don't put up with a lot on dates anymore. So if the person they're going on a date with makes an absurd claim like . . . whales are actually tiny fish that are made to look big in pictures, then instead of enduring said date, they take off and just leave, right then and there."

"Oh God, that seems harsh."

"Time is a valuable commodity, Aubree. You can't get it back, so why waste it on a two-bit chump who thinks whales are mini fish?"

"I guess so." I glance up at him. "Do you believe whales are tiny fish?"

"No, I think they were all blown up by Wayne Szalinski, and that's how they've come about."

I pause in our pursuit toward the restaurant. "Wayne Szalinski? Who is that?"

He turns toward me, eyes wide. "Who is that?" he asks as if I've insulted him. "Aubree, I know I'm older than you, but not that much older. You have to know who that is. It's pop culture. Everyone knows who it is."

"Doubtful," I say.

And of course, just at that moment, another couple walks by, so Wyatt stops them. "Sorry to bother you, but my girl and I have fallen into a bit of a debate. Would you be able to help us?" My girl, how do those terms just come so easily to him? He can say my girl and how I look beautiful, while I'm spouting off about the no-show of pleats in his shorts.

"Sure," the woman says.

"This is Aubree, and she says she doesn't know who Wayne Szalinski is, and I told her everyone does. Do you guys know?"

"Isn't that the dad from *Honey, I Shrunk the Kids*?" the man asks.

"Yes, it is," the woman says, and then I'm lucky enough to see the annoying grin that spreads across Wyatt's face as he turns toward me.

"See," he says. "People know." He thanks the couple, and we're on our way again.

"For the record, I've never seen that movie," I say.

"What do you mean you've never seen it? I think I saw it when I was in school once. It was a classic growing up."

"But, like you said, we're not the same age, so my class was probably moving on to something more new age."

I can practically hear his eye roll. "What are you? Thirty?"

"Twenty-eight," I say.

"Twenty-eight?" he nearly yells and stops us again. He gives me a scan, and when his eyes meet mine, he says, "Fuck, you are pretty young."

I chuckle, the sound feeling odd, but also . . . nice. "Thanks for the confirmation, I guess. Should I be calling you grandpa?"

"No," he scoffs. "I'm not that much older."

"How much is not that much?" I ask, liking how he's squirming.

"Seven years. Not bad."

"You're in your mid-thirties? Yikes."

"No." He shakes his head. "No yikes. There is nothing yikes about mid-thirties. Mid-thirties is great. You don't care about what people think about you, you have a more established career, and you're in tune with your body, which means you don't abuse it with late-night drinking and hangover cures. You get an honest night's sleep and understand the importance of vitamins, drinking water, and exercise. And if you want to host a dinner party, you don't have to ask people to bring something because you can provide the food yourself."

"Wow, you paint the mid-thirties like a theme park. All fun, all the time."

"You're welcome," he says in such a sarcastic tone. "Now, is there any wisdom I can impart on you?"

"Not sure, Granddad. I'll let you know if I think of something, though."

"Such a wise-ass," he says as we turn toward Provisions, the burger and fries joint here in Almond Bay.

He opens the door for me and presses his hand to my lower back once again when we walk up to the hostess.

"Hey, Aubree," Meredith says. Her eyes fall to Wyatt, and she lightly pushes her hair behind her ear. "Table for two?"

"Actually, we have a reservation under Frogmore? I believe I asked for a second-floor table looking out over the ocean."

"Yes, Mr. Frogmore, right this way." Meredith collects two menus and guides us up the wooden stairs to the second floor and the back deck. The sun is starting to set, and the sound of the ocean blocks out the people around us.

Wyatt pulls out my chair while Meredith sets the menus on the table. "Your server will be with you soon."

When she's gone, I lean forward and whisper, "Frogmore?"

He smirks and opens his menu. "Why give your real name when you can give a fake name?"

"Because it's weird."

"How is it weird?" he asks. "No one knows me here, so I might as well have some fun."

"They know you just enough to know that Frogmore is a fake."

He shrugs. "Let me add, when you're in your mid-thirties, you easily start not giving a fuck. Very freeing."

"Apparently."

I don't bother opening my menu. I know exactly what I like to eat here. The Hawaiian burger with fries and sweet and sour dipping sauce. The perfect combination.

"Hmm, there are a lot of burger choices. I don't think I've ever seen this many. Jesus, and look at all the dipping sauces."

"That's what they're known for here. The fries—courtesy of the farm's potatoes—are crispy and delicious, and they offer different dipping sauces to go with them."

"Okay, what's your favorite?"

"The Hawaiian." With one eyebrow raised, he glances over the menu.

"That has pineapple on it."

"And your point?" I ask.

"Burgers should not have pineapple on them."

"Says who?"

He sets his menu down, and with that signature smile, he says, "Says me."

"Oh." I cross my arms and lean back in my chair. "And who made you the authority of burgers?"

"The burger man."

I snort. "Oh, I see. And when did you meet the burger man?"

"To keep a long story short, I met him a few years ago when I was at a book signing in Omaha. He told me that he was the burger man, so I asked him what the dos and don'ts of burgers are. After he told me, I asked if I could impart that wisdom to others. He anointed me, and now we're here."

"Wow," I say with a shake of my head. "Is this how it's going to be for a year? You making up short stories about your life and expecting me to believe them?"

"Yes," he says with conviction.

"Ridiculous." I reach across the table and take his menu from him.

"What are you doing?" he asks.

"Ordering for you."

"Uh . . . how do I know you're going to order me something that I like?"

"Just going to have to trust me now, aren't you?"

He leans back in his chair. "That's what marriage is built on, trust. Well, here's my first test."

"I'VE NEVER HEARD OF HIM," I say while sipping my iced tea.

"You've never heard of Holt Green?" Wyatt asks, looking so perplexed that it's actually kind of cute.

Wait, I mean funny. It's funny . . . not cute.

I don't know why I'd say cute.

Cute is not a word I associate with Wyatt . . . I mean sure, he's attractive, but . . . ugh, never mind. Moving on.

"No. I don't pay attention to sports."

"But he isn't just sports. He's one of the highest paid players in the league. Your brother must talk about him."

I shake my head. "Ryland knows better than to talk baseball with me."

Distressed, Wyatt says, "Holt Green is the guy you see on all of those funny insurance commercials. He's also a spokesperson for Hopper Almonds. He does that one commercial where he's talking about the benefit of almonds, and he catches like ten in a row in his mouth without dropping one." I shake my head. "Uh . . . he was one of the guest judges on *America's Got Talent*."

"Wait," I say, placing my hand on the table. "Are you talking about the baseball player who gave Renita the roller skater slash singer the golden buzzer?"

"Yes," Wyatt says, tossing his hands in the air.

"Oh, I know who that is."

"See, I told you. Hate that you know him from a reality TV show, but yes, Holt Green would be my celebrity lookalike."

"That's great, but I didn't ask who your celebrity lookalike was. You asked me, then you decided to answer the question yourself."

"Excuse me for having a conversation," he says with a smirk.

"Here we are," the server says as she sets our plates in front of us. "Two Hawaiian burgers with a side of sweet and sour sauce for dipping. Enjoy."

"Thank you," I say, then grab my napkin and set it on my lap.

When I look up at Wyatt, he's examining his burger with his fork, lifting the bun and checking out the pineapple.

"It's not poisonous," I say as I pick up my burger.

"Looks like it could be."

"Stop, just take a bite. I promise you're going to love it."

"That's a hefty promise. What if I don't like it?"

"Then you have terrible taste buds, and I don't think we can go through with this plan."

"Ooo, the pressure is on." He wiggles his eyebrows while lifting his burger to his mouth. I pause, wanting to watch his reaction.

He takes a large bite, grabbing a taste of every layer of the burger. I appreciate that. Slowly, he starts chewing, his face remaining neutral. He sets the burger down, stops chewing, and then lifts his napkin to his mouth where . . .

"Don't you dare spit that out," I snap, causing him to chuckle.

He finishes chewing, swallows, and then grins at me. "Pretty good, Rowley. If you keep introducing me to flavors like this, I might keep you around." He takes another bite.

"Was the fake out necessary?"

He winks at me. "Keeping things alive, babe. Got to be on your toes with me."

Clearly. I shake my head and roll my eyes, but inwardly, I'm chuckling. He's such a goof.

"DO they offer a flight of dipping sauces?" Wyatt asks as he drenches his fry in the third bowl of sweet and sour sauce we ordered.

When I say this man can eat . . . he can eat. He devoured his burger in less than two minutes, then tackled his fries. They were gone very quickly as well. He's now on his third side of fries while I'm still working on my first.

And the worst part is, he has the body of a sculpted god. I've seen it. I've drooled over it. So where the hell is he putting all of this food?

Another reason men are so annoying.

"They do," I answer. "I could have told you that if you had paused your guzzling of the sweet and sour for a moment."

Fry halfway to his mouth, he asks, "Are you food shaming me?"

"No," I answer while I pick up another fry. "But I am shocked with how much you've been able to eat in one sitting."

"Didn't bother with lunch today, so I was starving. Here's something good to know, Aubree. I can be starving but I won't be hangry."

"Bad news for you," I say. "I'm a raging beast if I'm not fed."

"Why do you think I've brought you muffins every morning?"

I eye him, which makes him laugh. "It would be best if you don't poke the beast."

"I'm glad that you're acknowledging your beast-like qualities.

It makes me feel more at ease going into this marriage. I didn't want to be the only one who thought you were a beast. That's a heavy weight to hold on my shoulders."

"You poor man, how have you been able to survive?" I sarcastically ask.

"With a whole lot of grit and determination, that's how."

"The sacrifices you've made are incredible."

"Thank you." He presses his hands together and bows his head, causing me to laugh because he's so stupid. He's on another level.

I don't think I've ever met anyone as ridiculous as him.

Yet he's made you laugh. Apart from Mac's antics, not much has made me laugh lately. Maybe this year won't be that bad . . .

"Here is your check. Pay when you're ready," our server says, dropping off the bill.

I go to reach for it, but Wyatt swats my hand away. "Jesus Christ, woman. What the hell do you think you're doing?" The insult on his face is comical.

"Paying for dinner."

"No, you're not. Not when I'm here."

"I have money, Wyatt."

"Good for you, but you don't use it around me."

"Really?" I ask, placing my napkin on the table. "That's how it's going to be?"

"Yes," he says, pulling out his wallet and laying down a few bills. "I appreciate your hard work and the fact that you make money, but I'm the kind of man who will pay for our outings, our dates, and everything in between. Don't fight me over it. It's a sword I'll die on." He snaps the billfold shut, pushes it to the edge of the table, and then picks up a fry and dips it in the sauce.

"So that's that?" I ask. "Discussion over?"

"On that topic, yes. Now, if you would finally like to tell me who your celebrity lookalike is, I'd be interested to see how you compare."

"What if I don't know?" I ask.

"Please, everyone knows who they might be in celebrity form.

Like if a director came up to you today and said, who am I casting in the movie of you, you have five seconds to answer or I'm not making the movie, who would you say?"

"That's really aggressive of the director, and they should probably work on their bedside manner."

"That's Hollywood, baby." He snaps his fingers. "They want answers right then and there. So who is it?"

Rolling my eyes, I give it a second and then say, "A younger Keri Russell."

Wyatt leans back in his chair, studying me. His eyes scan over my face, my hair . . . my chest and then back up to my eyes. After what feels like forever, he says, "Fuck, you do look like her."

I laugh. "That's quite the reaction."

"Because I had the biggest fucking crush on her growing up." He drags his hand over his mouth, still staring at me. "And now that I see it, I can't unsee it."

"Well, unsee it because I'm not fulfilling your creepy teenage fantasies."

He shakes his head. "Sorry to say, Aubree, but you are." He stands from his chair and walks over to my side of the table. He holds his hand out and says, "Come on, Keri, oh, I mean, Aubree, let's get some dessert."

"You realize just how irritating you are?"

"Yet you choose to be with me."

I lift from my seat, not taking his hand. We walk out of the restaurant, his hand on my back instead.

Yet you choose to be with me.

Sort of. I did choose *this*. Not him. And even though he's irritating, can eat a mountain of food in one inhalation, and sees the light in every-fucking-thing, I'm starting to believe I *didn't* choose badly.

"YOU CAN SERIOUSLY EAT dessert after your three plates of fries?" I ask Wyatt as we step out onto the boardwalk.

"You fail to realize the endless tank my stomach is. I could probably eat a whole pie at the moment but trust me when I say that when we part, and I'm in my room all by myself, curled on my pillow, I'll be wallowing in agony, regretting those three plates of fries."

"Knowing that, why did you eat them?"

"You only live once, babe. Got to seize the moment when you can. If I'm going to impress you with my eating skills, then I need to take the opportunity."

"Is that what you were doing?" I ask as we cross the street at a crosswalk. "Showing off?"

"Yup. Got you all tingly, didn't I?" He nudges me with his elbow.

"Not even a little."

"Dammit," he says, snapping his fingers. "Here I thought you were wishing you were the food on my plate."

"Oh my God," I nearly shout, causing him to throw his head back and laugh.

"Was that not the case?"

"No!"

He chuckles. "Hmm, maybe I have to entice you some more."

"There will be no enticing and no . . . eating," I say.

"Shame," he says, his voice full of mirth. "Not only am I good at eating, but I fucking love it."

My cheeks go red hot as he opens the door to The Sweet Lab for me, and he guides me in, his hand feeling like fire on my back.

I shouldn't let a comment like that get to me, but I honestly can't remember the last time anyone has gone down on me. Not that I should be thinking about it, but Wyatt brought me there. Matt was okay at it, but when he didn't make me come right away, he grew tired and stopped altogether. It should have been a red flag for me. So the thought of Wyatt claiming that he loves doing it, or at least insinuating it, makes me feel all weird and tingly inside. I don't want to have such intimate knowledge about Wyatt's talents.

That kind of knowledge makes my mind wander, and I don't want my mind to wander, not when this is contractual.

"God, it always smells amazing in here," he whispers in my ear, the feel of his lips near my head sending a chill down my arm. "It might be my new favorite place. Although that burger." He pats his very flat, very ripped stomach.

"Wyatt, two times in one day, how did we become so lucky?" Harriot says as she greets us.

"Can't keep me away. Also, I think it's about time I share a slice of pie with my girl, don't you?"

Harriot glances at me, and a large smile spreads across her face. "You know, I heard there was a new couple in town, but I didn't want to believe the gossip. Are you telling me it's true?"

Wyatt puts his arm around my shoulders and brings me into his broad chest. "Very true." He kisses the top of my head, and I watch Harriot visibly swoon.

"Well, isn't this some of the greatest news? We've been hoping you would find someone," Harriot says to me. "After what Matt did to you, then for him to come waltzing back into town as if he didn't insult the very place where you two fell in love. Just disgusting." Okay, Harriot, we don't need the backstory. "But here you are, with a bestselling author. How did this even come about?"

"My brother and her sister," Wyatt says. "They left me part of the farm, and well, when I found out, Aubree and I got in touch. It wasn't love at first call, that's for sure, but the more I spoke to her, the more I realized she was pretty awesome. Then I met her in person, and that was it. Game over."

Harriot clutches her chest. "So it was long distance?"

"Yup," Wyatt continues. "Lots of texts and phone calls and FaceTimes."

"Are you staying here for a while?"

Wyatt nods. "That's the plan."

"But I heard you're staying at the inn." Harriot's brow

creases. "Wouldn't it be more cost-effective if you just stayed with Aubree?"

I feel myself grow stiff with nerves because, yes, that would make sense. Why wouldn't he just stay with me or my family?

"I kind of surprised her by coming to Almond Bay. I didn't want to bombard her, so I booked a room at the inn. Hoping she invites me to stay with her once my reservation expires."

"Oh, I think she will," Harriot says in a conspiratorial voice.

"Me too," he says. "Until then, I'm going to enjoy these nights as much as I can."

"You've got a good one," Harriot says to me, and I realize . . . it's my chance to turn on the charm.

I place my hand on his stomach and curl in closer. "I'm really happy."

Harriot claps her hands in excitement. "Oh that makes me so thrilled to hear that. I was worried about you, Aubree. The whole town was." Wow, okay. Good to know. "You've had it so hard, and when Matt left, and then Cassidy died, and well . . . it's just been one thing after the other. We weren't sure you would let anyone into your life, and then here he is, looking at you as if you were the only woman on the planet. My little heart can't take this."

"Somehow he won me over," I say, unsure of what else to say.

"It was my wit and charm," Wyatt says with a wink.

God, he's good at this. I feel like a stiff robot, attempting to play along despite the subtle short-circuiting in my head.

"Oh, I'm sure of it. We've all become quite fond of you, Wyatt." I'm sure they have. Hard not to when the man walks around, joking with everyone, tossing out compliments left and right. He's likable, and it's annoying and frustrating, and also . . . nice. *Especially when I feel like I've been surrounded by dreadful stress since Cassidy died.*

"And me of you. This small town has captured me just like Aubree has captured my heart."

Okay, there's no way someone falls for that line. It's so blatantly—wait, is that a tear I see in Harriot's eye?

She lifts her hand and blots at the tear. "Oh, look at you making me all misty." She takes a deep breath. "None of this crying nonsense. You're here for dessert, so what can I get you?"

She was crying. What on earth?

"What's your favorite pie, babe? I trust your opinion."

He barely trusted it an hour ago when I ordered him a burger, but we won't go there.

"The cherry pie," I answer.

"Mmm," he moans in my ear. "Fucking love . . . *cherries*."

And once again, my face goes bright red because I know he's not talking about the same kind of cherry that I'm talking about.

"So should I do half a cherry pie for you two?" Harriot asks, completely oblivious.

"That would be great, Harriot. One fork will do," Wyatt says.

What the hell is he up to? One fork?

"Not a problem." Harriot moves around the bakery while Wyatt moves me to the register.

"Need a drink?"

"Water," I say, my mouth and throat dry.

"And two waters please, Harriot."

"Coming right up." She brings us the pie, with one fork, and then grabs us two waters. Wyatt pays, and when I think we're going to leave, he directs me over to the seating nook away from the main bakery, but right in front of a window so anyone walking by could see us sharing a pie . . . with one fork.

I've never met anyone who has been two steps ahead of a situation before, but here he is. Planning and making sure all of our bases are covered at all times.

Once we're settled and he pops open the short bakery box with our pie, he looks up at me, excitement in his eyes. "This looks phenomenal. Sometimes I forget how homey small towns can be. Look at this pie, it looks like it came straight from Granny's oven." He dips the fork into the pie, grabbing himself a big piece. He shoves it in his mouth and moans. "Fuck . . . me," he says in such a dirty tone that I actually feel my upper lip sweat. "This is fucking delicious." He takes another bite, completely forgetting that I'm over here supposed to share this pie with him. "Yup, this is really fucking good." He licks the fork. "Jesus, the cherry flavor is so rich." He dips in for another bite. Uh . . . hello. "And this crust. Buttery, flaky. The perfect texture. Not too sweet but not bland." He shoves another bite in his mouth. "Fuck . . . so good."

"Uh . . . do you plan on letting me have a bite?" I ask.

He pauses as he reaches for another piece, and then the look of realization on his face is so fucking funny that I actually snort.

"Jesus, I forgot I asked for one fork." He actually blushes as he hands me the fork. "Sorry, babe."

I stare down at the fork and then back up at him. "You licked this."

"Yeah, so?"

"So . . . you have germs all over it."

His brow lifts. "And your point?"

"I don't want your germs."

"Better get used to my germs, Rowley. We're going to be married."

"That means nothing."

"Means everything." He snags the fork from me and takes another bite of the pie, nearly half of it gone now. "You realize we're going to have to kiss, right? There's no getting around it, so consider this fork sharing our first kiss." He wraps his mouth around the tines and pulls everything off it. Then he hands me the fork and nods at me. "Your turn."

I stare down at the utensil and look back up at him.

"Guaranteed, I'll be the best kiss of your life. Just warming you up right now."

"How on earth can you have that much confidence?" I ask.

"I just know. I work wonders with my mouth." He winks and, once again, the innuendos.

Leaning forward and keeping my voice down, I decide to confront him about it. "You have made several references to oral this evening. You realize we made an agreement about keeping things platonic, right?"

"Yup, I remember."

"Okay, so then why are you acting like that is not what's going on?"

"This is who I am and how I talk." He dips his finger into some of the cherry pie filling on the box. "I suggest you get used to the sexual innuendos. It doesn't mean anything. I'm just playing around. Why . . ." He grins like a fool. "Are you getting aroused?"

"No!" I shout, pulling Harriot's attention.

"Everything okay over there?"

"Yes," I squeak. "Everything is great. Just, you know, trying to stop Wyatt from eating all of the pie."

"Wyatt, don't forget to share." She wiggles her finger at him.

"Yes, ma'am," he says before turning back to me. "So . . . not aroused?"

My eyes narrow. "Not aroused."

"Good to know, just means I need to work harder."

"Why the hell are you trying to make me aroused?"

He shrugs. "Because it's fun."

"Do you find it fun to be aroused with no relief?"

"Babe, I never said there wouldn't be relief."

"Dear God," I whisper as I stick the fork into the pie.

"Don't you mean . . . oh God?" That stupid smile is from ear to ear right now.

"No, it would be 'Dear God, make him stop.'"

"Any sort of begging works for me." He swipes up another dollop of cherry and sucks on his finger as I bring a piece of the pie up to my lips.

He watches me the whole time as I slide the fork in my mouth, wrap my lips around the tines, and pull out.

"Yeah, baby, just like that." He nods his head in appreciation.

I nearly choke on the pie.

I cover my mouth and chew. He is pleased as punch. Once I swallow, he asks, "How did my lips taste?"

"Salty," I answer. "And a little like garbage."

His face falls flat.

"Okay, I get it." He takes the fork from me. "You're in denial. Don't worry, I'll get you there."

"Get me where?" I ask.

"You'll see," he answers with a knowing wink.

Chapter Nine

WYATT

I stare up at the ceiling in my room, the buzz of the pie still pulsing through me.

That was some good fucking pie.

And a good burger.

And fries.

And . . . company.

Surprising. Aubree can be really fun. I'm not sure other people know that about her. At least people around town. They seem to be concerned about her happiness and the cards she's been dealt. But what I've found is that of course she's serious, but that's not her entire personality. She can be fun. She can joke.

She can take a joke.

Not many people can, but she takes it and sometimes gives it right back.

She's a good time with a difficult past, which *I think* puts her on the defensive most of the time. I can sense that she doesn't want to open up. She doesn't want to grow close, but it seems she might allow me into her circle.

Her very, very small circle.

I desperately want to ask her what Matt did to her. Why he was a dick and if there is anything she wants me to do to him to seek revenge. I might not be a murderer or an arsonist like some of the main characters in my books, but I know a thing or two about fucking around with people. I could make Matt's life a living hell and get away with it. And Amanda? Her ex-best friend? Fucking awful. I am still angry that she had the gall to brag about marrying Aubree's ex to Aubree. To . . . belittle her so callously. I'll never understand mean girls, but I'm glad that she used me as her shield at that moment. I don't know Aubree that well, but what I am is a good friend. *And I want to be that person for her.*

I grab my phone from the nightstand, and even though I spent the evening with her, I text her.

Wyatt: *Hey.*

Great opening. I know it will get her attention. Because she'll probably be wondering *why is he texting me and why is he only saying hey after we said goodbye like half an hour ago?*

And what an awkward goodbye that was. She was going for a wave, I was going in for a hug, and she ended up scraping her hand over my nipple, making it hard. I, naturally, pointed it out to her and asked if she wanted to feel it. She shook her head and walked away.

Not sure why she didn't want to feel it. Who doesn't like a perky nipple?

Apparently, Aubree.

My phone dings with a text, and I smile to myself.

Aubree: *Hi?*

Just what I'd expect from her.

Wyatt: *How was your night?*

Aubree: *Are you conducting a survey?*

I smile to myself and type her back.

Wyatt: *As a matter of fact, I am.*

Aubree: *Not sure you want to hear the results.*

Wyatt: *I can take the criticism.*

Aubree: Well . . . the food was good. The pie was delicious despite only getting a quarter of it.

Wyatt: But what about the company?

Aubree: I'd give the company a seven out of ten.

Wyatt: A seven? I'll take that. Not perfect, room to grow, but not so low that I'll fall into a deep depression wondering what the hell happened to me and how I got to where I am. Where could I improve?

Aubree: I think self-assessment might be best for you.

Wyatt: You want me to self-assess? Seems like you might not know what was wrong and that my score was higher than a seven.

Aubree: No, it was a seven.

Wyatt: Hmm *taps chin* Did I get knocked a point because I asked you to touch my nipple?

Aubree: That was unpleasant, yes.

Wyatt: Was it all the oral talk?

Aubree: Another thing.

Wyatt: And was it because I didn't hold your hand?

Aubree: No, I didn't want you to hold my hand.

Wyatt: Why not?

Aubree: Because that feels intimate to me.

Wyatt: More intimate than sharing a fork that I drooled all over?

Aubree: Please, I tried to block that from my mind.

Wyatt: Seriously. We swapped spit tonight, but you refuse to hold my hand. Why?

Aubree: I just think that's something that should be reserved for a real relationship.

Wyatt: Okay, so are we never going to hold hands?

Aubree: Why do you want to hold my hand so badly?

Wyatt: It's an easy thing to do that convinces people we're a couple. If we walk side by side without holding hands, we'll give off sibling vibes.

Aubree: Trust me, people will still think we're together. Matt never held my hand, and people still knew we were together.

I stare at her text, confused. Matt never held her hand? That's pretty shitty. I wonder why. I was always grabbing for Cadance's hand. *It's something I miss, if I'm honest.* Although, it's interesting that it's not Cadance's hand I imagine to be holding right now.

Wyatt: *Matt seems like a loser if you ask me. If you were my girl, I'd hold your hand.*

Aubree: *I don't know what to say to that.*

Wyatt: *You don't need to say anything. Just know that I'm here for you, for anything you need.*

Aubree: *Why?*

Wyatt: *What do you mean, why?*

Aubree: *I don't understand why you're being so nice to me. Like you swooped in, without knowing much about me, and decided to be my number one fan, my number one supporter. Why?*

Yeah, why, Wyatt?

Why are you so drawn to her, wanting to help her?

Am I overcompensating because that's what I used to do with Cadance, and now I need to expel that energy onto someone else?

Is it because we're connected by two people we lost, and I feel the need to be by her side? *Like kindred spirits?*

Is it because I can see sadness in her eyes, the same sort of sadness I see reflected in the mirror? I might not show it, but I sure as fuck feel it. I feel it every day I wake up alone in my bed. I feel it when I reach for my phone and see no text messages, none telling me how I'm missed, how I'm loved. I felt it when I was resting on Laurel's couch, alone on a Friday night with nothing better to do than watch *Overboard* for the fiftieth time on TBS.

Either way, I feel something toward Aubree, but I don't think she'd want to know that. She made it quite clear about not having handouts or pity directed her way. Not that I pity her, but I wouldn't want her to think this connection I feel is anything but genuine companionship. She's barely okay with our agreement. I don't want to scare her off with these thoughts in my head. Plus, as I learned from her, she doesn't do emotions or feelings. Opening up to her would only scare her away.

So I snap out of my head and lie.

Wyatt: This relationship is an investment. I want to make sure we're both taken care of.

Aubree: I'm taken care of, so there's no need to go out of your way.

Yeah, I thought she'd say that. She doesn't like help, she doesn't like pity, and she doesn't like to look lesser than. She holds her head high, does the work, and has no problem supporting herself, even if it seems like she's in a patched-up boat, slowly drowning day by day.

Wyatt: Well, I'm here if you need me.

Aubree: I appreciate it. But I'm good. Which reminds me, I don't need you coming by tomorrow with muffins.

Wyatt: Wasn't planning on it. I'm taking muffins to Rodney.

Aubree: Rodney? The railroad museum guy?

Wyatt: The very one.

Aubree: Why?

Wyatt: Why not?

Aubree: Are you friends?

Wyatt: Possibly, we shall see by the end of tomorrow. He asked me to stop by, I told him I would, and here we are. Are you jealous?

Aubree: Not even a little.

Wyatt: Okay, because even though I'm going to visit with someone else, it doesn't mean that you're not my number one. Because you are, Rowley. You're my number one.

Aubree: Not sure if that should make me happy or nauseous.

Wyatt: Maybe a little of both. Have a good night . . . Mrs. Preston.

Aubree: Jesus.

⸻

"YOU REALLY GOT ME A HAT," I say to Rodney as he stares up at me with the biggest eyes I've ever seen, glee and hope beaming from them.

"I did. Do you like it?" he asks.

I take in the plain black hat with a white stitched number on the front in a Times New Roman font. The number is simple: 576. That's it. That's all that's on the hat. I don't think anyone outside of the train community would know what this number means. But from the look in Rodney's eyes, he knows.

Smiling, I say, "Love it, but remind me what this number means?"

He takes the hat from me and runs his finger over the tight stitching, saying, "Engine 576, the one remaining J3 in the country. Located now in Nashville under preservation, this mighty engine was one of thousands and once carried freight and troops during World War II. It was one of the last J3s to have yellow skirting, giving it the nickname the yellow jacket. In 1952, due to dieselization, all of the other J3s were scrapped, but the 576 lived on in memory and history."

Oh.

Wow.

Okay. I see what we're dealing with here.

I pull on the back of my neck as Rodney hands me the hat back. "That's incredible, Rodney."

"I was surprised to see the engine number at the expo, but representatives from Nashville were there selling model kits with 576, and I just knew I had to grab you a hat."

"That was really kind of you. Thank you. Would you say this is one of your favorite engines?"

He nods. "I love the yellow skirting. Would you like to see the pictures I took of the pictures they had on display?"

Boy, do I love pictures of pictures.

"Would love it," I say just as the door to the railroad museum opens. I look up to find Hayes walking in. I nod at him. "Hey, man."

"Hey," he says. "What's up, Rodney?"

"Busy," he says as he taps away on his phone with one single finger, you know, the way old people do it.

"Look at this hat Rodney bought me." I hold up the engine hat, and Hayes smirks.

"That's awesome," he says, clearly not believing it.

I adjust the back of the hat and then slip it on, showing off my new headwear. "Fits like a glove, Rodney."

"Aha!" Rodney says as he flashes his phone screen toward me. "See the yellow skirting?"

"Oh yeah, look at that. Wow, slick engine."

Rodney brings the phone back to himself so he can stare down at the picture as well. "What a masterful design with the bullet nose." He sighs and then looks up at Hayes. "I got you a hat as well."

"You did?" Hayes asks. "Wow, you didn't have to do that."

"They were buy two, get one free. I thought we could be the three musketeers with our hats." He walks over to his counter and grabs two more hats, all with the same 576 stitching on the front. "Here you are."

He hands Hayes the hat, and he puts it on. As does Rodney.

Together, we stand in the middle of a railroad museum, wearing our matching hats with a beaming owner—he's so proud of himself.

"Wow," Rodney says, clutching his hands together. "We look great."

I inwardly chuckle. "So great that I'd love to take a picture of all of us." I pull out my phone and turn it to selfie mode. Hayes and I huddle with Rodney in the middle, who's at least a foot shorter than us, and together, we smile.

Rodney smiles so big that his eyes are closed.

What a cute old man.

Odd, but cute.

"Perfect," I say and then send it straight to Aubree. Can't wait to hear what she has to say. "Why are you here, Hayes?"

"Came to bring Rodney a note from my grandma. They've recently become pen pals."

"You didn't read it, did you?" Rodney asks, looking like he's about to bark if Hayes did read it.

"Never," he answers. "It's sealed with the wax that I recently got her."

"Excellent," Rodney says as he snatches the letter out of Hayes's hand, grabs the box of muffins I brought him, and rushes to his back room.

"What the hell is that about?" I ask.

"Pretty sure they're sending each other love letters. I got a sneak peek of my grandma's response once, and there was a red heart next to her name."

"How do you feel about Rodney possibly being your grandpa?"

Hayes chuckles. "Well, he gave me this bitching hat, so what do you think?"

I laugh and pull the hat off my head to get a better look at it. "At least the embroidery is really clean. It's good work."

"I have like three others like this. Not a 576, though. This is a new one."

"Wow, really?"

Hayes nods. "Yup. Can't even tell you what the other ones are, can't remember, but I try to wear them around Rodney as much as I can. I knew he went to a convention this past weekend, so I assumed he'd bring one back for me. Therefore, I didn't bother wearing one today."

"So that means you come in here often," I say.

"Yeah. I'll hang out with Rodney and keep him company from time to time. He's a pretty cool guy, a bit eccentric, but his heart is in the right place. And when I say right place, I mean with trains."

I chuckle. "Yeah, I thought my grandpa was into trains, but Rodney is showing him up." I glance toward the back. "How long do you think he'll be back there?"

"A while," Hayes answers. "He is most likely analyzing the letter. He writes her back right away. Were you guys supposed to hang out?"

"Not really. I don't know what was supposed to happen today. I just know I was supposed to come here after his convention, so I'm here."

"Man of his word, I like that." He nods toward the exit. "Want to head over to The Cliffs for coffee and a donut?"

"Sure, since he took the muffins and ran," I say. I glance toward the back again. "Do we need to say bye?"

Hayes shakes his head. "Nah, he'll just snap at you to leave him alone."

"Fair enough."

Hayes leads us across the street. We pass The Almond Store, and I don't miss the way Hayes peeks into the windows, looking for his girl. I remember when I was like that with Cadance. Always looking for her and feeling a sense of joy when I did see her.

If I saw her now, I'm pretty sure I wouldn't have the same sense of joy. More like bitter anger. *Just how long had she been unhappy with me? To be able to walk away so easily?*

So completely.

"Are you enjoying your stay?" Hayes asks as we make it to the other side of the road and walk to The Cliffs, a place of coffee and pastries to-go, sit-down breakfasts and, from the sign, they do catering.

"Yeah, hard not to fall in love with Almond Bay," I say as we enter the building. It almost feels like we're stepping into a barn with large plank wooden floors, wood shiplap all along the walls and ceilings, exposed beams, and turrets. Barrels of coffee line up along the register and the stairs that lead to the second floor. Self-serve scoops and paper bags are next to the barrels, as well as a rainbow assortment of licorice. Interesting combination. Along the right of the shop is the coffee and pastry bar, and toward the back seems to be the sit-down area.

Surprised I haven't come in here yet.

"Morning, Hayes," a burly man from behind the register counter says. "The usual?"

"Please," Hayes says, making room for me. "Have you met Wyatt yet?"

The man with more hair on his forearms than his head looks up at me. "No, I don't believe we have. I'm Hank."

"Hank, it's nice to meet you. I'm Wyatt."

Hank studies me for a moment. "Wyatt, are you the new guy everyone is talking about? You're going out with Aubree, right? My daughters were gabbing about it all morning."

I chuckle. "Guilty, that's me."

"Well, nice to meet the talk of the town. Apparently, you were spotted last night enjoying cherry pie with Aubree. Now all the cherry pies at The Sweet Lab are gone. Sold out."

Hayes pats me on the back. "Look at you being a trendsetter."

"Yes, so if you could be spotted eating something here, I'd appreciate it."

I laugh. "What do you need to sell out of?"

Hank drags his hand over his cheek as he looks at his barrels of coffee. "I have this one coffee brand no one will buy from me, and it's driving me nuts."

A sick feeling starts in my stomach. "What coffee?"

"Clearwater Coffee." Hank shakes his head. "Tastes like swill, and everyone knows it. Maybe if they see you drink it, they might give it another shot."

I swallow hard and mask my discomfort. Of course Clearwater Coffee is here. Cadance made a big push on the brand a year ago, trying to sell it up and down the coast. Looks like Hank fell victim to her big blue eyes.

"Ah, man, I'd love to do you a solid on that, but I've tasted Clearwater, and it's piss."

Hank lets out a boisterous laugh. "Dammit." He playfully smacks the counter. "And here I thought I was about to get rid of it. Might just compost it and take the hit. After word got out about the flavor, no one has touched it. Trust me when I say, never do anything wrong in this town because everyone will know about it. Luckily, I've recovered since trying to feed people the sludge, but it's been an uphill climb. The only thing that saved me was my omelets."

"He's being dramatic," Hayes says. "But the omelets are next level."

"Is that the usual?" I ask him.

Hayes shakes his head. "Nah, I like a simple cup of coffee with creamer and one of his bear claws. To me, that's his real claim to fame, but it seems the omelet obsession has made people overlook the bear claw."

"Well, if they're that good, I'll have to give it a try," I say. "I'll take the usual as well."

Hank points his finger at me and Hayes. "If I sell out of bear claws, you two can eat here for free."

We both laugh, and Hank rings us up. Neither Hayes nor I struggle financially, but Hank's generosity reflects small-town kindness. Rare. Genuine. I go to pay, but Hayes stops me, claiming he asked me to breakfast, so he'll pay.

I'm not going to argue. Sometimes it's nice to have someone else pay for me.

When finished at the register, Hank moves to the coffee bar and says, "Pick a seat outside. I'll have your drinks and donuts delivered to you."

"Thanks, Hank," Hayes says, heading out back. He says hi to a few people but doesn't stay to chat. He moves to the back deck to a table under a blue umbrella.

The ocean breeze cools the temperature from the sun's rays, and the salty scent is incredible. *I can see why people want to live here year-round.* I might soon be one of them. I forgot how much I appreciate the ocean until I'm around it.

"So you were caught sharing a pie with Aubree. Big news," Hayes says with a smirk.

"Apparently. Didn't know it was going to be the talk of the town."

"Everything is the talk of the town, especially when it's a new relationship. You should have heard the gossip when Hattie and I first got together, especially since Ryland and I were in a feud. It was all anyone ever talked about. We even had some rumors develop. That was exciting."

"Oh?" I ask. "Like what?"

"Stupid shit like I was hooking up with Hattie to get back at Ryland. I was going to get her pregnant and leave her. That I was only using her for music inspiration. You know, dumb shit."

"How did you calm down the rumors?"

"I didn't go out of my way, that's for damn sure. Just kept loving on Hattie and showing up for her. Showing the town that I'm not some dickhead trying to get something out of my girl."

Oh boy, that hits a little too close to home.

Hank walks up with a tray. He sets down two cups of coffee and two plates, each with a bear claw bigger than my hand. Okay, I can get on board with this.

"Thanks, Hank," Hayes says.

"Now remember, eat those slow. Let everyone see what the two stars of the town are feasting on."

We both laugh as he takes off.

"I'll be impressed if he sells out of bear claws," I say right before I take a bite.

Holy fuck.

Soft with a slight crisp on the bottom. Cinnamon and glaze and dough all mixed into one. Jesus, this is good.

"Wow," I say, taking a look at the pastry. "This is really good." I glance around and then say a little louder. "This is really freaking good." I hold up the bear claw, pretending to examine it, but I'm really showing the audience what I'm eating.

"Subtle." Hayes laughs.

"Just trying to help a guy out. It is good, though."

"My favorite," Hayes says and sips his coffee. "Not to be a gossip, but what's going on with you and Aubree? Hattie was telling me you two have been talking for a while? Funny because when we were at Coleman's together, you seemed to be telling me a different story."

"Yeah, sorry about that. I was trying to mask what was really going on."

"Fooled me," he says.

"Yeah, just protecting her wishes, but we've been talking a while. It got to the point that I hated the distance between us. I could work anywhere really, so I thought I'd stay for a week and see what she thought about it."

"How do you think she feels?" Hayes asks.

"Good," I answer. "She was really happy that I came, after

the initial shock of course. She was nervous about what you guys might think, but now that everyone knows, she's less tense."

Hayes slowly nods. "So you like her?" I can see he's attempting to test me, most likely set up by Hattie. I don't mind. This is where I shine.

"Love her," I answer, causing Hayes's eyes to widen.

He sets his coffee cup down. "You love her?"

"Yeah," I say, then really go for it. "Plan on proposing."

Hayes is about to take a bite of his bear claw but then slowly lowers it back to the plate. "Propose?"

This is far too comical. Here he was, thinking he was going to have a simple conversation about Aubree, but instead, he's getting a whole lot of information he probably wasn't expecting.

"Yeah. I love her, simple as that. I don't want to be away from her, and well, I think it would just make sense, you know?"

"Uh . . ." He smooths his hands over his legs as he shifts in his chair. "But haven't you, like, just met?"

"No, we've known each other for a while. I helped move Clarke and Cassidy into their farmhouse when Cassidy was pregnant with Mac. I spent some time around Aubree, and I thought she was fucking gorgeous." That's not a lie. I did. I still do. I had just gotten together with Cadance then, so I wasn't even considering a relationship with Aubree. Not that Hayes needs to know about that. *No one here knows about Cadance.* "And when I found out that I owned part of the land, it was easy for me to talk to her because, like the hormone-driven idiot that I am, I was interested. So yeah, we were talking and then I realized that my feelings were stronger than what I expected. We started out as friends, and now we've moved on to so much more."

Hayes slowly nods his head. "Wow, I mean, that's awesome, but I'm surprised. I didn't think you knew that much about each other."

"Do I know everything about Aubree? No, but that's what marriage is all about, finding out more about each other."

"Are you staying with her in her house?" Hayes asks.

"Not yet, but starting this week, I'm moving in."

"Does she know you're moving in?" Hayes asks on a chuckle. "Because Aubree is not great at sharing her space."

"Yeah, we talked about it last night, but we came to the conclusion that it would be best to cross that bridge. She's wanted me to spend the night while I've been here, but I wanted to give her space, let her adjust." Total lies, but I am a storyteller, after all.

"Probably smart," Hayes says. He sips from his mug and then lowers it back to the table. He stares off at the ocean, still gripping the handle. "I think you'll be good for her." His eyes return to me. "Not that I know much about you, but what I do know, I think she needs. You're lighthearted and fun. You seem not to dwell on the negative, and she needs someone like that in her life."

"A reverse grumpy sunshine," I say.

Hayes raises a brow in question, causing me to laugh.

"Sorry, it's a book trope. Usually in books, the man is the grumpy one and the girl is the sunshine in the relationship. People love a grumpy hero and a female who can bring him to his knees. Aubree and I would be the reverse version. She's grumpy, and I'm sunshine, but she's still the one bringing me to my knees. Every fucking day."

"The Rowley women will do that to you," Hayes says. "At first, Hattie was the most annoying person ever, but then it was like it hit me all at once. I liked her annoying tendencies. I liked how she joked around with me, poked fun at me. It made me feel real, like I wasn't this man in a glass case that everyone wanted to impress or ask for something. She made me feel like I was an actual human."

I nod. "I get that with Aubree. Clearly, I'm not as famous as you, but I enjoy the fact that Aubree could give two shits about my books even though I know she's read them. I like that she fights back. I like that she doesn't let me get away with anything. She challenges me." Now that's all true. I do enjoy that about Aubree. *And it's something Cadance rarely did.* She was challenging, but she argued with me because she was a tad spoiled.

"It's the challenge," Hayes says knowingly. "We like the fucking challenge."

"We do," I say before taking another huge bite of my bear claw.

"So when do you plan to propose?"

"Soon," I answer. "Just have to get a ring."

"Wow, I didn't think it would be that quick." He shakes his head with a smile. "Fuck, man. You're going to make me look bad."

"Do you want to propose to Hattie?"

He nods. "Yeah, been trying to think of the perfect way to do it. I know Ryland, Mac, and Aubree would approve. But look at you, coming in full steam and just taking charge." He grips his chin. "I felt like I needed to win over the crowd first."

"There was history with you and Ryland, so the delay is understandable. I'm just the guy who had a piece of the farm and came right on in."

"Yeah, how the fuck is that fair?"

I shrug. "It's not. But I'm not complaining."

<hr>

WYATT: *It's happening. We're getting married.*

Laurel: You're serious? She agreed?

Wyatt: Yup, we're currently dating at the moment—fake dating—and I plan on proposing soon. Tonight I'm going to surprise her with my bags.

Laurel: What do you mean by bags? That could represent a variety of things. Like your suitcases? Or are we talking more intimate like . . . your bags, you know, testicles?

Wyatt: Jesus, no man with a right head on his shoulders is ever going to refer to his testicles as bags.

Laurel: It's just nice to clarify. So you're going to move in with her? How does she feel about that?

Wyatt: Probably not great, but it will be weird if I stay at the inn. I had to cover up for it already. If we're dating and going to get married, it only makes sense that I move in.

Laurel: *Do people know you're getting married?*

Wyatt: *I had breakfast with Hayes this morning and dropped the seed with him.*

Laurel: *What kind of seed . . .*

Wyatt: *Not THAT kind of seed. Jesus, Laurel, what is wrong with you today?*

Laurel: *Can't be sure. Okay, so you planted—I think that's the term we're looking for—the seed that you're going to propose. Smart, because he'll probably tell Hattie.*

Wyatt: *Not sure that he will. I think Hattie is looking for a proposal from him soon, and if I propose before Hayes, she might flip out.*

Laurel: *So then who would he tell?*

Wyatt: *My guess is Ryland, the brother, and Abel, the friend.*

Laurel: *Ahhh, smart.*

Wyatt: *Not just a hat rack, my friend *points at head**

Laurel: *So there's going to be a wedding.*

Wyatt: *There's going to be a wedding.*

Laurel: *Am I the only one who thinks this is completely insane?*

Wyatt: *THIS WAS YOUR IDEA!*

Laurel: *An insane idea! I mean, a smart, insane idea, but I didn't think it would work.*

Wyatt: *You underestimate me.*

Laurel: *Apparently. So am I invited to the wedding?*

Wyatt: *Uh, you're going to be my best woman.*

Laurel: *Wyatt, that's so touching. So when is it going to happen? Sooner rather than later? Can I bring a date?*

Wyatt: *It needs to be sooner rather than later, and of course you can bring a date.*

Laurel: *I'm assuming it will be in Almond Bay.*

Wyatt: *You assume correctly. Simple and small, I doubt Aubree will want anything big and flashy. Probably just a few friends and family.*

Laurel: *Crazy, but okay. Let me know when and where, and I'll be there.*

Wyatt: *I can always count on you, Laurel.*

Chapter Ten

AUBREE

Knock, knock.

Echo pokes her head into the doorway and says, "Can I come in?"

"Of course," I say as I close my laptop and welcome the distraction from the numbers I've been looking over for hours. I have no lead as to what's going on.

Instead of being outside today, I decided to come back to the office and look through the books with a fresh pair of eyes. And the fresh pair of eyes has done nothing to solve the problem. And since I wasn't finding a solution, all I could think about was what Wyatt said. We're spending a lot on farming our potatoes but not making the most dollars out of them. Which makes me think . . . do we need to cut down on the amount of potato fields like Wyatt suggested and use the land for something else, something that will bring more profit to the farm?

Ugh, I'd hate if he was right. He was literally here for two seconds before pointing it out, and it's something I've been trying to figure out for a while.

"What's up?" I ask. "How was your weekend?"

"Weekend was good. I settled more into my apartment. Hung up some curtains and potted some plants."

"Sounds relaxing."

"It was. It was nice." She takes a seat across from me. "I see that you did the chicken coop, which leads me to believe you didn't do any relaxing this weekend."

Relaxing? No.

Making huge, life-altering decisions? Yup.

"I'd like to say I did the chicken coop all by myself, but well . . . Wyatt helped me."

The slight hitch in her expression leads me to believe she must have heard talk around town this weekend. God, what she must be thinking . . .

"I heard he's been out here all weekend." She pauses, looking uncomfortable, and I don't blame her. The last time I talked to her, I told her how I thought Wyatt was up to something suspicious, and now she probably knows that we're dating. She has to be confused. If I were in her shoes, I'd be confused as well. She's the only one I told about my Wyatt suspicions . . . so maybe I can trust her to tell her what I agreed to this weekend.

"I know what you must be thinking," I say.

"I don't think you do." She laughs.

"Let me guess. Last you heard, I thought Wyatt was here to steal the farm away. You take a few days off and over the weekend hear that Wyatt and I are dating. And then of course he's here all weekend, helping me out. Hattie told me that people bought all of the cherry pie from The Sweet Lab because Wyatt and I were eating a pie together, and well . . . I must seem like a total hypocrite. I swear there's an explanation, but I need to be able to trust you as a friend to talk about this."

She chuckles and crosses one leg over the other. "Well, I guess you did know what I was thinking." That makes me smile. She grows serious and says, "When I say I'm looking for a friend, I mean it, Aubree. You can trust me, I promise. You have given me a new chapter in my life with this job and helped me find an apartment. My loyalty is with you and no one else."

"I appreciate that," I say. "Can you, uh, lock the door?"

"That serious?" she asks as she gets up.

"That serious."

She locks the door and then scoots her chair closer before sitting on it. "Okay, what's going on?"

I take a deep breath. "You're the only one I'm telling this to, okay? And I need you not to judge me either."

"I won't, I promise."

"Thank you," I say before taking another deep breath. Here we go . . . "Uh, Wyatt came into town, and I was rightfully annoyed. I knew he wanted something, and I was right. Long story short, a family cabin was supposed to be passed onto him, but because of a technicality, it goes to the first married grandchild in his family. That person will be his cousin, who apparently has no sentimental regard for the cabin and wants to knock it down when he gains possession. Wyatt owns a part of this farm that he doesn't want. So he asked me to marry him for a year in exchange for the land so he can get the cabin, and we're both happy." I let out a deep breath. "And I can't tell my family because they'll tell me not to do it and call me crazy, but I feel bad for Wyatt and his cabin because I know how much it means to want something . . . like this farm. And oh God, saying it out loud makes me sound like I've completely lost my marbles, but I haven't, I promise. I think this is the right thing to do."

Echo stares blankly at me for a moment before leaning back in her chair. After a few seconds, she says, "Wow, that's a lot to take in."

"Is it too much? Did I cross a line? Are you uncomfortable? If you need to excuse yourself, please feel free to do so."

She chuckles and shakes her head. "No, I mean, it's just not what I was expecting. I heard you two were dating, and that was confusing, but this . . . this makes the suspicions you had, the way he's been lurking around here, the gossip about you two in town —makes it all true. The dates out in public, that's to convince people that when you get married, you've been dating all along."

"Exactly," I say.

"That's actually pretty smart. And you get the farm, he gets his cabin, then you go your separate ways?"

"Yes," I say, feeling a little lighter now that I got that off my chest . . . and it seems like Echo is not going to judge me.

"Honestly, if I were in your shoes, I'd probably have said yes as well. Wyatt seems like a good guy, at least from what I've experienced and heard, so it's not like you're going to marry an ass. The deal seems fair. And you're both gaining something very important to you. I don't see what the problem is. Why do you have to be secretive about it?"

"Because of his cousin," I say. "Wyatt told me the moment he finds out about us getting married, he'll be pissed, which means we need to keep this farce a secret. We want to make him believe that we're together and we're in love."

"Ah, makes sense, and if the town knows about the lie, then that will probably get back to the cousin and ruin Wyatt's chances of getting the cabin." She scratches her cheek. "This feels like a well-plotted idea from the author who writes thrillers. Please tell me there isn't going to be a murder in the end."

"Only if he continues to annoy me."

That makes her laugh. "Is there a threshold for the annoyance?"

"There is," I answer.

"And what would that threshold be?" she asks.

"Anything embarrassing in public."

"Makes sense. I'd probably be the same way."

"Do you have any love interests or fake love interests?" I ask. "Possible marriage of conveniences in the works? You know, something so I don't feel so alone here?"

She chuckles. "Uh, no. I'm still trying to settle in. There is absolutely no room for love at the moment."

"But maybe something interests you here in town? There are some single men, you know. Like . . . Ryland or Abel."

"Are you trying to marry me off so you're not the only one?"

"You know it wouldn't hurt for you to step up here, ensure a friend's less lonely."

She leans forward and places her hand on the desk between us. "I like this friendship, Aubree, but I don't think we're at the place of taking a groom for one another."

"Damn," I say with a laugh, feeling much lighter. "Had to try at least." I let out a sigh and meet her eyes. "Thank you for the chat. All of this felt pretty heavy on my chest, especially with having to keep this a secret from my family, so I appreciate you being an outlet for me."

"Anytime." She clasps her hands together. "Actually, can I talk to you about something?"

"You mean the reason you came in here in the first place?"

She smiles. "Yes, but I do appreciate what we did talk about. I'm glad I could be there for you."

"Oh, I know. Is this about work?"

"It is. I was thinking this weekend about how we can best use every bit of the bees' hard work. I know we spoke about candles and lip balm, but what are your feelings about making beeswax food wrap?"

"What's that?" I ask.

"An eco-friendly version of cling wrap. I've seen some hype around it recently, and I thought that it might be something we can sell in the honey section of The Almond Store. I don't mind making them. It would keep me busy between my adventures of going out to different properties to take care of unwanted beehives and maintaining the garden and whatnot. I know a place where we can get some discounted fabric, and I can easily build an extension to the bee house where I could make the wraps, dry them out, and package them up."

"I think that's a great idea," I say. "People around town would easily buy them, and I feel like tourists might find them a neat and unique gift, especially grandmas. You know they love the kitschy things."

"They really do."

"I can help you extend the bee house if you want."

"That would be great. I have a few appointments this week to take care of some hives, but maybe we can at least map it out later in the week?"

"Sounds good to me."

"Great." She pats her legs. "I need to go make some more bee boxes. The owner of the house for one of the appointments today sent me a picture, and it's an enormous hive under the floorboards of their barn. They just found it and have a wedding this week. I'm hoping we can grab a big stock of honeybees from them."

"Well, be careful."

"I always am." She stands from her chair. "Thanks for the chat, and don't worry, your secret is safe with me."

"I appreciate it, Echo."

She waves and takes off. I lean back in my chair and pick up my phone, where I see a text from Wyatt. A picture. Confused, I open it and see him with Hayes and Rodney, all wearing the same hat, a very generic hat with the number 576 on it. Odd.

Aubree: *What's with the hat?*

After I text back, I stare down at the picture and take in Wyatt's smile. Straight white teeth, he must have had braces growing up. Scruff gracing his jaw—didn't bother shaving this morning. And a few crinkles in the corners of his eyes, showing off his mid-thirties, something I hate to admit I like about him.

Not that I should be admitting anything I like about him, but I do like that.

Can't tell you why.

I just think it's nice that he's not just older than me, but by seven years.

He's also wearing a shirt that seems to cling very tightly to his chest today. His pecs are defined, pressing against the fabric. Once again, not something I should notice, but I do.

Oddly, the most disturbing thing about the picture is that it looks like he fits right in with this town and all its eccentricities. Like he belongs in the railroad museum, laughing it up with Rodney. As if he belongs in this small town of Almond Bay and should have been here all along.

My phone dings with a response.

Wyatt: *Rodney got it for me at the train convention he went to this past weekend. It's engine 576, the last standing J3 from the World War II era. Duh, Aubree.*

I snort. Ugh, why can he make me laugh so easily? It's infuriating.

Aubree: *Didn't know you were a train nerd.*

Wyatt: *Just one of many things you need to learn about me. I think trains are pretty neat. I like planes as well, and I'm a fan of automobiles. Basically, I enjoy all sorts of transportation other than human-propelled toboggans, suspension railways (elevated monorail that dangles from the tracks), and any horse/reindeer/elk-powered sled for obvious reasons.*

Aubree: *I have so many questions.*

Wyatt: *Please, ask away.*

Aubree: *1. How do you know that many forms of transportation? 2. What human is propelling a toboggan? 3. There are monorails that dangle? 4. What about horse-drawn carriages?*

Wyatt: *I'm so glad you asked. 1. My protagonist in THE NIGHTLY WALKER (NYT, USA Today, WSJ bestseller, thank you) was an educator on all things transportation, so I researched different forms. 2. There are many versions of a human-propelled toboggan. You would be surprised. 3. Yes, there is a monorail that dangles from the tracks in Germany, and there is no way in hell you would ever see me on that thing. The only objects I approve of dangling are tits and testes. 4. I do not approve of any sort of animal-led carriage or sled, especially in any major city. The animals are treated horribly. Look it up. You'll never think a ride in Central Park by a horse-drawn carriage is romantic ever again.*

Aubree: *That was . . . a lot to take in.*

Wyatt: *Want more? I have other forms of transportation I can talk about as well.*

Aubree: *No, really, that's okay.*

Wyatt: *If you ever change your mind, I'm your guy.*

Aubree: *Won't be changing my mind.*

Wyatt: *Fair. So how's your day so far? Do you need anything from me? Currently, I'm lounging on the back deck of the inn with a pad of paper and a pen, plotting an idea for my next book.*

God, he's nice. Not sure Matt ever asked me if I needed anything, and we were actually dating. I knew Wyatt had a good heart because he was Clarke's brother, but he just seems to go the extra mile.

Aubree: *I'm good. Is the plot about a marriage of convenience?*

Wyatt: *Actually, it is. The heroine marries her stepbrother so they can both take advantage of the trust fund the stepfather left the daughter. But what the daughter doesn't know is that the stepmother and stepbrother are in cahoots, and they're actually lovers who killed the father together.*

Aubree: *Umm . . . wow, that's pretty dark and twisted.*

Wyatt: *Has that Lifetime movie "My Stepson, My Lover" vibe.*

Aubree: *Just a little.*

Wyatt: *Smells like a bestseller to me.*

Aubree: *How does it end?*

Wyatt: *Can't be sure. Sometimes I like to make the good person win, and sometimes I can picture them gurgling blood out of their mouth as they see the person who betrayed them right before they die. So you know, just depends on the mood.*

Aubree: *You say that so casually. Don't you care about playing with readers' feelings?*

Wyatt: *All I care about is if they have feelings toward the book.*

Aubree: *What do you mean by that?*

Wyatt: *Well, if they read my book and my words don't elicit any sort of emotion, good or bad, then I didn't do my job. I didn't captivate them. But if they read my book and they rain over me with praise and love for a job well done, or one-star me because they were pissed about a choice I made as an author, I'm happy because guess what? I made them feel something.*

Aubree: *You like one-star reviews?*

Wyatt: *I mean, no. I could do without them, but I read them because sometimes they go on and on about how I should have done something differently, that they're mad a character ended up dead, or I didn't write the love story they expected in the end. Sure, it sucks having to see people not like the end product, but I still pat myself on the back because I was able to make them think, feel, and escape into a world where they could immerse themselves so deep into a storyline, that they have their own opinion on how it should have worked out.*

Aubree: I see what you're getting at. Yeah, I've read books I haven't been happy with, but it was because I was so involved in the story. If I didn't care about the story, then I probably wouldn't have developed an opinion. I would have just . . . forgotten about it.

Wyatt: I'd rather have a reader be mad at me for not writing the story they pictured in their head, than forget about the words that I wrote.

Aubree: So if I told you I completely forgot about what The Maid in 5B is all about, you'd be pissed?

Wyatt: You're bluffing, no way you forgot about that plot. That plot still lives in the soul of everyone who's read it. Don't fuck with me, Aubree.

Aubree: LOL. Sensitive much?

Wyatt: With The Maid in 5B, yes. I put my entire soul into that book.

Aubree: You could tell. One of your best.

Wyatt: Wait . . . hold on, was that . . . was that a compliment? I'm screenshotting this and printing it out. My wife, Mrs. Preston, she complimented me! Huzzah!

Aubree: And now I take everything I said back.

Wyatt: Can't, you already put it out there in the universe. Don't worry, I'll be sure to give you a signed copy as a wedding gift. I know it will be your most treasured possession.

Aubree: And I'm going now. Bye.

Wyatt: See you later . . . wife.

I LOOK up into the rearview mirror of my parked truck and wipe under my eyes. Fresh from the shower, hair still wet, I drove into town to pick up Hattie because Hayes was meeting her at the farmhouse, and she needed a ride. Plus, I wanted to check out the space in The Almond Store to see where we can move things around.

Good to go, I hop out of my truck and head toward The Almond Store wearing a simple sundress with a built-in bra, one of the comfortable outfits I like to wear after a long day out on the farm.

The bell above me rings when I open the door to the store and find Hattie by the register closing up.

"Hey," I say when she looks up.

"Hey, almost done here, and I'll be ready to leave."

"No rush. I wanted to check out the store to see where we can add a cooler and a honey spot."

"Oh, I was thinking over there on the right. The cookbooks need to go. They are the worst sellers by far. I know Cassidy had good intentions with them, but there are like two recipes that include almond extract, so they're pointless for us to sell. They focus more on actual almonds than the extract when we're trying to sell the extract. They have to go."

I walk over to where the cookbooks are, and she's right. Some of them look bleached by the sun.

"I sold one of these to Hayes when he was trying to get back into your good graces."

"Yeah, that was the only one that was sold in like a year. And he doesn't use it."

"That doesn't shock me." I lift one of the books and flip through it, a collection of dust particles flying up at me. "What will you do with them if you don't sell them?"

"Donate to the library. What you see is all that's left in stock. So we can easily just donate what's left and be done with them. It opens up the space there, and we can start talking about how you want to set up the honey station."

"It's perfect," I say. "Might have to build some new shelves, though."

"I can have Hayes help me. Just let me know whatever you and Echo need, and we can make it happen."

"Perfect," I say, walking over to the center islands in the store. "Think you can free up some space over here in the front when we have the honey ready to sell? It would be nice to have it front and center at first, so people know it's new."

"Yes, of course," Hattie says while she turns off her iPad and moves to my side. "I'm always moving product around, especially if I want it off the shelves."

"Besides the cookbooks."

"The cookbooks are trash. Those don't deserve center island space. The second island is always the extract and vodka, our best sellers. And then the front island is whatever I want to get off the shelves that week."

"Very smart. Well, I'd love some center island space for the new honey line. Echo is working on balms, candles, beeswax wrap, and of course honey."

"I'm excited. I love having new things in the store. I'm especially excited about the almond honey."

"Me too. She's fine-tuning it, and we'll taste test soon."

"I'd like to be a part of that taste testing." Hattie raises her hand.

"Of course you'll be. Are you ready to go?"

"Yes, let me grab my things real quick." She hurries to the back, leaving me alone in the main part of the store.

So crazy how a little while ago, we weren't getting along. Well, I wouldn't say not getting along. Tensions were high. The stress of Cassidy's death made me closed off, which, in turn, shut her out, and well, it was a recipe for disaster. Now . . . I'm grateful for being able to talk to her without those tensions and stressors. I'm grateful she's no longer in school and that she's here. I had a hard time being around her for a while because she reminded me so much of Cassidy, but now, it feels comforting. She has the same warm energy, the same smile, and the same joyful spirit.

"Okay, ready," she says, entering the main store with her bag and keys.

We head out the front door, she locks up, and then we walk around the store to the back, where I'm parked.

"Thanks for picking me up."

"Not a problem," I say as we get in my truck.

"Were you in town for . . . other things?" she asks, her voice full of innuendo.

"Uh, no," I say, starting my truck and pulling out of the parking spot.

"Are you sure you weren't here visiting anyone?"

"Oh my God, just say it," I reply as I make a right out of town.

"Were you here visiting Wyatt for an afternoon delight?"

"Jesus, Hattie."

She laughs. "What? Why else would you be in town?"

"Literally to pick you up. I just arrived, I grabbed you, and I'm leaving town now."

"Really?" she asks, disappointment in her voice. "You weren't here, sneaking around at the inn?"

"Uh, no."

"Huh." She sighs. "Well, he doesn't stay the night at your place."

"How would you know that?" I ask.

"Because Ryland and I have a text thread about you and Wyatt."

"Umm, pardon me?" I ask, blinking a few times.

"Yeah, we talk about you. I asked him if Wyatt ever spent the night, and he said never. And if you're not going to the inn for an afternoon delight, then . . . when are you doing it?"

"What on earth are you talking about?" I ask.

Hattie turns toward me in the car. "Wait . . . have you two not had sex yet?"

Oh, dear God. You see, this is why I don't do nice things like pick up my little sister at her place of work because these are the kind of questions I have to deal with.

"Don't you think that's a little private?"

"Yes, but this is what sisters are supposed to talk about."

"I have never once asked you about your sex life with Hayes."

"You should," she says on a wistful sigh. "It's the best thing that's ever happened to me. He's amazing. And trust me when I say we haven't stopped once we broke the seal. Which makes me think that either you are sneaking around in the barn or you haven't done it yet . . . oh wait." I glance over at her and catch her cringe. "Oh no, is he . . . is he bad at the sex?"

Lord fucking help me.

"He's not bad *at the sex*," I say, very irritated and uncomfortable with this conversation.

"Is he just average? That happens. It's okay. You might just have to teach him a bit, you know? Not that I can be absolutely sure about this, but I got the vibe from Cassidy that Clarke was never one hundred percent on, so maybe it runs in the family."

If I weren't driving right now, I'd throw myself out of the car. I'd just toss the door open and chuck my body onto the road to avoid the rest of this conversation.

"It doesn't run in the family," I reply even though I honestly have no freaking idea. Knowing Hattie has a voracious sex life, the last thing I want is for her to pity me for my average one—or lack thereof.

"Soooo . . . you *have* had sex."

I grip the steering wheel tighter. "What do you think, Hattie?"

"I mean, I'd say yes, but I just don't know when. I haven't even seen you two hold hands or kiss or anything."

"You've been around us like once, and I don't believe you knew we were together."

"Either way, you were giving off more brother-sister vibes than we're ripping each other's clothes off every chance we get. And you know Cassidy was in a lackluster marriage, holding out for someone else. I don't want that to be you. I don't want you caught up in a relationship that doesn't fully satisfy you, you know?"

"I get what you're saying, but you have nothing to worry about."

"Are you sure?" she asks. "Because you could tell me."

"Tell you what?" I ask, trying to tamp down the annoyance pulsing through me.

"Tell me that, you know . . . Wyatt can't deliver on the orgasms."

Mother of God, why is this happening to me?

Feeling my cheeks go red, I say, "That's nothing you need to worry about. All, uh . . . orgasms are accounted for."

"Really?" She claps her hands. "Yay, that's so exciting. So you have done it. How come you've been able to hold back since he's been here? I would not be able to do that with Hayes."

"It's called self-control, Hattie."

"I still wouldn't be able to do it. I'd be sneaking off in the middle of the night."

"What makes you think I haven't been doing that?"

"Have you?" she asks, leaning in closer. "Oh my God, does he meet you halfway, and you do it in a field somewhere?"

"I'd prefer not to get into details," I answer because frankly, she doesn't need to know I have zero details. "Let's just say we've kept it quiet out of respect for all of you."

"Wow." She shakes her head as we pull onto the farm and make our way down the dusty dirt road toward the house. "I'm impressed, slightly insulted that you won't give me all the details, but impressed."

"Why would I give you the details of my sex life?"

"Like I said," she answers, exasperated. "Sisters share those kinds of things."

"Well, I don't think we're that kind of sisters."

"We should be," she says as I loop around the house only to find Wyatt standing on the front porch of the guest house with a suitcase next to him.

Oh God, what does he think he's doing now?

"Ooooo," Hattie nearly screams in delight. "That's a suitcase. Is he moving in? Oh my God, we have this entire conversation about hiding your sex, and you didn't tell me that he's moving in? We'll have to tell Mac all about knocking on doors, and if she hears a whimpering animal, it's just her aunt Aubree having fun."

"My God, Hattie," I say as I put the truck in park. "What is wrong with you?"

She chuckles. "I just love this for you." She hops out of the car and waves to Wyatt. "We were just talking about you."

I quickly get out of the car as well so I can potentially interrupt her if she says anything inappropriate to him.

"Is that so?" Wyatt asks while his eyes meet mine. "Good things?"

Hattie pats his shoulder. "Great things. And I know I don't have to say this, but I think it's necessary. Thank you, Wyatt, for fully satisfying my sister. I know she needed it." And then she takes off toward the farmhouse as if she didn't just light me on fire with embarrassment.

Smiling broadly, he asks, "What have you two been talking about?"

"Nothing you need to know," I say, pointing at his suitcase. "What is that doing here?"

He spreads his arms wide and says, "Moving in, babe."

I glance over at the farmhouse where Hattie watches us, hands clasped in front of her chest. Which means I have no other choice but to step forward into his arms and allow him to hug me.

And I do just that, but I keep my arms tucked in close.

Whispering, I say, "Why the hell are you moving in?"

He leans in close and whispers in my ear, "Better to get used to it now rather than later. Plus, I miss you, my snookums. I want to be around you all the time."

"This makes me hate you."

He chuckles and then turns us toward the guest house, letting us both in, along with his suitcase. When he shuts the door, I turn on him and say, "You're not moving in here."

"Like it or not, it's going to happen, Aubree, so we might as well start it now. People are asking why I'm not staying here. I'd rather squelch any talk in case Wallace comes waltzing in, asking questions. Don't worry, I don't plan on jogging around the guest house, dick out. Everything will be tucked in tightly."

"I'm not worried about your . . . flopping appendage."

"You're not?" he asks. "Well, in that case, I prefer to sleep naked."

"Wyatt, can you be serious for one freaking second?" I ask.

"I can," he answers.

"Then please be serious because this is . . . this is different for me. I've never done this before."

"The marriage of convenience, I know," he says. "Neither have I, but—"

"I'm not talking about the marriage of convenience aspect. I mean living with a guy other than my brother. I don't know how to navigate this situation."

"Oh," he says softly. "Well, if that's the case, what do you want to know?"

"It's not about knowledge of the situation. It's about comfort and well, like . . . there are things I do at night."

He studies me for a second and then says, "Oh . . . like, relax yourself?"

"What?" I ask confused and then understanding falls over me. "No, not that."

"But do you do that?"

I feel my cheeks blush again. "That's none of your business."

"It is if I need to know when not to disturb you. I mainly get off in the shower. Just easier that way."

Oh my God, my cheeks feel like flames. I didn't need to know that. I didn't need that image in my head. And now all I'm going to be thinking about when he's in the shower is that he's pleasuring himself.

"By the ghastly expression on your face, I'm going to guess that's not what you expected to hear."

"No," I say, shifting uncomfortably.

"Well, it's shit we should talk about because we're going to be together for a year, and even though I like to say I have self-control, the fact of the matter is, there is no way I'm going to be able to sleep next to you with blue balls for a year. Sorry. Not happening."

"Sl-sleep next to me?" I ask.

"Yes, sleep next to you. Sleeping next to a beautiful woman, who is probably going to smell good. It's just nature. There's nothing creepy about it. It's not like I'll be thinking about you in the shower, but men wake up hard, and I'll want to take care of it. Maybe when I'm doing that, you can take care of yourself. We could have a self-pleasuring party every morning."

My nose turns up. "That is not something I'm participating in."

"Well, the option is there." He takes a seat on the bed and places his hands behind him, leaning back ever so slightly. "What else do you want to talk about? I understand that you have a period, so I can assist you with anything during that time. If you need feminine products or chocolate or someone to rub your lower back. Not sure what your pain points are, but I'm here for you. Also, don't worry about me snoring. That's not something I do. I'm very clean and orderly. I'll just need a small portion of storage. If you don't have anything under your bed, I can use that. I'm easy, Aubree. I'll make it as comfortable as possible for you, so you don't have to worry. Okay?"

"What about . . . the toilet seat?" I ask, trying to find anything to ask him at this point because everything he's saying sounds like it will be okay besides the self-pleasuring party. And despite everything sounding okay, I still have this sickening feeling. I'm not sure I want to do this. Or that I can do this.

"Pee with it up, leave with it down. And I even wipe the seat before I put down the lid because that's just polite."

"And what about . . . snot rockets."

The corners of his lips tilt up. "What about them, Aubree?"

"Do you blow them?"

I can see that he wants to chuckle, but he remains serious for me. "I do, but into tissues like every other decent human out there."

"Okay, um, what about, you know, your, uh . . . morning deposit?"

His cheeks grow even wider. "You mean my cum in the shower?"

"Yes."

"All washed down. Nothing to worry about there. I even rub some soap on the floor of the shower."

"Dirty laundry?"

"In the laundry basket."

"What about your bedtime?" I ask, crossing my arms. "What kind of hours do you maintain?"

"I work best with seven to eight hours of sleep, so if you're wondering if I'm a night owl, the answer would be no. I like to read before bed, and once I start feeling tired or ten at night rolls around, I'll turn off my light and go to sleep. Depending on the day, I'll wake up between five and six. I fell off my workout schedule for a moment there, but I started running again and doing pushups. In case you were wondering."

He fell off his workout schedule, and that's what he looks like? What does he look like when he's on his workout schedule? My God!

"What about . . . uh . . ."

"Let me stop you there," he says. "I can see that you're trying to find something that will displease you, but I can tell you right now, if I do something that you don't like, all you have to do is tell me. That's right, Aubree. I can change. I'm not a man stuck in my habits, so you just tell me, and I'll fix the problem."

"Fine," I say. "The problem is I don't want you living here."

"Ooo," he says on a wince. "That's the one problem that can't be fixed. Sorry. But anything else, I can adjust."

I sigh and lean against the wall. I know this is part of the deal, and I get it, but I didn't expect him to move in tonight. I would have liked to have prepared for what's to come.

Feeling defeated, I ask, "Are people really talking about how you're not staying here?"

"They are. Ethel even mentioned it, and you know when she mentions something . . ."

"Won't it be like you're trying to cover something up by moving in right away?" I ask.

"No, because I mentioned that it would be soon. Didn't give it a specific date. I'll keep my reservation at the inn just in case you change your mind after tonight, but we might as well give it a shot, right?" *May as well give it a shot?* I don't really see that I have a choice. By all standards, Wyatt is doing everything, saying all the right things, to placate me. *He's so selfless.* And that speaks to me in ways I don't want to analyze at this point. I said yes to marrying him, and this is the next logical step. And . . . as he said, we may as well give this a shot.

"I guess so," I say.

"Great." He pops up off the bed and comes up to me. With a smile plastered across his face, he brings me into a hug, and I stiffly lean into his chest. "Oh yeah, giving me the good stuff. God, you're so warm and inviting. This hug, it feels like you're accepting me."

"I don't even have my arms around you," I say.

"It's called sarcasm, Aubree."

"Which should indicate to you that you should read the room and maybe not touch me."

He lets me loose. "Doesn't hurt to share in affection."

"I don't need affection," I say as I straighten out the skirt of my dress.

"From the mood you carry around on a daily basis, I'd say that you do."

"Affection means nothing," I say as I move toward the bathroom and grab a scrunchie so I can throw my hair up into a messy bun. "Affection doesn't help, it just hinders."

I walk out of the bathroom to find Wyatt standing in the middle of the room, staring at me with a concerned look.

"Do you really mean that?" he asks.

"Yes," I say as I attempt to move by him to get to the farmhouse. Ryland and Hattie are probably having a field day with their speculation about what's happening in the guest house, but Wyatt stops me by pressing his hand to my stomach, not letting me by.

"Aubree, every human needs and deserves affection."

"Not every human," I say. "Some people out there have done terrible things and deserve nothing."

Softly, he says, "But you're not one of them, so you deserve affection."

"I don't want it," I say.

"Why not?" he asks.

"It doesn't matter. Let's get to the house so we can help with dinner." I try to move again, but he doesn't let me.

"Does this have to do with an ex?" he asks. "Or maybe your dad?"

My eyes snap up to his, and I pull away from him. "What do you know about my dad?"

He slips his hands in his pockets. "Just that he wasn't the best guy. He hurt you and your siblings, just little things that Clarke told me. That people around town have mentioned."

"Well, forget about it. Nothing about him has affected me as an adult." I'm saying the words, but I don't even believe them because I know they're not true.

Everything that happened in my childhood has affected me as an adult now.

The abuse.

The yelling.

The lack of structure and balance.

I'm the way I am today because of the things I wasn't granted as a child.

I'm cold and moody because I don't want to get close to anyone.

I'm meticulous and organized because I can't function without it.

I'm off-putting and distant because I'm trying to calculate in my head what needs to be done so I don't fall behind.

So I don't disappoint.

So my dad's words that he spoke to me, yelled at me, drilled into me aren't right.

You're a nobody.

You'll amount to nothing.

You're a waste of my time.

I don't want him to be right. I refuse to let him be right. So I stay on task. I don't get distracted. I take what I need and make sure I'm moving forward, not living in the past.

"Aubree—"

"I said forget about it, Wyatt. Okay?" My voice cracks, and I hate that. I hate that he gets a glimpse of that emotion in me because I keep my feelings locked up. *Tight. So no one can touch them.*

It's the only way to survive.

"Okay," he says softly. It's silent for a second, and then he says, "I can wait on moving in if you want."

Great, now he's trying to accommodate me because he caught me in a moment of insecurity. I'm not going to let it happen.

I straighten my shoulders and say, "It's fine. It's going to happen eventually, so it might as well be now. Let's just go eat dinner and be done with this day."

And on that, I move out of the guest house and straight to the main house with Wyatt trailing me.

⊏══⊐

"SO . . . YOU, UH, SPENDING THE NIGHT?" Ryland asks Wyatt as I clean the dishes off the table. Wyatt offered to help, but I told him to sit down. Hattie was chosen for bedtime duty by Mac, so they're upstairs, and Hayes is in the kitchen with me, packing up the food for leftovers.

"Moving in," Wyatt says.

"Moving in?" Ryland asks, his voice rising.

"Yeah," Wyatt says as if it's no big deal.

Ryland directs his attention to me and asks, "You're letting him move in with you?"

"I don't see what the big deal is," I say as I rinse off my last plate and stack it in the dishwasher. "We're in love, might as well live together." The room falls silent, and I can tell that was probably a bit shocking to them, so before Hayes or Ryland can say anything, I add, "I know this all seems new to you, but it's not new to us. You're just finding out about us because I was keeping it a secret. Now that it's out in the open, well, it's going to seem like we're moving fast when, to us, we're at a normal pace, probably the same pace as Hattie and Hayes. No one batted an eye when they moved in together."

"That's true," Hayes says. "She has a very valid point."

"See," I say, pointing at Hayes. "Listen to him." I shut the dishwasher with my foot, then head to the table where Ryland studies me. "What?" I ask, feeling the pressure under his stare.

"So . . . this is a real thing? You two."

"It is," I say. "Thanks for asking. Now, if you don't mind, I'd like to go to bed, and I believe my boyfriend will be joining me, right?"

Wyatt smirks up at me. "Would love to." God, the way he said that was full of innuendo my brother does not need to hear.

Clearing my throat, I turn to Hayes. "Thanks again for dinner. As always, it was delicious."

"You're welcome." He leans against the counter, a knowing look on his face. "Enjoy your evening."

"We will." I nod at Wyatt to follow. "Come on." I head toward the door, and Wyatt trails me. I don't give Ryland a chance to respond or Wyatt a chance to drape his arm around me. Nope, I charge right out of the house and straight to what used to be my sanctuary.

Once inside, I move to my dresser and pull out an oversized shirt just as the door shuts behind me. I turn toward Wyatt and hold up my shirt. "This is what I wear to bed."

His eyes land on the shirt and then back at me. "Okay. It's a nice shirt."

"But that's all it is, a shirt. Are you going to be freaked out if I don't wear shorts?"

"Uh . . . no," he says with a laugh. "Are you going to be freaked out if I only wear a pair of boxers?"

"No," I answer even though I don't want to see him with his shirt off. I've seen it already, and his chest is too nice. His arms are too toned. His body is too sculpted and perfect. *Sooo much hotter than Matt would ever be.*

It's fine. I'll just turn away from him.

"Great," he says. "Then it's settled. We are unbothered by each other's nighttime clothes. Good to know."

"Wonderful," I reply as I walk into the bathroom and shut the door behind me.

I lean against the door with my head tilted back and my eyes closed. *Oh my God, what is going on with my life?* A week ago, none of this was happening. There was no Wyatt in my life, there was no impending proposal, and there was no man in my bedroom ready to sleep in my bed, disturbing the peace and order I've been able to establish since Cassidy's death.

Now it feels like everything is all scrambled again, and I just . . . I just need to get my head on straight. *This is fine. Everything will be fine, Aubree. Deep breaths.*

I take a few seconds to calm myself down. Then when I can tell that I'm not going to fall into a panic attack—something that's happened a few times since Cassidy passed—I get ready for bed, taking my time with my skincare routine, making sure I brush and floss, and then go to the bathroom at the end.

Once ready, I slip out of the bathroom only to find Wyatt sitting on my side of the bed wearing nothing but his black boxer briefs. Even his back muscles are impeccable. Look at those things. I can actually see the definition of his scapula. Those are the types of muscles you see on a man who works all day, every day on the farm, not a man who types on his computer.

He turns around and says, "All done?"

"Yes." Then I point at where he plugged in his charger and set down his book. "That's my side of the bed."

"I could tell by the indent in the mattress, but I plan on sleeping there."

"Uh . . . but it's my side."

"I understand," he says. "But it's also the side closest to the door, which means if someone were to come in here in the middle of the night, you would be the first one attacked, and I'm not going to let that happen. Therefore, it goes my body, then your body."

I feel my expression turn into a frown. "I've lived here for a while, and no one's come into my house in the middle of the night."

"That's great to hear," he says. "But I'm not taking any chances. And I know I said I'd accommodate any problem you might have, but this is non-negotiable. I will sleep in front of you and protect you. You're my wife."

I twist my lips together, hating that his last sentence sent a small thrill up my spine. "I'm not your wife yet, and I'm not that kind of wife, you know, the kind you have to sacrifice your body for."

"You are to me," he says, stepping up to me now. He grips my chin with his forefinger and thumb and says, "As long as you wear my ring, use my name, and sleep in my bed, you are mine to protect. Get comfortable on your new side because that's where you'll sleep."

And then he moves off to the bathroom, not another word uttered.

Right.

Well.

That was . . . hot. Sexy. Mind-blowing.

No.

Don't go down that path, Aubree. Think . . . outlandish, alpha-ish, and overbearing.

A part of me wants to test his theory and see if he truly means it, but the other side of me is tired and just wants to pretend this night is over. From the hard day to the conversation in the truck with Hattie to Wyatt bombarding me with this new living arrangement, I'm ready to shut my eyes and look forward to a new day where I can establish some semblance of order.

So I settle into the untouched side of my bed and attempt to get comfortable. He already set up my charger and everything else that was on my nightstand over on this side, which is thoughtful, and I can tell he gave me the pillow I was using as well.

I will say this about Wyatt—he might be sarcastic and a joke-ster—and treads the thin line of annoying me and wanting me to push him off a cliff—but he's nice, he's considerate, and he's thoughtful. The only other guy I've known who is like him is Ryland . . . well, and I guess Hayes.

Every other man in my life has been a major disappointment.

Wyatt moves out of the bathroom, and I avert my eyes so they don't wander over his chest and below his waist. I don't need any thoughts of his body inside my head before I go to bed.

He slips under the sheets and blankets with me, and when I think he's going to pick up his book and start reading, he turns toward me and lifts on his elbow. "Hey," he says softly.

I keep my eyes fixed on the ceiling. "Hello," I answer awkwardly.

He tips my chin so I'm forced to look at him. "You don't have to avoid eye contact with me."

"I'm not," I say.

"You are. This doesn't have to be awkward, Aubree. We can mutually enjoy this."

"What does that mean?" I ask, nervous as to what he's alluding to.

He rolls his eyes. "Nothing like that. I'm just saying if you're someone who likes to cuddle or likes to be the big spoon or little spoon, I can accommodate. You don't have to lie stiffly, staring up at the ceiling like it's your first night in prison."

"Wyatt, I don't even hold your hand. Do you think I'm the type of person who cuddles?"

"Have you tried it?" he asks.

"Of course," I say even though Matt wasn't much of a snuggler—probably because I wasn't.

Because I'm rigid.

Because I'm emotionally detached.

Cold-hearted.

Reserved.

Aloof.

All my father's words and descriptions that Matt echoed.

"Have you?" Wyatt asks again. This time, he scoots closer.

"Uh, what are you doing?" I ask him.

"Humor me for a second, Aubree."

"Humor what?" I ask, scooting away, but he stops me by looping his arm around me and gripping my hip so I can't move away anymore.

"I just want to try something."

"What do you want to try? I'm not some science experiment."

"I understand that, but please, just for a few seconds, and if you hate it, you can push me away. Okay?"

"Will you leave me alone after?" I ask.

He nods. "Yes, but let me just try this first."

Wanting to just get to sleep and knowing his persistence, I give in. Whatever he wants to do, might as well let him so we can move on and sleep.

"Fine," I say. "But don't touch any private parts."

He smirks. "All private parts are off the table. Now turn away from me."

"Turn away from you?" I ask, confused.

"Yes, turn away from me."

Unsure of what he's doing, I turn away from him and tuck my head against my pillow while lying on my side.

I wait there for a few seconds, wondering what the hell he's doing, then I feel his warm body come right up behind mine.

His warmth to my cold immediately sends me into a panic.

"Wh-what are you doing?" I ask.

"Shh," he says as he moves in another inch.

He's very slow, deliberate, like he has a plan he's wanted to execute for a while and has finally got a chance. He's not going to make a mistake.

He slides his hand to my side and then moves in another inch so his legs touch mine and his chest is to my back.

I stiffen when his hand moves over my stomach.

And when he pulls me in the rest of the way, right up against his large, protective body, every part of me stills.

My pulse.

My muscles.

My breath.

Everything is put on hold as he scoops me against his body, and his head rests right against mine.

He's . . . he's spooning me.

Holding me.

Cuddling me.

My fight or flight kicks in.

I want to squirm away.

I want to donkey-kick my legs back, convincing him I don't want anyone near me.

I want to scream that this is not what we do.

But then, something is in the back of my head, something telling me that this . . . this is nice.

It battles and wars with the fight in my head. Telling me that this is not something I deserve, not something I need in life. I don't offer affection, and affection is never offered to me.

I feel like a scared cat, waiting to pounce, ready to flee, but with each deep breath Wyatt takes, the edge of panic creeping up my spine slowly abates. The uneasiness recedes. My body is slowly starting to relax as he holds me every second longer and doesn't want to leave.

Doesn't want to flee from me.

And that's how we stay. He doesn't say anything, just holds me with his face against my head and his nose in my hair. His arm around my stomach. His breath matching mine.

In and out.

Deep in.

Deep out.

I find my eyes starting to close.

My tension fades.

And with every press of his chest to my back as we breathe in tandem, I drop the worries, the stresses, the insecurities, and I allow myself, probably for the first time ever in my life, to enjoy a peaceful moment with another human without questioning if I deserve this.

If I'm worth it.

Chapter Eleven

THE SIBLINGS

Hattie: *Uh, are we not going to talk about it?*

Ryland: *You realize I'm about to go to bed, right?*

Hattie: *Yes, but you went up to your room before I could even discuss things with you.*

Ryland: *There's nothing to discuss.*

Hattie: *What do you mean there's nothing to discuss?*

Ryland: *There's nothing to discuss. This is Aubree's life.*

Hattie: *I'm fully aware, but we also know about Aubree's life. We know this is not the kind of thing she does. She's only ever had one other boyfriend, and Matt never moved in. This doesn't seem weird to you?*

Ryland: *Am I shocked? Yes, but she claims they've been talking for a while. Pointed out that you and Hayes probably moved in together in a similar timeframe to her and Wyatt, but we were just aware of you and Hayes.*

Hattie: *That makes sense, but aren't you worried?*

Ryland: *I'm always worried when it comes to Aubree. I'm worried that she won't ever open herself up. That she won't allow people to be in her life. That she'll let her past lead to loneliness. It's always on my fucking mind, Hattie. I know what she saw, what she heard, what she was told,* growing up. And I know that hurt her as she's gotten older. I see the distance in her eyes. I see the pain. I'm always, always worried about her.

Hattie: I'm worried too. I mean, I haven't even seen them hold hands or hug or kiss. I talked to her about intimacy today, and she nearly choked on her own spit. I don't want things to end badly for her. I know they did with Matt, and . . . she just needs to find happiness.

Ryland: I agree, but I don't think there is anything we can do.

Hattie: You could talk to Wyatt, maybe explain Aubree to him.

Ryland: I don't want to step in like that, Hattie.

Hattie: I want to trust that Aubree is talking to him, but I don't know, she just seems so stiff. I want to help her like she helped me with Hayes.

Ryland: I know, and your heart is in a good place, but there's nothing we can do at the moment other than support her. Keep talking to her, encourage her to step outside of those comfort zones she's made for herself.

Hattie: I just want her to find happiness, Ryland. I know you guys worried about me when Cassidy died, and I really appreciate the help and love you gave me, but now my head is out of the dark cloud that was Cassidy's death. I can see what's happening around me. I can see that Aubree is on autopilot. I can see that you struggle. I want to help.

Ryland: I'm fine. I struggle like every other person taking care of a child. Aubree . . . she will be okay. We'll keep our eye on her, and if we feel like we need to step in to help, we will. But she will be madder with us if we step in without her needing it. Let her find her peace with Wyatt.

Hattie: I know you're right. I just wish she was more affectionate, more open to him. Maybe she is in private. Ugh.

Ryland: It will be okay. Let her find herself. Wyatt will be good for her. I can feel it.

Chapter Twelve

WYATT

"I like your shorts," I say as Aubree walks out of the bathroom in her work outfit for the day. She's wearing jean shorts frayed at the hem and folded over at the waist. She paired them with a black tank top, put her hair up in a large bun on the top of her head, and tied off the strays with a bandanna.

She glances down at her shorts and then back at me. "They're regular shorts," she replies, looking confused.

"They're nice," I reply.

She eyes me suspiciously. "Why are you being weird?"

"What? I can't compliment my wife's shorts?"

She holds up a finger. "One, I'm not your wife." She holds up another finger. "And two, these shorts are a decade old, and nothing is nice about them."

"Well, I think they're nice."

She mumbles something I don't hear under her breath and then starts making herself a mug of coffee.

Last night, I threw up a Hail Mary. I do not doubt that Aubree has been hurt, damaged terribly by men in her past. She's so skittish, and I hate it. I hate that she feels she needs to be stiff around me and seems to be thinking all the time rather than relaxing. That she feels like she doesn't need affection. I wish she could just let loose, have fun, and stop trying to be so perfect all the fucking time. So last night, even though I knew she wasn't into touching and affection, I pushed the envelope and attempted something I had no right to try. But I couldn't let our first night in the same bed be one that left a bad taste in her mouth.

I didn't want her lying in bed, staring up at the ceiling, motionless and scared. *She's so isolated. Emotionally.* Even though we're moving into a contractual obligation with each other, I am, if not anything else, a damn good friend. I have always been affectionate, something I got from my parents, and I know the power of a good hug.

Hopefully, I'll become someone she can rely on and lean into for support *when she needs it.* Someone other than her siblings who have their own lives and their own worries. I want her to know that I can be a rock of support.

So I thought spooning her might be a good place to start.

I assumed that it would be a five-second thing, and she'd wiggle away, but she didn't.

Instead, I was shocked.

I felt her relax.

I felt her breath fall in line with mine.

I felt her slowly fall asleep and followed quickly after.

I woke up this morning in the same position, holding her, her tucked in tight to her pillow. Neither one of us moved or attempted any other position.

I considered getting up and going for a run. Even thought about showering, but I didn't want to leave the bed, where she'd wake up by herself. I wanted her to know that I was still there for her. The entire night, I protected her.

And that was what happened—she woke up in my arms, went completely stiff when she realized it, and then slid out of bed and went straight to the bathroom.

So . . . magical morning.

"What are you up to today?" I ask her while she sits on the edge of the bed and puts on her socks.

"Working," she says.

"Great, just what I was hoping." When she was in the bathroom getting changed, so was I. I'm ready in my work clothes, a pair of cargo shorts and a T-shirt. I also made the bed when she was in the bathroom. "What are we working on today?"

"We?" she asks, looking over her shoulder at me. "What makes you think this is a we moment?"

"Um, well, who else would I be working with?"

"Maybe yourself. Don't you have that stepson lover book to write?"

"Nothing is due for a while, so I'm free. Come on, this is our farm, technically. Tell me how I can help."

"Like I said, Wyatt, I don't need your help."

She goes to her travel mug of coffee, takes out the creamer from her mini fridge, and pours some into the steaming liquid. Fuck is she stubborn. Probably the most stubborn woman I've ever met. *And I lived with Cadance Clearwater for several years.*

"I know you don't need it, but I want to offer it. Make me do stuff, put me to work. Does something need to be built? Do you need help picking out chickens? Want to go over future plans? Let me be of assistance."

"Seriously, Wyatt. We've got it covered."

She puts a lid over her cup of coffee, and I can feel my frustration boil over, so instead of pushing her, I decide to step back.

"Okay," I say, moving over to where I put my shoes.

As I put them on, she says, "Okay?"

I look up at her expression of disbelief. "Yes, okay."

"Why don't I trust that you're just dropping this conversation and won't show up on the farm, doing something weird I asked you not to do?"

"You might not know this, Aubree, but I can listen. If you don't want me out there, fine. I'll do something else."

I finish tying my shoes and stand from the bed. "What are you going to do?" she asks, her voice almost in a panic as if she's worried that I'm going to do something completely unhinged.

"I don't believe that's any of your business," I say. I pocket my phone and head toward the door, where she stops me.

"Can you please just tell me if it has anything to do with the farm?" There really is panic in her eyes, so I shake my head.

"No, Aubree, I wouldn't mess your farm up, okay? The only thing I want to do is help, but since you won't let me, I'll do something else. I'll see you later."

She stops me again, and even though I know she hates communication, I can sense she wants to say something. "Um, are you . . . are you angry about, you know, not helping?"

She can't even look me in the eyes when she says it, and fuck, it makes me want to shake her, to beg her to tell me who has made her this way. Who has made her so skittish, so insecure around men? *So untrusting.* I probably know who, but I'd dearly like to ask what happened. I want to get to know her on a different level. To understand her better. *And not live with a stranger.*

This may have started with an idea, a plan, a handshake kind of deal, but with every day I get to know Aubree more, it's less clinical, less cut and dry. Some gray is being mixed into this deal, and the gray wants to get to know Aubree and see what makes her tick. With Mac, she's warm, attentive, and kind. She stirs Hattie, admires Ryland, and she dotes on her niece. She's firm but considerate to her staff. She's an incredibly smart, focused, and selfless person, but I doubt anyone but her family sees that.

In the short time I've spent with Aubree, I've realized that it's not that she's grumpy, but she's guarded. She's been hurt and has put up walls to avoid being hurt further.

I want to be the person she allows to peek over it. We might only be together on paper for a year, but I'd love the chance to be her friend. *I need her to give me a chance.* And that surprises me. Because a few weeks ago, I was a devastated mess about a disappearing fiancée.

"Am I angry with you? No, Aubree," I say as I tip her chin up with my finger. "I'm not angry. Do I want to help you? Of course. But I'm not going to pressure you. I want you to feel safe around me and that means letting you go at your own pace." I release her chin and reach for the knob, but she stops me again.

"Um, about last night."

"What about it?" I ask.

"I, uh . . ." She looks down at her coffee. "I'm not, you know, like that."

"Like what?"

"The cuddling type," she says, still avoiding eye contact.

"You told me that last night."

"Well, I didn't want you thinking that's what I need from you or anything. Like I don't need you to hold me every night or whatever." She tries to brush it off, but I see right through her.

"I know," I answer. "I truly know you don't need anything from me, Aubree. You're strong, you're capable, and you are so fucking smart. The last thing you need is my help, and I mean that. But it's okay to lean in, lean on someone. And if you feel like you need that, I'm here for you. I'm not your enemy. I'm not someone you need to worry about. I'm here for you, whatever you need, even if that's someone to hold you at night so you don't feel so . . . alone."

Her beautiful eyes flash up to mine.

Her teeth pull on the corner of her lip.

And then she says something very unexpected.

"Thank you."

And there she is. There is the woman who hides behind her gruff exterior.

Thank you.

"Any time," I say. "See you tonight. Want to go out to dinner?"

"Sure," she says, shocking me again.

"Okay, see you tonight."

⊏⊐

"WHY DOES it feel like it's been months since I've seen you?" Laurel says as she scoops me into a hug.

"Because you got used to me sleeping on your couch, being with you almost every waking hour, so a few days apart seems like a lifetime."

"That could be it. By the way, I can still feel your body imprint on the couch. Makes me miss you."

"That's so touching," I say as we head toward the jewelry store.

Once I knew Aubree wouldn't accept my help, I drove into town and called Laurel on the way, asking if she'd meet up with me and help me pick out a ring. She thought it was insane but didn't want to miss it. We set a time and a place to meet, nearly halfway between her house and my new one. But before, I stopped at The Cliffs. I went in to check on how the bear claw was selling, and lo and behold, Hank has sold out the past two days. I don't know if it's me or what, but I find it hilarious that everything I seem to touch—or eat—the town consumes immediately. Luckily, he saved one in case I came in, and Hank gave it to me for free along with my coffee.

I tried to pay, but he said my money wasn't good at his establishment, then proceeded to ask me what my eating schedule was like. He wants to let me know when the next new batch of cinnamon buns he's been working on comes out so people can catch me eating them.

Who knew I was going to become a small-town food influencer?

"How was the drive?" I ask Laurel as I hold the door open for her.

"Not bad. I had two meetings in the car, so the drive went by very quickly. On the way back, I'll be able to catch up on my true crime podcasts."

"Are you listening to *Blood on the Door*?" I ask as we walk into the jewelry shop.

"Yes, I'm on episode three, so don't spoil anything for me."

"I won't," I say, "but if you were wondering if it's the—"

She clamps her hand over my mouth, causing me to laugh. "Don't you dare."

When she releases me, I say, "Come on, I would never. But it's fun to tease you."

"More like torture," she says just as a sales associate walks up to us.

The man in a medium gray suit and red tie looks like he just woke up from the dead with his pale features and dark circles under his eyes. In a thriller, he'd be considered a suspect but would end up just being a creepy old man rather than the killer. He's the kind of person you put in a book to throw the reader off the scent.

"Welcome to Barbitz Jewelry. Is there anything I can help you with?"

"Looking for engagement rings," I say, my hands smoothing together.

"Aw, how nice. And I presume this is your fiancée?"

"You are presuming wrong," Laurel says. "I'm the best friend and here to make sure he doesn't pick out anything hideous."

"Ah, the voice of reason," the man says. "Well, my name is Gerald, and I'm happy to help you with anything you might need. I'll direct you to the rings, and you can browse. If you want me to take anything out, I'd be pleased to."

"Thank you," I say.

"Right this way." Gerald ushers us over to a long row of engagement rings. "Here you are. If you're looking for something simpler, those would be on the right down this way. Flashier would be over here on the left. And a healthy middle would be right here. I'll give you some time to peruse."

"Thank you, Gerald," I say before he moves away.

"What do you think she'd like?" Laurel asks.

"Simple," I say without even having to think about it. "She's very simple and not flashy at all."

"And how do you know that?" Laurel asks.

"She doesn't wear jewelry in the first place. She barely wears makeup. She has this fresh-face thing going on that's pretty. She keeps herself grounded, and dressing up for her is a simple sundress. I don't think she cares for heels but would rather wear her work boots."

Laurel's brow raises in question. "Um . . . wow, that's more than I expected you to know about her."

"Just observations." I shrug.

"Uh-huh, and what did you say about her non-makeup look?" Laurel asks.

I roll my eyes. "I know where you're going with this, and you can stop that. Nothing is going on between us. And I mean nothing. She won't even hold my hand. She's skittish most of the time when around me, or she's putting up a wall." Besides last night, but Laurel doesn't need to know that.

"Would you like her to hold your hand?" Laurel teases.

"No, I mean, yes, but not like in the way you're thinking. If we're going to make this look more convincing, she'll need to be more affectionate."

"Maybe she thinks you smell or something. I wouldn't want to hold someone's hand who smells."

"Be real, Laurel."

She laughs and scans the rings. "Well, she's skittish for one of two reasons. Either she's scared of you, which I don't think is the case given how she stands up to you, or something in her past prevents her from being intimate."

"It's definitely the latter," I say, spotting a simple ring with three stones that could be an option. "I don't know the extent of it all, but I do know she didn't have a great childhood, and it seems like her ex was a dick, so she's probably tainted from both of those." Not to mention evil Amanda.

"Are you going to try to fix it?"

"No," I answer even though last night was my first attempt.

"You are such a liar," she says, bumping into my shoulder. "I know you, Wyatt. She's a project to you, isn't she?"

"Christ, don't ever say that around her."

"Well, she is . . . right? You see her as a project."

Sighing, I turn to Laurel and say, "I don't like that she's been hurt. You can see her guard is up, and you can see the hurt in her eyes. It's clear as day, and I hate that."

"Which means you want to make it better."

I shrug. "If I can at least open her up, let her know that not all men are asses, then I don't see an issue with that."

"The only issue is . . . if she actually falls for you."

I shake my head. "No fucking way. She barely tolerates me. I don't think she sees me in a romantic way. There's no potential for this being anything but a friendship."

"So you're not even friends at this point?"

"Nope. I'd say mild acquaintances. I'd love to get to a point by the end of this where we split amicably and are still friends. Right now, I do not see that happening. I think she'll kick me out of the house and say good riddance."

"You'd still see her, though, because of MacKenzie, right?"

"Yeah, there will always be that connection, but she'll most likely avoid me, and that's what I don't want to happen. I just want to be friends, and if that means attempting to make her more comfortable around me and helping her through whatever pain she might be feeling, then I'll do that."

She nods and turns toward the rings again. "What about your pain?"

"What pain?" I ask even though I know exactly what she's talking about.

"Don't play dumb with me, Wyatt. You can't tell me that this new plan, this going off and playing farm and trying to make the town love you, isn't a distraction from what's really going on inside you."

"Haven't really thought about it."

"You haven't?" she asks in disbelief. "How come I don't believe that?"

"Because apparently, you like to think you know everything about me."

"I do," she counters as she points out a ring on the right that catches my eye. "And even though you don't like to admit it, I believe there is still some hurt inside you from how Cadance ended your relationship. That's not something you get over easily. I want you to move on and get better, but I don't want you to mask what's going on in your heart with a project, that project being a new wife."

I turn toward her and look her in the eyes. "I promise, I'm not masking anything."

"Okay, then did you tell her about Cadance?"

How did I know she was going to ask that? Oh because she's my nosy best friend who thinks she knows everything about me.

Which she does.

"I haven't," I answer. "And not because I'm hiding something, but because I just don't think it's necessary or it hasn't been the right time. Aubree is dealing with her own problems and doesn't like emotions, so she won't want to sit down with me and hear about how my fiancée broke up with me the night before our wedding."

"Maybe she does."

"Trust me," I say with conviction. "She doesn't." I then clear my throat and say, "Gerald, I think I found something I like."

"Lovely," he says, walking up to us. The entire time, I can feel Laurel's gaze on me. I know she wants to talk about this more, but thankfully, as Gerald pulls out the ring she pointed out, she drops the conversation, which is perfect because I was done talking about it.

⸻

"ETHEL, CAN I TALK TO YOU?" I ask as I find her rocking on the porch of the inn. I'm meeting Aubree for dinner in a few minutes, but I need to tackle something first.

I ended up getting the ring Laurel pointed out because it was perfect. A cluster of diamonds set on the top, while petals of diamonds are scattered down the sides of the ring, making it look like a cascade of flowers. It's earthy, natural, and none of the diamonds are so big that Aubree would be embarrassed by the size, something I feel like she'd think about. I stole a ring from her dresser top, and luckily, the ring we purchased was the right size. Laurel joked about it being a sign, and I just waved her off.

"Of course, dear. What can I help you with?"

"Well, it requires some discretion," I say.

She lifts from her rocking chair and says, "Say no more. Come to my office."

Her brown-and-gold kaftan blows in the breeze as she weaves me through the front doors of the inn and to the left, past registration and to an office in the back that overlooks the yard scattered in Adirondack chairs, yard games, and picnic tables.

"Shut the door behind you," she says as she takes a seat at her desk and folds her hands together, looking all sorts of business. I shut the door and take a seat across from her. "How can I help you, Wyatt?"

"I need this to stay between us. Think you can do that?" I ask, knowing full well it won't stay between us, but I'm okay with that.

"Of course," she says, her hand over her heart. "You have my full discretion."

"Thank you." I cross my ankle over my knee and say, "I plan on proposing to Aubree and need your help."

Her eyes light up as she sits back in her chair, a satisfied smile spreading across her cheeks. "Well, isn't that just wonderful news!"

"It is. We've been talking about the idea of marriage, and well, I think it's time to ask. I know it might seem soon to some people, but when you know, you know."

"I could not agree more." She clutches her heart. "And if anyone needs this love, it's our dear Aubree. She has been through so much. Those Rowley kids are survivors. As you probably know, Ryland took most of their father's mistreatment, Cassidy was there to hold everyone together, and Hattie was protected from a lot of the abuse in that family, but Aubree, she's a different story. She received a combination of everything. The abuse, the neglect, the lack of love. She fell to the wayside and didn't get to live the kind of childhood she should have. None of them did, but I always thought Aubree was the one who suffered the most. It's one thing to have a purpose during a time of struggle. It's another to be forgotten."

Jesus.

She was abused? I know things were hard for them, but . . . to hear that her father actually struck her, that . . . that creates a beast inside me that wants nothing more than to protect her.

"And then Matt treated her so poorly and left town without blinking an eye. Amanda was no better to her. A best friend does *not* marry one's best friend's ex. Not to mention, broadcasting that illicit decision." She sighs. *Nothing gets past Ethel.* "I didn't think she'd allow anyone else close to her heart." Ethel looks at me with beaming eyes. "Then you come along. I just couldn't be happier."

God, when I hear shit like that, it actually makes me feel guilty. Like what will the town think when we divorce in a year? Are they going to have something bad to say about me? I sure hope not. *Are they going to pity Aubree all over again?* She would hate that.

"Thank you," I reply. "I'm pretty happy too, but I don't want to celebrate too soon, not when she hasn't said yes yet."

"Oh she will," Ethel says. "I see the way she looks at you." Do you now? Is Ethel mistaking disdain for love? Because I've seen the way Aubree looks at me, and the only spark I can find in those green irises is a spark of fire, ready to attack—and not in a good way. "There's no way she says no to a man like you."

Things I need to remember—always visit Ethel when I need a boost in confidence.

"I appreciate that."

"So." She leans forward. "How can I help you?"

I smile and lean forward too. "About that End of Summer Jubilee . . ."

"SERIOUSLY, this is the best fucking pizza ever." I take another bite of the crust and revel in the crispiness.

"I don't think I've ever seen someone who looks like they want to make out with food before, but here you are," Aubree says.

"Yes, here I am," I say, eyeing the last piece between us. "I'd make out with this pizza any day."

She wipes her mouth with her napkin. "That's not disturbing at all."

I wiggle my eyebrows at her. "Jealous I'm not making out with you?"

Her expression falls flat. "Definitely not."

I chuckle and finish my crust.

When I first met up with her for dinner, she was turtling in a bit, shy and slightly awkward, but now that I've spent the past thirty minutes coaxing her into talking to me and sharing about her day, she's loosened up. This is my favorite side of her when she slightly lifts the veil and shows her true self.

It's when her true personality shines.

It's when she gives me shit but with a smirk.

"Tell me, Aubree, if you were to make out with a food, what would it be?"

"That's seriously the line of questioning you're going with tonight?"

"Might as well," I say as I point at the last piece. "Can I eat that?"

"I don't want to be the person who comes between a man and his lover, by all means." She gestures toward the pizza, and I smirk as I pick it up. See, when she loosens up, she's funny.

"Come here, lover," I say before taking a large bite. She rolls her eyes at me and takes a sip of her Diet Coke. "So . . . what food are you making out with?"

"I'm going to guess you'll keep asking me until I answer. Am I right?"

"That would be correct," I say. "So best you just give in and answer."

She sighs heavily and leans back in her chair as she taps her finger on the table. "Not that I want to answer such a ridiculous question, but if I had to choose, I guess it would be mac and cheese."

"What?" I ask, surprised. "Really? I don't think I've seen you eat mac and cheese at all since I've been here."

"Doesn't mean I don't love it. It has to be the right mac and cheese. I don't like to just eat any kind. The Cliffs makes the best here in town, but it's not on the menu every week. It's a special. Hank always lets me know when he plans on making it because he knows I don't want to miss it."

"Hank," I say, clutching my heart. "The best fucking bear claw I've ever had."

"The bear claw that he's close to naming after you, which Hayes is bitter about since he told you about them."

I lean forward. "Is Hank really saying that, or is that a rumor? Did you hear it from his mouth? Fuck, I hope he does. The cherry pie is already under consideration for a new name that includes me. Having two menu items in town would be a dream."

"You have problems."

"Problems or goals, babe?" I wink at her. After I swallow my bite, I say, "So mac and cheese is a favorite. Maybe I'll try to make you some."

"Please don't."

I scoff. "Do you think I won't be good at it? You don't know about my cooking abilities."

"Yes, I do. You told me you weren't great at cooking. Something about being able to only make a peanut butter and jelly."

I clutch my heart jokingly. "Mrs. Preston, look at you listening."

"You know, it's not a requirement to be so dramatic."

"But it's what makes you smile," I reply.

"Does it, though?" she asks, and I can see the slightest tilt of the corners of her mouth.

"Yes, it does. But back to the task at hand."

"And what task would that be?" she asks.

"Getting to know what makes you tick. What makes you happy. So mac and cheese is your make-out partner—"

"Can you not put it that way?"

"No, I prefer to use those terms because it makes you roll your eyes, and if you don't roll your eyes at me at least twenty times a day, then I'm not doing my job."

"Your job of what?" she asks. "Irritating me?"

"Precisely," I say while I lean forward and boop her on the nose, causing her eyes to roll again. "See." I point at her. "That's number fifteen. Well on my way to hitting my quota for the day." She mutters something unintelligible under her breath, but that smile still peeks through, letting me know I'm still in the clear with teasing her. "So if you were to have a threesome with your mac and cheese, who would you invite for . . . dessert?"

"I hate this game," she states.

"But you're obviously still going to play."

"Do I even have an option?" she asks.

"I think it's cute that you think there's a slight possibility, but no, there's no option for you."

"That's what I thought." She huffs but then gives her answer some thought. "If you're talking about my dream meal, because I think that's what you're trying to determine in your ass-backward way, I'd say a Caesar salad with croutons, but pumpernickel croutons because those are the best. Mac and cheese from The Cliffs, because Hank makes this incredible cheese sauce that is unbeatable. After that, I'd top it all off with some sort of ice cream sundae."

"Not cherry pie?" I ask, surprised.

She shakes her head. "Don't get me wrong, I love cherry pie, but I love ice cream even more. And I especially love it when it's a simple sundae, but I'd take any kind of sundae, honestly."

"How do you define a simple sundae?"

"Don't judge me, because I know this will come off as boring and bland, but I'd define it as vanilla ice cream, hot fudge, chopped peanuts, whipped cream, cherries, and chocolate sprinkles."

"Hell," I say, wiping my mouth with my napkin. "That sounds really fucking good right now. And would you eat that while watching something?"

"Uh . . . sure," she says, confused.

"Like what?" I ask.

"I don't know, a movie? That's a weird question."

"No," I say, "I'm trying to see what kind of movies and shows you like to watch."

"Oh, anything about murder." She answers so quickly that I actually feel my balls quiver.

"That's unsettling for me."

She chuckles, and it's such a sweet sound. I don't get to hear it often, but when it does come out, I enjoy it immensely. It makes me think that I'm doing all the right things.

"I find murder fascinating—"

"Once again, that's horrifying for me."

"I don't want to commit the murder. I just like the mystery and thrill behind the documentaries or movies. It's the same as you writing about it. I just really like action-packed things and suspense, and I don't mind a romantic interest there either."

"But it has to have a murder?"

"Obviously. If no one is murdered, then I'm not interested."

"Looks like I'm going to sleep with one eye open from now on."

"Probably best." She smirks.

Fuck, that smile. She's gorgeous on the regular, but when that smile comes into play, I can practically feel it pierce through my soul, like I was assigned the task in life to make her smile.

"Okay, so murder and ice cream. Got it." I stand from my chair and say, "Let's go."

"Where are we going?"

"Uh, to enjoy some murder and ice cream. Did you not understand that?"

"Apparently not. Where are we going to enjoy this murder and ice cream?"

"I'll show you," I say. I lend out my hand for her to take it, but instead, she sticks her hands in her pockets, giving me a clear sign that there will be no hand-holding. Okay. We'll have to work on that.

Maybe what I have planned will grant me my first hand-hold.

Chapter Thirteen

AUBREE

"Thanks, Ethel," Wyatt calls out as he gets into the driver's side of my truck—he insisted on driving—and takes off down the road, away from where we're supposed to turn to return to the farm.

"What are we doing, and why did you grab pillows and blankets from Ethel?"

"Can you not just sit back and allow me to surprise you?"

"No. I don't like surprises."

"Shocking," he says as he drives down toward the general store where Dee Dee Coleman herself is waiting by the curb with a bag.

Wyatt pulls the truck to the side and says, "Can you roll down your window?"

"What is happening?" I ask while I roll down the window.

Dee Dee walks up to the truck and hands us the bag. "Put it on the tab for you, Wyatt."

"Thanks, Dee Dee, you're the best. I appreciate you."

"Not a problem," Dee Dee says. "Have fun."

"We will." And then he pulls back out on the road and then

makes a left, right into The Talkies, our drive-in movie theater. That's when I see what's playing today—*The Shining*.

"How?" I ask. "How did you even know this was happening?"

"Had a hunch that you were going to like murder, so I texted around for some help. In that bag are fixings for a sundae, the perfect sundae defined by you." He rolls down his window and speaks to the attendant to purchase a parking spot for us.

I'm shocked, stunned, completely caught off guard that someone who isn't romantically interested in me has put so much thought into something so nice for me.

I'm honestly surprised I was so wrong about Wyatt. I learned at a very young age to be watchful of people. Watchful of their behavior and how it can change within a second. But I feel confident that he won't make changes to the farm that Cassidy wouldn't have wanted.

He's been helpful, patient, kind, and . . . sweet.

I don't get it. *What is the catch? Why is he so kind to me?*

He backs up into a parking spot that's not too close but not too far away either, and then hops out of the truck, only to jump into the back. I glance behind me to see him arranging the blankets and pillows Ethel let him borrow. When he's done, he knocks on the window and waves for me to come out.

With the bag of sundae fixings in my hand, I hop out of the truck as well and hand him the bag. He holds out his hand to help me up, but I step up onto the tire and then into the bed of the truck.

"Take your shoes off," he says as he does the same. So I follow suit because honestly, I'm so stunned and confused as to why he's being so kind to me when I've been, well, guarded at times, that I just listen. "Now, come back here. I've tried to make it as comfortable as possible. Let me know if you need me to move pillows or blankets around."

"No, this is fine," I say and then look him in his eyes. "This was really nice of you, Wyatt. You didn't have to do this."

"I know, but I wanted to."

"Why, though?" I ask before I can stop myself. In front of us is a commercial of a talking drink and pretzel singing a song about concessions, but I ignore it as I look for an answer from Wyatt.

"Why did I want to do this?"

"Yes," I say. "You're being so nice, and I'm not sure I deserve your kindness."

"That's where you're wrong," he says. "You deserve it and so much more. That's why I'm doing this, because I feel like you're someone who hasn't experienced kindness in the past, and well, you're due for it."

"My past isn't of your concern," I say, the words registering in my head just as they fall out of my mouth. I hate myself for saying it, especially since he's been so thoughtful. I blow out a frustrated breath. "Sorry. I didn't mean to say that. I'm just . . ." I drag my hand over my forehead.

"Guarded," he finishes for me. "I get it, Aubree. I really do. You don't need to apologize."

"I do because I shouldn't be so snappy with my responses. I see that you're trying to be my friend. I notice you trying, and I'm, fuck . . ." I look away.

"Not good with emotions, having a hard time opening up, not fully trusting of me yet," he says as if he can read my mind.

"Once again, I get it. It takes time, and hopefully, I can earn that trust as we move forward. Just remember, I'm here for you. I'm your partner in this, not your enemy. What we do with each other, what we say to each other, it's sacred. You don't have to worry about me spreading any truth or lies about you. This right here"—he motions between us—"this is a vault. Just you and me. Got it?"

I hate that I feel emotional, that if I fully let down my guard, I could possibly see myself with watery eyes and a grateful posture of relief. But I hold back. I just nod and whisper, "Thank you."

"You're welcome even though you don't have to thank me." He squeezes my leg in reassurance, then opens the bag from Dee

Dee. "Look at what this angel did for us. She provided us with a bowl and a spoon as well." He takes out the whipped cream can and pops it open only to tilt his head back and squirt some into his mouth. When he looks at me, his mouth is full, cheeks puffed, whipped cream ready to fall out of his mouth.

I chuckle. "That's a great look."

He swallows. "Yeah? Should I make it my new signature? Maybe it's my next influence on the town. Tomorrow, you'll see everyone walking around town with a whipped cream can in their pocket, mouths and cheeks puffed."

"If I do, we are no longer going through with this arrangement. No way in hell will I be able to deal with such an idiotic influencer."

"Then I better put the can down. I can't lose you, not now," he says dramatically. "Not when you're about to make my taste buds scream with delight over this perfect sundae."

"Once again, with the dramatics."

"I'm an author, babe. It's what we do." He winks and then hands me a bowl.

We split the pint of vanilla ice cream, divvy out the hot fudge, which Dee Dee also warmed up for us—seriously, he must be really good friends with these people for them to go to this trouble—and then we top it off with chopped peanuts, whipped cream, cherries, and chocolate sprinkles.

As I lean back with my bowl in hand against the pillows that Wyatt propped up, Wyatt grabs the speaker from the docking station and sets it between us just as the movie begins.

"Have you ever seen this?" he asks.

"It has murder. What do you think?" I reply.

"That would be a yes." He chuckles and then scoops some ice cream into his mouth. "I actually stayed at The Stanley Hotel in Estes Park once."

"That's where the movie takes place, right?" I ask.

"Technically, the inspiration, and before you ask, yes, the place was creepy as shit. It might have been just my head, but I was in there for one night and then told myself no more. Not again, and I fled. I stayed in a nice place on the main strip, devoured an entire tub of English toffee from the candy store, and watched reruns of *Friends* to shed the creep off me."

"Did it work?"

"Partially. I still felt like I had ghost on me for a week later."

"Explains the little streaks of white in your hair."

His mouth falls open in abject horror. "Pardon me?"

I let out a loud laugh, even surprising myself. I point toward his temple and say, "You have a few grays. That's mid-thirties for you."

"Wow, Aubree." He shakes his head at me and dips his spoon into his ice cream. "Just wow. And I thought we were becoming friends, but then you go and say something like that. You know what? I rescind my ice cream."

He reaches for my bowl, but I curl away from him. "You can't take my ice cream. It's mine."

"I can take whatever I want when you insult me with such hideous accusations."

"It's not an accusation, it's facts."

"Facts that you should look past, that you act like aren't there. You don't point them out." His voice grows to a low, comical growl. "You think I don't know about those grays? I try to color them with a Sharpie every morning, but they're not taking to the ink kindly."

"Shut up," I say with a laugh. "You do not."

"I do. I don't think I'm using the right shade. I've put in a color match request with Sharpie, but I'm still waiting on an answer. Told them if they can help a guy out, I will forever and always sign my books with their pens. But right now, Bic's imitation of the Sharpie is looking like my new best friend."

"Wow, quite the story there. Also, have you tried the Bic imitation?"

"Of course not," he scoffs. "Nothing is going to be better than Sharpie. Where's your head at, Rowley?"

I laugh. "Clearly not in the right place."

From the corner of my eye, I catch him running his hand over the hair near his temple, and it makes me laugh some more.

He's just so ridiculous. *I've never known anyone like him.*

And strangely, with every day that goes past, I like it more and more.

"FUCK, I love those twins so much," he says.

"I don't understand how they're so creepy. They're two nice girls in matching blue dresses, but they cause an ungodly shiver to roll up your spine."

"The best kind of shiver," he says. "And the innocent but not innocent factor makes them creepy. Stephen King took an element that seems to be harmless—Danny riding around on his little tricycle, enjoying life—but paired it with sinful music that makes your toenails curl. To then abruptly stop at the end of a hallway because two identical humans are at the end, calling your name . . . It's so easy, so simple, but packs a serious punch."

"Also, you have to mention the knee-high socks. This would be a completely different scene if the knee-high socks weren't involved," I say.

He studies the screen for a moment and then nods. "You're fucking right. The knee-high socks do pack a powerful, frightening punch. Gives that old Victorian picture in the haunted house vibe." I can almost see him making a mental note.

"Going to use that in your next book?" I ask.

"You can bet your pretty little face on it," he says, scooting closer. To my surprise, he pushes me forward, drapes his arm around me, and then settles me back onto him, pulling me in close.

"Uh, what are you doing?" I ask him.

"People are watching, Aubree. Do you really think your ever-charming and handsome boyfriend would let his beautiful and grumpy girlfriend watch two freaky, knee-high sock-wearing twins all by herself without the protection of his arm wrapped around her?"

"I'm assuming the answer is no?"

"You are correct. Now, in a few minutes, you're going to need to slip your hand under the cover of the blanket right to my crotch where you're going to make a motion that looks a lot like—"

"Oh my God, you can't be serious."

He lets out a roar of a laugh so loud that the car next to us tells us to be quiet. He waves an apology toward them and still chuckles near my ear. "No, I'm not serious, but fuck, that reaction was priceless."

"Glad I could entertain."

"You know, though, it might not hurt for you to sit on my lap and make out with me. I know I'm not mac and cheese, but if you can see past that, it might help our image."

"You think making out while watching *The Shining*, one of the creepiest movies ever made, is going to help our image? It's going to make us look like deranged psychopaths who get off on things like murder and creepy twins."

"Umm . . . don't you?" he asks with mirth in his voice.

"No," I say sternly.

He chuckles. "So then what do you think the collective opinion is of the red car over there to the right that is suspiciously rocking back and forth?"

I lift to take a look at the car in question and notice the steamed-up windows and the rocking. "Um, two horny people who apparently can't have sex in their home, so they've chosen a public place to do so."

"Do you have anything against public sexcapades?"

"No," I say as I lean back against his arm. "But I have something against the fact that they kept the speaker in their car. That means they're having sex while listening to the twins calling after Danny."

"Hmm," Wyatt says, thinking about it. "Not sure that would be the soundtrack I'd want while wielding a massive erection."

"Was massive needed in that sentence?" I ask.

"Of course," he replies. "You see, Aubree, by using adjectives, we're able to portray—"

"Skip the English lesson, please. I know why adjectives exist. I just didn't think it was needed at that moment."

"Why?" I can already hear the smile in his voice before he speaks his next words. "Does it make you wonder if my erection is massive?"

"You are so predictable," I say. "I knew you were going to make some sort of sexual innuendo. You seriously have a problem."

"Uh, no, I'm a guy. That's what we do. We think about sex all the time. Hell, I looked at a mailbox this morning and thought about sex."

"How on earth did a mailbox make you think about sex?" I ask, ignoring the movie in front of us.

"Do you really want the rabbit trail?"

"I do," I say.

"Okay, you brought this on yourself." He takes a deep breath. "I was driving around this morning, not going to tell you what exactly I was doing because that is a surprise—and yes, I know you hate surprises, but you will find out soon—anyway, I drove by this house with a mallard mailbox."

"Oh my God, please don't tell me you found sexual desire from a mallard duck?"

"Aubree," he says in a tone that says he's trying to be serious, but I can hear the underlying mirth. "Is your opinion of me that low that you would think I'd get off on the thought of a luscious feathery animal?"

"I don't know . . . maybe?"

"That's insulting. Animals don't do it for me, thanks. But . . . the feathers did remind me of a feather-down pillow."

"Dear God, you humped a pillow."

"No," he says in an annoyed tone, which makes me laugh. "But it reminded me of this hotel I once stayed in that had feather-down pillows. I was so insulted that they'd use such a thing—because you don't even want to know the horror that goes into anything that's feather-down—that I charged right to the manager's office of the hotel."

"And let me guess, you had sex with her."

"Uh, no," he says. "I did not because I didn't make it to her office, not when I slipped on a wet floor, flew up in the air, and landed on my back, throwing out the entire thing. And before you mention anything about me being in my mid-thirties and having old man back issues, this was mid-twenties for me."

"I was still in high school."

"Jesus," he mutters. "Not something to mention." I laugh, and he continues. "Anyway, they called the ambulance, even though I told them that wasn't necessary, and I was taken to the hospital and put on some painkillers. Well, that night, my nurse came in . . ."

"Oh my God, did you have sex with your nurse?"

"No," he says.

"Then my God, Wyatt, where is this story going?"

"You asked for the rabbit trail, and I'm giving it to you." He clears his throat. "The nurse was wearing a carrot pin on her scrubs, which took me back to a moment when I was twenty-one and at a Halloween party. I was dressed as a stoplight, and there was a woman dressed up as a naughty carrot. Her tits were propped up to her chin, and she was—"

"So you did it with a carrot?"

"No." He shakes his head. "She was too drunk, but her friend, who was dressed like a mallard, she and I did it in the bathroom that night."

I lift from where I'm resting on his chest and look him in the eyes. "Why didn't the actual mailbox mallard remind you of the slutty mallard at the Halloween party?"

"Because," he says so casually. "That's not how author brains work."

And then he pulls me back to his chest as if he didn't just expose himself as one of the weirdest humans I've ever met.

After a few seconds, I say, "What am I getting myself into?"

"A world of fun, babe. That's what you're getting yourself into."

━━━

WYATT POPS out of the bathroom, freshly showered and ready for bed. He let me take a shower first, which was nice, and while I was drying off, I heard him tapping away on his computer. I asked him if he came up with a new idea or if he was still reminiscing about the mailbox mallard, but he told me he was just answering some emails from his agent. He also said he'd include his rabbit trail in his next book.

"Surprised you're still awake," he says as he checks the lock on the door—his paranoia makes me slightly intrigued because there's either a backstory behind that or all his research for his books has turned him into a safety officer. When he's satisfied with everything, he slips into bed and turns toward me. "I thought you'd be passed out by now."

"Why would you think that?" I ask.

"Avoidance of the night we shared," he says.

"That doesn't sound like me." He lifts one brow, and that's all it takes to make me smile. "Fine, maybe that is me."

"So what changed?" he asks.

"Nothing." I shrug. "Guess I just didn't think about it."

"Or you were waiting up for me because you had so much fun tonight that you wanted to tell me in person before I drifted off to sleep."

"That's not it," I answer.

"Keep telling yourself that." He brushes a stray hair behind my ear, his fingers lightly caressing my cheek in the process. It makes me wonder what it would be like if this man was actually my real-life husband. Would he act the same way? Would he be as attentive, or is he doing all of this just for show to keep me happy until I say I do?

Even if he was, I can't blame him. There's a lot on the line for both of us.

"I was thinking about something tonight," he says.

"Oh?" I ask.

"Yeah, because well, we're getting married and that will entail a ceremony."

"Yes, that's usually what happens when people get married," I say.

"Which means we're going to have to kiss."

I feel sweat break out on the back of my neck. "Yes, that's something we've mentioned before." His hand slides under the covers to my hip where he gently grips me.

"And I mean nothing sexual about this, and I don't want you to think this is me trying to extend the date, but don't you think we should, I don't know, at least kiss each other good night so we get used to the feel of it?"

"The feel of kissing?" I ask, my nerves starting to shoot up.

"The feel of kissing *each other*."

"Oh . . . uh, why?" I ask even though I know why. I'm just trying to prolong this because I'm so nervous I could actually throw up.

His thumb rubs against my hip in a soothing motion as he says, "So when I kiss you on our wedding day, you're not completely disgusted with me."

"I'm not . . . I'm not disgusted with you," I reply.

"Then how come I can feel you slowly leaning back, farther away from me?"

"Am I?" I laugh nervously. "Oh, didn't realize."

"Don't you think it would be smart to try kissing if we're trying to sell this?"

"I mean, yes," I answer.

"Good," he says. "Then I propose every night before we go to bed, we kiss each other just to get used to the idea. How does that sound?"

I involuntarily wet my lips. "Sounds fine," I say, trying to hide the shake in my voice.

"Okay." And then to my surprise, he pulls me in closer so our knees knock together and our faces are only a few inches apart.

The smell of his soap mixed with his fresh breath hits me all at once as he says, "You ready for this?"

No.

Not even a little.

What if . . . what if he thinks I'm bad at it?

What if he regrets this deal after he kisses me? That would be so humiliating and not something I think I'd recover from.

"Uh, yes." Even though my insides are trembling with nerves.

But there's no stopping him because he leans in closer and then runs his hand up my side until he's lightly touching my jaw.

I hold my breath as he closes the space between us, and when his lips reach mine, I still, my mind whirling as he applies the lightest of pressure.

He's kissing me. Oh my God, he's—he pulls away before I can even reciprocate the kiss.

Oh God.

I had . . . I had dead fish lips.

They weren't even puckered.

"Great," he says as he moves away with a smile. "See, you didn't explode or anything. You're still alive and well." He casually wets his lips . . . probably because the death of mine sucked all the moisture from his. "You didn't get poisoned by my lips." He's trying to make a joke out of it, but I'm still in shock over how fast that was.

I wouldn't have even called it a peck. It was . . . a whisper of a kiss.

"Nope, no, uh, poison," I say, my stomach flip-flopping inside me. "Didn't die."

"Maybe I'm not so bad after all."

"You're not," I say, which makes him smile but, in return, makes me feel weak.

"I think I might be growing on you, Aubree." He smirks and pulls me up against his chest, somehow flipping me to my side at the same time. He curls up against me and holds me, snuggling in close just like the other night.

And as I lie there, slowly relaxing and sinking into his

embrace, I think about that kiss. Maybe next time I won't be so stiff. Maybe next time I'll kiss him back.

If we're going to pull this off, I'll have to kiss him back.

THE NEXT NIGHT . . .

"I've noticed a trend with you," Wyatt says as he checks the lock on the door.

"What's that?" I ask as I plug in my phone and lie flat on the bed, just my head tilted to look at him.

"You tend to wear Almond Store shirts to bed. The color varies, but they're all oversized."

"These are actually the shirts Cassidy ordered when the store first opened. She didn't notice the error on them until Ethel pointed it out when she went to buy one."

"There's an error?" he asks as he slides under the covers and moves toward me. "Where?"

I sit up and straighten my shirt out. "Right here. The 'O' and the 'N' in almond are out of place."

"Oh yeah, look at that." He smiles as he stares down at my shirt. "So did you just take a bunch for sleeping in?"

"Yup, and then we donated the others to a shelter in San Francisco. Hattie took them for us since she was going to school there at the time."

"At least they were put to good use. So I'm guessing that's all you wear?"

"Pretty much. I have a few others I trade out, but these are it."

"I like them. Might steal one for myself."

"Umm, isn't it the wife who's supposed to steal clothes from the husband?"

He holds up one finger. "First of all, really pleased that you referred to our scenario as husband and wife. Clearly, I'm rubbing off on you. Now, we just have to get you to start going on rabbit hole tangents about mallard mailboxes." I chuckle as he holds up a second finger. "And that shirt would fit me. There-fore, I might steal it. Fair game."

"Does that mean I can steal your clothes?" I ask, only teasing.

"Have at it, babe," he says. "Take whatever you want."

"I'm not going to wear your clothes, Wyatt."

"Why not?" he asks. "I'm going to be your husband after all. Might as well take advantage. Although, some shirts are off limits."

"And what would those be?" I ask.

He curls his lips to the side. "Nice try. If I tell you which ones, you'll make it your mission to grab those shirts specifically to wear. Not falling for it."

"I guess you're starting to understand me better."

"Oh, I can read you like a book," he says as he pulls me closer by the hip. "Normally, you don't talk this much, but you know what's coming, so you're procrastinating and prolonging our conversation."

"I . . . I don't know what you mean."

He gives me a *get real* look and moves in closer, cutting down our space to mere inches. "Good night, Aubree." He cups my cheek and very lightly brings his mouth to mine. This time, I'm prepared, and when he kisses me, I kiss him back right before he pulls away. Looking down at me, he smiles but doesn't say anything. Instead, he curls into my back and goes to sleep, leaving it at that.

Okay . . . but . . . was that better for him? Did he notice any improvement? Does he want to do it again tomorrow?

I guess only one way to find out.

———

THE NEXT NIGHT . . .

"You know I already checked the lock on the doors," I say to him as he finishes making sure everything is secure before slip-ping into bed, wearing the same thing he wears every night. A fresh pair of boxer briefs and nothing else. His hair is damp from his shower, and his chest is freshly lotioned—something I wasn't aware men did. But he does, and when the light hits it just right, he glistens.

Not that I've noticed his glistening chest in great detail.

"I won't be able to sleep unless I personally check it," he says as he moves in closer to me. "How was your day? Sorry I didn't make it out to the farm."

"You don't have to come out every day. I told you that. I'm fine."

"I know you're fine, Aubree, but remember, I'm here for support."

"I'm aware, and thank you, but seriously, everything is fine."

"Good," he says, his hand going to my hip like it has the last two nights. "Hey, can I ask you a question?"

"Of course," I say.

"Well, I wanted to check in with you and see where you were with me holding you at night. Wanted to make sure you were okay with that. I know we never talked about it. I just kind of . . . made it happen. Now that it's happened a few nights in a row, I want to make sure you're okay, that you don't want me to stop. Because I will."

"Oh, umm." I wet my lips as he peacefully waits for my answer. His patience and understanding are unlike anything I've ever experienced before. Growing up, my father was anything but patient. He was a tornado, sweeping through the house every night. We were always on high alert, waiting to see what kind of man would appear. Was he going to hurt us? Yell at us? Ignore us altogether?

But with Wyatt, he offers this sense of peace, of structure. I know what to expect from him, at least now that we're in a routine, and it's weird to say, but it's comforting.

I know every morning he'll wake up and work out, usually go for a run. Then he'll take a shower and spend his day either helping around town, visiting Rodney, or working on the farm. At night, he either asks me out to dinner or we spend the evening with the family. He jokes around with Ryland and Hayes and then helps me with the dishes. At night, he takes another shower, he lotions, maybe answers some emails, then he checks the locks and holds me.

It's a routine I'm starting to get used to, that I'm starting to count on.

"Is that a no?" he asks.

"What? No. Sorry," I answer. "Was just thinking. I, um, I'm not good with this kind of stuff, you know that. But I don't mind you holding me at night. So you know, if you want to keep doing it, you can." I shrug, trying to play my answer off as casual.

A light smile tugs on his lips. "Glad to hear it." Then he pulls me in close again, and his hand cups my cheek. "Good night, Aubree."

"Good night," I say right before he brings his mouth to mine once again. I brace myself, and when his lips connect with mine, I kiss him back, but this time, his mouth slightly parts. It's so small, but it's just enough that I follow his lead and do the same. And instead of one peck like the last two nights, this is different. This is a step up in intimacy. This is two kisses molded into one.

It's brief as he pulls away, but it was a small glimpse of what this man could really do with his mouth, and when he pulls me into his chest, I worry for a moment because . . . I think I liked that.

Wait, no, I know I liked that.

I liked it more than I should have.

THE NEXT NIGHT . . .

I curl into my pillow, listening to the sound of Wyatt typing away on his computer. He told me he had to address something and asked if it was okay that he took care of it before bed. I told him it was fine, and I rested in bed for a bit, but as he continued to type away, I started to drift to sleep, so I turned into my pillow, turned off my light, and now I'm resting my eyes just as I hear him click his computer shut.

He moves around the room, checks the locks, then slips into bed, only to slide across the mattress and right up against me, getting in his cuddling position. But instead of resting his head, he leans up on his elbow, hovering over me, and then I feel his hand come around to my jaw. He gently tilts my face in his direction. His strong grip not only sends a euphoric chill through my limbs, but it also creates the right angle for him to lean down and kiss me.

Just like last night, he parts his lips, and I part mine. His mouth works over mine as his hand holds me in place, and I sink into the mattress, relaxing as he kisses me once, twice, three times, and on the last one, his tongue runs across my lips, and I swear on this entire farm that I nearly moan from it.

But luckily, I clamp down on my mouth before I can let out the sound.

It stays trapped inside me, swirling around, making me feel dizzy and chaotic. Warm and fuzzy. Dazed and confused.

That kiss . . . that was short, but the perfect length to entice me.

I don't want to admit this, but God, I want more.

Keeping his head right next to mine, he says, "Good night, Aubree."

"Good night," I answer, but he doesn't move. He hovers above me, and I'm not sure why. Does he want another kiss? I wouldn't be opposed because we're practicing after all.

After a few seconds, he sighs, lowers himself to the bed, and drapes his arm over me.

Why did he pause?

Did I do something wrong?

This bouncing, pulsing energy that has my nerves rattling inside me takes hold of my voice, and before I can stop myself, I ask, "Is everything okay?"

"Yeah," he says, his body moving against mine as he holds me close.

"Are you sure? Because it seemed like you were mad about something."

"I thought you didn't do feelings," he says, his head now buried in my hair.

"I don't, but I just want to make sure that I didn't, you know, do anything wrong."

"Nope," he says simply. "Nothing wrong."

"Like nothing wrong with the kiss?"

"Especially nothing wrong with the kiss," he replies. "That kiss was . . . fuck, it was good."

I feel my cheeks heat as my nipples harden against my shirt from his approval. The praise, the gruffness in his tone, the male satisfaction as he holds me close.

It makes me feel . . . amazing.

Should I be happy about that or not?

AND THE NEXT NIGHT . . .

"How are you in bed before me?" I ask as I pull my hair into a loose bun on the top of my head.

Wyatt's eyes fall to the high hem of my shirt before he moves them back up to my face.

"I took a shower before dinner. I was really fucking dirty from helping Parson out in the field." His eyes roam over me one more time as he wets his lips.

Ignoring his wandering eyes, I slip into bed with him and say, "Parson was happy that you helped him out today. He told me how grateful he was for the help, especially when the tractor got stuck."

"See," he says as he turns toward me. "I am helpful on the farm."

"Never said you weren't helpful," I reply as I cast the room into darkness by turning off my light. "Just that you don't have to be on the farm every day."

"What if I like being on the farm every day?" he asks as his fingers dance down my arm, creating a wave of goosebumps.

"Well, I mean . . . that's, uh . . . that's up to you," I say as a blast of nerves hit me all at once . . . because I know what's coming.

I know what we've been developing over the past few nights.

The intensity has grown.

The countdown in my head until I can slip into bed with him has kicked up.

And today, when I was washing my face and getting ready for bed, I realized that this light, airy feeling in my chest was the anticipation of how he might kiss me tonight.

"Well, I like being on the farm." He dances his fingers down to my wrist where he encircles it and then slowly lifts my hand over my head and pins my wrist to the pillow. "I saw you looking at me through the office window."

"What?" I say breathlessly as he lowers his head. "No . . . no, I wasn't."

"Damn," he says with a devilish grin. "I was hoping to catch you. You didn't watch me at all?"

"I, uh . . ." He brings his face so close our noses are nearly touching. "I was, um . . ." I wet my lips. "Working."

"Maybe next time," he says and then whispers. "Well, good night, Aubree."

"G-good night," I say just before his mouth descends on mine.

At first, he's soft, exploratory, just like last night, but when I think he's going to pull away, he applies more pressure as his mouth opens.

His body leans into mine.

And his mouth opens and closes along with mine, causing my mind to reel and my body to sing.

It's so good.

His kisses are so delicious.

So addictive.

I cup his face softly and mold my lips against his, parting my lips as his tongue connects with mine.

Oh my God, yes.

My grip intensifies as I take a chance and slip my tongue against his.

"Fuuuuck," he mutters as he pulls away and stares down at me, his chest heavy, his eyes searching.

I run my tongue over my lips as I keep my gaze on his. "That . . . uh, was that okay?"

"Yeah, more than okay," he says right before he brings his mouth back to mine. This time, his body sinks into my side, the heaviness of it now falling into me like a weighted blanket. He parts my lips again, and his tongue dances across my tongue, tangling and twisting, our mouths opening wider.

He's so good at this.

His command, his pressure, the feel of him holding me in place but also treating me as if I'm fragile. It's unlike any kiss I've ever experienced. And I don't want it to end.

It's why I move my hand to the back of his neck.

It's why I shift, making more room for him.

It's why I continue to run my tongue over his, causing him to groan softly as he returns the stroke.

This is unexpected, but it's also what I thought might happen tonight. Because the tension every night has been building. The kisses have grown. And now that he has me pinned against this bed, making out with me, using his tongue, making me feel things I don't think I've ever felt, I'm slowly starting to melt.

To accept this.

To be okay with it.

To *want* it.

"Jesus Christ," he says, lifting up and releasing my hand. He stares down at me, his breath heavy, his eyes searching. It takes him a moment, but then he says, "Fuck, I'm sorry, Aubree."

Wait . . . what?

"Sorry?" I ask, feeling confused and disoriented. "Sorry for what?"

He tugs on his hair. "That was . . . fuck, that was too much."

"Oh," I say, feeling foolish.

He's right, that was too much.

Right, this isn't a situation where I should want this or accept it. This is . . . business. What was I even thinking getting lost in his mouth and his hold and everything else that I was just lusting over? "Yeah, I'm sorry too. I don't know what came over me."

"Don't apologize." He shakes his head. "You did nothing wrong."

"Well, it takes two people to kiss."

"It does," he says. "But I'm the one who slipped you the tongue."

"And I slipped it right back."

"Well then, I guess we're both horny motherfuckers who've lost their minds."

I know it's a line that's supposed to make me laugh, but I can't seem to muster up the enthusiastic laugh he deserves. I just smile instead because moments ago, I was feeling something. I was feeling alive. *Which is much more than simply horny.* "I guess so."

He lies flat on his back and takes a deep breath. "Fuck, I'm sorry. It's been a while for me, and I think I just got lost in it."

A while? That seems hard to believe.

"How long is a while for you? Because I bet you it's been longer for me."

"Now that you say that, I think my answer will make you mad."

I turn toward him and prop my head on my hand. "Tell me."

"Over a month." He winces while my mouth falls open.

"Oh my God, that's nothing. Try years, Wyatt."

"Years?" His eyes widen. "How is that possible? You're . . . you're you."

"Exactly, I'm me, and there aren't a lot of people lining up to be with me." *People leave me, pity me, and mock me . . . but do not show sexual interest in me.* And when this man beside me showed interest in a mere kiss, he pulled away and apologized. I think that about sums up how appealing I am to the opposite sex.

He sits up as well to look me in the eyes. "Don't downplay yourself like that, Aubree, as if you wouldn't make any man happy. You're so fucking smart, and loyal, and protective. You're a hard worker and thoughtful."

"Yes, all attributes that scream desire to have sex with me," I say, which makes him flip a switch from complimentary to mad.

His brows turn down.

His face frowns.

And he grows tense as he says, "Those attributes make you sexy, and if a man can't see that, he's a fucking moron. But if we have to relate your physical attributes to what makes you sexy, then you have the nicest, bubbliest ass I've ever seen, your tits are firm and perky and look amazing without a bra, and those lips, Aubree, fuck me can they bring me to my goddamn knees. Your beautiful face? It stuns me, especially when I'm rewarded with one of your hard-won and glorious smiles."

I glance away because I was not expecting that at all. How do I process what he just said?

He hooks his finger under my chin, though, and forces me to look at him. "In case you need me to spell it out for you, it isn't you, it's them."

I swallow, my nerves shaking, my body wanting to curl into him and say thank you . . . my brain wanting to deny everything he's saying. "It's nice of you to say that, Wyatt. But look at what you've had to do to even get me to stop pushing you away. You've had to physically insert yourself into my life. Any other guy would think that's too much trouble."

"Then he's not the right guy, and he doesn't deserve you."

I smile softly, knowing we won't agree on this, so I drop it and turn away from him.

"You don't believe me, do you?" he says, clearly not getting the hint that it's the end of the conversation. "That's fine." He wraps his arm around me and pulls me into his chest. "Looks like I'll just have to prove it to you."

Chapter Fourteen

WYATT

"I'm not going," Aubree says as she gets dressed in the bathroom.

"Aubree Rowley, you are going, and that's final," I say back, raising my voice. I didn't even call her Mrs. Preston, which just shows how serious I am.

She pokes her head out of the door and says, "I don't do town events."

"You do now," I say. "Since you're attached to me, and I do town events."

"Why do you have to be someone who does town events?" she asks as she heads back into the bathroom.

"It was all part of the plan to get people to like me in this town, so I had a backup plan if you tried to run me out of it. That plan was making friends with everyone, which made me a town event person."

She steps out of the bathroom, fully dressed in a pair of green shorts and a matching peach and green top. She pinned her curly hair up into a thick bun with a few tendrils framing her face, and she put on mascara and some light makeup.

"You had a whole plan?"

"Would it even be me if I didn't plot out an entire action plan of how to get your hand in marriage?"

She shakes her head, the slightest smile on those plump lips. "Wow, seems like I had no choice in this matter."

"I would like to say you did, but in reality, you were doomed the moment I waltzed into town."

"Seems like it." She stuffs her phone and her wallet into a tiny purse with a long string. She slips on her sandals, and that's when I take her all in, fully dressed and looking gorgeous.

Hold on a second . . .

"Uh, why are you all dressed up?" I ask.

"I'm not going to a town event in my work boots."

"Wait, so this whole time you were getting ready and giving me shit about how you don't do town events, you were planning on attending the End of Summer Jubilee all along?"

She offers me an evil grin. "Wyatt, would it even be me if I didn't give you a hard time about the things you want to do?"

"Ooo, I see what you did there." I waggle my finger at her. "Clever."

"Thank you. I'll meet you at your vehicle. I have to grab a sweater for Mac. Ryland texted me that she's chilly."

"You were so invested in going that you had organized to take Mac a sweater?"

"Yup." She smirks and then heads out the door to the farmhouse.

We've been bickering all morning about attending the End of Summer Jubilee, and how she's not going. And she planned to attend all along. Christ.

I don't need this kind of stress today.

Do you know why?

Because in my pocket right now is the engagement ring I picked out for her a few days ago, ready to be placed on her finger with the help from a few people in town, Ethel leading the parade.

The last thing I need is for Aubree to stay home. Although, if it came down to it, I would have dragged her out of here like a sack of potatoes over my shoulder. I have no problem doing that.

I lock up the guest house, and while Aubree heads into the farmhouse, I wait for her at my SUV. I drag my hand over my face and think about this past week. The progress I've made with her, the jokes and laughs we've shared over dinner . . . our new nighttime ritual, a ritual that I sort of wish wasn't just a night-time thing because fuck, those lips.

I'm addicted to them.

And today is evidence of that because when she walked out of the bathroom just now, they were all glossy and begging for me to taste them again. I know that's the last thing I should be thinking about. She's supposed to be a friend, a business partner, not my own personal make-out buddy.

But fuck me, I can't stop myself.

And the whole idea behind the kissing was so that she could be less stiff around me, especially with what I have planned today. But the only thing stiff between us now is my goddamn cock.

Morning showers have been fun, but nighttime showers are a requirement. I say I'm washing the stink away when, in reality, I'm stroking myself, trying to get my head straight before I jump in bed and start kissing her.

So why not stop the kissing? Well, for one, I like it too damn much. And two, the last thing I need is for her to be tense when I propose. I need her to kiss and hug me and act like it's the best thing that's ever happened to her.

You must be wondering why I am not cluing her in on the proposal. *I do know she hates surprises.* But I want a genuine reaction from her. Call me crazy, but I haven't been too impressed with her acting skills. I want people around us to feel her surprise and, even though she might not love me and this is all for show, I know that when she does say yes and she kisses me, it will be believable—because we've been practicing.

The first kiss, I know she was scared.

The second, well, she kissed me back, and I felt a zing of lust rush up the backs of my legs.

The third, hell, I was enamored because she gave me more.

And after that, it's felt like a frenzy I couldn't control. And I know she feels it too because she's returning the same kisses. But last night was too much. My hand was seconds away from running up her shirt to her breast. I was ready to take it to the next level even though that's not what we're supposed to be doing.

Aubree pops out of the house and heads down the stairs, looking irritated. "Uh, everything okay?" I ask.

"I need to change."

"Why?" I ask just as I look down and see a giant red paint stain on the front of her shorts. "How did that happen?"

"Let's just say Mac isn't good at cleaning up. Be right back."

"Okay," I say.

As she walks away, I text Ethel.

Wyatt: *Running slightly behind. Aubree had to change, got paint on her clothes. Everyone still in position?*

Ethel: *We're good over here.*

Wyatt: *Awesome, thank you.*

Ethel: *Do you have the ring?*

Wyatt: *In my pocket.*

Ethel: *Good. Now leave the rest to us.*

Wyatt: *See you soon.*

I pocket my phone and am surprised to see Aubree approaching. Instead of her shorts and shirt, she's now wearing a light blue sundress with sleeves. The blue makes her eyes pop, and the dress's silhouette highlights her every curve.

Jesus, she's beautiful.

How she thinks she's not a catch is beyond me. Any man would be fucking lucky to call her his. And here I am, stealing her away for a year. Maybe by the end of it, I'll help boost her self-confidence so she won't second-guess her worth when she decides to venture out into the dating world again.

"You look great, Aubree."

She tugs on her dress. "It isn't too short?"

"No," I say as I peer around her to check out her ass. "Seems perfect to me."

"If my skirt blows up during this event, you will be responsible."

"Why am I responsible?" I ask as I open the door for her.

"Because you're making me go to this thing."

"Stop, you were going anyway." I tug on her seat belt and hand it to her. "Buckle up, babe."

Then I move around to the other side of the SUV and hop in.

Just to test the waters and see how comfortable she is, I place my hand on her thigh and glance at her.

"Uh, what are you doing?" she asks, clearly not accepting my audacity.

"Attempting to prepare you for affection." I smooth my thumb over her inner thigh, and she swats my hand away, laughing.

"That tickles, you can't do that."

"Your inner thigh tickles?" I ask as I put my hand back where it was.

"Yes, very ticklish, so don't."

"Interesting." I rub my thumb again, and she shifts her leg.

"Wyatt, stop, or I'll end up punching you out of survival, and I don't think you want that, do you?"

"I'm not opposed to love taps."

"This would not be a love tap. This would be a full-on fist to the face."

"Ouch." I chuckle as I turn onto the main road that leads to town. "That seems rather brutal." I place my hand back on her thigh, but I don't move my thumb this time. "What about hand-holding? Where are you with that? Still on the same page?"

"I don't know," she says, unsure.

"It's fine if you don't want to hold my hand, but maybe you can loop your arm through mine, something like that, which keeps us close together but doesn't require you to do something you don't want to do."

"I can do that."

"Perfect. I was also thinking that you can sit on my lap when we sit down."

"That shouldn't be too difficult to stomach."

"Funny," I deadpan, which makes her chuckle. "And then there's the whole scene I have in my head where we get caught making out by the inn. Serious tongue action, possibly some inappropriate groping—"

"That won't be happening."

I laugh at the disgusted sound in her voice. "Wow, the only other thing that would have suggested you were disgusted at the mere thought of us making out was if you threw up in your lap."

"Almost did. Good thing I have control of my gag reflex."

My eyes shoot to her playful ones, and I can't help but laugh.

This is the real Aubree. When she isn't hiding behind a wall, behind her feelings—behind the world that once crumbled around her—this is the woman we get to see. Playful and fun. Witty and sarcastic. If this continues, it's going to be a really fucking easy year.

I clear my throat and say, "Uh, gag reflex, huh?"

"Oh my God, you're such a guy."

"Guilty," I say. "But do you blame me?"

"Yes, I do. You could have easily not made a comment. You could have been sophisticated and moved past it."

I scoff. "Babe, if there is one thing you need to know about me, it's that I'm anything but sophisticated."

"Very true," she says. "I don't think anyone who writes about a killer fucking his prey right before slashing her throat could be sophisticated."

"It was a consensual fuck. The throat slicing, well, that was because she was a cuddler, and he wasn't. She had to go. But hot scene, right?"

"Weirdly, yes."

I tap my temple. "All from up here and experience."

"I'm hoping the fucking part was from experience and the murder part was from your head."

"An author never tells." I catch her twist her lips as she stares me down, causing me to laugh. "Fine, the fucking part was all real. The murder part was a fantasy."

She shakes her head. "You have so many issues."

"But here you are, letting me touch your thigh and discussing your gag reflex. So am I the one with the issues, or are you?"

"You," she replies, making me laugh again as we turn and see cars lined up all along the street. Thankfully, we can park behind The Almond Store in the private parking section, something I discussed with Ethel since she warned me that it would be crazy down here.

She was right.

Once parked, Aubree and I get out together, and I offer her my arm. She loops her arm through mine, and we head over to the inn, where the main event is happening. See, we don't have to hold hands to look like a couple. We got this.

Cars take up every parking spot on the side of the road as well as parking lots and even side streets. Music blasts from the inn's lawn while the sound of generators blowing up bounce houses can be heard in the far distance. Flower garlands are draped from lamp posts to the shops up and down the street to the business signs. Every shop in town has their doors open, welcoming floods of customers. I underestimated the town's population because, holy fuck, am I going to propose in front of all these people?

What the hell was I thinking?

Ethel didn't mention how big this event was going to be. I just assumed a few townspeople milling about, catching up on the latest gossip while sharing a drink and snacks. But this . . . this is something else.

It's what some might call a hullabaloo.

Food trucks, drink stands, and vendors line up along the inn's lawn. Ropes and cones are blocking entrances, directing the crowd to the flow of traffic. Maps are being handed out, live music is playing, and those blown-up wind men who you usually find outside car dealerships, but for some reason, they're flanking Five Six Seven Eight, catching the attention of everyone in town.

"Wow," I say. "This is not what I expected. A lot of people are here."

"Exactly why I don't like coming to these things, but here you are, trying to be the best friend of the town. Look what you got us into."

I chuckle. "Yeah, this was my mistake."

This was a big mistake.

"You know, it's never too late to turn around," she says.

Tempting, very tempting.

I shake my head. "Can't turn around now because I told Ethel I'd be here. And if there is one person in town I can't disappoint, it's Ethel."

"It's scary that you know that already."

"Like every good author, I do my research to determine what I'm getting myself into." *Except how big this festival was. Clearly.*

We make our way to the inn and walk through the front door, heading straight for the back lawn where a dance floor is set up along with a stage and a full band, Hayes being the lead guitarist. How the hell did Ethel make that happen?

From the look on his face, I'm going to guess he's not too thrilled about being up there as he strums along to a cover of *Why Do Birds Suddenly Appear.* Yikes, I hope he's not up there because of me. If he is, I'm going to owe him big time.

And just like out front, the area is packed. Circles of people are everywhere, hovering over high-top tables, firepits, and picnic tables. Some people dance, and others wait in line for food while kids run around like maniacs, chasing each other.

So many people.

Tons and tons of people.

Yeah, this was a huge mistake.

There is no way Aubree will cope with being surprised in front of all these people. I need to tell her what's going on. Give her a heads-up.

"You know, I actually need to tell you something," I say,

turning toward her.

"If it's about the murder sex thing, I really don't want to know."

"No, it's not about that," I say. "I actually, uh—"

"Aunt Aubree!" Mac yells as she runs up to us, wearing a cute pair of pink overalls. Her hair's tied up into wonky pigtails. "You're here. You're here."

"I am," Aubree says with a laugh.

"Come dance with me."

Aubree cringes. "Ooo, you know, that's not something I know how to do well."

"Yes, you do." Mac pouts. "You're the best dancer."

"Yeah, go and show off your dance moves," Ryland says, joining us. "Show the town the dance moves you do with Mac in the kitchen."

Aubree gives him a death stare as she tosses Mac's sweater at him. "Those dance moves are not for the public."

"Why not?" Ryland smiles. "They're so good."

"Yeah, they're so good." Mac bounces up and down. "Come on, Aunt Aubree. Pwease!"

Oh hell, good luck saying no to that.

Aubree sighs in capitulation and takes Mac's hand. "Okay, but you better dance with me."

"Why wouldn't I?" Mac says as they take off toward the dance floor.

"She's a good aunt," I say, watching her walk away as Ethel starts her next song.

That's when Ryland turns to me and says, "So Ethel told me you're proposing."

Christ. I nearly choke on my own saliva. I was not expecting him to say that.

"She . . . she told you?" I ask.

"Yeah, she did. Told me you were planning a proposal and that I needed to be here." From the stern set of his eyebrows, I guess he's not too happy about finding out about the proposal through Ethel.

Call me crazy, but I assumed Ethel would sing a love song, and I'd propose afterward. I didn't think she was going to tell Ryland. That means she definitely told Hayes. Who else did she tell?

"Uh, yeah. I was planning on proposing," I say, pulling on the back of my neck. "Is that, uh, is that okay?"

He looks me in the eyes and in a very serious tone, asks, "You tell me. Do you love her?"

Man, do I hate lying to him, but at this moment, I know I need to pull out an award-winning performance.

"I do," I say, giving him the same eye contact. "Very much so. And I know it might seem soon to you, but I just don't want to wait around. We've both talked about wanting to get married, so I figured, why wait?"

Ryland slowly nods. He looks out toward where Aubree and Mac dance together. Aubree moves their arms up and down while Mac jumps and twists, her legs flailing about. Even though Aubree made it quite clear she's not a dancer, the smile on her face and the way she looks at Mac shows me that there is so much more to Aubree than she likes to show. She has many layers, and when you get to the very core, the heart of her, it's easy to see she's such a beautiful, loving soul.

"She's been through a lot, Wyatt. As someone who has lost a sibling, I know you can understand that."

"I can," I say. "And I know she's been treated poorly in the past." I'm very aware I don't know the extent. "I know how fragile yet strong she is, and I have no intentions of breaking her or hurting her."

"Good," Ryland says as he places his hand on my shoulder and then turns to me. "Because if you fucking hurt her, not only will I hurt you but Hayes and the rest of this fucking town will too. Got it?"

Jesus . . .

"Yes," I say.

"Okay then." He nods toward the back of the inn. "Rodney is waiting for you."

"What do you mean?" I ask.

"He has his train ready. Ethel said you'd be coming in on his train while she sings *At Last.*"

"Uh, that's not what was discussed," I say, glancing toward Ethel, who seems to be giving us a dangerous look, one that says *get a move on.*

"Well, that's what she told me. You are to be unveiled by a train."

"I don't want to be unveiled by a train. I just want to propose, simple as that."

Ryland claps me on the shoulder and says, "You involved a former Broadway star in your proposal. Did you really think it was going to be a simple proposal?"

"I did," I answer.

"Fool." Ryland shakes his head. "Dude, you're being unveiled by a train."

"This is not what I asked for." I glance behind us. "Is there really a train back there? Because I didn't ask for one. I don't even have any likeness toward trains. We never discussed anything about a train," I say with a slight panic because if a train is involved, what else is involved? Are there train sounds? Are there outfits? Is there a whole Broadway number planned? And I didn't tell Aubree, and she's out on the dance floor. What the hell am I supposed to do?

"Really? She made it seem like you were all in on the train," Ryland says. "Very excited about the train."

"Not all in on the train," I say. "Think we can skip the train?"

Ryland shakes his head. "No, I don't think there's any skipping the train. Ethel has this thing mapped out, which, by the way, why the fuck did I have to hear it from her? Why didn't you tell me what was going on, or Hayes, for that matter, since you two have been talking?"

Yeah, why didn't you do that, Wyatt? Maybe because you're an idiot and didn't think this all the way through. I didn't think about Ethel's dramatic side. I didn't consider the family. I didn't think about the possibility of an entire town plus all their friends and family being here. Given that this isn't a real relationship between Aubree and me, I didn't think about the steps I'd take if I planned on marrying someone for love. The only reason I'm doing a big proposal is for the show of it, so if Wallace ever asks around.

I didn't consider the family's feelings—a huge miss on my end.

"Shit, man, I'm sorry," I say. "I guess I was just so wrapped up in this jubilee proposal that I completely forgot to talk to you and Hattie about it. I promise that moving forward, that won't happen again."

"Good," he says. "And good that you can admit to your shortcomings and mistakes. That will bode well for you when you're married to Aubree. She's very strong-willed."

Uh, yeah. Found that out on day one.

"She is, one of my favorite things about her." A clearing of a throat is projected through the microphone, and when we both look up, we find Ethel staring at us with daggers ready to fly from her eyes right at us.

"Better get in the train," Ryland says.

"But I don't want to get into the train. I actually need to talk to Aubree for a moment."

"Sorry, no can do, you have to get in the train. That was my job, to get Mac to distract Aubree and to get you to the back."

"I understand, but I just have to say something to her real quick."

"Nope." Ryland pushes me toward the back. "To the train you go."

"Ryland, seriously."

"Seriously," he says back with strong conviction. "You get back there, or else Ethel is going to have my head, and do you really want to do that to Mac, have her lose another important person in her life? Now. Get. Back. There," he says, shoving me along until I'm moving in the direction he wants me to go. "You don't want Ethel on your bad side."

"No, I don't, but—"

"No buts, get in that train." He gives me one last shove. I'm fighting a losing battle. So I follow the path to the back of the inn only to stop dead in my tracks.

What the actual fuck?

More people.

So many people.

But instead of milling about on the lawn, drinking and eating and having a merry old time, these people are lined up, all wearing green leotards and bonnets in the shape of flowers. They're stretching, cracking their necks, and practicing dance moves.

This can't be real.

I tentatively walk forward, taking in every long-sleeved leotard and colorful flower bonnet until I see it, right there, plain as day.

A train.

But not just any train. A kiddie caboose. You know the type of trains that you see in the mall, carting around unruly children? Yeah, that kind of train, and sitting proudly at the engine is none other than Rodney, dressed in a pair of blue-and-white-striped conductor overalls, matching hat, and red bandanna tied around his neck. With the joy in his expression and the pride in his chest, this man is ready to deliver the future groom to his bride.

Jesus Christ, I should have discussed Ethel's plans with her.

Why are people dressed as flowers?

Why are there *so many people*?

Is this a whole Five Six Seven Eight production? Will there be the snapping of thumbs? Possible jazz hands?

Will there be a pas de bourrée?

I don't even know what that is, but will there be one? Am I required to do one? I can barely do a kickball change.

"You're here," Rodney says. "Finally. Get in the back." He thumbs toward the caboose.

"Uh, I'm a little confused," I say. "What exactly is happening here?"

"He arrived? Where is he?" Dee Dee spots me and heaves a sigh of relief. "My God, what took you so long?" She's sporting a clipboard and a headset, looking all kinds of official. "Get in the back of the train. The music is about to start."

She pushes me toward the back of the train while a few people dressed up as flowers step into the other carts. Will this thing be able to tote all of us? Seems questionable.

"Can I ask what's going on?" I ask. "I thought Ethel was just going to sing a song, and I'd propose to Aubree, but now there's a train and people and, wait . . . are those confetti cannons?"

"Yes, with biodegradable confetti. Now sit down."

"Wait, I don't understand what's happening."

"It's called the proposal of a lifetime, Wyatt."

"But—"

She walks off before I can ask more questions.

Leaning forward, I tap a leotard-clad woman on the shoulder and say, "Pardon me, miss, but do you know what's going on?"

She glances over her shoulder and looks me up and down. "If you don't know what's going on, then that's a big problem." And then she turns back around.

Helpful.

I drag my hand over my face as I sit in this tiny train, all crouched in together. My knees to my nipples.

Yup, Aubree is going to kill me.

Kill me dead.

Dee Dee starts shushing the crowd, quieting them down just as Ethel's voice singing *At Last* filters to the back of the inn.

"That's our cue," Dee Dee says. "First group, go."

A wave of purple flower bonnet dancers extend their legs and start floating toward the lawn, leaping in the air. I lean to the left, dangerously testing the balance of my caboose as I attempt to get a view of what's happening. If I just lean a touch more . . . yup, I spot her. Aubree. She's standing in the middle of the dance floor all by herself, looking confused as flower people start circling her.

Hattie has joined Hayes on stage and stands behind him, her arm looped around his shoulders as he plays. A crowd starts to form, and oh my God, Aubree is going to murder me when this is all over.

The music picks up, and more of the dancers file out onto the main lawn on Dee Dee's direction.

"And smile. And smile. And smile," Dee Dee says while making a smile motion with her finger. "That's it. Remember your positions."

Can I ask what my position is, because if I knew things were going to be this extravagant, I would have, for one, said no, and if I didn't get my way, I would have at least asked to be a part of the rehearsal. I had plenty of time to rehearse this week. And if I didn't, I would have made time because right about now, I'm feeling all sorts of nervous.

Not because I'm afraid she's going to say no, but because I'm terrified I'm going to humiliate myself.

Humiliate her.

For the love of God . . . humiliate Ethel!

"And go train," Dee Dee says.

Wait, what?

Go train?

Rodney starts the train, and we jolt forward.

"Jesus," I mutter as I grip the handle in front of me.

"You ready?" Dee Dee asks as I start to move toward her.

"No," I say. "What's happening? What do I do?"

"If you don't know what you're doing in that caboose, then I can't help you." She holds her headset and says, "And go train."

We jolt forward again, this time picking up the pace as we head right out to the dance floor.

And I can guarantee you I've never felt more ridiculous in my entire life as I sit in the back of this kiddie train with my knees practically up to my neck because my large body is not supposed to fit into a small cart like this. Dancers move around with petals in their hands, starting to cover me as they walk along the train, indicating there will be a grand reveal.

That's me. I'm the grand reveal.

The prize at the end of this drama piece.

Yup, Aubree is going to murder me in my sleep tonight. There's no doubt about it.

Ethel coos into the microphone, her voice carrying through the cliffs that lead to the ocean. And even though I'm terrified about what will happen next, I can admit that Ethel's voice is actually really good. A part of me assumed that the quirky former Broadway star now inn owner wouldn't quite live up to the hype, but she does. I'm really impressed.

But enough about Ethel, back to me.

Still covered by what I can only assume are felt petals attached to a dowel, the train moves around in a circle on the dance floor. Around and around we go until . . . we come to a stop.

The music dies down, leading into instrumentals.

And then . . . the petals lift, and I am revealed. Like a fat man in a tiny suit—get the reference? But instead, I'm the six-foot-three man in the kiddie train caboose.

I look around, taking in the scene unfolding in front of me. A crowd has circled the dance floor. Ryland and Mac are near the stage, right next to Hayes and Hattie. Abel is to the left as well, standing next to Echo. Loads and loads of dancers are lying on the ground, their flower heads acting as a pathway to the one and only red-faced Aubree standing a few feet away, her hands clutched together, her nostrils flared.

When our eyes meet, her eyes narrow, indicating her displeasure. But it's so brief that I think I'm the only one who catches it before she plasters on a smile. A smile so bright that if I didn't know any better, I'd be convinced that Aubree is thrilled to see me. Huh, maybe her acting skills aren't as bad as I thought.

As the music softens, Ethel steps down from the stage and approaches us, holding the microphone.

I look at her.

She looks at me.

And when I don't move, she slowly mouths, "Get. Out."

Oh right.

Remove myself from the train.

That's if I can get out of this thing.

My feet seem to be stuck in the confined space, so I do a little shimmying back and forth. I place my hands on the edges of my seat and lift, popping my rear end out and unfolding my legs to a stand.

There we are.

With a smile on my face, I step out of the train with one leg, and just as I start to step out with the other, Rodney jolts the train forward—most likely assuming that I've extracted myself already—and I lose my balance, tumble forward, and land face first onto the dance floor.

The crowd makes a resounding *ooooo* sound as my chin scrapes across the not-so-smooth parquet tiles.

Motherfucker, that hurt.

"Oh God," Aubree says as she steps forward, but I hold out my hand to stop her.

"I'm . . . I'm fine," I grunt as I stand quickly, my chin and my ego the only things that are bruised.

"Where's your shoe?" Ethel asks from the side of her mouth.

"Huh?" I ask.

"Your shoe," she says, staring down at my foot.

I glance down, and lo and behold, my shoe is not on my foot. I look up to where the train is departing and say, "It must be in the train."

"Dear God in Heaven," Ethel murmurs and then says into the microphone, "Rodney, stop the train."

He stops it and looks at Ethel, confused.

"His shoe is in there. Can someone grab his shoe? He needs his shoe," Ethel says in an annoyed tone.

One of the flower ladies reaches into the caboose of the train and pulls out my shoe. She tosses it to the girl next to her, who drops it but then picks it up quickly and tosses it to the next person. And like an assembly line of footwear, my shoe is delivered to me.

I hold it close to my side, waiting for what's to come.

"What on earth are you doing?" Ethel asks. "Put it on."

"Right," I say before fumbling to put my shoe on. Once all footwear has been secured, I smile at Ethel, who nods and motions for me to proceed toward Aubree.

This is it.

This is the moment.

Settled and confident—false confidence—I reach into my jeans pocket for the ring and . . .

Wait, where is the ring?

I feel around in my pocket, coming up short.

"Do you have the ring?" Ethel asks through clenched teeth.

"I thought I did." I pat my pockets and then reach into them again.

Oh God, the ring was in there. Did it fall out when I tumbled out of the train?

I start searching the ground, looking around, scanning, but I don't see anything.

"This isn't funny," Ethel says. "You're ruining the moment."

Don't need the added pressure, Ethel!

"I thought I had it in my pocket. I put it . . ." My finger grazes over something metal when my fingers search my pocket once more. "Oh wait, here it is." I pull it out, and I lift it to show Ethel. The crowd around us cheers, congratulating me on my stupidity.

Meanwhile, Aubree stands there, frozen, watching me look like an absolute fool.

Isn't she lucky?

Clearing my throat, completely ready now, I kneel on one knee and hold the ring up to her as if I'm Rafiki, showing Simba off to Pride Rock.

Ethel steps forward and holds the microphone up to my mouth so the entire town can hear me confess my fake love to this woman who looks like she would like to crawl into her own dress.

And yes, as I look up at the way she tugs on the corner of her lip with her teeth and the blush in her cheeks, I realize this wasn't the best idea I've ever had. Everyone quiets down and waits for me to make a grand speech about my undying love for this woman. You know, sometimes as an author, you create these large scenes in your head, thinking it will be one of the greatest things you ever write, that it will add brilliantly to the storyline you're creating, but when they play out, they might not go as planned. They might fall flat.

They might end up terribly on the page.

And for me, it might not be executed the way I initially thought.

This is easily one of the weirdest, most embarrassing things I've ever been a part of.

But I go with the flow because, if anything, I'm flexible.

Hopefully, Aubree is too.

"Aubree," I say as I feel myself wobble from being on my knee longer than I want and holding up this damn ring. I should have talked to her first and then gotten down on my knee. Mistakes. All mistakes. "When I heard that I was part owner of the Rowley farm, I had no idea that deed would open me up to a love I've been looking for all my life."

"Aw," the crowd all coos together.

At least I have them on my side.

"Our first conversation was, well, angry at best." Chuckles. Yup, they're invested. "Our second was much different. I got to know you better, you got to know me, and quickly, you became who I wanted to talk to in the morning, during the day, and at night before bed. I found myself falling for someone I never saw coming. And now that I have you in my life, now that I can call you mine, call you my love, I never want to let go of that."

I shift on my knee, my arms burning from holding up this damn ring.

Aubree just stares down at me—still in shock, still blushing.

Please, Jesus, let her say yes. After all of this, let her say yes.

"So, Aubree Rowley, will you do me the greatest honor and be my wife?"

It takes her one second longer than I prefer to answer, but

when she does, she nods, and the crowd erupts in jubilation around us.

Ethel takes the microphone and shouts, "She said yes!"

More cheering sounds off.

The confetti cannons blast into the air.

And the music starts up again, this time playing an instrumental version of *Marry Me* by Bruno Mars.

On shaky legs, I stand just as Aubree goes to kneel. Together, we look like an engagement seesaw because when she starts to stand again, I go back down.

Urgh.

"Stay there," I say to her as I stand.

Everyone continues to cheer as I reach for her hand, but at the same time, she tries to wrap her arms around me for a hug, so I poke her in the stomach instead, causing me to drop the ring.

Christ.

I bend back down to pick it up, and I don't know what the hell she's thinking, but as I stand, she kneels again.

Motherfucker.

I snag her hand and pull her to her feet. I grip her finger, slip the ring on, and then hold up her hand for everyone to see. The crowd erupts again, still happy for us, despite the awkward display we just put on for everyone.

Some people shout, "Kiss!" while others clap and cheer.

Knowing we need to seal the deal, I smile down at her and try to put my arms around her, but at the same time, she lends her hand out for what I can only assume is a handshake.

Her fingers brush over my nipple as I bend down to hug her.

Her fingers bend back against my chest.

And there we are, my ass sticking out as I attempt to hug her, her trying to handshake my erect nipple.

This is not how I imagined this.

Whispering, I say, "What are you doing?"

"I don't know," she whispers back. "Should I kneel again?"

"For the love of God, no. Just hug me."

And thankfully, that's what she does. She wraps her arms around my back, I wrap mine around her shoulders, and we embrace.

For the hell of it, I kiss the top of her head and then raise my fist to the sky in victory, erupting the crowd all over again.

Well, that was . . . eventful.

Just as I start to let go of her, I hear a throat clear next to me, and I glance to the side to find Ryland standing there, holding Mac, waiting to congratulate us.

"You're getting married," Mac chants. "Can I see the ring?" Aubree holds the ring up to Mac, and Mac brings Aubree's finger close to her eye to examine it. "It's so pretty."

"Thank you," Aubree says.

"Congrats, sis," Ryland says. "Still trying to wrap my head around all of this. I didn't even know you were in love or even seeing anyone last week, and now you're engaged. Insane, but I told Wyatt if he hurts you, he's a dead man."

That shakes the confusion and shock out of Aubree because she chuckles. No longer wide-eyed and nervous being surrounded by her family. "Get in line. I'm not afraid to wield a shovel if he wrongs me."

And I fully believe that.

"Why would Uncle Wyatt hurt Aunt Aubree?" Mac asks.

"He wouldn't," Ryland says. "We're just joking."

"It's not nice to joke about hurting someone," Mac replies.

Ryland lets out a deep sigh, the kind of sigh every parent lets out at least once a day just as Hattie and Hayes join us as well. "I know, I'm sorry. I won't joke about it again."

"Your apology is accepted. Can we get cotton candy?" Mac asks, jumping up and down again.

"Didn't you already have a lollipop?" Ryland asks.

"Yes, but I want cotton candy now."

"How about we find something with protein?" Ryland says.

"Does cotton candy have protein in it?" Mac asks.

"No." Ryland shakes his head, and she pouts.

"I think I've had enough protein today. I don't need any more."

"Nice try," he says as he takes her hand in his. "Congrats, you two. I'll catch up a little later." He takes off, hand in hand with Mac, and all I can think of is how grateful I am that Ryland is in charge of her. I'm not sure I would have been able to step up to the plate like he did. He has the necessary patience required to raise such a young child.

Hattie and Hayes are next as they step up to congratulate us. Hattie pulls Aubree into a hug, and Hayes lends his hand out to me. I give it a firm shake as he says, "You just upped the ante on the proposal. Not sure I can top that. Someone else will be expecting something soon." He nods toward Hattie, and I laugh.

"Take your time and do it right. No need to rush. Also, Rodney has a train if you want to use it."

Hayes laughs. "You looked pretty sick in that thing, man. Like a man on his steed, riding into the sunset."

"I could tell you were envious." I rub my hands together. "Not everyone can look as cool as me."

"Very cool." He smiles, and then with a brow raised, he asks, "I have to ask, was there a reason you rushed into a proposal? Just curious."

"If you're implying something, the answer is no. We just want to be married is all."

"Are you assuming I'm pregnant?" Aubree asks, joining the conversation.

Hayes holds up his hand. "Not assuming anything, just, you know, making sure. Always good to have all the information."

"We're not," Aubree says.

"Shame," Hattie says. "I would have loved a shotgun wedding." She then pulls me into a hug and congratulates me. "I'm happy for you two. Now let me see the ring."

Aubree holds up her hand, and Hattie takes it. She examines the ring for a few seconds before she looks up at me. "Wyatt, I don't think I could have picked anything more perfect for her. This is . . . this is stunning."

Huh, maybe I know more about Aubree than I think I do.

Aubree glances down at the ring, then back at me. "It really is perfect."

Perfect, huh?

Some might count that as a win for me.

The train might have been a large loss. Along with the tumble out of it. The chin scrape and the seesaw attempt at a hug, but the ring . . . the ring is a win.

But I'm wondering, because Aubree has been pretty good at faking this entire endeavor, if she truly means it when she says the ring is perfect or if she's acting. Not that it matters, but you know, just for ego's sake, it would be nice to know if that comment was genuine.

"Thanks. When I was looking through all of the rings, I had something simple yet elegant in my mind. When I saw that one, it immediately reminded me of you."

That's not a lie. That's facts.

It felt like an Aubree ring.

Hattie clasps her hands together. "Isn't that just beautiful? They're so cute together. So perfect and right for each other. An opposites attract kind of thing, like me and Hayes. But you know, Hayes and I have been together longer, not that it matters, but we have, and sure, we live together, and so do you, but we've been living together longer. And if you're wondering if I'm saying all of this because I'm jealous that Wyatt proposed before Hayes, I'm not. Not even a little. I think it's great, especially since we just found out about you guys. Nope, not jealous. Thrilled actually. I'm so happy for you and not even the least bit jealous. Not even a tiny bit."

Hattie did not pick up on Aubree's acting skills. Because I'd say she's totally jealous.

"Hattie . . ." Hayes says.

She glances over her shoulder, a scowl in her eyes. "Yes?"

He pulls on the back of his neck, looking visibly uncomfortable. "It, uh, it seems like you might be slightly jealous."

Wow, dude. I even know to keep those kind of thoughts held in. Why does he think saying that out loud will help anyone?

"I'm not jealous of my sister. She deserves happiness," Hattie says. "I'm fine over here. Not irritated with you at all. If I think about it, I honestly don't even want to get married, no offense to you guys. But marriage, ew, gross. I don't want to be tied down to someone for life. I like having the option of just upping my life and running to whoever has their arms open and ready for me."

And now she's playing with fire.

"Excuse me?" Hayes says, falling right for her trap. These Rowley women are not to be messed with. "Can we have a moment?"

Proud of herself, Hattie walks off with Hayes.

Glad I'm not a part of that conversation. Nope, I have a happy fiancée, ready to . . . uh, why is Aubree looking at me like that?

Like she has murder on her mind but is masking it with the maniacal smile plastered across her lips.

Uh, Hayes, actually, can you bring that conversation back here?

Speaking softly even though we're alone, she asks, "What the hell was that?"

"Your sister? Oh, I think that was her—"

"The proposal, Wyatt."

Yup, that's what I thought she was talking about, but you see, always deflect at first. Clearly, it didn't work this time.

"Oh that." I place my hands on her hips, acting as if we're having an intimate moment. She's a loose cannon, and I have no doubt that my balls are at high risk right now. "That was not how it was supposed to go."

"And how was it supposed to go exactly?"

"Funny story," I say.

"I can already feel myself laughing," she deadpans.

Yikes.

Swallowing hard, I say, "Well, the train and the dancers and the confetti cannons were not my idea. That was all Ethel. When I thought about proposing, I asked her for some assistance. I thought it would just be her singing to us, but, well, she went a bit over the top. Dee Dee was involved. She had a whole headset and everything. I'm still trying to figure out who she was communicating with. Anyway, this was all on her, so don't hate me."

Aubree looks over at Ethel, who is back on stage, smiling and waving at us. We wave back.

"And that's what makes you new to town," Aubree says. "You never get Ethel involved in planning anything. It will only end badly."

"This didn't end badly. This ended up great for me. You said yes, and the whole town saw it."

She smooths her hand up my chest and speaks closely. "Yes, but you fell out of a kiddie train, scraped your chin, lost the ring, found the ring, and looked green the entire time. Not to mention, you have yet to meet my wrath when we're in private."

"Ooo." I shiver. "Don't tease me with a good time."

She rolls her eyes and pushes away from me. "You're so annoying."

A DECENT FIRE sparks in front of us as Aubree, Hayes, Hattie, Abel, Echo, Ryland with a sleeping Mac on his chest, and I all form a circle around one of the firepits at the inn. It's been a long afternoon turned into evening, and nearly everyone in town congratulated us. We spent a good half hour talking to Ethel, complimenting her and thanking her. She took pictures with us and then went around, boasting about how she was able to pull off the most epic proposal ever. Her words, not mine.

Pretty sure the train entrance brought down the epic-ness a notch or two.

Hattie sits on Hayes's lap, Echo and Abel are next to Ryland while Aubree sits next to me, holding a stick and poking the fire every once in a while.

"So any thoughts on the wedding?" Hattie asks.

"They just got engaged, babe. Do you really think they've

had time to think about it?"

"No," Hattie answers. "But Maggie comes into town tomorrow, and if you want help, you know she's your girl."

"Who's Maggie?" I ask.

"Hattie's best friend," Aubree answers. "She owns a wedding planning business." Aubree turns her attention to Hattie. "Is she bringing her boyfriend?"

"Yes," Hattie answers with excitement. "I'm so excited to see them together. They've known each other for some time actually. Her brother's best friend. She's had a crush on him for a while, but being the girl Maggie is, she never acted on it, besides the night of her brother's wedding. They made out, and well, he practically ran away. Anywho, they reconnected in Bora Bora, found love on the island, and are together. I'm so excited."

"We won't need her help," Aubree says. "We're just going to do something small. Probably just something at the courthouse."

"What?" Hattie sits taller. "A courthouse wedding? But . . . don't you want a big party?"

"No," Aubree says as she pokes the fire. "That's the last thing I want. I don't want the attention. I just want to be married and then move on with our lives."

I clasp her on the shoulder. "Isn't she so romantic?"

"Very romantic," Echo says, surprising me since she hasn't really said anything the entire time we've been in a circle around the fire.

"You're not going to have Mac as the flower girl?" Ryland asks.

"I really don't think it's necessary. We might just . . . I don't know, elope." Aubree shrugs her shoulders. But her siblings don't like that response because their expressions morph into anger.

"There will be no eloping," Ryland says. "I'll be walking you down the aisle, so erase the word elopement from your mind. Not fucking happening."

"Yeah, and I'm going to stand next to you with a bouquet in my hand as you stare up at the love of your life and say I do. No elopement."

"You know"—Aubree stares at the fire, looking like she's completely disassociated herself from the emotion of the conversation—"some might say that the wedding is about the couple, so if we want to elope—"

"No eloping," Ryland says again, this time stirring Mac awake.

"You're being loud," she says in a grumpy voice.

"Sorry," Ryland says as he rubs her back. "Let's get you home." He stands from his chair but stares Aubree and me down. "No eloping. You hear me?"

Now I'm all for making my bride happy, but I don't think I want to cross the brother of the bride. He seems like he could be really scary at times.

"Got it," I say.

"We're going to get back too," Hattie says while standing. "I'm starting to get cold."

Hayes stands and takes her hand in his. "Congrats, you two." He smiles softly. Hattie congratulates us as well, and then they take off.

Abel is the next to stand. "I'm passing out over there," he says, motioning to his chair. "A few more minutes and I would have been out cold, and how humiliating that would be if the town caught their doctor drooling in front of the firepit."

"Humiliating," I say as I shake his hand.

"Congrats, you two." Abel shakes his head. "Still trying to wrap my mind around this, because wow, but yeah, excited about the intimate wedding that's not an elopement that I'm inviting myself to. Night, you guys."

And then Echo rises.

I almost didn't recognize her at first when she came up to congratulate us. She didn't have her typical straw hat or overalls on, so it took me a second. Thankfully, I recognized her voice right away.

"Aubree, think I can chat for a second?"

"Of course," Aubree says as she stands and walks over to the side, in the dark where I can barely see them.

I watch as Echo says something to her, and Aubree nods. They glance in my direction and then turn their backs away from me.

What the hell is going on over there?

It almost looks like they're in cahoots, but I have no idea over what.

After a minute or so, they hug each other, and Echo takes off, leaving Aubree to join me once again in front of the fire. "Uh, care to share what that was about?" I ask.

"She was just saying how happy she is for us."

"Uh-huh, and why couldn't she have said that in front of me?"

Aubree glances over her shoulder at me. "She wanted to make sure you weren't threatening me to marry you."

"Did she really?" I ask.

"No." Aubree laughs. "Just saying she's happy for me and then asked me a work question. No biggie."

"Okay, because if you told her about us, you could tell me, you know. You don't have to hide it. My best friend knows about you and me."

Aubree pauses as she's poking the fire. "Who is your best friend?"

"Her name is Laurel. I met up with her this week. She helped me pick out the ring."

"Wait, she's your friend who is a lesbian, right? Not that her sexual preference defines her, but that was why you couldn't marry her?"

"Correct," I say. "So if you need someone to tell, that's okay, Aubree. Better that I know, though, so I can manage who knows about us and who doesn't."

She sighs and leans back in her chair. "Yes, she knows. I told her a few days ago because I was struggling with it all and needed someone to talk to. I figured she would be best since she's removed from the situation."

"I can understand that. Was she checking on you just now?"

"She was. Wanted to make sure I was good with how everything went down. I told her I could have done without the public display, but I was fine with the proposal and moving forward on everything."

"The public display was to solidify our standing in the community when Wallace finds out. Trust me, he's going to ask questions. There is no way he'll be okay with this. He'll try to prove it wrong any chance he gets."

"Seems like he's really fun," Aubree says, full of sarcasm. "When are you going to tell him?"

"Well, when are we getting married?" I ask.

She shrugs. "I don't know. When do you want to get married?"

"I was thinking next week."

Her brows shoot up. "That eager, huh?"

"I've been saving myself for marriage," I say in a teasing tone. "I'm ready to consummate."

"In your dreams, Preston." She fully turns toward me now and folds her legs under her bottom. "When is Wallace getting married?"

"A few months. I don't remember exactly, but we have a little time. I'd rather not wait, just in case he decides to elope before us. So the sooner, the better. Once we're married, I'll tell him."

"Think he's going to be mad?"

"Livid," I say. "There's no way he doesn't call bullshit on it, but I can handle that side of things. I just need you to pretend to love me."

"You make it hard."

"Do I?" I ask, teasing her. "So I make it hard?"

"Dear God, Wyatt," Aubree says as I laugh out loud. "Can't you be normal?"

"No," I answer. "Sorry. Also, can we talk about your reaction to the proposal? Were you trying to shake my nipple? What was going on there?"

"Uh, I had hundreds of people watching me. I didn't know what to do. You could have given me a heads-up. You know, let me know that you were planning on proposing."

"In my mind, I was hoping for your real reaction to the proposal."

"Well, you got that. Doesn't get more real than what you experienced."

I push my hand through my hair. "Yeah, didn't think about the fact that you might be awkward and try to shake my nipple."

She rolls her eyes. "I wasn't trying to shake your nipple. God, you're so dramatic. I was attempting to shake your hand."

"Once again, that's so romantic."

"I was confused and caught off guard. You weren't the one standing on the dance floor while flowers twinkled their toes all around you with Ethel singing directly to you."

"Nope, I was the clueless asshole, floating in on a kiddie train looking like a fucking white knight on the wrong steed."

She chuckles. "I really enjoyed when you fell out of it and landed flat on your face."

I press my hand to my sore jaw. "Yeah, I know, you laughed way more than you should have given I face-planted."

"It was nervous laughter."

"Liar," I say.

"You're right, I'm lying, but I still enjoyed it. I also liked the panic on your face when you thought you'd lost the ring."

"I actually felt my balls tickle my stomach in fear. Ethel would have made my life a living hell if she went through all of this trouble and I lost the ring. She would have been devastated."

"Possibly would have ended the proposal in tears."

"And not the kind of tears you should have shed when I got down on one knee."

"Once again, a heads-up would have been nice."

"I'll remember that for next time."

"You plan on doing this again?" she asks.

I shrug. "Possibly. It's been a fun experience so far."

"Only someone with some serious issues would call this arrangement fun," she says as she stands from the chair and shivers before rubbing her arms.

"Are you cold?"

"Yeah. The wind off the ocean is starting to cut through the fire, and I don't think I can take it much longer."

"Not a problem. I'm ready to leave too. Just means we can move onto stage two of the proposal."

She crosses her arms over her chest and asks, "Does stage two involve removing clothing?"

"You said it, not me," I say.

"Not going to happen, Preston."

"Says the girl who stuck her tongue down my throat last night." I playfully bump her shoulder.

Her jaw falls open in shock. "You started it."

"But man, did you finish it."

"Ugh, you're infuriating sometimes, you know that? We both got carried away. We're both apparently very horny, so it was bound to happen. Trust me, not happening again, and since we understand how to kiss each other, I don't believe there's a need to kiss each other good night anymore."

"You don't think so?" I ask.

She shakes her head as we start heading toward the inn.

"The point was to get used to each other, and we're used to each other now."

"Yes, your excitement over my proposal really showed that."

She points her finger at me. "Your fault, remember that. I could have been all giddy and excited if you had let me in on the secret. Any reaction is a product of your missed opportunity to communicate."

"It's called spontaneity. Can't we have any?"

"Remember . . . I don't like surprises."

We walk up the back steps to the inn, and I open the door for her.

"How are we supposed to have an eventful marriage if you don't like surprises?" I ask her as we walk through the back hall of the inn to the main living space, where a few people enjoy coffee and treats.

"I don't want it to be eventful. I want it to be mundane and boring. I want to know what every day is going to be like. I want a schedule, a routine. I don't want anything to throw that off."

I shiver. "You know, the way you talk like that, it really gets my gears going."

She looks up at me with a comical expression. "Gears going? I can practically hear the dirty talk now."

"There they are," a voice says just as we move to the front of the inn. When I look up to see who it is, I'm met with the same woman I saw outside of The Hot Pickle. What's her name again? Amalie?

"Congratulations on the engagement," she says, rubbing her hand over her pregnant belly.

"Thank you, Amanda," Aubree says while stiffening next to me.

That's right, Amanda. And the husband is Matt, who doesn't seem to be . . . oh wait, there he is, carrying a plate of treats in one hand and a cup in the other.

"Quite the proposal. I especially liked how you shook hands. It really screamed romance."

Man, either she's a rotten bitch spoiled to her very core with mold growing on her bones and algae seeping into her heart or the baby that's growing inside her is an itty-bitty alien from a far-off planet implanted inside her . . . *and* is making her act like an absolute rude ass.

The alien thing would be interesting to talk about, but I'm probably going to be realistic about this and chalk up her attitude to moldy bones and algae heart.

"I was caught off guard and nervous from everyone staring at us," Aubree responds as she moves in closer to me, definitely not the normal, confident ballbuster. What kind of hold does this girl have on Aubree? Just like the last time they engaged, Aubree has lost all her confidence around her.

"You never were one to enjoy being the center of attention. That's probably from when you were growing up, never wanting to be in your dad's violent path, always attempting to blend into the background."

Who does this woman think she is? Just saying Aubree's personal business like that.

"You would think your fiancé would know that about you and plan a more private proposal." She glances over in my direction with her nose curled.

Yeah, it's the fucking moldy bones on this one. No alien is that fucking rude.

Too bad she has no idea who she's dealing with.

"Thank you for your observation, Andrea." See what I did there? "But you must not realize how much this town loves Aubree. How much they cherish her. They wanted to make this day joyous for her. They wanted to celebrate with us."

"They have always been fans of the Rowleys, haven't they," she says, interrupting my tirade. "Although, I'd say their love was more directed at Cassidy and now Hattie."

Oh wow.

"Then again, they probably rally around Aubree because she was always the one . . . left out, right, Aubree?"

Aubree curls into me. Fuck, she's so uncomfortable.

"Could explain why you had such an odd reaction."

"It wasn't odd," I say. "It was genuine. She gets nervous when the focus of attention, but I've never seen a smile so big on her lips. I've never seen a town come together so thoughtfully for one person, and I've never felt more love than I have today. You can make all the snide comments you want, but we know they aren't a reflection on the love we have for each other, but a reflection on your unhappiness and attempt to make other people feel how you feel day in and day out . . . miserable."

And then I take a leap of faith and reach down to take Aubree's hand in mine, to let her know that I'm here for her, that she's not alone. I wait for her to pull away, to reject me holding her hand, but she doesn't.

Instead, she entwines our fingers, pressing her palm tighter against mine.

She trusts me.

She believes me.

She believes in this connection.

It might not be love, but it doesn't need to be. We have a deeper understanding for each other, something that extends past the kisses we've shared this week or the agreement we made. This is an appreciation for one another.

Amanda places her hands on her hips, looking angrier than ever. "How dare you make such an assumption about me."

"Just like you made an assumption about Aubree?" I ask, squeezing her hand tighter. "You act like you were friends, like you know her, but you know nothing about her. You don't know the kind of strength this woman has as she works on her dead sister's farm day in and day out, living out her sister's dream. You don't know the loving heart she has as she helps her brother take care of their niece, who still struggles with the loss of *both* of her parents. And you have no fucking clue how this woman will set aside her life to help out anyone in town. The reason people are celebrating today is because Aubree let herself come first. She let herself have a moment. So don't come over here and try to shit on her happiness. I'm not going to allow it."

Amanda folds her arms across her chest and cocks one hip to the side. She's not done. It's clear as day in her body language and the uneasiness in her eyes. "Any author can make up nice things to say about someone, but do you really mean it? People have seen you two around town, and sure, you're next to each other, but you're never intimate. For two people who seem to be soooo in love, you sure don't look like it."

I'm about to say something when Aubree moves in closer to me, her hand still in mine, her shoulder pressing against mine. I can see that she's filling herself up with courage, and I squeeze her hand three times, letting her know that we're in this together.

"Amanda," Aubree says, sounding shaky. "I understand that we went our separate ways, but I would appreciate it if you didn't try to spread your unhappiness on me and our big day."

It's a simple comment. Not the insult I would have made if I were in her shoes, but it's just enough for Amanda to back off with a look of shock.

Maybe she didn't expect Aubree to stand up for herself. Maybe in all the time they've known each other, Aubree has never stood up for herself. Maybe Amanda has used her knowledge of Aubree's past to her advantage and walked all over Aubree like her dad did. Either way, the stunned look on Amanda's face was all the indication Aubree needed to walk away.

Hand in hand, Aubree tugs me away from the negativity and straight out the inn door. She doesn't let go of my hand and she doesn't say a word. She vibrates in anger, so I don't say a word either. Instead, I keep by her, squeezing her hand, reminding her that she's not alone in this.

When we finally get to my car, I bring her to the passenger side and open the door, but she doesn't get in. She turns toward me instead and looks up at me.

"That was . . . that was embarrassing. I'm sorry."

"Why the hell are you sorry?" I ask. "There is nothing to be sorry about. You weren't the one being an asshole. I'm sorry you had to deal with that."

"She's just . . ." Aubree looks away. "She's not the best person, and I hate that she brings up the past. She knows me so well from that period of my life. I don't like it being brought up, or for people to know about it. I just hate that you had to hear it."

"Are you afraid I'm going to judge you?" I ask.

Her eyes find mine. "No," she answers. "I mean, you . . ." Her voice shakes. "You . . . you defended me."

"Of course, I did," I say. "Do you really think I'd just stand there and let her make you feel bad about yourself? No fucking way. From her husband's silence, just standing there eating petit fours, my guess is that she's very unhappy, and she's projecting that unhappiness on you. Her problem, not ours."

"I guess not." She glances away, but I can tell something else is on her mind, so I tip her chin and have her look at me.

"What are you not saying?"

"It's stupid." She shakes her head.

"Nothing is stupid. Just tell me."

"I shouldn't even be asking," she says.

"Aubree." I force her to look me in the eyes. "Ask."

She heaves a heavy sigh and then says, "Did you mean it?" Her eyes look impossibly large as she stares up at me. "It's okay if you didn't mean it, but I was just wondering—"

"Did I mean what?" I ask.

She wets her lips and then softly says, "Did you mean the words you said to Amanda, or was that . . . was that something your author brain was able to come up with on the spot?"

Fuck. This woman has no clue how incredible she is. She underestimates her heart, her looks, her strength. *Fuck, I hate how hurt she's been.*

I bring our connected hands to my lips and press a gentle kiss on her knuckles. "I meant every word of it," I say. "There are things I can lie about when it comes to this relationship like how we met and this fake love I have for you, but there are things I can't lie about. And that's who you are as a person. Your very core, your morals, your values, those are all true. That's not something I can make—"

I don't finish what I'm saying because her hand loops around my neck, and she pulls me down to her mouth, where she kisses me and kisses me hard.

Shocked for a second, I still, but the moment her tongue parts my lips with hers, I follow suit and place one hand on her hip as I press her up against my SUV, my mouth exploring hers just as much as she's exploring mine.

Fuck, these lips. They're unlike anything I've ever kissed before. Full and soft but tentative and timid at the same time. They're eager, yet they don't fully go all in. They wait for me to take charge, and I really fucking love being in charge.

I bring my hand to the side of her head, pressing up against the SUV, and push my pelvis against hers as I angle my head to the side, giving us both better access as her tongue wanders into my mouth.

So sweet.

So delicious.

She has such a hard outer shell, but on the inside, she's warm and—

"Get a room!" someone shouts a few feet away, startling us both.

I pull away as Aubree's hand goes to her mouth. She looks just as stunned as I feel.

"Oh my God, I'm sorry," she says quickly. "I don't . . . I don't know what came over me."

Seeing that she's visibly stressed and unsure of herself and her actions, I decide to lighten the mood. I don't need her overthinking this because if she starts overthinking it, then I'll do the same, and that's the last thing I need.

So I say, "I think you were terrified about closing out the good-night kiss, so you felt like you had to get one more in."

Her expression falls flat and that irritated look I've become so fond of reappears. "Thank you for that."

"Thank you for what?" I ask.

"Reminding me why I find you so unbearable."

I open her car door and gesture for her to get in. "Anything for my lady."

She shuts the door on me and buckles herself up.

If I wasn't so stunned by that kiss right now, I might even laugh at her reaction. But hell. That was . . . that was not something I was expecting.

I've kissed her before, and I've liked it. I've liked every second of it.

But that kiss. I felt it all the way down to my toes.

I felt it in the pit of my stomach.

I felt it knocking on my head, telling me something was there. Something I'm ignoring and not ready to face just yet.

And because of that, I push it all to the side and to the back of my mind where I won't touch it.

I won't even go near it.

Because I'm afraid if I do . . . I might get hurt again.

Chapter Fifteen

AUBREE

"Oh my God, this will be so great," Maggie says as she claps her hands together, far too excited about a wedding I don't want.

When I came into The Almond Store to talk to Hattie about stocking up on honey this week, I forgot about Maggie coming in. I blame the commotion from yesterday . . . that kiss, and the awkward night I had of trying not to breathe too heavily while Wyatt held me last night. I considered kicking him away, telling him not to curl into me, but every time I got the courage to say something, I remembered how well I sleep when he's snuggled into me. And I really value my sleep. So I didn't kick him away. But I sure as hell booked it out of the guest house this morning and went straight to work. On a Sunday. I did everything I could think of, which included scouring the potato fields for any wayward trash that seemed to be dragged in by the wind from careless litterers.

And my avoidance served me well up until the point when I was starving. Wyatt texted me if I wanted him to make me lunch, and I politely declined, hightailed it out of the farm, and came into town. I was going to grab a chicken salad sandwich and discuss honey, in case Wyatt asked.

But instead, I ran into an overzealous Maggie and her new boyfriend.

"I really don't want to make a big deal out of this wedding," I say. "Seriously, we're probably just going to find a courthouse and do it that way."

"I refuse to let that happen." Maggie caps the pen she was using to outline a—what she calls—simplistic yet chic wedding. "It will be in the barn, the family will sit on hay bales covered in lace—"

The doorbell rings above the front door, and I thank the high heavens for the distraction until I hear Mac's voice yell, "Maggie!"

Then her little feet patter across the floor, and she leaps into Maggie's arms.

"Hey there, Mac. How are you?"

"Good." Mac looks over at Brody, Maggie's boyfriend, and asks, "Who is this?"

"This is my boyfriend. His name is Brody."

Mac looks him up and down but ignores him and says, "Aunt Aubree has a boyfriend, and they're getting married."

"So I heard," Maggie says in an evil tone as if she just realized her key to making her barn wedding dreams come true. "I was just talking to your aunt Aubree about her wedding."

"Maggie," I warn, seeing where she's going with this.

"And you know what she told me?"

"Maggie, I swear."

She just smiles at me and says, "That she doesn't want a wedding."

Mac's head whips around to me, and those big eyes that grow three times their size in seconds stare back at me. "You don't want a wedding?"

Yup, Maggie did it all right.

"I just don't want a big one," I answer gently.

"But . . . that means I can't be your flower girl, and Uncle Ry Ry said I could be your flower girl."

Ryland, who leans against one of the islands in the store, arms crossed, just smiles back at me as if he knows exactly what he did.

You know what? It's not fair to use a child to get what you want. There should be a law against that. Just because you have a child in your life doesn't mean you can use them to your advantage. Although I would say many parents would disagree with that statement. It's probably one of the benefits of having a child, besides the whole fulfilling part of raising a human and the unconditional love thing.

"You would be the most beautiful flower girl," Maggie says.

"And Chewy Charles could be the ring bearer. I told him last night. He would be so sad, Aunt Aubree."

Dear God.

Sighing, I say, "Fine." The bell rings above the door again as I finish, "We can skip the courthouse wedding and have it here."

"Oh really?" Ethel chimes in from the entrance.

No.

Noooooooo.

I turn around to find Ethel and Wyatt standing at the door, their faces lit up with smiles.

And Wyatt is with her?

How did a simple chicken salad sandwich turn into this?

"We're going to have a big wedding?" Ethel asks. "I meet with the Peach Society tonight. We can discuss everything."

I hold up my hand. "Not necessary. Maggie here is going to be planning it."

"But I'd love to join the meeting to discuss," Maggie says. "But tonight won't work. We're supposed to go out to the burlesque club for dinner."

"Oh, they do a lovely job," Ethel says. "Have you been?"

"No," Maggie says. "But we were going to go with Hayes and Hattie . . ." Her head swivels to me. "And you guys should come too. You and Wyatt. On the way there, we can talk all the wedding things, and then, Ethel, I can meet up with you tomorrow."

"That would be perfect." Ethel clasps her hands together.

"Uh, hold up a second," I say.

"Burlesque club, huh?" Wyatt chimes in before I can strike the meetup between Ethel and Maggie. "Sounds great. We'll be there."

"Wait," I say. "Hold on a second."

"Perfect," Hattie says. "Now all of you need to leave so I can close up and get ready. Ryland, you good if we all take off tonight?"

"Fine by me. I have a date with Mac and the *Paw Patrol* movie."

"We're going to have gummy worms in our popcorn," Mac says excitedly.

The group starts discussing what kind of candy they like in their popcorn. I feel like I just got run over by a semi-truck. How did this go from me attempting to avoid Wyatt to us having a town wedding, planned by Maggie, with Chewy Charles involved, and a road trip to the burlesque club to talk about it?

I don't understand what just happened.

⊏══⊐

"WOULD YOU LIKE A DRINK?" Wyatt asks me as we take a seat on a two-person couch behind Hattie, Hayes, Maggie, and Brody.

"Uh, it's a requirement for me," I say, my mood less than excited.

I've been to the burlesque club before, and it's a lot of fun. Dinner, drinks, and a live show with crowd interaction. But I've only been with friends, never with a man, let alone my soon-to-be fake husband. Red velvet couches all face the center stage with bistro tables in front, providing little space for food and drinks. Large red and gold curtains are draped in front of the stage while lights from the floor and the ceiling are all angled down, waiting for the performers.

I'm just glad we're not in the front row like the rest of our party because I'm not up for any interactions. I barely got dressed. I'm only wearing a high-waisted skirt and skintight cropped top because I knew Hattie and Maggie would dress up, and I always succumb to peer pressure when it comes to going-out clothes.

I didn't even bother to gather Wyatt's reaction to the outfit. I just grabbed his arm and pulled him toward the waiting SUV that Hayes was driving. We then spent the entire thirty-minute drive discussing wedding specifics. Flowers and decorations and locations in the barn where we could get married. I cut her off about the barn and told her if we were getting married on the farm, we'd get married under my favorite tree.

And I don't know why I said that because that should be reserved for a real marriage, not this one, but I was so mixed up with all of the questions and the ideas that I blurted it out, which in return made Hattie cry and say how perfect it would be.

So yeah, now we're getting married under my favorite tree, Mac is the flower girl, Chewy Charles will be carrying the rings, there will still be hay bales, and because of Wyatt, The Cliffs will provide mac and cheese—his idea.

Oh, and don't forget the cherry pie instead of a cake—I almost offered sundaes but clamped my mouth shut.

It's as if we're developing a wedding based on the existing relationship and inside jokes I have with Wyatt when, given we've only known each other for just over a week, we shouldn't know each other this well already.

Yet we do.

Hence the drink I need.

"What can I order for you?" Wyatt asks as he drapes his arm over the back of the couch and crosses one of his ankles over his knee, looking all casual in his black jeans and button-up black shirt with the sleeves rolled up. He's taking this whole planning in stride. He's unfazed, actually smiling about the entire thing.

"Anything with alcohol," I answer.

"Well, if that's the case, I'll order you a Jager bomb just to see how you can handle it."

"Why do you have to be so mean to me when I'm clearly distraught?"

He chuckles and tugs a strand of my hair. "I'm sorry, Mrs. Preston. What can I get you to help you in your time of need?"

"Something fruity and delicious with a high alcohol content."

"That I can do. Do you want something to eat too?"

I nod. "I love the appetizer sampler. Buffalo wings, potato skins, artichoke dip, and a side of nachos."

"Is that for two?" he asks as he twirls my hair around his finger.

"Yes, but if I swat your hand away, don't take offense. I'm on edge."

He chuckles and turns more toward me. "Want to talk about it?"

"Aw, look at you two," Hattie says, interrupting. She holds her phone up and says, "Smile."

Of course Hattie will document every second of this. She's just like Cassidy, wanting to savor every moment, especially when it comes to love.

Wyatt wraps his arm around me and pulls me in closer. My hand falls to his thigh, and together, we smile. "Gah, you two are adorable." Our server appears in a scantily clad outfit, and the first thing out of Hattie's mouth is, "That's my sister behind us, and she just got engaged to her boyfriend. They're getting married next week, and we're here to celebrate."

"Well, you came to the right place," the server says before taking everyone's orders. Wyatt orders us the appetizer plate as well as a whiskey for himself—not sure why I find that attractive, but I do—and a Malibu sunset for me, which already feels relaxing.

"So," Wyatt says, still twirling my hair. "You're on edge? I know a good way to take care of that."

I'm still leaning in, my hand on his thigh because Hattie

keeps looking back at us like this is her best day, which it probably is, because her best friend is in love and her sister is supposedly in love and she's in love, which means everything is great and wonderful in the world. And this is exactly why I can't tell Hattie the truth about my arrangement with Wyatt. She'd be devastated. She was devastated when she learned Cassidy wasn't truly in love with Clarke. She wouldn't want me to be in the same situation. *Oh the irony, especially between sisters who couldn't be more different.*

"And what way would that be?" I ask.

"Take your skirt off, and I'll tell you."

I slowly turn to face him. "Excuse me?"

He chuckles. "Don't look so offended."

"I'm not offended, but just confused as to where that came from."

"You think you can waltz around in that outfit and not warrant comments from me about how insanely hot you look?"

"Correct me if I'm wrong, but one, women can dress however they want, men are the ones who need to control themselves, and two, we don't say things like that to each other."

"We don't?" he asks as he continues to twirl my hair. "I thought we were here to pump each other up."

"We're here to exchange goods. Meaning, my hand for your land, like you said."

"Yeah, but that doesn't mean we can't be each other's number-one hype man or woman."

"Uh-huh, and what exactly do you mean by that?" I ask.

"Meaning, if you look good, I'm going to tell you. If you like the way my ass looks in these jeans, feel free to say something. It's not bad to compliment each other. We're at this for a year, so we might as well be each other's number-one fans when we split. Don't you want that?"

"I mean, I don't need the ego boost as much as you clearly do."

"I don't think it'll hurt," he says. "So if I say you look insanely hot tonight, take it as a compliment from a friend."

"Okay," I say.

"And you know, if you want to return the compliment, that won't hurt you either."

"Yeah, sure, when I think the compliment should be returned."

His expression falls, and I laugh.

"I'll have you know, these are my hot pants. I wore them just for you."

"Hot pants, huh? What makes them so hot?" I ask.

"Every time I wear them, I orgasm."

"Dear God," I reply, making his head fall back as he laughs. "Do you really think that's something I want to know?"

"Possibly. Could be a newlywed question that's asked of us."

"Who is asking what pants do you constantly orgasm in?"

"People . . ." he drags out.

"You're an idiot."

He chuckles some more just as our server drops off our drinks. We thank her, and I suck down a large gulp, not even bothering to taste-test it.

Wyatt, on the other hand, swirls the amber liquid in his glass and then takes a sip.

"You going to guzzle that whole thing down?" he asks me.

"Possibly," I say. "Have you ever been to one of these clubs? They make you interact. And I'm going to need alcohol to interact."

"What kind of interaction are we talking about?" He picks up a piece of my hair again. "Are you going to get dressed up like one of the waitstaff and start strutting around? Because that's something I have to see."

"No." I scoff at him. "But sometimes they call the audience for help and don't take no for an answer. You know when you pay the cover fee and sign the release? That's part of it. When you come here, you have to be prepared in case they call on you."

"In that case, I don't think I'll drink at all. I want to be completely sober to soak in every last moment if they call on you."

I lift the bottom of his glass to his lips and say, "Oh, you'll be drinking." And then together, we take a few large gulps.

———

"OKAY, these are some of the best potato skins I've ever had. Holy shit," Wyatt says as he stares down at the potato in his hand.

"It's one of the reasons I said yes to coming, knowing I'd be able to order some."

"We might need more," he says before taking another bite. "Fuck, they're good. The crunch they get on the outside is impeccable."

"Didn't know you were a food critic."

"Uh, given my popularity with the town and my food choices, I think you should know that by now. By the way, did I tell you that By the Slice is going to design a pizza around me, name it after me, and even suggest a dipping sauce for the crust?"

I have a carrot midway to my mouth when I stop. "You're kidding."

"Nope," he says, his chest puffed, fully proud of himself.

"How the hell did you manage that?"

"I'm telling you, those bear claws and cherry pies are selling like hotcakes, and the other proprietors want a piece of this popularity. I'm going to be doing a taste-test with Keesha later this week. I was trying to come up with a cool name for it. I was thinking something simple like The Wyatt, but then I thought it would be cool to call it The Thriller Killer, presented by W.J. Preston. Has more of a posh ring to it, don't you think?"

"The fact that you've put this much thought into it really annoys me."

"Why?" he asks as he wipes his mouth with a napkin. "Envious?"

"Perhaps," I admit. "You've been in town for two seconds. The Rowleys have been here all our lives, and we are a staple in Almond Bay with The Almond Store. We should have something named after us."

"Do you have something named after Keesha?" he asks.

"No, are you naming something after her?"

"Dedicating my next book to her and plan on having the detective take her namesake."

"You're lying."

"Nope. Have it all written out. She's thrilled."

"Wow." I shake my head and pick up a buffalo wing. "You really have stuck your head up the town's ass, haven't you?"

He smirks. "Yes, but if it makes you feel better, I've stuck my head up your ass the furthest."

I press my hand to my heart. "That is one of the most beautiful things you've ever said to me."

"I know." He winks, and I just continue to shake my head at him.

———

"WHEN DOES THIS SHOW START?" Wyatt asks as he looks down at his watch.

"In about twenty minutes. They like to get people fed before they start anything. That way, the waitstaff isn't constantly moving in front of everyone."

"Makes sense."

Hattie turns around on the couch and leans on the top as she talks to us. "Did you get the potato skins?"

"What do you think?" I ask.

"Hayes was moaning over them over here."

"Can you not say moaning?" Hayes asks, making her chuckle.

She cups his face and says, "Those were the sounds you make in the bedroom."

"Trust me, I'd take you over the potato skins any day."

"That's what I told Aubree," Wyatt says. "She didn't believe me."

Brody turns around as well and says, "I'd take the potato skins. Sorry, Maggie."

Maggie turns as well and addresses all of us. "He's only saying that because I told him I'd marry their boneless buffalo wings over him earlier. He's salty."

"Not as salty as those fries." Brody makes a chef's kiss. "They were spectacular. Who knew a burlesque club would have such good food."

"Are you having a good time, you two?" Hattie asks us.

Wyatt smooths his hand over my bare thigh as he says, "The best."

His hand moves higher, making my stomach twitch with warmth as it slowly slides under my skirt. I attempt to keep a smile on my face while he strokes my thigh, sending this bolt of unexpected lust straight between my legs.

"I'm glad," Hattie says. "Hayes just ordered another round for everyone, so enjoy."

"Thank you," Wyatt says, lifting his empty glass toward their table.

When they all turn around, I half expect Wyatt to stop touching me, but he keeps his hand where it is and continues to run his finger lightly over my skin.

I don't think Matt ever touched me like this. He never casually claimed me as his person in public, but here's Wyatt, having no problem doing so, and he's not even romantically interested in me.

Quietly, I say, "Your hand is up my skirt."

"Yeah, it is," he says casually.

"Okay, just wanted to make sure you knew, in case you lost it."

"Nope, I know exactly where it is."

"Did you know that no one can see you stroking my thigh, yet you're still doing it?"

"Just relaxing you, Mrs. Preston," he says.

"The alcohol is doing just that."

"I can tell." He turns his head to look at me. "An hour ago, you would have broken my fingers off if I was touching you like this."

"Not true," I say.

"Such a liar."

"No, I don't break your fingers off when you hold me at night," I reply.

"That's different," he says.

"How so?" I ask.

"That's for comfort."

"Mm-hmm," I answer. "And what's this for?"

"To see how far I can go before you stop me."

I turn toward him and put my arm on the back of the couch. "Why would you do that?"

"Because I want to show you that even if you try to ignore me all day, I'll still be here at the end of it, touching you, being by your side, kissing you good night."

"You say that as if you want more," I say. "I thought we said this was all platonic."

"It is." With a smirk, he adds, "But it doesn't hurt to play."

Yet he removes his hand from under my skirt to lift his newly replenished drink off the table and brings it straight to his lips.

I do the same. But whereas he takes a sip, I take a gulp.

⸏

"WHAT DO you think of your drink?" Wyatt asks me as I set the empty glass on the table and curl my legs up on the couch so I'm facing him.

"I like it a lot."

He grins and pokes my cheek that's smiling. "I can tell. Are you feeling tipsy, Aubree?"

"No, are you?" And that's a huge, fat lie because, whoa boy, do I feel good.

"Uh-huh," he says skeptically just as another drink is set on the table for me.

"Hey, I didn't order that."

Hattie turns around and says, "That's from us, enjoy the show."

I pick up the drink and position the straw in front of my mouth. "If I didn't know any better, I'd think my sister's trying to get me drunk."

"I think she's doing a good job with it," Wyatt says while he drains the rest of his drink by opening his mouth wide and letting the amber liquid flow right down his throat.

"I think one more of these, and I might be sitting on your lap," I say as I look at my pretty sunset-colored drink. So delicious.

"You don't have to wait, babe. Sit all you want." He gestures to his lap, but I shake my head.

"No, that would be too much, don't you think?"

"Hattie is sitting on Hayes's lap," Wyatt points out.

I lean in close to him and whisper, "That's because they're sex freaks."

Wyatt lets out a roar of a laugh. "I didn't know sitting on someone's lap made you a sex freak."

I shake my head. "No, I'm serious. I heard them once in the middle of . . . coitus, and it's unlike anything I've ever heard before. It was violating my ears on all accounts. And Hattie even told me she'll have multiple orgasms. That can't be a thing."

Wyatt tilts his head to the side, questions in his brow. "You haven't had multiple orgasms in a night?"

"No," I scoff. "I was lucky if I got one. It's okay, though." I take a large sip of my drink and talk a little quieter. "I have a vibrator that does the trick when the man can't."

"You do, do you?" he asks. "Can it make you come twice in a night?"

I smile and nod. "It can."

"Do you ever use it when I'm in the shower?"

I frown. I'm feeling loose at the moment. Hmm, maybe these

drinks are starting to get to me. "No, I've been too nervous. But .
. ." I place my hand on his thigh as I lean in even more and say,
"When you went on a run the other day, I pulled it out and had
fun."

His tongue runs over his lips. "Did you think about me?"

"Why would I think about you?" I ask. "That seems
weird."

"Weird?" he asks as he turns toward me as well and runs his
finger over my arm. "I've caught you checking me out without a
shirt on."

"I don't check you out. I just examine."

"Oh, there's a difference?" he asks.

"Certainly," I answer. "Checking you out requires a tongue
hanging out of the mouth, like this." I demonstrate, holding my
tongue out and looking him up and down. "Now examining, that
would be like this." I casually tilt my head to the side and slowly
look him up and down. "See the difference?"

"Yeah, I do." A smile tugs at the corner of his lips. "So if I
were to look you up and down like this . . ." His intriguing and
hungry eyes roam over my body, starting at my head and moving
down my neck to my chest, where he pauses for a moment or
two, then lifts back up. The entire time, I feel like I'm being
scanned by X-ray vision. "That would be examining, not
checking out."

"Correct," I say in a wobbly voice before taking a large sip of
my drink. "Now, when the women in their scantily clad lingerie
sets start strutting across the stage, if your tongue is hanging out
while you watch, that would be . . ."

"Checking them out," he answers.

I boop him on the nose. "Good job."

"I don't plan on checking them out, though," he says.

"No?" I ask. "Just examining? Well, don't judge me if you see
me with my tongue hanging out."

"Oh yeah?" he asks. "Do you like checking out women?"

"I like the female body. I think it's a beautiful thing. And I've
kissed a girl or two in my lifetime, felt a boob once. I think they're

nice. I think they're so nice that I like to play with my own breasts sometimes."

His smile grows even wider. "You like your tits played with, Aubree?"

"Oh yeah. Love it so much. Matt was okay at it, but I think I'm better."

"What makes you better than Matt?" he asks.

"Many things, but he just loved shoving the whole thing in his mouth, as if that's what I want. He never understood the art of teasing, you know? He wouldn't play with my nipple. He wouldn't circle his finger around it or flick it or pinch it. He'd lick it on occasion, but that didn't do much. I wanted more from him. So much more."

"Shame," Wyatt says as he drags his finger up my shoulder and circles it. "I love playing with nipples."

"Really?" I ask. "Do you play with your own?"

"No." He shakes his head. "But I don't mind if my girl plays with them. Turns me on."

"Interesting." I tap my chin before taking another sip of my drink. "What else turns you on?"

"Going down," he says without even thinking about it. "I love eating pussy."

"Oh." My cheeks redden because I'm not sure I've ever heard a man say that, especially with such conviction. "I remember you saying that. Love to, uh, put that out there, don't you?"

"Because I love it," he says. "So fucking much. If it were up to me, I'd start every night with my woman sitting on my face. Where it goes from there, I don't care, but fuck do I want that pussy on my tongue."

Good God, why am I getting so hot right now?

So flustered.

So . . . turned on?

Probably because I've never really had a man go down on me and do a good job. Probably because they treated it more like a chore than something they enjoyed doing. Probably because it's been a really long time for me, and Wyatt keeps touching me and kissing me and looking at me as if I decided to sit on his face right now, he'd be the happiest motherfucker in the room.

"Well, that's, uh . . . that's valuable information," I say. "Thank you for sharing it."

His hand curls around my neck as he pulls me in closer. "What about you, Aubree? What do you like?"

Men who like eating pussy.

Men who don't mind stepping up for me.

Men who will curl into me every night because they know it comforts me—even though they don't know the real reason is because it helps distract my mind from the terrors it plays when the lights turn out.

But I can't say that.

I don't want him to know.

"Umm," I say as I awkwardly bring my drink between us and sip. "Well, you know about the nipple thing."

"Logged that away," he says as his thumb strokes the column of my neck. I like that, a lot. I like the possession of it.

"And I like my vibrator."

"Yup, established that." His finger runs along my jaw.

"And, you know . . . I like playing with a man's dick."

He wets his lips again. "Tell me . . . Mrs. Preston, how would you play with mine?"

I don't know if it's the alcohol or the way he's holding me so possessively, but I actually hear myself answering.

"I'd kneel between your legs," I say while my hand falls to his thigh. His teeth pull over his bottom lip. "Undo your pants and gently pull you out."

"Then what?" he asks.

"Run my tongue along the underside of your cock until you're fully erect."

"Fuck yes," he says as his hold on my jaw grows tighter.

"Then I'd lower my head and circle your cock with my tongue, over and over again, until you were panting."

"I would fucking love that, baby," he answers. "Would you make me desperate to come in your mouth?"

"I would—"

"Welcome, ladies and gentlemen!" the emcee for the night shouts into the microphone, startling both Wyatt and me away from each other.

"Shit," he whispers while softly looking back at me.

Shit is right. What the hell were we just doing? Did I tell him I'd lick the underside of his cock?

I think I did.

The audacity.

He drives his hand through his hair and sighs back into the couch.

Yeah, I feel that sigh all the way down to the marrow of my bones.

"We're so excited to have you here tonight . . ."

The emcee continues to talk about the show, but the pounding of my pulse drowns her out as I try to catch my breath.

I peek a look over at Wyatt, and he does the same. When our eyes meet, he keeps them locked for a few seconds before they drop to my mouth and back up again.

I do the same.

And when our eyes lock, I can feel it, this electric energy bouncing between us. It's worrisome but also exciting. It shouldn't be happening, but oh my God, I can't stop myself from leaning into him, letting him touch me, stare at me, and make me feel unlike anything I've felt before.

He was right. I avoided him for a reason today, and that was because I felt something. Something toward him. Something I shouldn't be feeling, but I can't help.

I've grown accustomed to having him around.

I look forward to him holding me at night.

And I crave his witty comebacks that provoke an eye roll from me.

But tonight, tonight it feels different, and I don't know why.

Tonight, it feels like something's going to happen. Someone

will break, and I just hope it's not me.

———

"WOW," Wyatt says as I start sipping my fourth drink of the night. "She was an amazing singer." He swirls the last of his whiskey and drains it.

"I really liked her outfit." I turn toward Wyatt and place my hand on his chest. "For a moment, when she flung her head around and her boobs bounced everywhere, I thought her titty tassel was going to fall off."

Wyatt chuckles. "That would have been a great show ender." He then pushes a strand of my hair behind my ear. "Why are you sitting so far away?"

His eyes are glazed over, and I can only imagine mine are as well. I'm most definitely drunk. There isn't a part of my body that doesn't feel like it's floating on a cloud, nor is there an ounce of me that cares.

Yup, this girl is feeling good. Capital G, goo-ood. Oh yes. So good that I've contemplated going up on stage myself to shimmy at the crowd. When that thought came into my mind, I knew I was drunk.

"Am I sitting far away?" I ask.

"You are," he says as he places his arm around me, cups my hip, and then pulls me all the way up against his side. "See, that's better."

"Ooo, you're warm. There's a breeze, and it's making my nipples all tingly and hard."

His eyes fall to my chest and then back up to my eyes. "I can't tell."

I puff my chest out and then run my finger over my hard nipples. "See, hard as stone."

His teeth pull on his bottom lip as his eyes meet mine again. "You're going to get yourself in trouble if you keep stroking your nipples like that."

"Oh," I say, glancing around the room. "Do you think they

get mad about that kind of stuff here? I mean, I don't know why they would. The lady that was up two songs ago touched her crotch at least five times while she thrust it at us."

He chuckles. "That was a bit aggressive."

"I liked her top, though, and I was jealous of her boobs. They were so big."

"Why were you jealous?" he asks as the next person comes on stage. "You have great tits, Aubree."

"You haven't even seen them. For all you know, I could be stuffing my bra."

"Are you?" he asks.

"No, but I did in high school when I was as flat as the freaking wall. I found a great way to make tissues look real."

"Welcome to the interactive portion of the night," the new singer says. "I'm Lady Marmalade, and I'm looking at all these couples out here and wondering why none of you are taking advantage of this moment. Can we dim the lights, please, and cast our fellow patrons in the dark?" The lights dim, and the woman with bright red hair, red lingerie, and black knee-high boots so large that I think they'd swallow my entire leg snaps her finger, lighting up the club with music.

"What's going on?" Wyatt whispers.

"Ooo, I think she might be doing the Simon Says game."

"What's that?" he asks.

"You'll see."

"Now that the mood is set, I want to see everyone find a comfortable place to sit." She spins and whips her head around with the music. "And when I say comfortable, I mean, you better be on each other's laps."

A few people in the crowd let out catcalls.

I'm not one of them.

"And if I see you're not participating, I think you all know what will happen. You'll be brought up on stage."

I turn toward Wyatt and say, "If you want to leave, we can."

"Mrs. Preston," he says as he spreads his legs and sits taller on the couch. "Sit on my goddamn lap."

"Are you sure? I don't want to—"

"More than fucking sure," he says before wetting his lips.

Well, in that case, don't mind if I do.

I slip one leg over his and then straddle him so my back is to his chest. "Is this okay?" I ask him as his hands find my thighs.

"Fucking great," he says.

"Now that we're comfortable," Lady Marmalade says. "I think we kick it up a notch. Who is ready for some Simon Says?"

The crowd cheers some more, me included this time because I'm completely gone at this point. I'm drunk. I'm horny. And I'm sitting on Wyatt's lap. Hattie wanted me to have a good time. Well, here I am, ready to do whatever is told of me.

"Now listen closely." The music starts to play, and Lady Marmalade takes the reins of the room. "For our lappers. Simons says, put your hands on their hips." Wyatt places his hands on my hips. "Simon Says, put your hands on their thighs." Wyatt slides his hands down my thighs, sending this wave of anticipation straight to my core. "Simon says put your hands on their tits." I watch other men and women slap their hands on their partner's chest but not Wyatt, though. He slides his hands up my thighs, to my hips, up my rib cage, and as I hold my breath from his incredible patience, he slowly covers my breasts with his very large palms.

And then . . . I hear a low growl fall past his lips.

Dear God.

"Now, move them side to side," Lady Marmalade says. Wyatt holds still, doesn't move, doesn't even breathe.

"Ahh, Simon didn't say," Lady Marmalade says as she tsks some people . . . Brody being one of them.

He holds his hands up and shouts to us, "I like her boobs. I can't help it."

I laugh briefly, but that's until Wyatt caresses my hard nipples with his thumbs.

Fuck.

Me.

"For my sitters, are you ready?" Lady Marmalade says into

the microphone. I mean, I think I am, but I'm so distracted. "Simon says lean forward." Unsure of where she's going with this, I lean as far forward as Wyatt will allow since he's still holding me. "Simon says swivel to the right." I swivel my hips to the right just as Wyatt pinches the tip of my nipple.

"Oh my God," I moan quietly to myself.

"Simon says swivel to the left." I swing my hips to the left. "Simon says move in a circle." I swing my hips around in a circle. "Now give your partner a lap dance."

Fine by me.

Lady Marmalade gets what Lady Marmalade wants.

I lean back against Wyatt's chest, lace my hand behind me, and grip the back of his neck. I slowly move my ass over his lap, using him as leverage. His hands slide up my body, and I totally get lost in the feel of him, in the sway of my hips, in the beat of the music.

It isn't until Wyatt whispers in my ear that I realize what I've done. "Simon didn't say, Aubree."

"Huh?"

My eyes open wide, and I catch Lady Marmalade staring straight at us, as well as Hattie, Hayes, Brody, and Maggie. I pause my hips as my cheeks flame red with embarrassment.

"Well, honey, I think I wouldn't be able to help myself either if I were in your position." The crowd laughs, and I slowly slink off Wyatt's lap as Lady Marmalade tells the crowd to start clapping together.

The music kicks up, and she starts her number, singing but of course, as Lady Marmalade.

I turn toward Wyatt and whisper, "Sorry about that."

He shifts in his seat, keeping his eyes ahead, and says, "It's fine." But it doesn't look fine. It looks like he's . . . irritated. I don't think I've ever seen him look like that. He's always laughing, acting like the fun-loving guy everyone wants to be friends with.

But right now, his brows are set in a stern line, and he's actually leaning away from me.

"Uh, excuse me," he says as he gets up from the couch and moves through the crowd toward the bathroom.

"Oh God," I whisper, feeling foolish.

"Everything okay?" Hattie asks as she leans back.

"Um . . . I don't know," I say. "Let me go check."

I stand as well and adjust my skirt as I move through the crowd and straight back toward the bathrooms, where I see Wyatt disappear into one. Since they're all single toilets, I lean in close to his door and knock.

"Wyatt, it's me. I just wanted—"

The door flies open, and I'm caught by his strong arms before I fly too far forward. I'm pulled into the bathroom right before the door slams shut behind me.

Locked.

And then I'm pressed up against it, only for Wyatt's mouth to come crashing down on mine.

I'm so stunned at first that I don't kiss him back, but when he hikes me up and wraps my legs around his waist before pinning me against the door again, I realize exactly what's going on.

And I want it.

I want it more than anything I think I've wanted in my life.

I grip his cheeks, and I open my mouth for him as his tongue dives and twists against mine. His hands slide up my sides, under my shirt, and to my bra, where he pulls the cups down and presses his palms right to my tits. And he squeezes.

"Fuck," I say as I come up for air. "Wyatt, what's . . ."

"I need this," he says. "Fuck, do I need this." That's when he pulses his hips into mine, and I feel just how much he needs it. "Tell me you want this, you want me."

His lips move down my jaw, to my neck, and I hold him as my entire body melts into him. "I want you, Wyatt."

"Good," he replies as he moves his mouth down my body, lifts my shirt, and then sucks my nipple between his lips.

"Oh my God." I clench my legs around his waist. My hand slides up his neck to his hair, and I tug on it as he tugs on my nipple.

With his other hand, he moves up to my other breast, and he gently starts massaging it, making me feel all kinds of crazy just before he pinches it between his fingers.

"Wyatt," I moan as my head hits the door.

The scruff of his beard mars my skin as he slides his mouth to my other breast, taking my nipple between his lips and then fully sucking on it.

His hips thrust into me.

His hands start to own me with every pass over my skin.

And just as I start to settle into the feel of him, he releases me, letting me stand back up on my own.

"What—" I start to say, but then the man is on his knees, and his hands are moving up my skirt, reaching the waistband of my thong.

He looks up at me. "I need you on my tongue. Stop me now if you don't want this."

Umm, is he insane? There will be no stopping this. None.

I don't say a word, just move my hand over his hair, which is all the invitation he needs. He pulls down my thong, and I step out of it right before he slips my thong into his back pocket. Then he lifts one of my legs over his shoulder, spreads me with his fingers, and his mouth is on me.

Warm, wet, delicious.

"Oh my God," I say, completely taken aback by the way he presses his tongue against my clit. Taking long, languid strokes, he makes sure to lick every part of me.

This . . . this sensation is new.

The fury of his mouth.

The sharpness of his tongue.

The heavenly moans as he tastes me over and over again.

"So fucking good," he mutters before he returns his mouth.

Diving.

Addicted.

Giving me so much pleasure with every single simple stroke.

He kisses me.

Sucks.

Applies just enough pressure that I'm clawing at the man, my mind swirling, my body reacting. It takes about one minute for him to drop to his knees and bring me all the way to the edge.

"God, Wyatt," I say as I tense. He must be able to tell because his mouth moves in more, his tongue, right against my clit, flicking and flicking . . . and flicking.

My body lights up, tension coils at the base of my spine, the air around us seems to still while he works his mouth over me until I'm standing on my toes, ready for release.

"Wyatt . . . I . . . I . . . oh, fuuuuck," I drag out as he licks me one more time, and I tip over the edge, my orgasm rocking through me at such a powerful force that he has to press his hand to my stomach to keep me from toppling over.

And as pleasure rips through me, he doesn't stop. He keeps using his mouth over me until I can't take it anymore.

"No . . . no more," I say as I breathe heavily, my back firmly against the door.

He lifts away from my skirt and looks up at me, the most satisfied smile crossing his lips.

His tongue moves around his mouth, licking up every last drop before he says, "Fucking delicious, Aubree."

He stands from the floor, and he helps me adjust my skirt.

"Christ, I needed that," he says.

He needed that?

Uh, I'm pretty sure I just forgot my name. If anyone needed that, it was me. One hundred percent I needed that.

He takes a step forward and lifts my chin.

"You okay?" he asks.

I nod. "Yeah, I'm . . . I'm okay." Feeling wobbly, I lean into him, my pelvis brushing against his . . .

Wait . . . holy shit.

Is that his . . .?

I move my hand between us and brush my knuckles over his very present erection. Oh my God, it is. "Wyatt," I whisper.

"Yeah?"

"You're so hard."

"I was hard the moment you sat on my lap. When you started moving, that was the end for me. I knew I had to get up and calm myself down." I move my palm over the bulge now. "When you followed me, that was the end of it," he says. "I couldn't hold back."

"You need a release," I say as I start to kneel before him, but he stops me.

"No, you don't need to do that."

I slip my hands to the button of his jeans and undo it, along with the zipper. "I more than want to," I say before sinking all the way to my knees.

"Fuck," he mutters as he grips my hair with one hand.

I tug down his jeans and his briefs, freeing him in one swoop, and oh my God.

Wide-eyed, I look up at Wyatt. "Jesus, Wyatt."

His cock stretches forward, long and thick, with the most perfect head I've ever seen.

"Baby, you don't—"

He doesn't finish as I grip the base of his cock and then lick along the backside, along a vein that leads all the way to the head.

"Fuck . . . me," he says as he leans forward and props his other hand against the door behind me. His legs spread wider, and he angles his body, making it easier for me to access him.

I run my tongue along his length a few times, loving how he twitches and groans with every pass. His reaction empowers me, making me want to give him so much more.

When I reach the head again, I swirl around it a few times, his quads tensing right in front of me, before I open my mouth wide and bring him all the way to the back of my throat.

"Fuck." He slaps his hand against the door. "Your mouth, fucking velvet," he says as I take him all the way to the back of my throat again, letting him feel me lightly gag before pulling him out. "Too good, baby. Too fucking good."

His hand that's holding my hair curls into a fist as he gently guides me up and down his cock. Every time I bring him in, I open wide, and when I pull him out, I suck hard. I can tell he . really likes it because he wants me to move faster, so I do.

I open wide and suck hard, repeating the process until his legs shake and he's visibly on the edge. That's when I pull all the way off him.

"Fuck, why?" he asks as he breathes heavily.

I don't answer. I just swirl my tongue around the head again, letting my tongue play with the slit until he's shaking in front of me.

"Going to come," he says on a short breath.

So I take him all the way to the back of my throat again and slowly pull him out just as his cock swells, and he comes in my mouth with such force that I think it startles us both.

"Fucking hell," he whispers as I swallow and start licking his length again, cleaning him up until he's finished.

Letting go of my hair, he loops his finger under my chin and encourages me to stand. First, though, I place him back in his briefs and zip up his jeans and button them up. Then I stand, and he lifts me from the ground and brings me to the countertop.

When he sets me down, he cups my cheek and leans in to press a sweet kiss to my lips.

It's short and doesn't hold the kind of passion our initial kiss held when he first pulled me into the bathroom, but it shows me that he appreciates me.

Then he grabs some paper towels, wets them with warm water, and wipes my knees down. When our eyes connect, he says, "I don't like that you had to kneel on the bathroom floor for me."

"I don't mind," I say.

"I do," he replies as he cleans my knees. When he finishes, he tosses the paper towels in the trash and rests his hands on my hips. "Are you okay?"

"I'm . . . I'm great," I say, feeling so freaking alive. Like he just breathed a bout of fresh air right into me, awakening every last inch of me from this dark and dreary state I was in.

Sure, I know I'm drunk and my happiness is heightened, but I can't remember the last time I felt this good.

This cherished.

This needed.

And if I were honest with myself, I think I've been feeling this way for a while. I just haven't allowed myself to fully feel it. I've been stubborn, misleading myself, saying that I don't like this man and don't need him in my life. When, in reality, I think . . . Oh God, I think I like Wyatt.

I think I like him more than a friend.

More than the agreement we came up with.

I like him as a person, as a man.

And I don't know if I should be elated or terrified.

"Good." He pulls on the back of his neck. "Listen, Aubree," he says when his gaze meets mine. Uh-oh, why don't I like that look in his eyes? Why does it look like he's about to say something I won't like? Something that might be soul-crushing, especially right after the revelation I had.

"You, uh, you don't need to say anything." I stop him because I don't want to hear it. I don't want to know what's going through his head. I don't want to be disappointed and brought down from my high.

"But——"

I press my hands to his lips. "Really, it's fine. Everything is cool." I hop off the counter and take a deep breath. *Just ignore whatever he was going to say and move on. You don't let him say that he regrets what happened between us, then you'll never know.*

Simple as that.

I move toward the door and unlock it. "Ready?" I ask as I hold my hand out to him.

He stands there for a minute, contemplating what he wants to do . . . wants to say, but he resigns as he walks up behind me. But instead of taking my outstretched hand, he places his hand on the small of my back, guiding me back to the main stage.

And if that isn't telling of how he's feeling, I don't know what is.

Chapter Sixteen

WYATT

Aubree leans against her headrest, curled in and sleeping while a sober Hayes drives us home.

And as I sit here, I can feel the bunching of Aubree's thong in my back pocket.

I can still taste her on my tongue.

I can hear her soft moans as she moved closer and closer to her release.

I drag my hand over my face. Fuck, what was I thinking?

I wasn't. I wasn't thinking at all, and that's the problem. I let myself get lost in the moment. I took advantage of her drinking, my drinking, and I lost control.

Now . . . fuck, now what am I supposed to do?

How am I supposed to navigate this?

It was one thing to kiss her and get lost in her mouth, but now that I know what her pussy tastes like, what her mouth on my cock feels like, I'm thrumming over here, wanting more.

I want so much more.

I want to know what it feels like to be inside her. I want to see the look on her face when I enter her. I want to feel her contract around my cock when she inevitably comes. I want all of it.

But from the way she cut me off tonight, the casual way she just moved on . . . She's always kept her cards close, but this, this I don't know how to navigate.

And we're getting married in six days. Fucking married.

This was supposed to be a business transaction, and now it's turning into something that feels like there's more to it. It makes me wonder if we should get married at all. Because if I'm having feelings for this girl, should I mess with my heart, a heart that's already been broken and barely pieced back together? Should I mess with it and marry someone I could see myself falling for?

That doesn't seem smart.

Because what happens when she doesn't feel the same way I do? What happens when a year is up, and I'm head over heels in love with her, and she wants a divorce?

Fuck.

It wasn't supposed to happen this way. She was supposed to be cranky and not fun to be around, making this an easy transition from marriage to divorce. But of course I had to keep pushing her out of her comfort zone. I had to keep showing her that I was someone to trust, someone she could be honest with, and the more she opened up, the more I wanted to get to know her on a deeper level.

I'm not there yet. I know that. I know there are things she hasn't told me, but fuck I so want to know them. I want to spend days getting to know all of those secrets, preferably with both of us naked.

But I don't think she's there.

Hell, I know she's not there.

"Do you need help carrying her out of the car?" Hayes asks as he pulls up to the guest house. Hell, we're home already?

"Uh, I got it," I say.

"I'll grab the guest house door for you." Hayes hops out of the car and so do I. I move to Aubree's side and open the SUV door. Carefully, I pull her into my arms, making sure her skirt is held tight so no one sees anything.

Hattie mumbles something to me, but I can't quite understand what it is, so I just tell her to have a good night.

Brody and Maggie are passed out in the back, so I don't even bother with them. Good luck to Hayes when they get back to his house. I wouldn't want to be in charge of getting everyone out of the vehicle, especially Brody. He's a pretty big guy.

"Thanks for the ride," I say to Hayes as he opens the door for me.

"Not a problem. Do you have it from here?"

"Yeah," I answer. "Thanks, man."

"Sure thing. Hit me up for some coffee this week."

"I will." I offer him a nod goodbye, and he takes off, shutting the door behind him.

Carefully, I set Aubree on the bed, then lock up the house so I know that we're all set with security. Then I move around the room, taking off my clothes, going to the bathroom, and brushing my teeth. Once I'm ready for bed, then I can get her ready.

I wash my face, swish around some mouthwash, and head into the bedroom, where Aubree is still passed out.

Wanting to make sure she's comfortable, I grab one of my T-shirts—because I'm fucking possessive like that, and I at least want her sleeping in one of my shirts when I can manage it—and I remove her crop top. I try not to notice the thin lace of her bra, but fuck, it's hard not to when I see her dark nipples clear as day through the fabric.

The way they puckered so beautifully between my lips and how responsive she was when I played with them. Fuck me, I want to play with her again. Obviously, not now. I'm not even sure it's an option for the future.

So I drape my shirt over her head as she starts to stir awake.

"It's just me," I whisper. "Getting you dressed for bed." I pull the shirt all the way down and then move my arms up to her bra to remove it. I slip it off without exposing her and toss it in her laundry pile. Then I undo her skirt and pull that down as well.

"I'm tired," she mumbles.

"I know, babe," I say. "Do you think you can go to the bathroom and brush your teeth real quick?"

She mumbles something but stands. I help her to the bathroom, where she takes care of business and then brushes her teeth. Her eyes are closed the entire time. I help her wash her makeup off because I know from nights out with Cadance that Aubree won't want to sleep with that on. I struggle for a moment, looking for the right products, but once I figure it out, it's smooth from there. If I didn't care about this woman, there is no way in hell I would have applied her retinol cream or moisturizer.

When we finish, I help her over to the bed and pull back the covers. She settles into the pillow and curls up, so I drape the blanket over her. She mumbles something.

"What?" I ask, leaning down.

"Hold me," she repeats.

A warm sensation spreads through me. Let's call it satisfaction because despite the agreement, the craziness of this week—of tonight—she still wants my arms wrapped around her when we're in bed together. That gives me the kind of ego boost that puffs my chest and makes me want to give her so much more.

"Give me a second," I say, and because I'm a glutton for punishment, I lean down and press a soft kiss to the top of her head.

I check the door one more time, plug both of our phones in, then slip under the covers with her. Instead of pulling her toward me like I do every night, I move toward her and wrap my arm around her stomach. She snuggles into my chest and then sighs.

I press a kiss to her head one more time, then rest my head on the pillow, feeling wide awake and wired.

I lost control tonight, and I liked it.

I tasted her, and I loved it.

I crossed a big line, and I want so much more.

I'm utterly fucked.

I NEED TO LEAVE.

I need to run.

It has to be no earlier than five thirty, and I'm wide awake.

Thinking about last night. *All* of last fucking night.

Talking with Aubree, touching her gorgeous hair freely, touching her soft, soft skin, moving my hips as she rocked over me . . . *her clit in my mouth. Fuck, her taste. The sounds she made when she came. The look in her stunning eyes as she watched me from her knees. The feel of her hot, warm mouth around my cock.*

Christ, just thinking about last night has me wired.

It's why I need to leave and go for a run to get rid of some of this pent-up energy.

And stop. Thinking. About. Aubree.

I slip out of bed and grab a pair of running shorts from my bag. I don't bother with a shirt because I end up taking it off anyway. I move to the bathroom, where I brush my teeth and change.

When I exit the bathroom, I glance over at Aubree, who has shifted on the bed, but she's still sleeping, so I grab my running shoes and head out of the guest house, not wanting to make too much noise.

I shut the door behind me quietly and then take a seat on the stoop of the stairs, allowing the cold chill of the morning to hit my heated skin. It starts chilly, but it warms up quickly, especially when I start moving.

I slip on my socks and my shoes, taking my time to tie them as I still try to get my bearings. My body is exhausted, my mind is wired, and I'm battling with what the fuck to do with my current situation. I stare out at the rising sun, loving the orange light that settles over the horizon.

I drag my hand over my face and let out a deep breath.

How did this happen?

Over a month ago, I was going to lose the one thing that was most important to me, the cabin. And even though my heart felt tender, bruised, and broken, I was determined to keep my family's legacy alive. *Whatever it took.* I'd fake it until I made it, so to speak.

And here I am, engaged again, yet under very different circumstances.

I'm not in love.

I'm in lust.

I'm not thinking about the future.

I'm daydreaming about the night before.

And I can't get it out of my mind.

I can't shake it.

My body hums for more.

My tongue begs for another taste.

My cock pleads for me to find her mouth again.

Everything in me says one more hit, one more taste. That's all I need to subdue this nagging, growing, itching feeling of needing her. But my head is telling me it's all a lie. One more hit will not satisfy the ache. It will only ignite it.

Which means I need to talk this through.

I reach for my phone but realize I left it in the guest house.

"Shit," I mutter.

She's probably still sleeping, so I just have to be quiet.

I quietly open the door to the guest house and start to slide my body through the narrow opening, not wanting to bring any of the chilly air into the room—and as I lift my head to look for my phone, I catch Aubree scrambling around on the bed before sticking something under her pillow.

So . . . she's awake.

I shut the door behind me, ready to ask her if she's okay, when I hear the telltale sound of vibrating coming from under her pillow.

"What, uh, what are you doing?" she asks with panic in her eyes.

"What am I doing?" I ask while pointing at my chest. "The better question is, what are you doing?"

"N-nothing," she answers, looking anywhere but at me.

I take a step forward, the vibrating sound increasing. "Aubree . . ."

"Yes?" she asks, still avoiding eye contact.

"Are you getting yourself off?"

"No," she says as her cheeks darken with embarrassment. "Wh-why would I do that? That's not, I wasn't . . . aren't you going for a run?"

I take in her appearance, freshly awake from bed, the hint of mint in the air indicating she's brushed her teeth. The red in her cheeks only makes her look that much more adorable. Combine that with the image of her masturbating while I'm gone, and something in my brain switches.

This hunger I've felt for her all night takes over, and before I can stop myself, I take off my shoes and socks.

That taste.

Those sounds.

I need them all over again.

I'm taking the hit.

"No," I say. "I'm not going for a run." And then I kneel on the bed.

"Wh-what are you doing?" she asks as I reach under her pillow and take hold of her vibrator. I turn it off and toss it to the side.

"You don't need that," I say as I tear down the bedding and spread her legs.

"Wyatt," she whispers right before I lower my body flat on the bed and bring my mouth right to her pussy.

I spread her and press my lips to her inner thigh, lightly caressing her soft, sensitive skin with kisses while my fingers spread her pussy, revealing her glistening clit. I practically shiver with excitement as I move my kisses closer. Beneath me, she attempts to wiggle me closer, to bring her arousal to my mouth, so I press my hand to her stomach, holding her in place.

"Wyatt," she groans in frustration.

I pause and look up at the combination of distress and anticipation in her eyes. "You want my tongue, baby?"

"Yes, badly."

"You'll have to wait," I say as I torturously run the tip of my tongue over her pubic bone and along the juncture of her thighs, getting close but never close enough.

I love the struggle in her muscles. The patience that's wearing thin. Her arousal grows with every pass of my mouth, wet and so fucking ready. I was wrong last night. *She. Wants. This.* She wants me just as much as I want her.

My cock pulses against the mattress, wanting so much more. Wanting inside her.

"Fuck, I love this," I say as I start to move my hips against the mattress, easing some of the growing tension in my lower back. "I could eat this pussy all fucking day."

"Then . . . do it," she says in desperation.

Smiling, because I love seeing how much she wants this, I press my tongue to her clit. I don't move, I don't lick, I just hold my tongue there, wanting to gauge her reaction.

And to my fucking delight, she moans loudly as her back arches off the mattress. "Yes, Wyatt."

That's all I need to snap my plans of a slow, methodic way of pleasuring her.

Continuing the pressure, I flatten my tongue against her clit and then slowly drag it up, feeling her arousal all around my tongue.

"Oh . . . my . . . God," she moans.

And she was going to get off on her vibrator. I'm so much better than anything she could do herself. I want her to realize that and keep it in her mind. I want her to remember every second of my tongue between her legs. *Because there is no way I will forget her delicious taste.*

I dip in for more, continuing the slow, languid strokes, prepping her for what's to come as I grind my hips into the mattress at the same time, the friction of my cock against the mattress spurring me on.

"So good," she says. I love the way she vocalizes and doesn't hide her feelings.

And Christ, she's got to have the best-tasting pussy I've ever had the luxury of going down on.

Sweet, bare, and responsive. Everything I want in a woman.

Wanting more, I slide my hand under her shirt to her breasts, where I find her nipples already hard. So fucking hot.

I run my fingers over them lightly at first, thinking back to her words from the night before.

"He wouldn't play with my nipple. He wouldn't circle his finger around it or flick it or pinch it. He'd lick it on occasion, but that didn't do much. I wanted more from him. So much more."

Fucking selfish prick.

Well, I'm not, and these fucking incredible breasts are going to get everything they love and more.

The hardened nubs tug against my fingertips as I circle her nipples, then pass over them, continuing the movement until her head thrashes from side to side and her breathing picks up.

"Yes," she whimpers. "Just like that."

After a few passes of my tongue and a few teasing rubs of my fingers, I pinch her nipple at the same time as I suck her clit between my lips.

"Oh my God!" she yells as her back arches off the mattress. "Oh fuck, Wyatt." Her hand falls to my head, her fingers tangling in my hair—one of the best feelings ever.

"That's it, baby."

I continue to suck on her clit while my finger rolls her nipple, pinches, and lightly tugs.

She moans.

She quakes.

She tugs on my hair.

It's so fucking hot.

While she tenses around me, I take her legs and drape them over my shoulders before I release her clit, and then, with the tip of my tongue, I flick rapidly over her clit. Immediately, she lets out a delicate moan as her legs clamp around my head. Her body lifts, and she says, "Wyatt . . . I can't . . . I'm going . . ."

I lift my mouth off her for a second to say, "Come, baby. Come all over my tongue."

And then my mouth is on her again. My fingers pinch her nipples. My tongue runs rapidly over her clit.

Her body tenses, her back arches, her fists clench into the sheets, and in a matter of seconds, she's yelling out my name, her pleasure tipping over the edge as her orgasm rocks through her.

"Oh God, oh fuck. Yes . . . yes, keep going," she moans. "More, Wyatt." I keep flicking, loving how wet she is. I lap up every ounce of her as the tension slowly ebbs from her orgasm.

I lazily let my tongue explore her pussy until she's sated and relaxed on the bed.

Spent.

Satisfied.

That's when I lift and stare up at her, a beautiful, pleasured smile crossing over her lips as her eyes open to meet mine.

"Fuck," she whispers, catching her breath. She covers her eyes with her arm. "You're so good at that."

"I better be," I say as I lift some more, the pain of my erection almost knocking me back down. While I was going down on her, I practically humped the mattress, getting off on her moans, on the taste of her, but now that I'm all riled up with no release, there's only one thing to do—go take a shower.

I lift off from the bed, my erection painfully obvious in my briefs, so I head for the bathroom, but she calls out to me. "What are you doing?"

I glance down at my tented briefs and then back at her. "Release, baby," I say.

She props up on her elbows and says, "Come get a release over here."

I shake my head. "That's not why I did that to you."

"I know," she says. "But . . . don't you want me to help you?" The way she asks, insecurity lacing through her voice, there's no way I could deny her.

"More than anything," I say. A smile lights up her face as I move toward the bed again. "Where do you want me?"

She reaches for the vibrator she was using and says, "Lie down."

I do as I'm told and ask, "What are you doing with that?"

"Having fun," she says, surprising me.

I lie down, and the tip of my cock peeks past my briefs, but I don't do anything. I let her take charge, and she straddles my thighs and turns on the vibrator. I place my hands behind my head as she brings the vibrator down to the tip of my cock.

"Fuuuck . . . yes," I drag out, already knowing this will be amazing.

"Does that feel good?" she asks.

"So fucking good, Aubree," I say as I stare up at her and her fucking angelic face, her orgasm-stained cheeks. Her hair curly and flowing over her shoulder and back, and those eyes, lit up with intrigue, looking like she's ready for a show from me.

I'll fucking give her one.

Anything she wants at this point.

I just want to come, and I want her to watch me come.

Keeping my briefs where they are, she brings the vibrator down my length to the base and back up.

"That's it, baby," I say. "Tease me. Make me so fucking hard."

Her eyes briefly fly to mine, then focus on what she's doing. She lifts and says, "Spread your legs."

I do as I'm told, and she straddles only one of my thighs as she brings the vibrator down between my legs and right to my balls. And because she doesn't have any underwear on, I can feel how wet she still is from her orgasm. *Fuck, that's going to make me even harder.*

"Take your shirt off. I want to see those gorgeous tits," I growl out. And thank fuck, she does. "Jesus, fuck," I say as I grip the sheets under me tightly.

"Oh fuck, that's . . . Jesus." I nearly feel my eyes roll to the back of my head as she presses it against the spot right behind my balls. "Shit, Aubree."

My cock springs up, now resting on my stomach, twitching from the new pleasure that I didn't fucking know existed.

And that's where she keeps the vibrator, clearly happy with my reaction that she doesn't stop. With her other hand, she takes the rest of my cock out of my briefs and then leans down and licks the tip.

"Fuck me," I say as my hips lift. "Shit, I need, I need more, baby."

"What do you want?" she asks.

"Whatever you're willing to give me," I answer.

Smiling, she removes the vibrator for a moment and lowers my briefs until they're completely off. Then she brings the vibrator back to my balls and runs it along the sensitive seam a few times, then to that special spot again, and that's where she keeps it.

"Don't move. I want that staying there."

"Trust me." I gulp. "It will."

Smiling, she then climbs on top of me, hovers over my lap, and I nearly blackout as she starts to lower down, but instead of posing my cock at her entrance like I thought she might, she lowers her pussy on top of my cock right over the ridge.

Warm, wet, and addicting. That's all I can think as she starts to rub herself along my length, dry-humping but without the clothes between us.

Her hands fall to my chest as she takes a deep breath, her hips moving faster now.

"Jesus fuck, Aubree," I say. "You're so fucking hot."

"You're so huge," she replies, her head falling back. "God, I'm going to get off again."

"Let me hear it, Aubree," I say as my teeth clench together. The feel of her smooth pussy gliding over me, combined with the vibrator, brings me to the fucking edge. "Shit," I say as my balls tighten. "Fuck, I'm going to come."

Her fingers dig into the skin on my chest as she rides me faster, harder.

Her teeth fall over her bottom lip.

The muscles in her neck contract.

And the sexiest moan falls past her lips as she comes again on top of me.

"Yes, God . . . yes," she cries as every one of my limbs goes numb, my body tightens, and I groan as my cock twitches and comes all over my stomach.

"Mother . . . fucker," I say, loving how she continues to ride on me as I finish coming.

I grip her hips, and my dick jolts under her.

She flips her head back and lets her hair fall down her shoulders and back as she catches her breath.

She's so gorgeous.

The slope of her neck, that head of hair I want to dive my fingers into. Those perfect tits. I want every inch of this woman.

I don't want bits and pieces. I want more, so much more, and I know I can't ask.

I can't tell her, not when we have an agreement.

Not after last night and her cold detachment after we came.

She rolls off me and grabs the vibrator before turning it off. She lies flat on the bed, her arms spread as she looks up at the ceiling.

"You okay?" I ask her.

She drapes her arm over her chest, still breathless. "I'm . . . I'm still contracting."

Shit, that's hot.

Wanting to feel it, I lean on my side, spread her legs, and then slowly slip my fingers inside her. She groans as her pussy contracts around them.

"Jesus Christ," I say before removing my fingers and bringing them to my mouth. Her eyes are on me as I lick her arousal off my fingers. "You taste like goddamn heaven," I say.

Her eyes squeeze shut, almost in disbelief. *And she thought multiple orgasms by a man wasn't a thing.* Fuck, she's had selfish lovers.

Then I take the vibrator and switch it on. Her eyes widen for a moment before I rest it right against her clit.

"I want one more from you, Aubree."

"I don't think . . . I don't think I can." She breathes heavily.

"Yes, you can," I say. Her breasts are anything but big, less than a handful, but they're round with small dark nipples that have my mouth watering. Images of her last night in her lace bra scour through my mind as I lower my mouth to the little nubs and run my tongue around in circles, focusing on her areolas.

"Come on, baby. I want to hear those sweet moans one more time."

She tenses as her breathing picks up.

"You're close, aren't you?" I ask.

She nods as she presses her lips together, so I switch off the vibrator.

Her eyes shoot open, and her mouth falls open in protest. "Wyatt, don't stop."

I drag the vibrator up her stomach to her breasts and switch it on, letting it run over her nipples, over her cleavage, and under her breasts.

"I don't want an easy orgasm. You have to earn it," I say.

"How . . . how?" she asks, clearly in distress.

"Tell me how much you like my mouth, my cock, my fingers. The more compliments, the closer you'll get to your orgasm."

Her tongue peeks past her beautiful lips before she wets them. "No one has ever given me oral like you. Just thinking about you going down on me gets me wet."

Christ.

I didn't think she'd go along with my plan, but here she is, divulging how she feels, and I'm fucking living for it. I drag the vibrator to her stomach.

"Your pussy tastes so fucking good. It's all I can think about."

"I barely felt your fingers, but they're so long . . ."

"I'll use them on you, Aubree. I want to fucking use them."

Her breath hitches as her teeth pull on her bottom lip while I bring the vibrator right to her pubic bone.

"What about my cock?"

"It's huge," she answers, which brings a smile to my face. "I loved sucking on it. I loved riding it."

"Good," I answer right before I bring the vibrator to her clit.

She screams a resounding yes that echoes off the walls of the small space as her back arches. I bring my mouth to her right nipple, drawing it past my teeth and against my tongue.

While her breathing becomes erratic, I continue to work her, to play with her, to bring her to another apex because all I want is to hear her one more time. See her collapse into pleasure one more fucking time . . .

"Oh God, yes, Wyatt. Oh fuck, I can't . . . I don't think . . . mmmmmm, fuck." She grips my head, keeping me on her breasts so I nibble on them, tugging with my teeth. I'm probably pulling a little too hard, but she doesn't seem to mind.

It actually seems to spur her on even more as she lifts into the air, silence falling past her parted lips.

"Aubree, baby, I want you to come again. Give me that orgasm. Let me hear it."

She writhes.

She thrashes.

She digs her fingers into my scalp.

"Fuck, Wyatt . . . oh God."

"You're close. Come, baby . . . come for me."

She groans, drapes her hand over her eyes, and then her body tenses. Her mouth falls open. A feral cry flies out of her as she convulses beneath me, her entire body shuddering as she moans out my name.

So fucking hot.

I keep the vibrator on her sensitive clit until she squeezes her legs together, and I know there's nothing else she can give me at the moment. So I turn it off and toss it to the side. Then I move down to her pussy, spread her legs one more time, and press a soft, caressing kiss against her clit.

I watch her wet her lips as she slowly relaxes into the mattress, looking like she was just put through a vigorous, soul-defining exercise.

After a few seconds of her catching her breath, she opens those beautiful eyes and looks up at me as I move toward the top of the bed. Her expression reads satisfied but also confused.

I brush a piece of hair out of her face and then gently cup her cheek. "You okay?" I ask her.

She lightly nods her head.

"Then why does it look like you're stunned?"

"Be-because I am," she says. "I, uh . . . that was unlike anything I've ever experienced."

"Trust me when I say, me too. Not sure I've ever come like that before, but fuck would I do it again."

She smiles but then worries her lip as she looks away. I know that avoidance. I can practically hear the wheels in her head turning as she tries to piece this together and make sense of it all.

"God, Wyatt," she whispers. Please don't say it, please don't say it. "What are we even doing?"

She fucking said it.

Just like last night, she's pulling away and distancing herself. She realizes that she gave in to temptation, and now she's slowly trying to back away. And just like last night, it doesn't hurt any less.

"I, uh, I don't know," I say even though I know damn well what *I'm* doing. I'm starting to like a girl I shouldn't fucking like. I'm starting to develop feelings.

Cravings.

Addictions.

Needs and wants.

Looking unsure, she says, "I don't know if we should be doing this. I don't know if we should be crossing this line."

And just like that, poof, all of the hopes and needs and wants vanish without a trace.

This was what I was afraid of, of her saying those exact words. Not because I don't agree, but because I *do* agree with her. We shouldn't be doing this. It's dangerous, given our situation. But a big part of me wanted her to live in a state of delusion with me, where we didn't think about the future. A part of me wished that we could shove all of the complications away and just fucking enjoy. Live in the moment. Explore every last part of each other.

I tug on my hair in frustration, knowing that I have to agree with her. "I know," I reply and blow out a heavy breath. "Fuck, I'm sorry, Aubree. I'm apparently having a hard time controlling myself."

"It's fine. We don't need to apologize. I think just be more careful."

"Yeah, I agree," I say, sitting up. "Uh, I think I'm going to take a shower, if that's okay?"

"Yes, um, can I just wash up real quick, and then I'll get out of your hair."

"Sure," I say as she lifts from the bed and puts on my T-shirt. She walks over to the bathroom but then looks over her shoulder at me. "Thanks for taking care of me last night."

"Here in the guest house . . . or in the club bathroom?" I can't help myself.

She smiles. "Both." Then she shuts the bathroom door, and I lie flat on the bed, gripping my hair.

Fuck.

Me.

———

SITTING on a bench in the park right across from The Talkies, I stare out at the hazy ocean as I hold my phone, contemplating if I should talk to Laurel.

I mean, who am I kidding? If I don't talk to her, I might lose my fucking mind.

I pull up her name in my phone and text her.

Wyatt: *Do you have a moment to talk?*

I sip my coffee from The Cliffs. Christ, this coffee is good, which means it's not Clearwater Coffee. On the walk over here, I downed a bear claw, knowing that this afternoon, I'll have to go to the gym at the inn—Ethel gave me permanent access—and work it off.

My phone beeps with a text.

Laurel: *Yup, I'm free. Want me to call?*

I don't bother texting her back. Instead, I dial her number, and she picks up on the first ring.

"What's going on? Everything okay?" she asks as a hello. Leave it to the lawyer to get straight to the point.

"Not really," I say, slouching on the bench.

She pauses for a moment and then whispers, "Did she call off the wedding?"

"No, nothing has changed there. Planning on Saturday. You can still come, right?"

"Do you really think I would not make it to your wedding that's fake, but not really fake? I'm there for the drama."

"There better not be any drama."

"Very true. We don't want any drama. Okay, so if the wedding is still set, then is it your parents? Are they pissed?"

"Uh." I scratch the side of my jaw. "I haven't told them yet. I didn't want to tell them out of fear that they'd mention something to Wallace."

"Probably smart, but does that mean they won't be at the wedding?"

"No," I say. "I'll tell them we eloped. My parents did the same thing, so I know they'll understand. I do think they're going to have a hard time understanding that it's Aubree I married and it's not even been two months since I was supposed to marry someone else, but you know, that's a bridge I can cross when it happens."

"So then, what's the problem?"

I squeeze my eyes shut. "Fuck, Laurel, I don't know how this happened, but . . . I think I like her."

There's silence.

"Uh, what do you mean? Define like? Are we talking friends here or . . . more than friends?"

"More than friends," I answer.

"Ohhh my," she coos into the phone like a teenager. "Hubba, hubba, our boy has feelings."

"Laurel, I'm serious. This isn't good."

"I'm sorry, but I don't see how this is an issue. Is it not good to like your future wife? Huh, I must be old-school then because I thought that was a great reason to like someone."

"Not when you're going into this marriage on a business deal. This should have been platonic, and well . . ."

"You guys had sex," she finishes for me, her voice far too excited. How come she doesn't understand the severity of this?

"Not quite," I say. "But pretty close to it."

"Oh boy, let me guess, you went down on her."

"You know"—I sift my hand through my hair—"details are not important." She laughs, and it just annoys me. "Laurel, this isn't funny. I'm serious, this is a problem."

"Let me get this straight. You hang out with this girl for two weeks, you strike up a deal, you're getting married, and then you go down on her, and you're in all kinds of panic because now you're starting to like the woman you're supposed to marry this Saturday when, in reality, you shouldn't like her because this is a business deal, not an opportunity for a love affair."

"Exactly," I say with relief.

She gets it.

"You're being an idiot."

Or not.

"I'm not being an idiot," I defend. "I'm being sensible."

"Really?" she asks. "Is it sensible to push away feelings you might have for a woman only to marry her and live with her for a year with no chance of shaking off the feelings, only giving them the opportunity to continue to grow the more time you spend with her? Seems pretty stupid to me."

"Well, when you put it like that . . ." I mutter.

"Seriously, what's the big deal? So you like her. Deal with it. Seems like an ideal situation to me because this could be the chance to maybe fall in love again."

I shake my head. "I don't think . . . I don't think there's a chance for that. Or at least, a chance at reciprocation, and I don't want to get hurt again. I don't think I can take another rejection."

"What do you mean there isn't a chance for reciprocation?" she asks. "You don't think she likes you?"

"I don't think she'd open herself up like that. She's . . . she's damaged, Laurel. She's been hurt by many men. I'm not sure the trust is there."

"But it's also been two weeks at most. How do you know that six months from now, she won't feel the same way about you? That she won't trust you by then?"

"But what if she doesn't?" I ask. "I don't think I can stomach falling for her, only for her to never feel the same way. I don't want to put in the time and put my heart at risk only for it to be crushed."

Laurel sighs over the phone and then grows serious. "Do you remember our senior year in college, when I met Ginny?"

How could I forget Ginny? She was the one woman who put Laurel into a tailspin after she broke up with her. Laurel questioned everything about herself. The way she dressed, the way she wore her hair, the way she acted around people, and the way she represented herself. She went into a deep depression, stopped eating, and really turtled in on herself. It took a long time to get Laurel back to the same woman she once was.

"I know where you're going with this," I say.

"If you do, then why are you questioning opening your heart again? You saw what I went through. You saw how I was able to —with your help—open my heart again. I suffered so much heartache, and here I am, dating someone new and loving that I have a person I can go out on dates with and talk to before I go to bed. Are you saying you'll never open yourself up again?"

"I don't know," I say. "This is so complicated. We're two damaged souls trying to connect and get what we need in life. She hasn't really opened up to me, but I haven't opened up to her. There's still a wall, but the attraction is heavy. She doesn't even know about Cadance and that I was engaged to another woman two months ago. I thought I loved Cadance, Laurel, but here I am with feelings for a different woman. I was going to fucking marry Cadance because I thought I was in love with her. Fuck, Laurel, I'm so confused."

Surely I should still be grieving a lost relationship, but I couldn't give two fucks about Cadance at the moment. I no longer care that she's out of my life. *What does that say about our relationship? Was it just infatuation?* Have I simply replaced Cadance with the next willing woman to sleep with me? Or do I actually see the chance of more with Aubree . . . *which terrifies me if she doesn't feel the same way.*

"Tell me this," she says. "Do you think you can go a whole year sleeping next to this woman in a small guest house and keep your hands to yourself?"

I snort. "Fuck no."

"Exactly, which means you'll have to take a chance on something. You have two chances as far as I see it. You can take a chance on your willpower and keep your hands to yourself for a year, or you can take a chance on your heart, and see if the person you're going to marry in a few days very well might be the person you're supposed to spend the rest of your life with. Now you just have to figure out what you're going to do."

"THANK YOU FOR BEING HERE TODAY," Maggie says as we sit in front of her on Hayes's couch, ready for whatever presentation she's put together. To say she's in her element would be an understatement.

I met up with Aubree in town, where we picked up some cheese, crackers, meats, dried fruit, and nuts for a charcuterie board to take to Hayes and Hattie's house. We didn't say much to each other as we shopped around, but we did look like a couple, which was what was important. Dee Dee checked us out at the register, and as we were leaving, she said she planned to put together a newlywed special at the front of the store of everything people would need to help celebrate our wedding.

Just what we need, more attention, especially when I have this burning itch to put my hands all over Aubree. My brain tells me not to go there.

On the drive over to Hayes and Hattie's house, Aubree quickly put everything on a tray, not even bothering to make it look nice. She grumbled the entire time, saying something along the lines of, this is why you don't ask people if you can bring anything. She also grabbed two jars of a special kind of pickle. They were the last two in stock.

And now that we're here, with our poorly constructed charcuterie board on the island and pickles in the fridge, Maggie has sat us down and is about to present her wedding ideas to us.

Hands together in front of her, she says, "Now, this might seem a bit overwhelming, and if at any time you want me to stop, I can, but I had a long chat with Ethel this morning, and I really think we've put something together that will be quaint like you want, but also a beautiful celebration of love." She claps her hands together three times. "Brody, you may enter with the first board."

From the hallway, Brody walks in, holding a large board against his chest.

"Excuse my lack of professionalism in this presentation. I can only be as professional as what is handed to me."

"I told you it would be fine," Hattie says from the side where she and Hayes sit together, his arm draped over her shoulders. Hmm, I should be touching Aubree too.

I take that moment to press my hand to her thigh while saying, "No need to impress us. We're just excited to get married."

"Well, I want you to know, this is not how I normally work, but like I said, I was given magazines, a printer with minimal ink, glue sticks, and markers."

"She's being dramatic," Hattie says.

"Shush, we don't need your commentary." Maggie clears her

throat. "Hayes, the mood music, please."

"Alexa, turn on wedding music," he says before kissing Hattie on the cheek.

"Playing wedding music, instrumentals on Amazon Music," his Alexa says.

Maggie stomps her foot. "Hayes, I gave you a list of songs you could play on your guitar."

"I know."

"Why aren't you playing them?"

"Because I wanted to play with Hattie this afternoon instead."

Hattie chuckles and pushes at his chest. In return, he grips her chin and turns her head toward him, only to kiss her very passionately in front of everyone. Lucky son of a bitch. I wonder what Aubree would do if I turned her head and kissed her passionately like that in front of everyone.

Probably accept it, but then tell me how we shouldn't be doing that kind of stuff later when we're alone. The rhetoric that's been a real wet blanket on my needs.

At least I would have been able to kiss her, though.

Brody turns to Maggie and says, "They got to play while I was attempting not to glue my fingers to your poster board?"

"Listen," Maggie says, quieting everybody with her stern voice. "The side chatter is very unprofessional, and I'm trying to be professional." She gestures toward us. "We have a newly engaged couple getting married on Saturday. This is DEFCON 1 status. Okay? We will need the entire town to help us pull this off, and I'd like to start making decisions without having to listen to you two make out." She motions to Hattie and Hayes. "And you complaining about not making out." She gestures to Brody.

"I just really like you," Brody says, almost with a pout.

Wow, does he really think that's going to work—

Maggie's expression softens as she walks up to him. "I really like you too." She lightly kisses him on the lips and then whispers something in his ear that makes him smile.

Christ, it did work.

I'm going to bank that for possible use later.

She kisses him one more time and then clasps her hands together. Brody stares at her as if she's the best thing that's ever happened in his life. So . . . my assumption is they're going to get married soon as well. If Brody has anything to say about it, they will.

"Okay, as I was saying, we have decisions to make and not a lot of time. So, Brody, if you could turn the poster board for us, I'd appreciate it."

Brody turns the board around, and we're met with a neatly organized collage of pictures and ideas. At the very top, in bold lettering, it says Mr. and Mrs. Preston. Below is a picture of the barn, hay bales, lace, and bulb lighting. Rows of old dining room tables with mismatched chairs, lace runners, and wildflowers. A picture of The Cliffs with a bowl of mac and cheese next to it, which I think is funny. The tractor is used as a backdrop for the bar, and there's a layout of a dance floor and what the tables would look like lined up—although that's more tables than I'd expect. And then of course a bouquet of wildflowers strung together by jute. There are a few other things, like favors and the wedding party and . . . Chewy Charles. It's very well put together.

Stepping to the side of the poster board, Maggie holds up a wooden spoon and starts painting a picture for us.

"The wedding starts at dusk, right before the sun sets. String bulb lights illuminate the barn, and hay bales are lined up row by row but covered with burlap and tweed. Hayes plays a soft melody of *Wildest Dreams* and *Love Story*. The procession starts, led by Hattie, followed by MacKenzie and Chewy Charles." I hold back my snort because she's truly trying to paint a pretty picture for us. "Then the bride steps out, and there isn't a dry eye in the barn. She's so beautiful there will be sonnets written about her. The town will have no other choice than to clap because she's breathtaking, like a gust of angel breath caressing the farm."

"What about the groom?" I ask. "Is he angel's breath?"

Maggie's eyes fall to mine. "His jawline will make people

weep."

I wink at her. "That's what I like to hear."

She smiles and continues. "The couple says their I do's, and then they're announced as Mr. and Mrs. Wyatt Preston. The cheers will make the cows one farm over lift their ears with interest. Potatoes will sprout new eyes. The bees will flitter about, proud of their new owners." Dear God. "And then, while you're off taking pictures during the golden hour, the tables will be arranged and set up. Tables from around town will be brought in along with chairs. They'll be quickly decorated while a dance floor is assembled. This will be the busiest time, but guests will enjoy some spiked cider and bear claws in the barn while talking about how beautiful the new couple is."

"Because of the jawline," I say.

Maggie points at me with her wooden spoon. "Precisely. Once pictures are done, we'll introduce the new couple, the family, as well as Chewy Charles, because that has been told to me by a spicy four-year-old. Then we feast on mac and cheese from The Cliffs and cherry pie for dessert. Wildflowers will be used for décor and the bouquets. Invitations will be e-vite because we don't have enough time to print, but I think that's okay. I would say we're looking at about . . . one hundred and fifty people—"

"What?" Aubree practically yells. "Where are you getting that number from?"

Maggie looks stunned. "Uh, Ethel gave it to me."

"Ethel?" Aubree asks. "She's not in charge of the guest list. I wasn't even planning to invite her."

"Ooo, that would be a bad idea," Maggie says. "I know I'm not from here, but just from what I know, not inviting Ethel would be a black mark on your name."

"Babe, we have to invite Ethel," I say.

"But if you invite Ethel, you have to invite Dee Dee," Aubree says. "And if Dee Dee is invited, then the whole Peach Society is invited. If the whole Peach Society is invited, then Rodney will want to come—"

"You're not going to invite Rodney?" Hattie asks. "He drove your knight in shining armor onto the dance floor on a locomotive. You don't think that deserves an invite?"

"A locomotive, Aubree," I repeat because this seems like a lot of fun.

"Be that as it may," she says, looking at me with those stern eyes. "I don't think one hundred and fifty people should be at the wedding."

"What is your ideal wedding party size?" Maggie asks.

"I don't know . . . ten?"

"Ten?" Maggie shouts, then quickly calms herself. "Ten is . . . very intimate. Ten might be too intimate. If it were ten, I don't think we'd be invited." Maggie motions to herself and Brody with the wooden spoon. "And even though there are times when I'm terrified of you, I'd still like to witness your marriage. Plus, Ethel and Rodney are a must for the invite, given what they did for the proposal."

"I second that." Hattie raises her hand. "On all the accounts, even the terrifying part."

Aubree snaps a look at her sister, who curls into Hayes.

"Fine, we can expand the guest list to twelve."

Maggie winces. "Again, I just don't think that's enough people. You see, normally I wouldn't blink an eye when paring down the guest list, but the problem is, Ethel has made it quite clear that this is a town event. She stated that the proposal was a town event, and now the wedding is a town event, and it won't happen on time unless the town is involved. Therefore, it seems like we're going to have to include the town."

"Then we just elope," Aubree says. "I'm not into the big wedding thing."

"It might seem big," Maggie says. "But in reality, it's actually quite small and intimate. You won't even be able to tell."

"Trust me, if I'm up there saying I do and notice more than ten people staring up at me, I'll be able to tell." She turns to me, and with those pleading eyes, she says, "Let's just elope."

Oh boy.

Here's the thing. Right now, I'd do anything to make Aubree happy. Reason number one: I got her into this mess, and I want to make it as smooth as I can for her. Reason number two: this guy, **thumbs toward himself** is currently crushing on his fiancée, and well, he wants to keep her happy. Reason number three: I don't care for a large wedding either.

But the problem with all of that is, we *need* to convince the people of the town that we're a couple so when shit hits the fan with Wallace, and he comes charging into Almond Bay— because he will—he won't be able to prove our relationship is fake.

And that's what matters the most.

But I can't say that in front of everyone, so I calmly place my hand on Aubree's thigh and say, "Babe, I know this is overwhelming, but think of it this way. These people love you, and they want to help you. Plus, your brother has already told me that he'll murder me if we elope, and as much as I would like to elope with you, I want to do the right thing by your family. You all have been through a lot. Let's make this a day for celebration."

Her eyes connect with mine, and for a moment, it's almost as if there's appreciation in them. Appreciation for my comment, appreciation for understanding her family dynamics.

On a sigh, she turns to everyone and says, "Fine, but we are not having one hundred and fifty people."

Maggie claps her hands in excitement. "Brilliant. What is your cap?"

"Fifty," she says.

Maggie winces but then nods. "Okay, that's doable. I think we can manage that. Ethel will have to be cutthroat, but I think we can manage. Now." Maggie lets out a long sigh. "What are you going to do about a dress?"

Aubree shifts uncomfortably and says, "Well, I just thought I could wear Cassidy's, if that would be okay." She glances over at Hattie.

"You want to wear Cassidy's dress?" Hattie asks.

"I mean, if that's okay. If not, I can find something else. I just thought it would be the easiest, cheapest option."

"Money doesn't matter," I say quietly, just in case she needs to know that.

"Thank you," Aubree whispers.

But then Hattie presses her hand to her chest and says, "I think . . . that would be so sweet."

"Are you sure? You weren't going to wear it when you eventually get married?"

"Does it matter?" Hattie asks. "We could all wear it. Kind of like sisterhood of the traveling pants but with a dress."

That makes Aubree chuckle. "Well, if you're cool with it, then I'd like to wear it."

I'm shocked that she'd want to wear something so senti-mental to a wedding that's all for business, but then again, maybe it's a strength thing. What we're doing on Saturday, getting married for convenience, can't be easy on Aubree, and maybe if she has her sister there in spirit, it will be easier for her to walk down the aisle.

That makes a lot of sense.

"I think it will be perfect," Hattie says. "Are you going to wear the veil with it?"

Aubree shakes her head. "No, that's more your thing."

"If I can step in for a moment," Maggie says, raising the wooden spoon. "If you'd like, I could fasten together a flower crown to go with the wildflower bouquet. Even something that resembles more of a headband."

"Oh sure, that would be fine," Aubree says.

"Wonderful. I have something in mind that'll work perfectly. And just so I can report back to Ethel, who is my supplier at the moment, I need a verbal yes to what I have going on here." With her wooden spoon, she points at certain aspects of the wedding —the tables, the lace, the wildflowers, the barn, and the food. And with every slap of her spoon to the poster board, we give her a verbal yes. That's until we reach the cherry pie.

"No," Aubree says.

"What?" I ask in surprise. "Babe, that's our special pie."

I can practically hear the eye roll she's holding back. "I think we should have more options for those who might not like cherry pie."

"Uh, didn't you hear?" I say. "We're trendsetters. Everyone in town likes the cherry pie."

"Just in case," Aubree says in an annoyed tone. "Also, there will be no trains at the wedding."

"Aubree," I say in a challenge. "How could you do that to Rodney? He's probably polishing up the locomotive right now, getting it ready for another debut."

"No trains," she says, practically putting her foot down.

"No trains it is." Maggie speaks behind her hand to Brody. "You're going to have to tell Ethel that."

"Why me?" he asks, visibly shaken.

"Because I don't want to be the bearer of bad news, honestly, Brody." She lets out a deep breath and then smiles at us again. "Okay. If we're all set here, I believe we have some cheese and crackers to tend to."

"Hold on a second," Hattie says. "I thought you wanted the ceremony under the tree."

Oh, that's right. I peer at Aubree as her lips twist to the side. I know what the tree means to her. Would she want to get married there, in her sister's dress? Or would she save that for someone who means more to her than I do?

"The barn works," Aubree says, and because I'm crushing on this girl, a stab of disappointment hits me in the gut. The dress is fine, but the tree . . . she's saving that. "I don't want to move too many things around on the farm."

"Are you sure?" Maggie asks. "Because we can make it happen."

"No, the barn is great."

"Wonderful. So . . . cheese and crackers?"

"Great, I'm starving," Brody says as he puts down the poster board.

Maggie loops her arms around his waist and stands on her

toes to kiss him sweetly on the lips. "Thank you for being my easel."

"Anything for you," he says as he kisses her, slowly moving his hand right to her ass.

God, that's irritating.

I miss that. The ability to freely and wholly love someone. To touch them and grab them and kiss them however you want, whenever you want. I know now that Cadance wasn't the right person for me. I'm still questioning why because there was no closure there, but even with that, I don't want to be with someone who doesn't want to be with me. But that doesn't stop me from missing the way I held her hand and didn't think twice about it. Kiss her with everything in me and not worry about what she might say after.

I want the ability to hold and to cuddle and to run my hand up Aubree's shirt without her stiffening or wondering what I'm doing.

Christ, I want her.

I want her bad.

And I have no idea how this happened. How all of a sudden, I can wake up in the morning and feel perfectly content because I have my arm around her. Or how I can smile when I see her, all dirty from working on the farm, looking like a hot mess, but still think she's beautiful.

I don't get how I could just know of a woman one day and then want more the next.

And I want her to want more.

I want her to want to get to know me, to want to be with me.

To give this a fighting chance and not treat it as a contract.

"Can I speak to you for a moment?" Aubree asks as she stands.

"Yeah, sure," I say, standing as well.

Without taking my hand, she walks out toward the back deck, where a beautiful, still pool expands across the yard with a picturesque view of the ocean, offering peace and serenity. I need to get myself a house like this because Jesus, Hayes knows what he's doing.

When Aubree shuts the sliding glass door and walks me farther out to a firepit and bench area, she takes a seat, so I join her.

"Everything okay?" I ask.

"Sort of," she says as she stares out at the ocean. "Just wanted a second to breathe and thought that if I did it alone, it would look like I was mad at you."

"Are you mad at me?" I ask.

"No." She shakes her head and rubs her hands over her thighs. "Just overwhelmed. I didn't think this wedding was going to be a thing, and now it's a thing, so I'm starting to get anxious. I feel like we're doing it for everyone else but us, and then I think, why would we do it for us? This isn't a real marriage filled with love. This is a business transaction, so we should be doing it for everyone else because it's a show, you know? And we need to perform, but then it made me sad for a second because I'm going to wear Cassidy's dress, and why would I do something senti- mental like that if this wedding isn't sentimental? But then again, I'm nervous and a little scared and worried, and she was the closest thing to a motherly figure that I've had in my life, and I just thought that she should be there, and that felt dumb and——"

"Hey," I say, gripping her chin so she has to look at me. "Shhhh, you're starting to freak out."

"I know because this is all so much." Her scared eyes peer up at me.

Wanting to offer her comfort, I say, "If you want to call it off, we can call it off. Like I said, I can walk away, give you the land, and figure something else out. I'm not opposed to that, Aubree. This was a lot, me asking you to do this, and when I came up with it, it was completely selfish. I didn't think what this might do to you mentally. All I thought is that you would get the land, and it would be fine, but . . . now I see the toll it's taking on you."

"Stop," she says, shaking her head. "I'm not taking the land from you. I'm going to earn it. You're going to get your cabin, and all of this will be over in a year." See, when she says things like that, it brings me right back to reality. This is a business transaction to her, and that's all it will ever be. And I don't blame her. That's how I approached it. That's how I came into this. That's how I sold it. Why would she have any feelings other than that?

She shouldn't.

I continue, "But if you're uncomfortable—"

"I'm just nervous." She turns toward me on the bench, bringing one leg up as she faces me. "Aren't you nervous?"

I drape my arm over the bench and face her as well. "It hasn't hit me yet. Maybe when the day comes, I'll be nervous, but I'm also comfortable with you," I say as I take a chance and place my hand on her leg. I rub my thumb over her soft skin. "If I wasn't comfortable with you, I'd probably be terrified." I swallow and tilt my head down as I ask, "Are you comfortable with me?"

She's silent for a second, which feels like hours before she answers. "If I wasn't comfortable with you, I wouldn't want you to hold me at night," she replies so softly that I almost don't hear her.

But her answer brings a smile to my lips. "Would you even say that we're . . . friends?"

"That's asking a lot," she says, the corners of her mouth twitching up. "How could I be friends with someone who walks onto my farm on day one and starts picking apart everything I could be doing better?"

"I wasn't picking it apart," I say. "Just . . . being an ass to drive you nuts."

"Do you think that was a smart idea?"

"No, but my plan worked."

"And what plan was that?" she asks, her head slightly tilting, looking so goddamn beautiful that it makes me want to pull her in close and claim her as mine.

"A plan that I shall never unveil," I say. "That's between me and my plotting book."

"And this is why you should never get involved in any business dealing or relationship with an author. Because they will plot every second of it until they get their way."

"Sad you didn't figure that out sooner," I tease. "Instead, you fell for the good looks and the charm."

"Good looks I'll give you. Charm? Not so much."

I smirk. "Hey, as long as you can admit to the beauty that is my face, that's all I care about."

"Oh my God." She rolls her eyes and playfully pushes at my chest.

I love this. Seeing her like this. Smiling and joking. Not tense or worried. We all need this Aubree in our life—this lighthearted woman who has spent most of her life worrying and trying to make something of herself.

Maybe I can be the one who helps her show this side to others.

"You feeling better?" I ask her, wanting to take her hand in mine so damn badly.

"Better about marrying you? Not sure I'll ever feel good about that." Her smile lets me know she's teasing.

"Baby, you could do a lot worse than me," I say, right before I lean forward, cup her chin, and place a short but sweet kiss on her lips just because I want to remind her exactly what I'm capable of.

When I pull away, her eyes almost look dazed as they peer open to me.

"Now, let's get in there before they eat all the fine cheese we picked out," I say as I stand from the bench.

And just to test the waters, I hold my hand out to her to take.

She looks up at me for a moment, stands . . . and then takes my hand.

I hold my breath, not wanting to scare her away, because Jesus Christ, she's holding my hand.

Everyone, stay calm.

I SAID, STAY CALM!

Chapter Seventeen

AUBREE

"Our wedding is going to be so dreamy," Wyatt says as he flops on the bed when we return to the guest house.

"Why are you like this?" I ask as I take my shoes off and sit on the bed.

To my surprise, he tugs on my shoulder, forcing me to lie down next to him. He props himself up on his elbow to look down at me.

"Tell me it wouldn't be as fun if I were normal."

"It would be a lot easier," I answer.

"But not as fun." He rests his hand on my stomach.

"Are you trying to prove a point?"

"Yes," he says, his hand moving to the waistband of my shorts and the hem of my shirt. What does he think he's doing? "That even though you might not have asked for this intrusion in your life, you're beyond grateful for it because I've added color to your world. Loads and loads of color."

"You're obnoxious."

"Another way to describe fun. I'll take it." His fingers dance over a small patch of exposed skin.

364

I look down at his hand and back up at him. "What do you think you're doing with that hand?"

"Nothing," he says.

"Uh, it seems like you're doing something."

"And what would that seem like?" he asks.

"Like you're trying to slip it under my shirt."

"Ew, why would I want to do that?"

The way he said ew was unexpected and actually makes me laugh out loud.

"Gross. I don't want to touch you," he continues.

"Then you better stop," I say.

"Can't, my hand is stuck."

"Really, Wyatt?"

He smirks. "How about we play a game?"

"If you suggest strip poker, the answer is no."

"Like I said a few seconds ago, ew!"

"Stop." I laugh as I try to push him away, but while I do it, his hand slips under my shirt, and his warm palm presses against my stomach.

"Wyatt," I say in a questioning tone. "What did we say about this?"

"I'm not doing anything," he says, his thumb stroking just below my breast, making me hyper aware that he could easily turn me on at this moment.

"You are when you nearly touch my breast."

"Ew, you have breasts?" His hand flies out of my shirt, and he shakes it above me as if he's trying to get a bug off his fingers. "Gross."

Because he makes me laugh, I reply, "That's not how you reacted when you were sucking on them."

His brows shoot up, and he points at his chest. "Sucking on your . . . tits? No, that doesn't sound like something I'd do. I'm a dignified man, and dignified men don't suck on tits."

And this is why I like him, this right here. He saw how stressed I was at Hattie and Hayes's. He noticed how quiet I was on the way home, and instead of letting me sulk away by myself, he's flipped the mood around. He takes my wandering mind full of doubts and questions and puts me in another headspace, where I forget about the past, the worries that rest heavily on me, and the pressure, and settles me into a fun and carefree place.

"What do dignified men do?" I ask.

"Smoke cigars and talk about their loafers."

I snort. "Oh wow, I had no idea. It's weird, though, because I haven't seen you smoke a cigar or wear loafers even once, let alone talk about them."

"And are you with me every second of every day? I think not. Therefore, you don't know what I do all the time," he counters, living in this imaginary tomfoolery with me.

"Then how come I never smell smoke on you?"

The corner of his mouth tugs up in a smile. "You smelling me, babe?"

"Hard not to when you force yourself on me."

"Now, when you put it like that, it seems like I'm some sort of predator."

"Uh . . . my hand for your land?"

"Hey now, hold on a second . . . I only said that because it was catchy," he says while I chuckle. "If this were my book, I would put that slogan on shirts. I didn't really mean it . . . fully. Just in a comical sense. You are more than welcome to leave this agreement. The door is right there." He gestures toward the door.

"This is my place," I counter.

"Yeah, but I've grown accustomed to it and don't want to leave. Plus, I'm getting close to squatter's rights, and that's a badge I would wear with honor. So it was nice knowing you, but if you don't mind, I intend to enjoy myself this evening." He pushes me toward the edge of the bed.

"Hey," I playfully yell. "What are you doing?"

"Claiming my bed."

"Don't knock me off." I grab his leg to keep myself on the bed, but he attempts to shake me off. Good thing for me, I have an impeccable grip. I wrap my arms and legs around his thigh and shin, and I don't let go. The entire time he shakes, I can feel my shoulder graze his junk, my head . . . my ear.

That's when he stops, laughter in his voice. "Christ, if I shake any more, my dick is going to act like a Q-tip in your ear."

I laugh just hard enough to surprise him. "Wyatt, there is no way that thing will fit in my ear."

That makes his brows shoot up in surprise. "Why, Aubree Rowley, are you saying I have a giant, beefy slayer of a cock?"

Oh my God, this man.

"And that is exactly why I can't stand you most of the time," I say as I release myself from him and move up on the bed. "The exaggerations with you. My God."

"I wasn't exaggerating, just repeating what you said."

"I did not say you had a giant, beefy slayer of a cock. I just said it wasn't a Q-tip."

"Which means . . ." he says, motioning with his hand. "You believe I have a giant, beefy slayer of a cock."

"We are done with this conversation." I move farther up on the bed and turn away from him, but it's only for a moment because he tugs on my hip, flipping me to my back.

He hovers over me and says, "Are we done because you're getting turned on thinking of my cock?"

"Yes, Wyatt," I deadpan. "That's exactly why."

"Knew it," he says playfully. "I fucking knew it."

"Good God," I say as I plant my hand on his face and push him away.

He chuckles and moves off the bed. "By the end of this marriage, you're going to be thinking of my giant, beefy slayer every second of every day."

"Keep wishing, Wyatt."

"ALL LOCKED UP," Wyatt says before hopping in bed.

"I know, I checked." I turn toward him and ask, "Is there

more to why you check the locks other than research for your books?"

"What do you mean?" he asks as he tucks his hand under his pillow, facing me.

"I don't know. You seem very vigilant about it, and I wasn't sure if it was because something happened to you in the past."

"Are you asking me a personal question?" he asks.

"I am. Don't you think I have the privilege of knowing? I'm going to be your wife after all."

That makes him gently smile. "True." He lets out a deep breath. "Okay, yeah, something happened to me."

"Really?" I ask as I press my hand to his bare chest, wanting him to know he can trust me. "Do you mind telling me?"

"No," he says, letting out a deep breath. "Probably best that you know." He rests his hand on my hip, tugging me a touch closer, and I allow it because I know when I'm talking about something serious, I like the comfort of being closer to someone. I play with the short strands of his chest hair. I've never been particularly tactile, but strangely, showing affection to Wyatt seems almost natural. "I, uh, I was twelve."

"Twelve?" I ask. "That's so young."

"Yeah, tell me about it. It was just my mom and me at home. Dad was off on a business trip and Clarke was at a sleepover. My parents always locked the door every night, but we didn't have extra measures, like a bar that you propped up against the door or even an Ada-lock. Nothing that I would prefer now."

"I don't have those things," I say.

"And that's why I sleep here, and you sleep there, farther from the door."

"It's not that much farther."

"It's far enough for me to be the first to be attacked." His hand curls around my hip as he continues. "Anyway, Mom and I stayed up later that night. It was a Friday, and we had a fun movie night with popcorn and peanut M&M's, our favorite nighttime treat. I was helping Mom clean up in the kitchen when we heard our dog, Millipede, start to growl."

"You named your dog Millipede?" I ask.

"Yeah, why not?"

"Not a typical dog name."

"Sorry, should we have named him something generic like Kevin?"

"Kevin would have been better than Millipede, but continue. Sorry for the distraction. I was just surprised by that detail."

"It's fine," he says and sighs again. He starts to tense up, and I can tell we're getting to the hard part of the story, so I continue to smooth my hand over his chest. "Millipede was growling, but we just thought he saw the neighbor's dog outside, so we let him out to go to the bathroom. That's when he started barking incessantly. Mom was getting annoyed, so she called Millipede in, and when he didn't come, she had to go out there to bring him back in."

"Oh God," I say, my heart starting to race.

"Nothing happened to her. But Millipede was going crazy. We ended up putting him in his crate that night because we didn't know what had got into him. We both got ready for bed, and Mom said good night. She went to her room, and I went to mine, where I turned on my reading light and started to read."

I am not loving this story.

"After reading a chapter, I remembered that Dad had asked me to put out the trash, and I'd forgotten, so I jumped out of bed and peered down the hall at Mom's room. Her light wasn't on, so I decided not to bother her. When I turned to head back into my room, I saw a flash of something in the dark. Something moving in the living room."

"Oh my God," I say, my heart nearly beating out of my chest.

"I assumed Millipede escaped his crate somehow, so I fumbled down the hallway in the dark, switched on the light when I reached the living room, and standing in the middle was a man in a hoodie with a knife in his hand."

I gasp as my hand flies to my mouth. "Oh my God, Wyatt. What did you do?"

"What any other teenage boy would do . . . wet myself. Right there, on the carpet of the hallway, I piddled."

"Wait, you peed yourself?" I ask. "You didn't scream? You didn't run? You just peed?"

"Yup. There was so much pee that it flooded the hallway, one of those never-ending pees, you know? The kind where you stand there—or sit in your case—and start laughing because there's so much pee. But I didn't laugh. I just watched the hallway fill up with pee, at least a foot of it."

My expression of shock and horror slowly slips away as I stare at Wyatt and the glint in his eye. "Are you lying?"

"Lying seems harsh. But spinning a story for your enjoyment? Now that's more like it."

"Oh my God, Wyatt," I say, swatting at his chest. "I thought you were being serious."

"About the peeing or the invader?" he asks.

"The invader," I growl.

He smirks. "Well, I guess that makes me a good storyteller, doesn't it?"

I flip to my other side, tucking my head against the pillow. "You're annoying, that's what you are."

He leans over me and smiles. "Don't be sour."

Staring at the wall, I say, "You know, I was trying to have a serious conversation with you, find out something interesting about you, and you took it upon yourself to turn it into a joke. Well, I don't find it very funny."

His expression softens as he rolls me to my back. He brings his hand up to my cheek and says, "I'm sorry, Aubree." He strokes his thumb over my cheek. "You want to know something? What I just told you, it was true, but in a dream I had when I was twelve. And the peeing, well, that happened too, but in my bed. My mom had to help me change my sheets in the middle of the night."

I stare up at him and look for any tell that he's lying. "Are you being serious?"

"Do you really think I'd lie about peeing the bed? Flooding

the hallway with pee because there's a murderer in the house, sure, but peeing the bed at twelve? That's something only my mom and I know. We didn't even tell my dad. She swore she wouldn't."

"So you really peed the bed at twelve?"

"Yes," he answers, looking very serious. So serious that I crack a smile.

"That's so embarrassing," I say.

He chuckles. "I know. Tell me about it. I will never forget the feel of wet boxers plastered against my dick."

"You know, the details aren't needed." I wave him off.

"Are you sure? Because there's so much more I can dive into, like the smell—"

"Oh my God, Wyatt, no." His boisterous laugh actually makes me chuckle.

"Your loss." He shrugs and then caresses my cheek again. "Do you forgive me now?"

"I guess so." I playfully sigh.

"Good," he says. "Now, where are we on those good night kisses? I can't remember where we left off."

"We left off with not doing any of that."

"Right . . . right," he says while nodding and looking away. "You know, I actually think we should revisit that—"

"Good night, Wyatt," I say as I turn away from him.

He chuckles and wraps his arm around me like every other night. "Good night, Aubree."

⊏⊐

"I'M GOING to shove my foot so far up your . . . ughhhh," I growl as I realize my computer doesn't have an ass I can shove my foot up.

I push away from my desk and drag my hands over my face.

"Why?" I say out loud to no one. "Why is this so hard? Why am I freaking failing at this?" I stand from my chair and start pacing the office floor. "This should be easy. You look at the numbers, you figure it out, and then you fix the issue. But I can't figure it out. I can't figure out why there is a problem with our numbers."

The door opens to the office, and Wyatt sticks his head in. "Uh, everything okay in here?"

"No," I say as I shove at my chair, feeling really irritated.

"Yeah, didn't seem like it." He glances around the room. "But you're in here alone, which is slightly concerning, given I could hear you talking."

"I was talking to the numbers," I say out of pure frustration as I toss my hand toward the computer.

Wyatt fully steps into the office, wearing a pair of gray Chino shorts and an untucked button-up shirt with the sleeves rolled up and the top few buttons undone. His hair is styled, he's left the scruff on his jaw from the night before, and he's looking all kinds of handsome as he moves farther into the office.

And here I am, in a pair of cotton shorts, a ratty old shirt, and my hair tied up into a bun because I thought that if I was at my epitome of comfort, I could figure this whole thing out with the books.

I was so, so wrong.

"The numbers, ahh, I see," Wyatt says, approaching me as if I'm a stray, ready to run away.

"I feel like you're patronizing me."

"Aubree, why the hell would I want to do that? I know better at this point. Why don't you tell me what's going on, and maybe I can help you."

"No," I say, shaking my head. "This is my problem, not yours. I can figure this out on my own."

"Mm, yeah, seems like it." My eyes shoot to him, not appreciating his sarcasm. And he notices right away. "Uh, yeah, excuse the tone of that last comment. It's just frustrating to see you frustrated but you won't let me help. And I understand that you are a woman running her business, and the last thing you want is for some man to come in and tell you what you're missing, but sometimes it's good to have another pair of eyes on things, you know?"

"I don't need your help, Wyatt."

"Yup, completely get that, and I don't need to help you. But maybe I can help calm you down. Why don't I take you for lunch? Hank told me they're serving mac and cheese at The Cliffs today. I told him to reserve me a seat on the deck. Come join me."

I shake my head. "I need to figure out this problem."

"I get that," he says calmly. He's silent for a second and then says, "Did you know when I'm writing, I get stuck at times, and even if I plotted out a whole book, I sometimes have a hard time moving from one scene to the next. I wonder if it will be whiplash to the reader, if the connection makes sense, if the scene I'm writing is even worth it. I start questioning every little thing, and I can't get out of that mindset until I take a break. Fresh air, a run, or sometimes just sitting at a coffee house, staring at nothing, will get me thinking about the story in a different light. Maybe you need to just take a breather for a second."

"Or I can power through," I say as I take a seat at my desk.

Wyatt closes the space between us and perches on my desk. "Aubree, I'm telling you right now, powering through will only frustrate you. If you're so worried, bring your computer with you. If you want, you can look at it on the way into town and even while we're waiting for our meals. But at least change up your location and get some fresh air."

"No, I'm just going to stay here."

"Great," he says in a chipper voice. "Then I'll stay too."

"Wyatt, come on."

"Come on, what? If you're going to be stubborn, then I want to be stubborn, which means you get to have me here in the office with you while you attempt to figure out your issue with the numbers. Oh hey, is that a pencil?" He picks up a pencil off my desk. "Wow, haven't seen one of these in a while. You know, I like to use pens when I take notes and plot. My favorite is—"

"Oh my God, fine, I'll go to lunch," I say, standing up and unplugging my laptop. "I'm not going to sit here and let you annoy me with your drivel about pencils."

"How did you know it was drivel? I didn't even get to tell you what my favorite type of pen is, which is a big thing in my world. Pens matter, and writing materials matter. Ever consider that, Aubree?"

He follows me out of the office, and I hop into the four-by-four, which he quickly gets in as well.

"Hello, I'm talking to you," he says.

"And I'm ignoring you."

I start the four-by-four and take off down the dirt road toward the guest house.

"Why? You know, if you paid attention to what interests me, maybe you could get me a nice gift for our wedding, like a bouquet of my favorite pens."

"My gift to you is saying I do," I say.

"Solid gift, but I think I'd like something a little extra."

"I don't dry heave while saying it," I reply.

"Mmm, solid response, but I was thinking more along the lines of pens . . . or, I don't know, some lingerie that you could show me later."

I glance over at him and catch that teasing smirk of his. You know, when he says stuff like that, it makes me believe that he might possess feelings toward me other than me being the key to his cabin, but then he tacks on that smile of his, and I know it's Wyatt just being Wyatt.

"Why does the woman have to be the one who wears the lingerie for the man?" I ask. "Why can't it be the other way around?"

"Baby, if you want me in a thong, all you have to do is ask. I have no problem strutting around for you."

"Dear God, please don't." He laughs some more as we pull up to the guest house. "Just going to change real quick."

"Why?" he asks. "I think you look good as you are."

I glance down at the hole in my shirt and then back up at him. "Your standards are low for looking good."

"Nah, Mrs. Preston, you set the bar high."

I don't bother to respond to him. I just hand him my computer and then move into the guest house, where I find a pair of jean shorts that have been freshly washed. I pull those on and trade out my holey shirt for a Hayes Farrow Stadium T-shirt. Hattie found a bunch in his house and asked if I wanted one. Of course I'll take anything free. It's really soft and one of my favorite shirts now. I move over to the bathroom, where I throw on a bit of mascara just for the show, then I slip on my Birkenstocks and loop my pack containing my wallet over my shoulder and head back outside, where Wyatt waits by his car. When he spots me, I catch his eyes scanning me, taking me all in.

"That was fast," he says.

"Did you want me to put on my ballgown and curl my hair for you?"

He opens my door for me and says, "Curling the hair would have been too much, but the ballgown I would have immensely enjoyed."

I get into his SUV and say, "Not sure you're at ballgown status."

"I'll get there, babe."

He shuts the door and then moves around to his side. When he gets in, he sets my computer on my lap and then buckles up and starts the car. When he pulls out, he puts his hand on my seat and then backs up, using one hand to turn the wheel and straighten out. I don't know why I think that's hot, but I do.

What's even hotter is how he rests his hand on my leg when he drives down the road. Not sure why he's placed his hand on my leg, but I like it. Therefore, I don't tell him to move it. It's probably one of those things where he tries to get me used to him, used to his touch.

"Want to talk about your problem?" he asks.

"Not really," I say.

"Why?"

Because it's embarrassing that I can't figure it out.

Because I don't want you to think I'm a failure and can't handle this farm.

Because my sister left me to grow this business, and I can't seem to do that.

"Just tired of thinking about it," I answer.

"Hmm, doesn't seem like it." His thumb rubs along my thigh in a soothing motion that simultaneously relaxes me and turns me on. "Seems like you don't want to talk about it because you don't want to tell me something."

"What could I possibly want to hide from you?" I ask.

"Your pride," he says as he stops at a stop sign and looks over at me.

How?

How does this man already understand me so easily when we haven't known each other that long? Am I really that transparent?

"Tell me I'm wrong," he says, growing serious.

I look away, unable to sit here under his stare.

"I know I'm not wrong," he says, continuing to drive. "There's nothing wrong with being a prideful person, Aubree. But what makes you an even better person is being able to set aside that pride and ask for help. Especially when you're having a hard time making sense of something."

"Are you saying I'm too prideful to ask for help?"

He nods. "I am."

"Well, I'm not."

"Okay, prove it," he says.

"Fine," I say, not letting him win this. Even though telling him seems like he's winning . . . Ugh, I'm too irritated and exhausted to battle. "I can't make sense of our numbers. Our output of potatoes, extract, and vodka is great, but the income is lower than what I'm calculating. I can't quite make sense of it all, and I don't understand why. I feel like I'm failing Cassidy, and if I don't figure it out soon, it could be an issue."

He continues to rub my thigh. "Okay, well, do you want me

to look at it? I probably won't know the answer, but I don't mind. We can even talk it out. Tell me what you see . . ."

I look out the window, my mind so tired, but my heart telling me I want to do this myself. And that's exactly the problem because if this was Cassidy, she wouldn't do it herself. She never did it herself. She was always asking for help, never too prideful to seek out the right person to aid her in whatever she needed.

So why am I so against this?

Maybe because my father told me I would never amount to anything. That I was a waste of space and I have this inner need to prove him wrong.

"What's going on in that head of yours?" Wyatt asks as we pull into town. "It seems like it's running a mile a minute just from the way your lips are pursed."

He pulls into a parking spot that . . . oh my God. It says it's reserved for Wyatt Preston. I can't even right now.

Hayes Farrow, one of the leading singer-songwriters in the country, doesn't even have his own parking spot, but my fake soon-to-be husband does. The charm this man possesses is out of this world.

He puts the SUV in park and turns toward me.

"What's going on, Aubree?"

I let out a heavy sigh as I stare down at my lap. "I just feel like I need to do this myself," I answer truthfully.

"I can understand that," he replies. "When I first started writing, I was trying to prove my creative writing teacher wrong. He told me that my ideas were predictable and barely researched. That my sentences were juvenile, and my vocabulary was immature. I set out to prove him wrong and the C he gave me in class. I told myself that if I could become successful all on my own, I could prove to him I'm much better than the C grade he gave me. And when I first started, boy, did I fucking fail. It wasn't until I started asking for assistance, interviewing crime analysts and forming a group of like-minded author friends, that I found some success. It takes a visionary to start a project and a village to complete it." He lifts my chin with his finger. "Don't be caught digging a ditch by yourself with a spoon. Take the help from the person with the excavator."

Then he steps out of the SUV and moves around to my side. When he opens the door, he leans over my lap and unbuckles my seat before taking my hand in his. I'm tense at first, but I relax when he gently squeezes it.

He starts to tug me, but I don't move.

"What's wrong?" he asks.

"I . . . I think I need help," I say, his words running through my head.

It takes a visionary to start a project—that visionary being Cassidy. It takes a village to complete it—that village being me and my siblings and this town.

He's right, I can attempt to do this myself, but it would be so much easier with help. I told myself at a very young age that I would never be like the cold, distant, horrible man that my father was. A man who would spend his nights in front of the television drinking. A man who thought of his children as his servants, not his loved ones. A man who thought the world owed him something from the misfortunes he suffered. He never did anything to fix his life. He relied on bitterness and booze to propel him from day to day.

And here I am . . . bitter, resentful, not letting anyone help out.

That was what my dad would have done. He would have sat back, not letting a soul offer him a hand. The only help he took was from his own children.

Help in raising his own children.

Help in making him meals.

Help in carrying him up the stairs when he was too damn drunk to do it himself.

I don't want to be like him.

I refuse to be like him.

"Okay, then let's get you some help," Wyatt says. "Want to work while we eat? Talk it out?"

"Yeah," I say softly. "I think I'd like that."

"Okay." He clutches my computer to his chest. "I got you, babe. Come on."

He takes my hand in his and then helps me out of the SUV. When he shuts my door behind him, I stop him and say, "I'm sorry that I'm so stubborn. I appreciate you sticking around, even when I push you away."

His expression softens as he says, "I'm here for you, Aubree. I'm like a boomerang. You keep tossing me away, and I keep coming back."

"One day, I'm sure that string will break," I answer, feeling far too insecure and inefficient. Not worthy of his time.

He grips my chin and shakes his head. "No, that string tying us together, it's unbreakable. Nothing you can say or do to me, Aubree, will make me snap. This is forever, this bond. Even after a year of marriage, we will still be tied together when we go our separate ways."

"You might be regretting that sooner rather than never."

"Impossible," he says as he guides me toward The Cliffs.

Given his special parking spot, it's not much of a walk, but from the car to the restaurant, Wyatt waves high to a few people, shakes two hands, and compliments someone I've never met before on how adorable their baby is. He came here to immerse himself in the town and find a bride—well, he's impressively done both. Oddly, I think one of the reasons I find myself drawn toward this man is because he's so friendly, kind, and understanding.

Growing up, we didn't have a lot of understanding in our house. Cassidy did her best, as did Ryland, but at the end of the day, we were all kids and should not have had to act like adults at such a young age. Dad didn't have patience with us, he was never kind, and he was not one to walk around town, shaking hands.

Wyatt . . . he's the complete opposite, and I find that immensely attractive.

When we reach The Cliffs, he holds the door open for me and immediately says hi to Hank at the register.

"Wyatt, how are you?" Hank says in a greeting.

"Great now that I got my girl to take a break for a second to eat lunch with me."

Hank smiles at me. "She's always been one of the hardest workers I know."

"Thank you," I say shyly, very pleased with the compliment. Sometimes I feel like I walk around this town invisible. I was never the outgoing, loving one like Cassidy. Or the entertaining, funny one like Hattie. Or the solid, reliable one like Ryland. I've just . . . done what I have to do and never spent too much time interacting with the town if I don't have to. It's nice to have a compliment.

"Go ahead and grab a seat. I'll send someone over to take your order."

"Thanks, man," Wyatt says as he brings me through the restaurant—as if I haven't been here before—and right to the back deck. He then brings me to a table in the far corner, right up against the railing so the ocean is the only thing we see. "My favorite table."

"You have a favorite table?" I ask as he pulls out a chair. I reach for mine, but he pulls me toward his chair instead, taking a seat and bringing me onto his lap.

"Yup, come here often for a bear claw and coffee. My physique begs me to stop, but I can't."

"Trust me when I say your physique is unaffected."

In a shocked voice, he asks, "Are you saying you like my body, Mrs. Preston?"

"Don't push it," I say as he wraps his arm around my waist. "By the way, there is a perfectly good chair over there for me to sit on."

"Yeah, but when you sit on my lap, I can feel like a manly man."

"Do you really need the ego boost?"

"Yes, because you don't tell me how hot or strong I am enough."

I turn toward him and pat his cheek. "Aw, poor baby. You need to fish for compliments."

"I do." He pouts his bottom lip. "So if you can offer me some compliments, I'd greatly appreciate it."

"I just told you, you have a great physique." Leaning in, I whisper, "And I'm pretty sure I told you how big your penis is the other day."

A stupid grin spreads across his face. "You know, I actually forgot what you said. Can you repeat?"

"No," I deadpan, causing him to chuckle.

"Dammit."

"Hello, the soon-to-be newlyweds," our server says as she sets down some silverware and two glasses of water in front of us. "How are we this afternoon?"

Wyatt's grip on me grows tighter as he says, "Fantastic. Aubree was just giving me a compliment about how—"

"She doesn't need to know that," I say, poking him in his side.

He chuckles and looks up at the server. "She's so shy when it comes to compliments. Go ahead," he encourages. "Tell her how—"

I clamp my hand over his mouth and say, "Two mac and cheeses please, a side salad with ranch for us to share, and this water is great. Thank you."

The server smirks and nods. "Got it. I'll put that in for you."

Then she takes off.

"Aubree, now she won't know how big my penis is."

"Wow, what a shame," I say sarcastically as I try to get up from his lap, but he holds me in place.

"Where do you think you're going?"

"Uh, to the seat across from you."

He shakes his head. "No, that doesn't suit me. I prefer for you to sit on my lap . . . well, actually, if I'm being totally honest, I prefer for you to sit on my face, but I'm not sure Hank would allow that here."

My cheeks flame as I say, "You would not prefer that."

"Aubree," he says in such a flat tone that I turn to look at him. "If it were between eating the mac and cheese you just ordered for me or eating your pussy, I'd choose your sweet, delicious pussy any day. For every fucking meal."

"Wyatt," I whisper, feeling like my entire face is about to explode from the heat.

"Yeah?" he asks, looking so sure of himself.

"That's . . . that's . . ."

"Hot? I know."

"I wasn't going to say hot."

"What were you going to say? Tempting? If that's the case, we can leave right now so you can sit on my face."

"Oh my God, I'm not sitting on your face."

His bottom lip is in full pout mode. "Why would you say such a mean thing to me? Have I not been kind to you? What did I do to deserve such a harsh punishment?"

"Stop it," I say as I open my computer. "You're being ridiculous."

"I'm being truthful," he says as his lips nearly caress my ear.

"Well, stop being truthful."

"You want me to lie to you?" he asks. "Okay, well . . . uh, I think you smell terrible, and I hate that you're sitting on my lap right now. It's sickening actually."

Seeing where this is going, I turn to face him and catch that brilliant smile on his lips. "Wyatt . . ."

"Hmm?" The expression on his face is so light and breezy, you'd think this man has never faced heartache or tumultuous times. That or he's really good at just staying positive and lighthearted no matter what happens to him.

"Remember what we said about . . . the sex part of all of this?"

He nods. "I do."

"Okay, so then, let's keep that in mind."

"I am." His grip on me grows tighter. "It's not like my hand is up your shirt right now, caressing your nipple. Because it can be." He pauses. "Do you want it to be?"

"Dear God, Wyatt," I say as he chuckles. "Are you always like this?"

"You've been with me for two weeks, you tell me."

I resign with a sigh. "You're right, you are." I pull up the Excel sheet and say, "Think I can pull up a chair next to you?"

"Nah, I'm good like this." He rests his chin on my shoulder.

"You don't think it's a little excessive?"

He glances around the deck. "No. I think it's necessary. Not sure people are seeing just how much we are in love. You sitting on my lap is sealing the deal on this façade."

"Uh-huh," I say, my heart slightly plummeting from the use of the word façade. "So how does you telling me to sit on your face help the façade?"

"Great question that I'd love to answer," he says. "You see, from the mere mention of me pleasuring you with my tongue, you grew a beautiful shade of pink. Now, people from the outside looking in would assume that's a blush, a blush from something I said, which means we're madly in love with each other. See how that works?"

So it's *all* for show. It always is. Not sure why I think it's for any other reason. This right here is why I can't develop feelings. What he says and how he touches me makes me believe there could be more. When this isn't reality at all. This is one big production, and I'm along for the ride.

Which means I need to start getting caught up in the charm of it all, enjoy the friendship—yes, friendship—we have, and keep moving forward.

"Clever," I answer.

"They don't call me the plot king for nothing."

"Do people really call you that?" I ask.

"No," he says sadly. "But I'm hoping it might catch on. Think you can jump on my socials and comment as a loving reader and start calling me the plot king? See if the word spreads?"

"That wasn't part of the initial deal. You'll have to pay extra for that."

"Not a problem . . . do you take tongues to the clit as payment?"

"Jesus Christ, Wyatt."

He chuckles and squeezes me even tighter. I try not to sink into his warm hold, but my body betrays me, and I slip into the ease of his personality.

———

"I CAN SEE why you love this so much," Wyatt says as I remain on his lap while he feeds both of us.

If I were someone watching us, I'd think to myself—*get a freaking room! Can't they keep their hands off each other for one second? There's a perfectly good chair on the other side of the table, use it.*

But that must be the skeptic in me because all we've received are smiles, cooings of appreciation, and even a pat on the back from Hank after he hand-delivered our meals.

Wyatt has really won over this town, and that's something to marvel at. My family has been here forever, and I wouldn't say everyone in town agrees with us, but Wyatt is winning over every person.

"Glad we have this for our wedding. I was going in blind with your food choice, putting all my faith on your taste buds, and it looks like I can trust them."

"You better," I say as I wipe my mouth with my napkin. "I've had your dick on my taste buds."

He snorts so hard that he has to pick up my napkin and dab his nose.

"Fuck," he mutters as he finishes cleaning up. "Mac and cheese is now lodged in my nasal cavity."

"You're not the only one who can be crude," I say, pleased with myself.

"Apparently," he says on a light chuckle before taking a sip of his water. "And you're right, if you allow the sweet taste of my dick on your tongue, then I should trust any food choice of yours."

"Sweet, huh?" I ask. "More like salty."

"Uh, doubtful," he says in a scoff. "I eat at least three pounds of pineapple a week. My dick offers mouthwatering nectar for anyone who comes eye to eye with it."

"A great example of a man thinking he's doing the world a service by producing cum for anyone interested."

"Not just anyone, babe. You, great-tasting cum for you."

"I honestly can't with this conversation."

He chuckles and wraps both of his arms around my waist while placing a gentle kiss on my neck that sends shivers all the way down to my toes. "You started it."

"No, any unnecessary and filthy talk is always started by you. I was just trying to give you a taste of your own medicine."

"Well, keep it coming—see what I did there—because I love when you talk about my dick on your tongue."

I shake my head and then lean back into him. "Are we going to discuss the farm at all? Or are we just going to talk about fellatio this entire meal?"

"Ooo, fellatio, great word. I mean, I'm all for that topic, but I can sense that you're wanting to move on, so yes, let's talk about the farm."

"So what do you think is going on?" I ask. "What am I not seeing?"

Growing slightly serious, he scrolls through the spreadsheet that he's been looking through while we've been eating and he says, "I see what you mean about the numbers seeming less, but the units sold are higher. There is something off. Have you spoken to Hattie about what she's selling the almond extract at?"

"No, I can see it on my end. It's the regular price."

I feel him nod. "And the only source of income is from the store?"

"No," I say. "The website as well, which is what Cassidy set up right before she started to get really sick."

"You sell products online?" he asks.

"Yes, just the almond extract and vodka. We want to move the honey over there as well as some other products, like cookie mixes and whatnot, but we haven't gotten to that aspect of the business yet. Only so much we can do at a time."

"Understandable," he says. "Who does the fulfillment for the online store now?"

"Esther. She's in charge."

"Is she in charge of the website?"

"I was taking care of it for a bit, then Hattie for a second, and now I believe Esther has fully taken it over. At least that's what was in the process of happening when I spoke to Hattie last."

"What's the website?" he asks.

"What do you mean? We sell goods."

"No." He chuckles. "What's the name of the website?"

"Oh." Since I'm already connected to The Cliffs's Wi-Fi, I pull up my web browser and type in the website. It takes a few seconds, but I show him when it comes on the screen. "It's simple. Cassidy wanted it to be so much more, but she didn't have the time, and none of us are webmasters."

Wyatt takes a moment to look over the very basic Shopify website that Cassidy set up. With a white background and basic blue font, there isn't much to it other than a homepage with a picture of the storefront, a shop page, and a contact page. She wasn't even able to add the about us page she mentioned when she first started putting it together.

"It's pretty basic," Wyatt says. "But it does the job." He clicks on the store and scrolls down, looking over the pictures of our products. Our two products. "I like what she did with the pictures, capturing the feel of the store." He clicks on the almond extract and then balks. "Holy shit."

"What?" I ask.

"Is that how much you sell your almond extract for?"

"What do you . . ." My voice fades away as my eyes land on the price. Two dollars and ninety-eight cents. "What the fuck," I say as I bring the computer closer. "Does that really say what I think it says?"

"Uh, if you think it says two dollars, then yes."

"Oh my God, we sell it for twelve dollars." I stare down at it, thinking about when Cassidy put this up. *It was just as she started feeling unwell.* She wanted to do something when she was lying in bed, something that made her feel like she was contributing. She must have missed putting the one in front of the two to make it twelve dollars, not two.

I lean back against Wyatt, feeling a sense of frustration and relief at the same time.

"Do you think that's the problem?" he asks.

"Yes," I whisper as I move back to the Excel sheet and sort the products by almond extract. "That easily explains the higher volume of sales with lower income." I let out a relieved sigh. "God, Wyatt, I've been driving myself crazy over this. And I should be mad about this, furious that no one caught this, but I'm just relieved." I lift and look him in the eyes. "Thank you, Wyatt. I thought . . . I thought it was something I was doing wrong. That I was failing Cassidy."

His expression softens as he lightly cups my cheek. "You're not failing her, Aubree. You're preserving her legacy through this farm, the store, and Mac."

I wet my lips, my emotions getting the better of me as I say, "That means a lot to me, Wyatt. Thank you." And then, because the relief outweighs the frustration, I grip his cheeks and press my mouth to his.

His hand falls to my thigh while the other holds my back, and he kisses me back. It's slow and thoughtful, with a hint of hunger as our lips part and our tongues lightly tangle.

The world around us falls to the wayside as nothing else exists besides us—me sitting on his lap, his grip holding me tightly as our mouths explore each other.

Comfort and reprieve pull me into a tight hug while I get lost in Wyatt and the way he captures me so easily with his kisses.

I forget that we're in the middle of town, in a popular restaurant where anyone can see us.

I forget that this is a platonic relationship.

I forget that he's not my man but a business partner.

None of that matters as I move my tongue deeper into his

mouth, my body igniting into a burning inferno as his hand slides farther up my thigh.

I shift on his lap and straddle him so I have better access to his soft lips. My hands caress the rough stubble of his beard while I melt further into him, my lap now moving over his bulge. My mind returns to the other morning when I rode him, feeling his thickness between my legs. I want that again. Badly.

I want to know what it feels like to have him fully inside me. To own me. To do whatever he wants to bring me pleasure.

I feel almost desperate for it, so desperate that I start to move over his lap, causing him to groan in my mouth.

"Umm, Aubree." My sister's voice halts me mid pulse.

I'm knocked back into reality as the bubble we were just in fades away, and the salty smell of the ocean returns. The light from the afternoon sun shines down on us, and the clatter of forks and plates from around the restaurant floats between Wyatt and me.

Oh my God.

I pull away, my eyes connected to his.

Wyatt has a satisfied smile across his lips while I feel horrified.

Clearing my throat, I glance over my shoulder where Hattie stands by the table, a shocked but gleeful look on her face.

"Oh, hi there," I say as I attempt to shift off Wyatt's lap, but he holds me in place. Not sure if that's because he wants me to remain seated on his lap or because he wants me to hide his very obvious erection.

"What, uh . . . what are you doing?" she asks.

"Um, you know, just enjoying the afternoon," I answer awkwardly.

But of course Wyatt, being Wyatt, leans forward and whispers, "She was trying to get me to have sex with her right here."

"Wyatt," I snap, which makes him laugh. I look back at Hattie and say, "I was not doing that."

"I don't know." Hattie smirks. "It kind of seemed like you were."

"I wasn't." I stick my chin up. "I was trying to . . . feed him."

Mentally, I toss my hands up in surrender because that is honestly the most ridiculous thing I've ever said in my life. *I was trying to feed Wyatt.* What is wrong with me? I've probably been hanging out with Wyatt far too much.

"Feed him?" Hattie snorts while Wyatt chuckles, the rumble of his chest knocking against me.

"Well, you were giving me all the good nutrients, babe. Thank you."

I turn on his lap and fold my arms across my chest. "Well, now that he's been fed, I think it's time we leave."

"Nah, I'm good right here," Wyatt says. "I'm actually still hungry, so if you could feed me some more, I'd appreciate it."

"He does look malnourished," Hattie says. "Maybe you should take him back to the guest house and really give him a feast."

Wyatt points at Hattie. "Now there's an idea. Babe, we should listen to your sister."

I look back and forth between Wyatt and Hattie and say, "I hate you both."

They laugh together before Hattie says, "No, you don't. You love us."

"Barely," I mutter.

Wyatt wraps his arm around my stomach and rests his chin on my shoulder. "Why don't you tell Hattie what you figured out."

"Is it something sexual?" Hattie asks as she takes a seat at our table. That's when I see Hayes walking toward the table with two smoothies.

"No, it's not something sexual," I say as Hayes pauses and looks among all of us.

"Uh, what did I just walk in on?"

"Aubree feeding Wyatt her tongue," Hattie says as she lifts up from her chair and lets Hayes take a seat. He then pulls her onto his lap and hands her, her smoothie. Hattie thanks him with a soft kiss and sips her drink.

Is this a thing? Where women sit on their men's laps?

Apparently, because Hayes holds Hattie tightly, just like Wyatt holds me. The only difference is that they're madly in love, and we're just mad.

"Having an afternoon delight?" Hayes asks. "In public nonetheless."

"My girl gets what my girl wants," Wyatt says with such cockiness in his voice that I truly wonder how he can be so good at acting. He's an author, not an actor. Maybe it's the multiple personalities he has in his head.

"Smart man," Hayes says before sipping on his green smoothie.

"So what do you want to tell me?" Hattie asks, bringing the conversation back—thankfully.

Enough of this afternoon delight stuff. I'm embarrassed as it is and fretting the private conversation I'll have to have with Wyatt about how I accidentally got out of control.

"I haven't said anything because, well, I didn't want to worry you, but the numbers have been off with income when compared to what we're selling in units." Hattie's expression morphs from joyful to concerned.

"What do you mean?"

"We're okay, but I was struggling to make sense of why we weren't bringing in as much as we should have. Well, I just figured it out with Wyatt. We've been selling the almond extract on the website for two dollars, not twelve."

"What?" Hattie nearly shouts, pulling the attention from around the restaurant. She waves and smiles at some patrons and then leans forward. "What do you mean we've been selling it for two dollars?"

"I'm assuming when Cassidy created the website while she was sick, she accidentally entered the wrong number, forgetting the one in front of the two. And I know the website has been the last thing on our minds, just some passive income while we've focused on the store, the farm, and Mac. It just slipped right by us."

"How much have we lost?" she asks.

"Not sure, but I can speak with Esther when we get back to the farm and explain what's been going on."

Hattie presses her hand to her chest. "She's going to be so upset that she missed that."

"I'll take the blame," I say. "Tell her it's something I should have noticed before passing the website over. I'll get it fixed. Thankfully, we caught it before the holiday season."

"True." Hattie leans against Hayes. "God, Cassidy would have been so mad at herself."

"She wasn't doing well then. I should have double-checked her work."

"We all should have," Hattie says. "An expensive lesson to learn, but I guess we know what to do moving forward."

I nod. "I'm just relieved I figured it out." I swallow hard. "I hate feeling like I'm failing."

The table grows quiet because I know it's rare that I share such thoughts or feelings I experience.

"You're not even close to failing," Hattie says as she reaches across the table and takes my hand. "You're the glue of this entire operation, Aubree. Without you, we'd be drowning. Ryland would be struggling without the support you offer him daily. I probably wouldn't be with Hayes because you're the one who stepped in and helped us. You're the one who ran the store and the farm at the same time, keeping it afloat. We've relied on you heavily. If it weren't for you, we would all be in over our heads. You're not failing. You're helping us thrive."

I don't know if it's her words of affirmation or if it's the relief I'm feeling, but my emotions climb up my throat, growing tight as my eyes water.

Don't cry, Aubree.

Don't freaking cry.

But it's useless. I blink, and a single tear rolls down my cheek. I quickly wipe it away, humiliated that I showed such weakness. I half expect Hattie to gawk at me, but when I glance up at her, she offers me a soft smile and a squeeze of my hand.

"We'll let you two finish your lunch."

She gets it.

She understands.

The last thing I want right now is a crowd, staring at me as I try to get myself together.

"Thank you," I say, keeping my head tilted down.

They offer their goodbyes, and when they're gone, I feel Wyatt turn my head toward him. "You okay?" he asks softly.

"Yup," I answer as I take a deep breath. "I should actually get back—"

"Aubree."

My eyes meet his. "Yes?" I ask.

His hand presses against my cheek, and his thumb rubs across my skin as he says, "You can be yourself with me. You don't need to swallow the emotions. You can let them out."

"I'm fine," I say despite my throat tightening again.

"I know you're fine. You're strong. One of the strongest people I know, but even the strong are allowed to feel weak for a moment."

My lip trembles.

My eyes water.

And before I can stop myself, another tear rolls down my cheek.

He smiles softly, bringing me into his chest. I wrap my arms around him and allow myself to *feel* at this moment, on the back deck of The Cliffs where anyone could see me fall apart.

But for some reason, as I rest my head against Wyatt, shame doesn't eclipse me.

But rather, comfort and peace start to surround me.

Relief.

Like for the first time in my life, I don't have to put up a wall. I can let it crumble because nothing bad will happen to me, not when I'm in Wyatt's arms.

"ECHO, ARE YOU BUSY?" I ask as I step up to her bee house, well, more like a shack. She's in the midst of expanding.

"Nothing I can't step away from," she says as she removes her work gloves and turns toward me. "Everything okay?"

I glance over my back to make sure Wyatt is nowhere near us, and I tug on her arm and move toward the back of the bee house. "Echo, I think there's a problem."

"A problem with what?" she asks, her face growing concerned.

"With me."

"Okay," she drags out. "Care to explain?"

I twist my hands together and whisper, "I'm falling for Wyatt, like . . . really falling for him."

A smile plays on her lips as she says, "I knew it."

"What?" I ask, surprised. "Oh God, is it obvious?"

"Not to anyone else, but to someone who knows your situation, yes, it's obvious. I've watched you slowly become warmer around him. I've watched you hold his hand. Lean into him. I've watched the way you look at him. I told myself I was imagining it, but it seems I wasn't."

I lean against the bee house and press my hand to my forehead. "Oh God, do you think he's noticed?"

"Probably not," Echo says. "And so what if he does?"

I drop my hand to my side and stare back at Echo. "So what? Uh, Echo, I'm not supposed to be falling for him."

"Says who?"

"Says our agreement. Says him. I know it might seem like the man is all over me, because he is, but he's just pretending. Trust me, he's drilled it into me that this is all a façade. When he calls me baby, when he's holding me and kissing me? It's just a job for him. Meanwhile, I'm over here, soaking up every ounce of him and wishing that it was real. Like . . . how? How did this happen? How did I happen to fall for an irritating, annoying, sarcastic man who grates on my nerves?"

"Does he grate on your nerves, or does he see you for who you are and push you past your comfort zone?"

I look over at Echo and say, "I came here to be delusional, not for you to point out the obvious."

She chuckles. "Come on, Aubree. Is it so bad that you're falling for the man you're marrying in a few days?"

"Yes," I nearly shout. "He doesn't feel the same way."

"Have you asked him?" She lifts a brow at me.

"How the hell am I supposed to ask that?" In a whiny voice, I say, "Hey Wyatt, I was wondering if you like me the way I like you." I shake my head. "Come on, there is no proper way to bring that up."

"Sure there is. You sit him down, look him in the eye, and say, 'I know you're probably not expecting this, but over these past two weeks, I've come to the realization that I like you more than a friend.'"

I nearly gag.

"That is not something I want to say to him."

She chuckles. "Well, you could break it down like that."

"And then what? Have him tell me thank you, and that he likes me as a friend? That's just asking to be humiliated."

"Or," she says, "he could say something like . . ." In a deep voice, she continues, "Aubree, I've come to find you quite attractive in the past two weeks as well, and I'd like to explore the possibilities of a real relationship."

I gawk at her.

Unblinking.

Unmoving.

And after a few seconds of silence, I say, "That's a terrible impression of him. He'd never say that."

She rolls her eyes dramatically. "Well, then what would he say?"

"Uh . . ." I drop my voice and say, "Aw, Aubree, you loving on me? That's so cute." I clear my throat and say, "It would be condescending but not condescending. It would be confusing, and he'd joke about it, and as he teased me, I'd melt, right there, on the spot."

"I think he'd be more sensitive toward your feelings."

"Or he'd be so stunned that the only way he'd know how to react is by joking about it. And I couldn't take the joke. I like him too much to have my feelings teased."

"But if you like him, don't you think you should at least let him know, especially since you two are getting married?"

"I don't—"

"Aubree?" Wyatt calls out, and I feel all the blood drain from my face.

"Oh my God," I mouth to Echo. "Do you think he heard us?"

"Aubree, where are you? I can hear you."

"Holy fuck!" I whisper. "Oh my God. Oh my God."

"Shhhh," Echo says, gesturing with her hands for me to cool it. She clears her throat and shouts, "Back here."

My face burns as I whisper, "What are you doing? Oh God, don't say anything to him."

"I won't," she whispers back just as Wyatt appears and pauses as he looks at us both, huddled together, probably looking anything but innocent.

A grin spreads across his face as he says, "What are you two doing?"

"Nothing," Echo says casually as I shout, "Talking about you."

Echo glances at me in shock as fear takes over me. Fear that he heard what we were talking about.

"Talking about me, huh?" He casually leans against the bee house and folds his arms over his chest. "What in particular were you saying?"

Echo casually waves her hand. "Oh, you know, nothing—"

"Your penis," I shout again.

Yup, penis talk. That seems safe. I'd rather him think I'm talking about his penis than the feelings I have for him.

"My penis?" he asks. "What exactly were you saying?"

Echo looks at me for help, but I come up short. That's apparently all I have in me, so Echo improvises and says, "Just that she thinks it's nice."

"Nice?" he asks, looking over at me.

My cheeks are so hot right now that I truly think it would be easier to burn on the spot than finish this conversation.

"Yeah. Nice."

"I see." He glances back and forth between us, his perceptive eyes probably picking up on our blatant lie. "Well, can't hear that enough. Although, I'd prefer that my dick is referred to as mean rather than nice. A nice dick presents the idea that it doesn't do the type of punishing it's able to do. Rather just presents a gentle time, like an afternoon picnic under the sun. A mean dick, now that's something to be proud of. A mean dick strips you away from the picnic, bends you over the park bench, and takes what it wants while giving at the same time."

Echo looks at me.

I look at her.

She glances at Wyatt.

He smiles at her.

And then both of them look over at me.

Smiling awkwardly, I ask, "What does a neutral dick do?"

Wyatt lets out a roar of a laugh as he walks over to me and takes my hand in his. "Why don't I show you." And then with a quick goodbye, he moves me away from the bee house and Echo and toward the four-by-four.

"What's going on?" I ask.

"I want to show you something."

He helps me in, then hops into the driver's side.

"Who gave you permission to drive this?" I ask.

He starts it up and grins at me. "Mrs. Preston." And then he jolts us forward, flying us down the dirt road of the farm and straight toward the guest house. "You know, I have a feeling you weren't talking about my dick back there."

Oh yeah, what gave it away?

"But if you don't want to tell me, that's fine," he says. "And for what it's worth, the nervous chatter about my penis to cover up what you were talking about, I didn't hear anything. So no need to worry."

Ease settles in my chest. "Well, we weren't talking about anything, you know, bad. If you're worried about that."

"Not worried in the slightest. Can't possibly think of anything that would make you say anything bad about me. I'm the picture-perfect man."

"Dear God," I mutter, causing him to laugh just as we pull up to the guest house. He turns the engine off and hops out. I do the same, and he meets me by the house and takes my hand again. "Can I ask what this is all about?"

"Be patient," he says as he opens the door to the guest house. I half expect him to show off some sort of redecorating, but when nothing is changed, I wonder what the hell he's really doing. "Sit here," he says.

I sit on the bed, then watch him grab his laptop and bring it to me. He takes a seat so our shoulders bump against each other.

"Now, you might hate this, and I'll take no offense, but I was bored today. You won't let me work on the farm, and Maggie and Ethel won't let me near the wedding planning, so I did something."

"What did you do?" I ask.

"I made a website."

I groan. "Wyatt, did you make us a wedding website? Seriously, I don't think that's necessary."

He chuckles and shakes his head as he opens his laptop. "No, I made a website for you."

"What?" I ask as he plugs his password into his computer. When the screen lights up, a website for The Almond Store and the farm come into view. A beautiful, professional picture spans the banner across the top of The Almond Store website. Tabs along the top look like divider tabs from a notebook. One for the shop, the farm, the store, and our story. My throat grows tight again as I stare down at the beautifully constructed, professional-looking website.

He clicks on the tab that says Our Story and up pops a picture of Clarke and Cassidy when she was pregnant.

"Here," he says. "If you want to read it. I hung out with

Hattie today, and she helped me with some details and I pulled from what Clarke had told me."

I shakily take the picture, and I read through the beautiful write-up about Cassidy and Clarke. Where they met, the love they shared—even though I know they weren't in love—and the legacy they built together. I try not to cry at the pictures framed in white, like Polaroids. Or the beautiful picture of Cassidy at the bottom with Hattie in front of the store.

Or the picture of Cassidy and me in front of the potato fields.

But when I read the paragraph at the end, the one that talks about me and the farm and the changes I've made to carry on Cassidy's dreams, I let the tears fall.

I let them cascade down my cheeks, not feeling the need to wipe them away, to hide and make sure no one sees me.

Instead, I openly turn toward Wyatt, my tears staining my cheeks. "This is . . . this is so incredible, Wyatt."

He smiles softly. "So those are happy tears?"

"Grateful tears," I say, and then I cup his cheek and lean into him, pressing a soft kiss to his lips before pulling away. "This is more than I could have ever asked for. Why did you do it?"

"Wanted to do something nice for you. Something helpful. You're setting aside your life for a year to help me, and I want to do as much as I can for you."

"It's not necessary," I say but look him in the eyes. "But this is . . . this means a lot to me."

"I'm not stepping on toes?"

No, you're making it that much harder for me not to fall for you.

You're making it so freaking easy to say I do on Saturday.

You're proving to me that my brother isn't the only decent man on this planet, that there are men out there willing and wanting to be kind and thoughtful. That they don't live with a bottle in their hand, ready to verbally attack you.

"No." I shake my head. "You're not. This was incredibly thoughtful, and I'm grateful, Wyatt." And because I can't help it, I kiss him one more time, but this one lasts two seconds longer.

When I pull away, his eyes slowly open, and a lazy smile spreads across his face.

"Well, I'm not done yet. I still have to figure out the shop for you, but I figured this was a good start and something that will keep me busy and out of your hair."

"Which is the most important thing of all," I tease.

"I'm just here to please."

Yet it feels like he's here for so much more than that.

It almost feels like Cassidy sent him, like Cassidy knew something all along. Because with every day I spend with Wyatt, with every night he holds me, it's like the dark gray cloud hanging over me is slowly parting, and a glimpse of the sun peeks through.

Chapter Eighteen

WYATT

"Laurel," I say as she hops out of her car and runs up to me. With open arms, I pull her into a hug and embrace her tightly.

"Ahh, look at you." She pulls away to give me a once-over. "You look all . . . groomy."

I chuckle and glance down at my dress pants and tucked-in button-up shirt. "I try."

She runs her hand over my cheek. "Didn't shave, though."

I shrug. "Aubree likes the scruff."

She raises her brow at me. "Oh, have things progressed since we last spoke?"

I shake my head as I glance toward the car where a woman stands. She has long blond hair, a sleeve tattoo, and wears a maxi dress. She looks exactly like who I'd picture Laurel with. This girl has a type. "No, same old, same old. But that doesn't seem to be the case with you. Care to introduce me?"

Smiling brightly, Laurel holds out her hand, and the woman by the car takes it. "Wyatt, this is Rhonda. Rhonda, meet Wyatt or . . . W.J. Preston as you know him."

Rhonda takes a deep breath and holds out her hand. "It's a

pleasure to meet you, Wyatt. I've read nothing but great things from you and heard nothing but brotherly things from Laurel."

Smiling, I lean forward and say, "Is she giving away stories about my personal life?"

"Very much so and I've loved every one of them."

I point at Rhonda while I speak to Laurel. "I hope you made her sign an NDA."

"In your dreams," Laurel replies. "I think she might have an Instagram account dedicated to just you and your secrets."

"I'm really here to capture content for it," Rhonda jokes, making me like her already.

"You know, Rhonda. I think we might be really good friends."

She nods. "I think so too."

Laurel looks around, taking in the farmhouse and the guest house. "Where is the bride-to-be?"

"Getting ready." I thumb toward the guest house.

Laurel leans in close. "How is she feeling? Does she seem nervous?"

I shake my head. "No, not at all. Really calm, actually."

"That's good." Laurel takes my hand in hers. "And what about you?"

I can tell what she's trying to hint at, and I tack on a smile for her. "Fine."

"Are you sure?" she asks. "Because I know you, Wyatt, and it's the night before your wedding. Given what happened last time, I can't imagine you don't have any concerns."

"This isn't for love," I say as I glance at Rhonda.

"It's okay," Rhonda says seriously. "Laurel told me, and I've been sworn to secrecy. This stays off the IG account."

I chuckle. "Thank you." I turn back to Laurel and say, "There's no chance of my heart breaking this time. It's business. That's all."

"Really? Because that's not what you made it seem like the other day when you said you liked Aubree."

"I have a crush on her." I shrug, trying to play it off like it's nothing because if I think about it too much, I'll start worrying, and I don't want to worry. If I worry, Aubree will worry, and she's skittish. I don't want to give her any impression that I'm not fully in this.

"Yes, but it wasn't long ago when your heart was broken." Laurel squeezes my hand. "You never talk about what happened. You never talk about her. And honestly, I'm worried about you. I need to know that you have healed." She takes a step forward. "I know this was all my idea, but I honestly didn't think you would go through with it, and now that you are, I just . . . I want to make sure you're okay."

"I'm fine," I say.

"Wyatt—"

"Laurel," I say in a stern voice. "I said I'm fine. Okay?"

She sighs and takes a step back. "Okay."

Feeling guilty, because I know her heart is in the right place, I pull her into a hug and whisper into her ear. "I'm better. I know Cadance wasn't the one for me. I'm trying not to think about it because I don't want to be nervous and make Aubree nervous. Just trying to chill. But thank you for worrying about me."

That eases her mind because she hugs me back and then pulls away.

I glance over at Rhonda and say, "I'm sorry you had to hear my stern voice. Not something I'm proud of."

"Oh yeah, I was really shivering over here."

I let out a hearty laugh. "Yup, I think we're going to be great friends." Just then, I hear the guest house door shut, and I turn around to find Aubree standing at the door, her hands connected in front of her, looking so fucking gorgeous that my heart skips a beat.

She chose a simple light green dress for the evening with off-the-shoulder sleeves and a longer hemline. Her hair is half up and half down with her curls perfectly defined. Her subtle makeup makes her eyes pop, and those gorgeous lips are coated in a gloss, beckoning me to taste them again.

The past few days have been interesting between us, to say the least.

I've worked on the website. She's worked around the farm.

I've helped bring in hay bales for the ceremony. She's helped Maggie set up décor.

We decided on a brunch wedding instead because I told her I wanted to take her somewhere after, and I needed travel time. She easily agreed. Maggie was not happy about the change but went with it. That's when we volunteered to help, and she accepted it.

At night, we haven't said much, just slipped into bed where I held her.

No good night kisses.

No not-so-innocent caresses.

Nothing.

The last time I tasted her lips was when I showed her the website, and now, I'm practically drooling every time I see her, hoping for a spontaneous kiss when she's grateful for something.

Maybe she'll give me one tonight. Shyly, Aubree waves, and I walk over to her. When I reach her at the steps of the guest house, I take her hand in mine and whisper, "You look gorgeous, Aubree."

Her cheeks pinken as she says, "Thank you."

With her hand in mine, I bring her over to Laurel, and I say, "Aubree, this is my best friend Laurel and her girlfriend, Rhonda."

"We haven't really given each other titles yet," Laurel says, but Rhonda steps in.

"She's my girlfriend."

Laurel smirks and shakes Aubree's hand. "It's so nice to meet you. Wyatt has said a lot of great things about you and the not-so-great things, I ignored and didn't believe."

"Laurel," I reprimand, which causes her to chuckle.

"It's fine," Aubree says. "I still say not-so-great things about him."

"Wow," I say. "Thanks a lot, babe."

Laurel smirks as she looks back and forth between the two of us. "You guys are cute."

"You think so?" I ask. "Not sure Aubree would say the same thing."

"No, you're cute. Annoying but cute."

"That's what I wanted his author bio to be," Laurel says. "But he said he wanted to stay aloof with his readers, making them think that he's a secret serial killer."

Aubree eyes me. "Wyatt? A secret serial killer? I heard him scream when a bee chased him the other day."

"Hey now," I say as I nod toward Rhonda. "We have company over here. Can we act like it?"

Aubree chuckles. "How on earth did you deal with him for so long?"

Laurel shakes her head. "I think it's a love-hate relationship. The annoyance is heavy, but the laughter outweighs it all."

"Hmm, seems to be the spell he casts on everyone," Aubree says as she looks up at me, and for a moment, a moment so small, it almost seems like she means that. Like I've cast a spell over her. If only. It would make these feelings I have for her so much easier to deal with.

"Hey," Ryland calls from the farmhouse. "Mac wants to show you guys Chewy Charles's bow tie. Can you converse in here?"

Chuckling, Aubree says, "Chewy Charles is Mac's stuffed animal. He's very important. If he licks you, it's normal. If her fingers turn into spiders and crawl over you, also normal. There's also Chewy Chonda. He's the new horse Wyatt brought with him."

"Okay, one question. Do I like the licking and the spiders?"

"Yes to the licking. Be scared of the spiders, but don't try to hurt them."

"Got it," Laurel says while tapping the side of her head. "Did you hear that, Rhonda?"

"Loud and clear. Licking yes, spiders no."

Chuckling, we all head up the stairs to the farmhouse and into the living room, where Mac sits on the couch with Chewy Charles next to her. Chewy Chonda, thankfully, is on the other side. Glad he's still approved. A red bow tie has been fastened around Chewy Charles's neck while Mac is wearing one of Ryland's ties over a poofy white dress.

Dear God, if this is what it means to marry Aubree, then I'm all fucking in.

⸺

"I'M JUST GOING to help them to their car. I'll meet you in the house," I say to Aubree, who offers a wave to Laurel and Rhonda.

Dinner consisted of the regular gathering, but this time with Laurel, Rhonda, Maggie, and Brody. Of course, when Hayes arrived, Laurel tried to play it cool but lost it when she heard he's been working on new music. She sat next to him and asked him pretty much every question under the sun about his career. She then proceeded to apologize but then kept asking him. Hayes was the chill guy he always is and answered every single one.

Instead of having one of us cook, I had By the Slice deliver pizza and then topped everything off with Aubree's favorite ice cream sundae. I caught the smile on her lips when she saw me set up the fixings for dessert, and I didn't miss the way her shoulder brushed up against mine when she dug into her sundae.

The entire night, she let me hold her hand and drape my arm over her shoulders. She even sat on my lap for a while. I took advantage and held her when I had the chance. I even kissed her head a few times, and even briefly on the lips in the kitchen only to be caught red-handed by Mac, who screamed "ew" and ran away.

It felt real.

It felt like we were a true family, coming together the night before a small wedding.

It felt like Aubree belonged to me, like she was prepared and ready to give herself over to me.

And it made me feel this deep, guttural possession every time I looked at her. Like my brain was screaming, "Mine. Mine."

I have no right to claim her like that, but it didn't stop me from internally creating a moat around her, making sure no one could get to her besides me.

"Did you have a good night?" Laurel asks as we walk over to her SUV.

"Great night," I say.

"Seemed like it," Laurel says and then turns to Rhonda. "Think you could give us one moment?"

"Not a problem." Rhonda quickly gives me a hug and wishes me luck for tomorrow and then hops in the car.

I turn to Laurel and say, "Before you give me the concerned friend speech, I just want you to know that I like Rhonda a lot, and I approve."

Laurel shyly smiles. "I like her a lot too. I'm glad you guys get along."

"Now"—I fold my arms over my chest—"tell me about how you're concerned for me."

She tilts her head to the side. "I'm not concerned. I'm actually relieved."

"Relieved?" I ask.

She nods. "Yes, because she likes you."

My heart stutters in my chest. "What do you mean she likes me? Did she tell you that?"

"No, but I could see it. I know the difference between acting and when someone is truly infatuated with another person, and she's infatuated with you. She didn't leave your side all night. Any time you touched her, she leaned into it. And the way she'd look at you from across the room when you were apart, it was like she was hoping you'd find her again."

"Stop, that's not true."

Laurel presses her hand to my forearm. "Do you really think I'd pump you up like this if I didn't think it was real?"

"No," I answer.

"Exactly. There's something there, Wyatt. I think after the wedding, you talk about it. Get this over with first, and then approach the subject of dating your wife."

I chuckle and push my hand through my hair. "Shit, this is so backward."

"It is, but I kind of like it. But I want to make sure you're ready for a relationship. You were with Cadance for a long time."

"I was with the wrong person for a long time," I say.

"And you've hesitated to talk to Aubree about how you feel. Is it because you're unsure of how she'd react, or you're not ready? If it's the latter, do not let her know how you feel. You have to be ready for her. She's been hurt and damaged, so if you can't be the man *she* needs, don't say anything."

"I'd never hurt her," I say. "She's been hurt too much. I won't be the one who does that to her."

"Good, then weigh your options. If you're ready to open your heart again, go for it. But if you don't think you can risk it, please . . . please don't pursue her, okay?"

I nod. "I understand what you're saying, Laurel."

"Good." She pats my chest. "Now, I'll see you early in the morning. You're coming to the inn?"

"Yup, I'll bring coffee and muffins."

She pats my cheek. "That's a good boy."

She hugs me, and I help her into her car, then wave at Rhonda one more time before shutting the door and heading back to the guest house. When I step in, I notice right away that Aubree is in the bathroom, so I switch out of my clothes and slip on a new pair of boxer briefs just as she opens the door and walks out in one of her large Almond Store T-shirts. The more she wears them, the more they turn me on.

"Everything okay with Laurel?" she asks.

"Yup. She's great." I move past Aubree, dragging my hand over her stomach as we squeeze by each other, and head into the bathroom, where I take care of business, wash my face, and brush my teeth.

Once done, I turn off the light and check the locks as Aubree slips into bed. When I feel comfortable that everything is secure, I slip into bed with her and turn toward her, immediately placing my hand on her stomach to roll her toward me.

"Hey," I say as her makeup-free face stares back at me.

"Hey," she says, curling into the pillow.

"You good?"

She nods. "I'm good."

"Because if you weren't, you could tell me."

"No, I'm good."

"I know tomorrow is kind of weird and maybe a little scary, so if you want to back out—"

"I'm not backing out," she says, her eyes fixed on mine. "I'm in, Wyatt. I told you that."

"You did, but I just want to be sure. You have an out. I'm giving you one."

"I don't want an out," she says. "We're getting married tomorrow. That's happening. I'm not nervous, I'm not scared, and I'm not changing my mind. You asked me to marry you, and I said yes, so we're getting married."

And fuck does that hit me hard. It was the same thing with Cadance, only with a different result. I asked her to marry me, and she said yes, but in the end, she didn't show up.

She didn't show up for me.

And Aubree, who has been nothing but annoyed by me, pressured by me, somewhat blackmailed by me, she's showing up. She's here for me. We're in this together, and fuck does it break something inside me.

I roll to my back and stare up at the ceiling, my breath growing heavy.

"Wyatt," Aubree says as she lifts up to look at me. "Are you okay?"

This heavy weight seems to secure itself on my chest as my worlds start to collide. It's like I buried it away for so fucking long, and now that I'm here, with a woman guaranteeing me that she will marry me tomorrow—even though she doesn't love me—I'm reminded how I felt when Cadance didn't show up.

I never fully worked out those feelings.

I stuffed them away and let something else take over my mind. That something being the cabin. Then Aubree. Making her happy and content. *Do I just keep focusing on other things and not dealing with my grief?*

"Hey," Aubree says as her hand falls to my chest. "Is it something I said? Because I'm sorry—"

I shake my head. "No, it's nothing you said," I say while blowing out a heavy breath and dragging my hands over my chest.

"Are you sure?" she asks. "If you brought this up because you want an out, then that's fine, Wyatt. Just know that I won't take the land for free."

I'm silent for a second, trying to calm myself. This is exactly why I don't talk about Cadance.

Because I was fine.

I wasn't even thinking about her. I don't even love her anymore. I'm not sure I ever truly loved her like I should have. Maybe she did us both a favor, but it doesn't neglect the panic I feel right now on the night before my wedding. The realization that this could happen again, my heart could be tampered with again.

"Wyatt," Aubree says soothingly as her hand slowly rubs against my chest, "is that what you want? You want an out?" When I don't answer right away—because I'm still trying to calm myself—she starts to pull away, shifting her warmth off me. And that's when I snap out of it and grab her hand to prevent her from moving away from me.

When our eyes connect, I say, "You'll become Mrs. Preston tomorrow, have no doubt about that."

"Okay," she says. I catch her throat contract when she swallows. But the wary look in her eyes knocks me in the stomach, and I realize how much I probably just worried her, so I prop myself up on my elbow to look her in the eyes.

"You did nothing, Aubree. If anything, you did everything, and I just think it hit me all at once what you're actually doing for me." Yes, it's a deliberate lie, but the last thing I want to do is freak her out about Cadance and my concerns. "Guilt is a consuming thing."

She wets her lips. "Are you sure?"

"Positive," I say as I gently shift her onto her back and move in close. I cup her cheek gently and stroke her face with my thumb, staring into her beautiful eyes. "Everything is fine as long as everything is okay with you."

"I'm fine," she answers. "I want to do this tomorrow."

"Promise?" I ask her.

She nods. "Promise."

And because insecurity rushes through me, I say, "Can we also promise something else? That no matter where this adventure leads us, we don't let anything come between us? We're only good together as a unit. The minute we part is the minute this unravels."

"Are you afraid I'm going to mess this up?"

"No," I answer. "But this is a year of commitment. When it's over, I want to make sure we're still each other's number-one fans. We need to promise to treat this like a marriage. We talk things through, we work through any issue, and we never go to bed angry with each other. Can you promise me that?"

"Yes," she answers, sounding slightly breathless.

"Good," I reply. I run my thumb over her cheek a few more times and then say, "Thank you, Aubree. I don't think you'll ever know how much this means to me."

"It means just as much to me," she replies.

"I know," I answer and then stroke her cheek a few more times. "Okay, I should let us get to bed."

Her hand lands on my chest before she says, "Are you sure you're okay?"

"Positive, babe," I answer as I lean down and press a very soft kiss to her lips. When I lift, I catch her eyes fluttering open, and for a very small second, as she stares up at me, I almost believe that Laurel was right and Aubree has feelings for me. But I can't focus on that now.

I need to focus on Aubree showing up and saying I do. Once she's officially Mrs. Preston, I can focus on my feelings . . . and possibly hers.

———

WYATT: *How are you feeling?*

Aubree: *Good. You?*

Wyatt: *Great. Laurel just fixed my tie, said it was crooked. Did you get the flowers and muffins?*

Aubree: *I did. I nervously ate two.*

Wyatt: *Are you really nervous?*

Aubree: *I think anyone in this position would be nervous. You have to be a little jittery.*

Wyatt: *Solid as a rock, babe.*

Aubree: *I don't believe you.*

Wyatt: *LOL. Okay, maybe my ass keeps clenching, but that's neither here nor there.*

Aubree: *What every bride wants to hear about their groom before they walk down the aisle—that their groom has been clenching their ass all morning.*

Wyatt: *Here to serve. Hey, sorry I bolted out of the guest house this morning. I forgot to set my alarm and told Laurel I'd be at her hotel bright and early.*

Aubree: *It's fine.*

Wyatt: *I wanted to make sure you slept well and everything. With all the commotion, I'm finally getting the chance.*

Aubree: *I always sleep well when you hold me.*

Wyatt: *Mrs. Preston, that almost sounds like you can tolerate me.*

Aubree: *Don't push it.*

Wyatt: *LOL. Are you ready for this?*

Aubree: *Ready as I'll ever be. Currently, Chewy Charles is licking my leg. Mac taped sandpaper to his mouth so it felt like a cat's tongue. Not sure what's going on there, but it's distracted me.*

Wyatt: Is it weird that I want Chewy Charles to lick me now so I can know how it feels?

Aubree: Yes.

Wyatt: Dammit. How're Ryland and Hattie?

Aubree: Hattie keeps tearing up, especially when she helped me into Cassidy's dress. And Ryland, well, he's just casually observing. Hasn't said much other than to ask me if you were going to make me happy.

Wyatt: What did you say?

Aubree: I said the most happy, because you were giving me land for my hand.

Wyatt: And don't you forget it . . . wench.

Aubree: Wench?

Wyatt: Trying something new. Did it fall flat?

Aubree: Very.

Wyatt: Noted. I'll stick with babe. Oh, Laurel is beckoning me. Time to head to the farm. See you down the aisle, babe.

Aubree: See you down the aisle . . . ass clencher.

Wyatt: **Clutches heart** You woo me with your romance.

———

I SHIFT on my feet as Mac makes her way down the aisle in a poofy white dress with Chewy Charles tucked under her arm. She chucks—yes, chucks, *not tosses*—flower petals at the people lining the aisleway, sitting on hay bales. Ryland, from the side, tries to "dance mom" her—aka, show her what to do—but she completely ignores him as Hayes nails an instrumental version of one of his songs. Don't ask me the title. I can't freaking think of it at the moment because Aubree appears at the end of the aisle, Hattie joining her on one side and Ryland on the other.

My heart stutters in my chest as I take in my bride.

Her simple white dress frames her torso but flares at her hips. The long sleeves hang off her shoulders, showing off her long, elegant neck. Her hair is loosely pulled back with a few curly tendrils framing her face while a cute crown of flowers sits on the top of her head.

She's . . . fuck, she's easily the most beautiful woman I've ever seen, and she's walking toward me, ready to commit to me. Ready to be mine.

And I swear to myself, at this moment, as her eyes stay fixed on mine, I will never do anything to hurt her. I will protect this woman with everything I have in me. She's my responsibility now, and I'll be damned if anything happens to her.

Hayes wraps up the music just as Aubree reaches me. I offer Ryland a handshake and Hattie a hug before I take Aubree's hand in mine. Leaning in close, I whisper so only she can hear me. "You look so beautiful, Aubree. You . . . you took my breath away."

When I pull away, her eyes smile up at me as we turn toward Ethel, our officiant. It was a requirement, as was the locomotive parked off to the side that we could take pictures on. The people on the hay bales, mainly proprietors around town, are people Ethel found worthy enough to be here, as well as Brody, Maggie, Abel, and Echo.

The barn is decked out in mums, spanning from cranberry to orange to yellow. The tractor has been pulled to the front of the opening and decorated in mums as well as hay bales, offering a pretty backdrop for pictures. There are bulbed lights strung throughout, which doesn't make much sense to me because it's a morning wedding, but I wasn't going to argue with Maggie. The town really came together to make this wedding happen, which is a testament to the Rowleys and the way they've impacted this community. I know I joke about winning Almond Bay over with my charm, but I'm not the reason all these people are here. Aubree is.

They want to see her happiness.

I don't blame them.

I want to see it too.

I don't pay much attention to what Ethel says because I'm mainly fixated on Aubree and the way she keeps looking up at me. How there is a slight tremor in her hand, and how even though she's strong as hell, meeting me up here at the end of this aisle, I know deep down, she's scared.

That's why I squeeze her hand tight.

It's why I look her in the eyes when I say our vows.

It's why when I place her ring on her finger, I make it clear that this is a promise I never plan on breaking.

And when Ethel announces us as husband and wife, I step in close to her, grip the back of her head, and seal that promise with a kiss. A kiss that garners a loud cheer from the attendees.

When I pull away, she smiles up at me, and then together, we walk down the aisle, hand in hand as Mr. and Mrs. Preston.

"OH MY GOD," Aubree whispers to me as we finally have a moment to ourselves.

Pictures took about an hour, which felt weird, given the circumstances, then we were ushered into our first dance, where Hayes played music for us and Ethel sang. I swayed back and forth with Aubree in my arms, watching her look around and attempt to smile at everyone taking pictures.

In all honesty, she's been a big trooper through all of this.

"I think this is the first second I've had to breathe," she says as she dips her fork into her mac and cheese.

"Kind of a whirlwind for a second, huh?" I ask as my chair is pulled up right next to hers, and my hand rests on her thigh.

"More like a tornado." She looks around the tables of people all enjoying their food. "I can't believe it actually happened. That we're actually married."

"Tell me about it." I hold up my hand and stare down at my black tungsten ring. "Feels like I was always meant to be your husband." She gives me a *get real* look, which makes me laugh. "Are you saying you don't feel that way, Mrs. Preston?"

"Let's not kill the mood with how I feel."

"Already looking into divorce lawyers? At least save it for after the honeymoon."

"We aren't going on a honeymoon."

"So you think," I say. "I moved the time of this wedding for a reason." I look down at my watch and say, "Actually, you're going to need to speed it up on that mac and cheese if we're going to make our flight."

"Our flight?" she asks, looking stunned.

"Yeah, babe. Did you really think we were going to get married and not fly off somewhere?"

She leans in close and whispers, "What the hell are we going to do on a honeymoon?"

I wiggle my eyebrows, and she places her hand on my face to stop me. With her hand on my face, I say, "So does that mean boning is out of the question?"

"Oh my God, do not call it that."

I laugh as she removes her hand. "Seriously, though, I'm taking you somewhere . . . oh, which reminds me." I pull my phone from my pocket, and I turn on the camera. I lace my arm around Aubree, and I say, "Hold up your ring and smile for the camera."

I take a picture of us both, and then I shoot it off to Wallace with the text, newlyweds.

"Did you send that to your cousin?"

"Yup," I say. "And let the drama begin."

———

"ARE you finally going to tell me where we're going?" Aubree asks as she looks out the rental car window at the large ponderosa pines.

"Look to the right, up ahead," I say as a wooden sign comes into view.

I catch her reading it. "Welcome to the town of Canoodle, where's . . ." She pauses. "Oh my God, are you taking me to your cabin?"

"Yup," I say with a grin. "My grandpa's neighbor, who watches over the cabin, has prepared it for us. I told him I was

415

bringing my new wife, Aubree, and said we were spending time together in the cabin. He was more than happy to change out the sheets and have the cleaning service run through it."

"Seriously?" she asks. "That's . . . that's really sweet, Wyatt. I'm excited to see it."

"I'm excited for you to see it," I say as I feel the temptation to take her hand in mine and kiss her knuckles, but I refrain. Technically, we're not in front of anyone, so why would I do that?

"So this is Canoodle, huh?" she asks. "I wish I was seeing it in the light."

"I'll show you around tomorrow," I say as I follow the road that curves around the lake. "There are some cute shops here as well as great places to eat. The lake is beautiful to walk around, and of course the cabin property is as peaceful as it gets."

"I can't really tell in the dark, but the trees seem tall."

"Very," I answer as I turn down Pine Lane. "And also in the morning, you'll see the beautiful mountains framed by giant boulders."

"I've never been too far from Almond Bay, so this is exciting," she says as she stares out the window.

"Really?" I ask, but then give it some thought. If her dad wouldn't even tell her she was beautiful, what makes me think he'd take her anywhere other than where they live? "Sorry, that was an insensitive question."

"It's fine," she says with a shrug. "At least that wasn't my first time on a plane. My first time was when Cassidy and I flew to San Diego for a weekend. She got these really cheap tickets, and we decided to make a weekend of it. First time on a plane for both of us. We held on to each other for dear life. But I will say this, we didn't have first class seats, that's for certain."

"Well, I'm glad I could offer you a new experience."

"Thank you," she says sweetly, the same voice she's used all day. At first, I thought she was putting on a show for everyone, but once we left the farm and headed into San Francisco to catch our flight, and her tone stayed the same, I wondered if it was because her stress levels had lowered.

Either way, I like it.

I especially like it when she teases me while using that voice.

I make a left to head down a dirt road toward the cabin and say, "Heads-up, the cabin is an old A-frame. It still has its original wood paneling, with the only update being the bathroom. I plan to make a few adjustments here and there, but I want to preserve the old cabin feel as much as possible."

"I'm sure it's perfect," she says just as I make another left and then pull into the short driveway of the cabin.

"There it is," I say, happy that the outside light was left on.

"Oh, it's so cute," she says as I put the rental car in park and turn it off.

We both step out of the car, and I retrieve our luggage from the trunk as she takes it all in.

Crickets sound off in the distance as the silence of the forest envelops us. The smell of fresh pine fills the air, as well as a dewy mist, indicating the night is upon us. Through the leaves and branches of the trees, the glittering stars shine down upon us, and even though there are neighbors, they are nowhere in sight, offering complete privacy.

"Wow, it's dark here and quiet."

"Just what an author loves," I say as I walk up to her with our luggage. "Go on, the key is under the welcome mat."

"Doesn't seem very safe," she says.

"No one is doing anything illegal here in Canoodle. Trust me, the town is like Almond Bay, one big family."

"Says the guy who checks the locks every night because he peed his pants."

"Hey now." I point at her. "That was told in confidence. I don't expect you to throw it back in my face."

She chuckles. "Never should have told me."

She grabs the key from under the mat and unlocks the door. The kitchen light was left on as well, so we aren't fumbling around as we enter.

The first thing I notice is the smell of the wood all over the cabin.

The second thing is a note saying congratulations.

The third thing . . . just how right this feels.

How homey.

"Fuck," I mutter as I take in the open-concept cabin with a wood-burning fireplace in the corner, worn-out furniture in the living room, and a kitchen sink with a red-and-white-checkered curtain underneath it to block the view of the pipes.

"What's wrong?" Aubree asks.

"Nothing." I drag my hand over my face. "I can't believe it's going to be mine." I turn toward her and say, "You did this. You helped make this happen. Thank you so much, Aubree."

Her cheeks flush as she says, "I'll be saying the same thing to you when I own the deed to the rest of the farm. It worked out. Did Wallace ever text you back?"

I shake my head. "No, but I'm sure he's trying to figure out what happened."

"Did you talk to your parents?"

"Yeah, I called them while you were packing. They want to meet you. Said they were happy for us, but definitely want to meet you. I told them we can arrange for that after we get back to Almond Bay. But I did mention the cabin, and they said they'd contact the family lawyer in the morning. They'll need a copy of the wedding certificate, but once we turn that in, it's all mine." They asked many more questions like *how did I find, date, and marry a new woman in such a short space of time.* But Aubree doesn't need to know about that.

She softly smiles. "I'm happy for you, Wyatt. I know how much this means to you." She looks around the space. "And I can see why. It's very homey, feels like a place where many memories are made." She places her hand over her mouth and lets out a large yawn. "Gosh, sorry."

"It's fine. You must be exhausted. After the day's excitement combined with the nerves and the long travel, I'm sure you're ready for bed."

"Yeah, I am," she says.

With both bags in hand, I nod toward the stairs. "Bedrooms are that way."

She follows the way to the stairs and starts to climb them but turns around. "Do you need me to take my bag?"

"Uh, no," I say, which makes her laugh. "I can handle it."

"I know you can handle it, but I didn't want you to think I'm using you as my mule."

"I'm your husband, you are my wife, and I'll treat you as such. I'll take care of the bags."

"Okay." She smirks and heads up the stairs.

After the wedding, she changed into a pair of leggings and a crop top with a long-sleeved flannel shirt. She looked all kinds of cute, and now that I'm getting a great view of her ass in those leggings, I'm appreciating the outfit change. Not that she didn't look stunning in Cassidy's wedding dress because she did. But I like Aubree casual and comfortable like this. I think it's when her best self shows.

When we reach the top of the stairs, she looks between the two bedrooms across from each other with a bathroom between.

Now, if it were up to me, I'd plop both of our bags in the bedroom on the right and call it a night. She's my wife, so she's sleeping with me. But given this is the first time we're offered multiple beds, I don't want to assume she'll sleep with me. So even though it's painful, I ask, "What bedroom do you want to take?"

"Oh," she says, looking between the two. "You can have the big bed. I'll take the bunks."

Of course she'd say that.

"Are you sure?" I ask. Are you sure you don't want to sleep with me? Share a room? Let me hold you while you fall asleep?

"Yeah, I'm much smaller than you." She takes her bag from me and moves into the bunk room while I mentally curse myself out for even giving her the option. There should never have been an option. Fucking idiot.

"Do you want to use the bathroom first?" I ask her.

She shakes her head. "You're faster than me. You can use it first."

"Okay," I answer as I bring my bag into my room, but before I set it down, I look over my shoulder and ask, "Are you sure about the bunk beds?"

She smiles back at me. "Positive." And then she starts unpacking.

Yup, you're a fucking moron, Wyatt.

Chapter Nineteen

AUBREE

The bathroom door shuts, and I take a seat on the bottom bunk as I let out a heavy sigh.

Holy shit, what a day.

I can't believe that I stood in front of my friends, family, and some people from town and took Wyatt's hand and placed a ring on it. I can't believe I said I do. And most importantly, I can't believe the fluttery, magical feeling I felt the entire day, as if it was all real.

That the kiss we shared when pronounced man and wife was real.

That the pictures we took of me leaning into his embrace was real.

That the first dance we shared with Ethel singing in the background was real.

It wasn't.

It was all fake.

It was all for show.

And what a show it was.

Then he whisked me away, looking like the doting husband

stealing me away for a few days. And as I sit here, in the cabin that brought on this entire plan, all I can think about is how I wish he felt the same way about me. Or how I wish I wasn't feeling so drawn toward him and didn't rely on him for comfort or peace of mind. I wish that weren't the case at all, but it is.

And now that we're alone in this cabin with two bedrooms, all I can think about is how disappointed I am. How I'm going to have to sleep in this bunk bed alone, with Wyatt a few feet away, enjoying a bed all to himself.

Is he happy about it?

Does he wish I asked to sleep with him?

Probably not, or else he wouldn't have asked me what room I wanted to be in. He would have just put our stuff in one room.

That's fine.

Going into marrying him, I knew that I was carrying these feelings and that he probably didn't reciprocate them. And now that we're married and he has the cabin—or he will have it when the paperwork goes through—there's no need for him to continue to woo me and keep me on his good side.

Totally fine.

The bathroom door opens, and he says, "All yours."

I lift from the bed, grab my shirt for the night and my toiletry bag, and move into the bathroom, but not before he stops me with his hand on my stomach. Shoulder to shoulder, I peer up at him.

"Are you sure about your bed?" he asks.

"Yeah," I say even though I want to say no. Even though I want to tell him I desperately want him to hold me tonight. Even though I wish he'd ask me to sleep with him.

"Okay." He studies me for a few seconds and then says, "Thank you again for today. It means so much to me."

"We both won today," I say.

"We did," he says, his thumb rubbing over my stomach and making it flip with butterflies. "I'm going to make sure everything is locked up."

"Sounds good," I say, moving into the bathroom and closing the door.

I set my things down and stare into the mirror as an annoying bout of emotions hits me all at once.

I like him so much.

Too much.

To the point that I actually feel my throat grow tight over the thought of not sleeping with him tonight. What would he do if I just showed up at his door and asked if I could sleep with him? The worst he could say would be no. Then I'd have a really clear idea of where he stands.

I brush my teeth, contemplating what to do. I know if Cassidy were here and I asked her, she'd tell me to go for it, to throw caution to the wind and put myself out there. She never took what she wanted when it came to her feelings. I know she'd use her past mistakes to help me decide.

I spit out my toothpaste and rinse my mouth. When I dry it, I look in the mirror again and whisper, "I don't know, Cassidy, should I go for it?"

Deep down, I know she'd tell me to do it. If he doesn't want me, he doesn't want me, and I'll move on. But I'll never know unless I try.

I strip out of my clothes, including my underwear, and I put on one of my Almond Store shirts, this one black with white writing. I finger comb my hair and then splash some water on my face before drying it off. I grip the counter and take a few deep breaths.

Just do it, Aubree.

Just go in there and ask if you can sleep with him.

If he says yes, that's when you make the next move.

You have to try.

I cover my hand over my face, my nerves ripping through me but my courage peaking as I open the bathroom door and bring my dirty clothes into the room. I deposit them by my bag, take a few more deep breaths, and then, on shaky legs, I move toward the hallway, where I catch Wyatt slipping into his bed. His muscular body flexes and retracts as he slides under the sheets. What I wouldn't give to feel his body, to explore it, to hear him moan the same way he did when my mouth was dragging over his cock.

And that's all the ammo I need to propel myself forward. I step into the doorframe just as his eyes connect with mine. His face draws into concern. "Everything okay?"

Twisting my hands together in front of me, I ask, "Please feel free to say no, I won't be offended at all, but, um . . . do you think I could sleep in here with you?"

His brow perks up. "Yeah, of course."

"Are you sure? I know you're probably excited to have a bed to yourself."

"Babe, you can sleep with me anytime."

And that's the last bit of courage I need as I move toward the bed. Since it's pushed up against the wall, Wyatt gets out and lets me slide in before he slips under the covers again.

"Thank you," I say. "Strange place and all."

"I get it," he says as he turns off the nightstand light, casting the room into darkness. "Do you want me to hold you?" he asks.

"Only if you're comfortable," I answer, this conversation between us far too polite for two people who just got married.

"I'm comfortable," he says as he moves in behind me, and then to my surprise, he slips his hand under my shirt and presses it against my bare stomach. Immediately from the warmth of his palm, a tingling sensation strikes up between my legs. My shirt is hiked up, I'm not wearing underwear, and I can feel his arm and body pressed against mine.

It makes my nipples hard.

It makes my skin tingle.

And it makes me feel like I have the power to move forward.

To make a move.

So I turn my head, lean back against him just slightly, and grip the back of his head, bringing his mouth down to mine.

Nerves rip through me as I lightly kiss him. It's short, sweet, and to the point. A simple good night kiss. When I pull away, I whisper, "Good night, Wyatt."

"G-good night," he stutters, making me smile as I rest my head against the cushiony pillow.

As I sink into the mattress and grow more comfortable, I feel his chest take a few deep breaths, which could only mean one thing . . . perhaps I turned him on.

Perhaps there is hope, so I wait a few more seconds, and then I lean against him again, twisting my head and reaching for his. Once again, I bring his mouth to mine. On a sharp inhale, he kisses me back. This time, his hand that's on my stomach floats up right below my breast, but before he can touch it, I pull away.

"Night, Wyatt."

He swallows loud enough for me to hear. "Yeah . . . night," he says, sounding flustered, which makes me smirk to myself.

I wait a few more seconds, eager to see if he makes a move, but when he doesn't, I know I'll have to go in again.

So I twist my head just enough, pull on the back of his one more time, and when I bring him down for a kiss this time, my mouth parts and my tongue slips into his mouth. He groans as his hand slides up to my breast, and he lightly brushes his thumb across my nipple.

My entire body heats from the touch, and I quickly pull away before it goes any further.

But it's too late because I can feel his erection pressed up against my backside.

He's turned on.

But so am I. That one swipe of his thumb has me already wet and wanting so much more. But I really want to see what he does, so I curl into my pillow, and I remain like that, taking a few deep breaths to calm myself.

And I wait.

And wait . . .

And just when I'm about to lose my mind, his hand moves down my stomach an inch.

Please God, let this be him closing in.

I take a few breaths, and then his fingers move another inch south. Yes, I nearly cry. Please, he wants this like I want this. I hold still, not wanting to make a sound. My cheeks burn, my pussy pulses with need, and my stomach flip-flops, begging for him to continue his pursuit.

It takes him a few more seconds, but when his fingers dance lower, right above my pubic bone, I turn on my back so I'm looking up at him.

"Aubree?"

"Yes?" I answer breathlessly.

His fingers stroke right above my bare pussy. "Are you not wearing underwear?"

"I'm not," I answer.

"Why not?" he asks.

And I know this is the moment. This is what I've been leaning toward ever since I hopped into bed with him. I either take the moment now, or I never do, and I don't think I could face another night by his side without having his mouth all over me or his hands . . . or his cock inside me.

I want it all.

I need it all.

So I sit on the bed and push him on his back. Then I reach for the hem of my shirt, and with all the courage I can muster, I pull my shirt up and over my head and deposit it on the floor, leaving me naked.

"Holy shit," Wyatt mutters as I lift and straddle his lap, nestling his erection right between my legs. "Fuck," he drags out as his hands move to my thighs.

"Tell me you don't want this, and I'll leave," I say. "I don't want to do anything you don't want."

"Baby," he says softly as he sits up and loops his arm around my back. "Fuck, do I want this more than anything." Why do I feel like there is a but coming? "But . . ." And there it is.

Humiliation falls over me, and I try to slide off him, but he stills me.

"Aubree." His eyes meet mine. "I want this badly, but I don't have protection."

Oh . . .

"Okay," I say, feeling relieved. "Well, I'm on birth control, so it's up to you."

His eyes study me for a moment. Then his hand loops behind my head, and his mouth comes crashing down on mine. He leans against the headboard as I continue to straddle him and get lost in his mouth.

Yes, is all I can think.

Thank God, yes.

I want this man so much. I want to feel him and touch him and not worry about what might happen or what he might say. I want him to look into my eyes, kiss my lips, enter me with his long, thick length, only to bring me to the edge and let me ride there for a while before he tips me over.

I grind my hips against his lap, my clit riding along the ridge of his cock, his underwear getting in the way of what I fully want, so I lean to the side, and while his mouth is still on mine, I help him get rid of the boxers, which he does quickly, and that's when I settle back on his lap.

My clit to his cock.

"Fuck, you're so wet," he says as I glide over him, loving how it feels.

"You're huge," I reply as I move faster. "God, so big, Wyatt."

Then my mouth falls to his again, and I part my lips, letting my tongue tangle against his and getting lost in the feel of his arm around me, his hand snaking up between us to play with my nipple. His legs spread, giving me a better anchor to ride him harder.

He grows beneath me, his cock stretching up along his stomach, and I use the angle to my advantage, focusing on the friction over my pussy.

I grind, and I swivel.

I pump, and I pull.

My stomach coils, and my pleasure climbs.

His mouth takes control, moving over my jaw to my neck, and then he curls down and lifts my breast to his mouth, where his teeth nibble on my nipple.

He licks.

He sucks.

He bites.

He squeezes.

He repeats the process over and over again until I'm panting.

I smooth my slit over his length, rubbing myself out, bringing my body to the height of my pleasure.

I moan with my head tilted back.

I call out his name with every little bite along my skin.

And when he brings his mouth back to mine, I groan into it when our tongues collide once more.

We're erratic, frenzied, trying to grasp onto each other as we seek out our pleasure.

"Fuck," I moan as he pinches my nipple. "Oh God, I'm close," I say as I rotate my hips faster.

"I want you coming around my cock," he says as he tips me back on the mattress and hovers over me. I stare up at him and his magnificent body. His defined pecs and sculpted shoulders. The contracting six-pack as he breathes heavily, staring down at me. He holds his long, girthy cock in his hand, and he's lightly pumping with a bit of pre-cum on the tip.

He's just as close.

So keeping my eyes on him, I slip one of my legs over his shoulder, and then I spread the other.

"Fuck . . . me," he says as he lowers his cock down to my entrance and slowly starts to push forward.

Immediately, my teeth fall over my bottom lip as I adjust to his size.

"You okay?" he asks.

"So perfect, don't stop."

And he doesn't. He continues to push forward while he grabs my leg that's over his shoulder, and when he bottoms out, we both groan together.

"Goddamn it," he says as his eyes squeeze shut. "Baby, I can already feel you contracting around me."

"I'm so close," I nearly cry as my entire body is lit up and ready to fall over just from him entering me.

"Me too. But let me catch my breath."

"No." I shake my head. "Please, I need you to fuck me, Wyatt. Fuck . . . me."

The fire in his eyes lights up, and he leans one hand against the headboard and braces himself as he plunges into me. He thrusts so hard that he bottoms out again and pushes me up toward the headboard. I raise my hands to keep my head from bonking into it, and he does it again.

I've never felt anything like it before.

Penetration has never done it for me, but with each thrust, I feel like he's touching a part of me that's never been touched before. He's pleasuring me in a way that I've never been pleasured before, and it's addicting.

I want more.

I want it harder.

I want it faster.

So I grip his hips, and I encourage him to move more. I dig my fingers into his skin.

He grunts.

He pulses.

He thrusts.

He twists.

And before I know it, I'm panting, calling out his name, feeling my entire body seize on me as I finally tip over the edge, and my orgasm hits me harder than I ever could have imagined.

"Oh fuck, oh God," I cry out. "Wyatt, I'm . . . oh God, I'm coming."

He grunts some more, his hips flying frantically, the bed sounding like it's about to break, and then . . .

"Oh fuck," he cries out as he stills. His cock swells inside me, and he comes.

His moan is the sexiest, hottest thing I've ever heard.

I continue to contract around him as he slowly lowers his body toward mine, keeping his cock firmly inside me. He props himself up on his elbows and stares down at me. He gently moves a strand of my hair off my face and then leans down for a soft kiss.

I get lost in the feel of his lips and don't realize he's slowly removing himself from me. When he's entirely out, he lifts and says, "Be right back."

When he heads into the bathroom, I sigh into the pillow and squeeze my eyes shut.

Oh my God, I just had sex with Wyatt.

No, I didn't just have sex with him. I had mind-blowing, life-altering sex. The kind of sex that will live with me forever. A feeling that will never leave me. And I want to tell him that. I want him to know that this is so much more for me than just one night. I want him to know that I want to date him, that I'm ready to try something new and sneak out of the haze I've been living in.

But not now, not right after what we did. In the morning, when our minds are clear.

He walks back into the bedroom with a washcloth and gently says, "Spread for me, Aubree."

Feeling incredibly awkward, I say, "You don't have to do that—"

"I said, spread," he says in a sterner tone, so I spread my legs, and he takes his time cleaning me.

He then drops the towel and reaches for me. He picks me up into his arms and takes me into the bathroom, where he sets me down. Taking my chin in his hand, he leans in, lightly kissing me on the lips.

"You're so fucking beautiful," he says right before he takes off. When I hear him in the bedroom, I lean against the counter and let out a deep breath.

I hope he likes me back because I can't think of a way I'll ever get over this man.

I STRETCH my arms above my head as I arch my back against the mattress and feel the glow of the morning mountain sun filter through the window.

Soreness creeps between my legs, but it's the best feeling as I open my eyes and turn toward Wyatt, but come up short when I see that he's no longer in bed.

After I returned from the bathroom, he helped me back into my shirt. He was already in his boxers and brought me back to bed. I sort of hoped we would sleep naked together, or maybe he'd wake me up in the middle of the night and try to go for round two, which I would have easily been on board with, especially after the way he made me come the first go around. But he didn't. Instead, he held me all night, and that was that.

Now that it's morning and he's not in bed with me, worry starts to etch up my spine. Did I make a mistake? Did I judge him wrong? Is it going to be uncomfortable?

Worried, I tiptoe out of bed and try to stay as quiet as I can while I move to my bedroom. I don't hear Wyatt, but that doesn't mean he's not downstairs doing something, so I stay extra quiet when I grab my phone and take a seat on the bunk.

I check the time, and I know Echo is awake, so I text her.

Aubree: *I need advice.*

I stare down at my phone, and when I see the dots indicating she's texting back, I thank the high heavens.

Echo: *Uh-oh, what happened last night?*

Aubree: *How do you know something happened last night?*

Echo: *Really? You're texting me at eight in the morning after the first night with your husband. Something happened.*

Aubree: *You're right. Something did happen. I had sex with Wyatt.*

Echo: *Are we happy about that?*

Aubree: *I was. Really happy actually. And he seemed enthusiastic about it as well, but once it was done, it was like he reverted to how we were before we had sex. He held me last night, but there was nothing past that,* *and I woke up alone this morning. I don't know, I might be overthinking this, but something feels off. Do you think I freaked him out?*

Echo: *Who initiated sex?*

Aubree: *I did, but he was glad to participate. Very glad.*

Echo: *Okay, then maybe he's just giving you some space, you know? Like maybe he wants you to fully understand what happened between you two.*

Aubree: *I know what happened, Echo. Everything changed for me.*

Echo: *Then maybe you need to tell him that. Maybe you need to have that conversation.*

Aubree: *And if he doesn't feel the same way?*

Echo: *Then at least you know. But you can't be doing this, not for a whole year. It's better to set the expectations now. Set the boundaries.*

Aubree: *You're right. I don't think I could live with this on-and-off type sexual tension between us.*

Echo: *I know you can't. Now go talk to him.*

Aubree: *Okay. Thanks.*

Echo: *Any time.*

I set my phone down, and then, on a deep breath, I stand from the bunk and head down the creaky stairs of the cabin. When I reach the bottom, I glance out the back deck and marvel at the towering trees that seem to expand into the sky. Since the cabin is on a slope, it almost feels like we're in a tree house. I scan the deck but don't see Wyatt, so I move around toward the living space and spot him in the kitchen with his back toward me, hovering over the coffee maker.

I nervously clasp my hands together and say, "Good morning."

He turns to face me with a cup of coffee in his hands. His eyes immediately fall to my bare legs and then scan up my shirt to my face. "Morning," he says with a light smirk.

Unsure of how to respond and open the conversation, I tiptoe on my feet and say, "The floor is cold."

"Did you bring slippers with you?" I shake my head. *Because who packs slippers on their honeymoon?* "We can grab some when we go into town later."

"Okay," I say, feeling so incredibly awkward.

He sips his coffee, his eyes on me. "Something wrong?"

"Yes," I say before I can stop myself.

That makes his brows peak with interest. He sets his coffee down and leans back against the counter. "What's going on, Aubree?"

Here it goes.

I wet my lips, and in one fell swoop, I say, "Last night was something special for me. It meant something to me. I'm not sure if it meant something to you, but it was a huge step for me. I don't normally do this, but I don't think I can live a year in this purgatory of not knowing, so I just need to tell you, Wyatt, that I like you." Relief flies through me as the words tumble out. "I like you a lot and not as a friend but more than a friend. I've started to develop feelings for you and want you to know because if you don't feel the same way, then I want you to tell me now so I can set boundaries for myself. I don't want to keep slipping into your bed if you don't feel the same way. I don't want to—"

"Whoa, slow down," he says, pushing off the counter and walking up to me.

"I'm sorry, I just want you to know where I stand," I say nervously. "And don't feel like you have to say you feel the same way or that you don't want to hurt me. I just want you to—"

"Aubree," he says, closing the space between us. "I feel the same way."

I shake my head as he steps right in front of me. I press my hand to his chest. "Seriously, Wyatt, I know you don't want to hurt me—"

"Aubree," he says in a very serious tone. "I'm being fucking serious. I've had feelings for you for a while now, and I didn't want to scare you away because I didn't think you felt the same. Why do you think I kept touching you when no one was around? Why I kept trying to kiss you despite not doing good night kisses anymore? Why do you think I nearly lost my goddamn mind yesterday when you chose to initially sleep in the other room last night?"

"You lost your mind?" I ask, feeling like this can't be true, like this is all a dream.

"Yes," he says in exasperation. "The entire time I was getting ready for bed, I cursed myself for even suggesting you choose what bedroom to sleep in." He wraps his arm around my waist and pulls me into him. My hands fall to his chest as I stare up at him. "I want to date you, Aubree. I want to see where this can go because I think you're incredible, and I don't want to pretend I don't anymore. I'm tired of it." He cups my cheek. "I want to give us a chance."

"I want that, too," I say, feeling a wave of relief and excitement hit me all at once.

He smirks and then lightly presses a kiss to my nose. "Then if that's the case, Aubree Preston, will you date your husband?"

I chuckle. "Oh my God, Wyatt, could you be any lamer?"

"I could," he answers. "I could hold out my hand, introduce myself, and ask you where you're from, starting at the very beginning." When I don't say anything, he pulls away and holds his hand out to me. "Hi, I'm Wyatt—"

"Stop that." I swat his hand away.

He laughs, scooping me up in his arms, and he brings us over to the couch, where I straddle his lap. His hands fall to my thighs and move up toward my hips. Once again, he notices I'm not wearing underwear and lifts one of his brows at me.

"What have I told you about not wearing underwear?"

"Nothing," I answer. "You've actually told me nothing."

"Huh, I think you're right." His hands roam under the hem of my shirt. "Well, for future reference, if you don't wear underwear, I have free access."

"Free access?" I ask. "You realize this is my body, right?" My fingers play with his light splattering of chest hair.

"Not anymore, babe," he replies as he sinks further into the couch, bringing my hips right over his hardening erection. "You married me. That means you belong to me."

"Wasn't aware that's what I was signing up for."

"Always read the fine print, babe." His hands travel farther up my body, dragging my shirt with him until he removes it and leaves me naked on his lap. His hungry eyes roam my chest as he wets his lips, a look of satisfaction crossing over his expression. "That's better."

Fascinated that I don't feel self-conscious, I watch how he appreciates every inch of me, not even hiding that he's checking me out. "Getting your fill?" I ask him.

"Yes," he replies as his hands lazily run up my sides. "You have no idea how much I've been hiding this need to have you in my arms without you second-guessing it or questioning me."

"Why didn't you say anything?" I say as I start to rock over his hips, causing his teeth to pull on his bottom lip.

"Because I didn't want to scare you," he says, his hand connecting with my breast where he massages it. "Thought I'd marry you first so you couldn't get away." He leans forward and pulls my nipple between his teeth.

A hiss escapes my lips as I lean into his touch. This touch that I seem to be craving now that I've finally had him. He brings his hand up to my other breast and starts circling my nipple, over and over again, then lightly flicking it, giving me just enough to drive me crazy but never enough to be fully satisfied.

"God," I breathe out when he releases my nipple and starts licking it. "You're making me so wet, Wyatt."

He releases my breast from his mouth and says, "Stand up." When I look at him with a confused expression, he says, "Stripping down." He removes his underwear, and my mouth waters as his cock hardens against his stomach, stretching upward, ready for me. The idea of me turning on this man will probably never get old.

It feels powerful.

It makes me feel beyond sexy.

It makes me feel like I matter.

He holds out his hand to me, and I take it, starting to straddle his lap when he stops me and then turns me around.

"Sit down, Aubree," he says, taking my hips and guiding me down on top of him, my back to his chest. He leans me all the way back so my head rests on his shoulder and his hand wraps around my stomach. His erection presses between my ass, hard as a rock. Softly, Wyatt drags the tips of his fingers over my stomach and up to my chest. "Your skin is so fucking soft. It's addicting."

His fingers wander over my breasts, barely caressing my nipples before they move up to my neck where he lightly encircles at the base. Holding me still, he brings his mouth to my ear, where his lips brush against my lobe as he says, "Need inside you."

I need that too, desperately, so I sit up on my knees and bring his cock to my entrance, only to slowly lower down on top of him.

I have to take a few deep breaths as I lower because I'm still adjusting to him in a new and different position, which seems to add more pressure, a pressure I wasn't expecting.

"God, Wyatt," I moan as I lean against his chest, his hand still gripping my neck.

"Your pussy is so fucking addicting," he says on a groan as he starts thrusting up into me. "Fuck . . . me, Aubree. Warm . . . wet . . . fucking tight. Yes, so fucking good," he moans, sending a bout of chills down my arms. "Can't get enough." He runs his other hand up my stomach to my breasts, where he starts circling my nipple again. "Move for me, baby, fuck my cock."

So turned on, I anchor myself against him as he teases my breasts, and I start moving my hips around in circles, grinding on his lap and taking in the feel of him so deep inside me.

"That's it, Aubree," he encourages. "Keep going."

As I rotate on him, his lips move along my cheek, my jaw, my neck.

His fingers play with my nipple, stroking, flicking, circling.

His hand applies pressure to my neck, his thumb gliding up and down the sensitive column.

It's like he knows exactly how to handle me, how to bring me to the edge quickly.

"Wyatt," I whisper. "I'm close."

"I need more, Aubree. Squeeze me, baby."

Wanting him to come with me, I start moving my hips up and down, and every time I crash down on his lap, I squeeze my inner walls.

And with every squeeze, he moans deeper and sexier.

"Ohhhhh, fuck," he says as I drop down on him again. "Fuck yes, baby." He releases my neck and brings his hands to my hips, where he grips me tightly and then starts aiding my thrusts with his own. His body turns into a frenzy as he seeks out an orgasm. "Jesus fuck, it's so good." He slams me down again and again. "Fuck, Aubree . . . fuck . . ." He bites down on my shoulder, his hips flying now as he pumps up into me.

My tits bounce with his jostling, his legs smack against my ass, and his fingers dig into my skin. It's the best, most erotic feeling of my life.

"Touch your clit, baby. I want you screaming."

Nearly there, I bring my hand between my legs and massage two fingers over my clit, circling it over and over again. Combined with what he's doing, my release presses quickly at the base of my spine, my body ready to fall over the edge as tingles of pleasure jolt through my veins.

"Oh fuck, Wyatt," I yell as he pounds me down on top of him, over and over and over. "I'm . . . I'm coming," I shout as my pussy contracts, and my orgasm takes over, sending me right over the edge and into a wave of bliss.

Wyatt groans behind me as his hips still and his cock pulses inside me. "Oh fuck," he groans as I feel him come, his fingers nearly piercing my skin with how tightly they're holding me. His head falls forward, and he bites into my shoulder as he continues to come, both of us taking in every last second of it until we settle.

After a few seconds of heavy breathing and relaxing our bodies, Wyatt says, "Fucking hell, Aubree."

I chuckle and lean against him, completely spent. How did I not know that sex could be like this? So . . . incredible? Wyatt is such a selfless lover. "It's so good."

"It's phenomenal," he says, placing a kiss on my neck and then my shoulder where he bit me. "Fuck, I left a mark. I'm sorry."

"Don't apologize," I say, turning my head toward him. "I like it."

Growling, he holds my jaw in place and presses his lips to mine. "You very well might be the death of me if you keep that up."

"What a way to go."

―――――

"IT'S COLDER than I thought it would be," I say while slipping my shoes on.

"Take my sweatshirt," Wyatt says while he starts to tug it off.

"No, I don't want you to be cold." I stand from the couch.

"Babe, do you really think I'm going to walk around town with you and let you be cold?"

"No," I answer.

"So take the sweatshirt," he says, bringing it over to me.

I press my hands to his chest and smile up at him, still in awe over the fact that this is real, that we are a real thing. "I appreciate the gesture, but I'll be fine once we start walking in the sun."

"You're cute," he says. "But take the fucking sweatshirt."

I chuckle and take the sweatshirt, slipping it on over my long-sleeved T-shirt. And because he's so much bigger than me, it envelops me in his scent, the hem hitting me mid-thigh and the sleeves extending far past my hands. But oh my God, I love it.

I hug the sweatshirt close and say, "You're not getting this back."

He chuckles and lifts my chin only to place a soft kiss on my lips. "It's yours."

I take in his long-sleeved shirt and the way it clings to every part of his torso, including his thick pecs and rounded shoulders. "Are you sure you'll be okay?" I ask him.

"Yeah, and if not, when we get your slippers, I'll grab a sweatshirt for myself. Sound good?"

"Sounds good. Thank you," I say, kissing his jawline.

He smirks at me and takes my hand, leading me to the front door. "You know, when you let your guard down, you're quite pleasant to be around." I pause, only for him to look over his shoulder and laugh. "You're also sexy as shit when you're irritated. Thought that from day one."

"Is that why you enjoyed making me mad?"

"Yup, something about the fantasy of having angry sex with you really motivated me."

"Keep it up with those comments, and that fantasy very well might come true."

"Don't threaten me with a good time, Aubree. I know exactly how to press your buttons at this point." Funnily enough, he's not wrong. And it's amazing to be with someone who won't use that knowledge to malign me. He leads me out of the cabin and into the crisp mountain air where silence surrounds us, just the sound of the breeze blowing through the trees and the occasional bird chirping filtering through.

I sigh, taking it all in. The lengthy ponderosa pines that seem to be never-ending, the earthy smell of the leaves changing colors and falling to the ground, and the feel of total seclusion and privacy.

Turning toward Wyatt, I say, "I can tell exactly why you wanted to make this cabin yours. It's breathtaking here. I could get lost in here, forget all of my responsibilities and just soak in the nature surrounding us." I look around, catching a blue-winged bird floating through the air only to land on a tree branch. "One can truly find peace here."

"I have found peace," he says quietly. "This cabin was where I wrote the first sentence of my very first book."

"Really?" I ask, surprised.

"Yup, I was talking to my grandpa about a story idea I had. I was fifteen at the time, and he told me to write it down. He never thought of my aspirations to write as something silly. He supported them and even helped me flush out some ideas when I was stuck."

"You were pretty close, weren't you?" I ask as we walk up the road, hand in hand.

"We were. Very close."

"Can I ask you a private question?"

"Aubree." He chuckles. "We're married, and you've sat on my face. Pretty sure you can ask me anything at this point."

"Well, when you put it that way . . ." I peer up at him, and he smirks and then winks. And we're probably both thinking of what we did this morning. Hard not to, especially after I screamed his name loud enough to scare every bird away from the cabin within a five-mile radius. Clearing my thoughts, I ask, "If you were so close with your grandpa, then why did he not just leave the cabin to you? Why was it to one of the grandkids and not one of his kids?"

"Great question," Wyatt says. "He and his brother owned the cabin. His brother didn't have kids and didn't care for Grandpa's kids."

"Ha!" I laugh. "Seriously?"

"Oh yeah, hated them. He wasn't the greatest uncle in the world. My dad had a few choice words to say about him that I won't share, but Grandpa didn't want the cabin to be sold. He wanted it kept in the family, so they made a deal that the first grandkid to get married would inherit the cabin."

"Did your grandpa's brother ever visit the cabin?"

"Yup," Wyatt answers as we make a right and head into town. He told me it was a short walk, and he was right. I can see some shops up ahead. "He would come up to the cabin and have smoking and drinking benders. Grandpa's only requirements were no smoking his pipe in the house and no women. It was a family cabin, and he didn't want his brother bringing over a parade of women. He was known for partying and having a voracious appetite for women."

"Yet the things we've done in that cabin since we've arrived."

Wyatt laughs. "We're married, Aubree. That's different. We're allowed to do those things."

"I hope so. I don't want to taint your grandpa's requests."

We cross the street again, right into town. From what I can tell, the town centers around a large lake with the main street flowing around it, and businesses dotted all along the road. The town is a combination of western and mountain with log-like cabin buildings and saloon façades. It's cute and whimsical. Everything I'd want in a mountain town.

"My grandpa would have loved you."

"You think so?" I ask as we head toward the diner. Wyatt warned me that it's chock-full of trolls.

Yes, you read that correctly, trolls. The owner apparently collects them and has used her diner to display them on every surface she can. As a bipartisan of troll collecting, I'm fascinated to see what this troll haven might look like.

"I know so," Wyatt says. "He always wanted me to be with someone who was—as he put it—a bit spicy. Or in your case, a lot spicy. He wanted someone to challenge me, not fall in line with my day-to-day. He wanted someone who would push my buttons, make me think, and make me work to find peace. He never ever wanted anything handed to me, and baby, you were one hell of a hard catch to land."

"Hence the bribery at the beginning. Your grandpa would have been proud," I joke.

"He would have."

When we arrive at the diner, Wyatt reaches for the door just as it pops open. He steps back, and I catch a smile cross his face right before he says, "Fallon, how are you?"

"Wyatt?" a stunning woman says, pulling him into a hug. "Oh my gosh, it's been so long. How are you doing?"

"Great," he says and then holds up our connected hands. "Got married this weekend."

Her eyes fall to mine, and she says, "Oh, is this Cadance?"

Cadance . . . who the hell is Cadance?

Wyatt shifts but remains cheery as he says, "No, this is

Aubree Rowley. Her sister was married to my brother before he passed. Aubree runs the farm up in Almond Bay."

"Oh my gosh, I'm so sorry," she says, shaking her head. "Wow, what a dense thing of me to say."

"It's fine," Wyatt says. "We haven't seen each other in a while."

"And whose fault is that?" she asks, hand on her hip, looking so freaking cute. "But congratulations, that's so exciting. I actually got married myself."

"To Peter?" Wyatt asks.

Fallon laughs and shakes her head. "Wow, we really need to update each other. No, his name is Sawyer. He came into town after running out of his best friend's wedding, left only a shoe behind, and came rolling into Canoodle. He needed a place to stay, so he stayed at the cabins. Long story short, he became best friends with my grandpa, helped me renovate the cabins, and I fell in love. He's a screenwriter. You two would probably get along."

"Well, if that's the case, we should get together at some point."

"That would be so great. I'd say my grandpa would love to see you, but his Alzheimer's is taking over his memory."

"I didn't want to ask, but are you still caring for him?"

Fallon nods. "Sawyer has been a huge help. My dads are up here a lot, helping out as well. And then everyone in town. It's really been a community effort. Especially from Tank. You should go visit him. I know he misses your grandpa a lot. He'd love to see you."

"I'll stop by the hardware store and say hi. Plan on taking Aubree around and showing her everything."

"Good, and hey, now that you're married and taking owner-ship of the cabin, does that mean you'll be up here more often?"

"I hope so," he says.

"Well, I'll warn Jazz. You know she gets excited when you're around, loves talking all things stabby."

Wyatt turns to me and says, "Jazz is Fallon's best friend, and she likes to think that she's not eccentric like the rest of the town, but she might be the most eccentric besides the cat that's the mayor."

"Uh, that would be Beefinator, the grandchild of Beefy Boofcheck, the Saint Bernard."

"Wait," Wyatt says, looking truly concerned, more concerned than over the mention of that Cadance chick I'm still reeling over. "What happened to Miss Daphne Lynn Pearlbottom and her glittery fascinators?"

"Kicked to the curb," Fallon says. "Pearlbottom had no chance at reelection when Beefy's kin stepped in."

"Such a shame," Wyatt says. "Makes me think if I'm spending more time here, I need to pay closer attention."

"You do, especially in the mayoral politics. There is a small cult of Pearlbottom lovers who are ready to try to take over and win her back her spot."

"The drama," Wyatt says, "I love it."

Fallon smirks. "Well, I'll let you two go eat something. Stop by the cabins. I'd love to show you the renovations, and you can meet Joannie, my baby girl."

Wyatt's face softens. "You had a baby girl?" he asks.

Fallon smiles widely. "Yes, and she's perfect."

"Congratulations, Fallon. I'm really happy for you. I'll stop by for sure." Wyatt leans in and gives her another hug. "Good seeing you, Fallon."

"You too." She waves at me. "Nice meeting you, Aubree."

"Nice meeting you," I reply as Wyatt opens the door to the diner and guides me in by placing his hand on the small of my back.

We enter what I can only describe as a troll haven, but my mind is still yelling *who the hell is Cadance?*

From floor to ceiling, narrow shelves line the walls, displaying thousands of trolls, ranging from naked with bejeweled bellies to fully dressed. Tall. Short. A variation of hair colors combined with vibrant—yet dulled—clothing themed to the nineties trends. There are signs and license plates, and every paraphernalia an ardent collector would have in their arsenal, and this diner didn't cheap out on any of them.

"It's something else, isn't it?" Wyatt says, mirth in his voice.

"It really is," I say as he brings us over to a booth up against one of the walls. He sits across from me and nods toward the napkin dispenser covered in troll stickers. Really, nothing has gone untouched in the decorating of this diner.

And maybe if I wasn't at war in my head over this Cadance mention, I'd find it quite comical, but I can't seem to muster up the strength to push that aside and enjoy the moment with Wyatt.

And he must notice because he asks, "Hey, are you okay?"

I wet my lips and twist my hands in my lap as I look up at him. "Yeah, sort of. Just a little confused."

"About the trolls?" he asks. "I know, I think we all are."

"No," I say. "Not about the trolls, about what Fallon said."

His brow turns down. "What did she say that confused you?"

"She thought I was some woman named Cadance." I look him in the eyes. "You've never mentioned her."

"Oh," he says while he pulls menus from behind the napkin dispenser and hands one to me. "She's just an ex. Didn't think she was worth mentioning."

"Were you guys serious?" I ask.

He pulls his gaze from the menu and makes eye contact. "Does it matter?" he asks in an easy tone. Not mad, just curious.

"I guess not," I say. I glance down at my menu, the words and letters all swirling together because I have this weird feeling he's hiding something from me. It could just be my paranoia, though. "I guess we've never talked about those kind of things before."

"Do you want to talk about those kind of things?" he asks me.

I shrug. "We don't have to. I guess there isn't much substance that would add to our situation by talking about exes, especially mine."

"Because yours was a complete tool," Wyatt says and then

reaches across the table and takes my hand in his. He leans forward and kisses my knuckles before resting our connection on the table. "I think what's in the past is in the past, and we should just leave it there."

He lets go of my hand and returns to his menu, where I watch his eyes scan over it, his lips twisted to the side as he tries to decide.

What's in the past is in the past . . .

Why does that feel like anything but someone who is over the past?

That sounds like something someone still living in the past would say.

Chapter Twenty

WYATT

"How do you like the pancakes?" I ask as Aubree takes another bite of the banana granola pancakes I suggested she order.

Mouth full, she looks up at me and smiles.

"That good, huh?"

She nods, and I lightly smile as I glance back down at my barely eaten omelet. It was nice running into Fallon and hearing how well she's doing. I've known her for years. Since our grandpas were friends, we occasionally hung out at the Canoodle Cover Cabins. I didn't even think about running into her, which was naïve of me because the town is so small. I should have known she'd ask if Aubree was Cadance, but I've been so consumed by what Aubree confessed to me this morning that I didn't prepare myself for what the town might say to her.

And it hit me harder than I expected.

Just the mere mention of her name twisted my insides. But not twist in the way you're probably thinking, as if I miss her, because I don't. I don't miss her self-importance or her need to always be right. I don't miss her judgment of this cabin or this town. I don't miss the way she'd beg me to skip my deadlines and hang out with her. I don't miss the way she'd constantly want me to stop everything for her because she considered her life more important than mine.

That twist, the nausea that climbed up my throat from the mention of her name, stemmed from the reminder of the heartache I suffered. A slap to the face, waking me up from the haze I've been in since yesterday when I took Aubree's hand and made my vows to her. These feelings I have for Aubree are real. They're so real that the fear of losing her crept through me while I was talking to Fallon.

She lifts her cup of tea and looks over the mug at me. "You seem like you're thinking really hard," she says.

"Why?" I ask, my eyes connecting with hers. "Is steam coming out of my ears?"

She chuckles and sips her tea. "Yes, the steam coming out of your ears rivals the steam from my tea."

"Impressive. Didn't think my brain could work that hard."

She sets her cup down and picks up her fork. She's sitting cross-legged, which I think is adorable, and she stuffed her cloth napkin in her shirt because apparently, she likes her pancakes drenched in syrup, and she didn't want to get any drips on her clothes. Just made me like her that much more because I can see that she's truly opening up now. She's letting the walls down, something I've wanted her to do since day one.

"Care to share what you're thinking about?" she asks, looking slightly insecure, and I know exactly why.

"Nothing you need to worry about," I say.

"Why would I worry? Are you worried?"

"No." I shake my head.

She sets her fork back down and leans in closer. "Are you thinking about Cadance?"

Yup, I knew what I said earlier wouldn't stop her from asking about Cadance. Hell, it wouldn't have stopped me from asking about one of her exes. I would have kept pestering her about it until she told me all about the fucker who hurt her.

But I just got Aubree to confess her feelings for me. She's just starting to open up. The last thing I want to do is make her feel insecure about someone from my past, someone I'm trying to forget. I don't want Aubree knowing that Cadance slightly broke me. I'm the strong one between us. Aubree's been through so much. She needs a rock in her life, and I want that to be me. She doesn't need to see the rock cracked and crumbling.

"Am I thinking about Cadance?" I repeat her question. "No, I'm not."

She studies me, her eyes not letting up as I lift my mug of coffee to my lips. "Why do I feel like you're lying to me?" she asks.

"I don't know," I answer, hating that insecurity is already taking over her thoughts. "But I don't want you worrying about anyone in my past. There's nothing to worry about."

"Then tell me about her," Aubree says.

I sigh and set my fork down before moving out of my side of the booth and sliding in next to her. She turns toward me, and I rest my hand on her thigh as I look her in the eyes. "Aubree, I need you to listen to me, okay?"

She nods as those beautiful eyes peer up at me.

"Nothing good will come if we talk about exes that didn't matter. I like you a lot, and I'd rather spend our time getting to know each other on a deeper level, than the mindless people we dated."

She twists her lips to the side as she looks down at her lap. "You're right." She sighs heavily. "I'm sorry. I guess my insecurities are showing."

Just what I thought. Aubree is one of the strongest people I've ever met. She's brave and strong, and she doesn't take shit from anyone, but when it comes to feelings, when it comes to her heart, she's not as strong as I think she wishes she was. She's been hurt several times by multiple people. Starting with her dad, then Amanda, then Matt, and losing Cassidy on top of all of that, it hasn't been an easy road for her. She's going to guard herself, and she's going to fall into thoughts and notions that are damaging to the confidence she's been able to carry.

Telling her about Cadance and our engagement, our almost marriage, I'm not sure she'd be able to bounce back from that, at least not right now when we're so new.

"Aubree," I say. "You need to know that you don't have anything to be insecure about when it comes to me. I've said it from the very beginning. This is just you and me. We're in this together."

"I know." She leans her head against the tall booth seat. "I'm sorry." She grumbles to herself, shaking her head, "I'll be better."

"Stop," I say, having her look up at me. "You're perfect. Just offer me a little more trust. All I want is happiness for you." I smirk. "And now that you've finally given in to your feelings, you're going to find a whole lot of happiness."

Her face falls flat as she stares at me. "You're so lame, Wyatt."

"Lame? Ouch, babe. I thought that was clever."

"Yes, an old man like yourself would."

Now it's my turn to scornfully look at her. "I'm not *that* old."

"Old enough to know what dial-up Internet was like."

I point a finger at my chest and say, "Which makes me a fucking pioneer. You have no idea the kind of stress I suffered when I wanted to check my AOL messaging while my parents were expecting a phone call. It wasn't easy."

She pats my cheek. "Poor baby."

"That's right, poor baby. I should be compensated for the time I spent listening to that godforsaken screeching while the Internet connected."

"And who dare I say do you think should compensate you? And what would this compensation be?"

"Well, given you're a youth, I think it should be you. And frankly, I think compensation should be of the pleasurable kind."

"Something is seriously wrong with you if you can say something like that in a diner full of trolls. What is wrong with you?"

I grin and lean in close. "When you get to taste a pussy like yours, it's all you fucking think about, even when there are thousands of trolls staring me down."

She tilts her head to the side, her previous insecurities washing away when she says, "I don't know if I should be honored or horrified."

"Maybe a little of both."

―――

"I KNOW I've said this like one hundred times," Aubree says as we take a seat on a bench to look over the lake. "But Canoodle is truly adorable. It has the same feel as Almond Bay, but in the mountains. I can see why this place is so special to you."

I drape my arm behind her and pull her in close. "Yeah, so many great memories were formed here. I couldn't imagine what I'd have done if Wallace took the cabin."

"Still haven't heard from him?"

I shake my head. "No, and I won't until he's ready to strike."

"Are you worried?"

"No, not in the slightest. I covered all my bases. I'll just have to deal with his cranky ass, but I'm not worried about that, just annoyed."

"Well, I'm glad about that." She adjusts the paper gift bag at our feet. "Thank you for the slippers, by the way. And the blanket. And the fuzzy socks. And the sweatshirt."

I chuckle. "You're welcome . . . again."

"You didn't have to buy me all of those things, you know."

"Oh, I know, but now that you're my wife, don't you think I should be able to spoil you?"

"I don't know." She shrugs. "I don't get the dynamics sometimes. Like . . . am I really your wife? Feels more pretend to me. Are we, I don't know . . . dating? It's so backward, it's confusing."

I pull her in close to my chest and say, "You're my wife, we're dating, and we're seeing where this goes. Simple as that."

"You make it seem simple, but it doesn't feel simple."

"What doesn't feel simple about it?" I ask.

"Well, I feel like there is so much I don't know about you."

"Probably," I answer. "What do you want to know?"

"Your parents, you said they eloped, and they wouldn't be mad about missing your wedding. Were you close with them?"

"Yes," I answer as I run my hand over her shoulder, keeping her plastered to me. To my satisfaction, she leans her head against my chest and snuggles in close. "Since it was just us four, we had a strong bond. I know it's different from what you experienced growing up, but my parents were there for everything. I don't know, I feel bad talking about it."

"Because I had a shit father who abused us?" she asks. "Don't feel bad. It's not your fault. I want to hear about your childhood and the stories you carry close to your chest. It will make me believe that there are good people out there."

"There are," I say, kissing the top of her head. "Very good people, just like you and your siblings."

"Thank you," she says softly. "That means a lot, but tell me about your parents."

"Well, they met in high school," I say. "Broke up in college. During their senior year, my mom started dating my dad's friend from high school, which made him incredibly jealous. He told his friend he wasn't allowed to date her. It became a huge ordeal, and they actually got into a fight."

"Who?" Aubree asks.

"My dad and his friend. They had to be pulled apart. My dad broke his friend's nose."

"Oh my God," Aubree says. "He was really, really mad."

"Yeah, pissed. That night, he asked my mom out."

"What did she say?" Aubree asks.

"Told him to go to hell." I chuckle, thinking about the story. "It wasn't until two years later when they were back in their hometown for the holidays that they ran into each other. They were both single, and Dad took advantage of it. According to Mom, he wooed her. Brought her around to all of these Christmas activities, including ice-skating and cocoa in front of a bonfire. And when they just so happened to be under a mistletoe, Dad kissed her. After that, they were never separated again. A month later, they eloped, and well, they're still together to this day and madly in love. They always told me that when you know it's the right person, you know." I kiss the side of her head.

"Are you subtly trying to tell me after a few weeks together, a marriage, and some sex that I'm the right person?"

I laugh. "Well, when you put it like that . . ."

She bumps her shoulder with mine. "We will see where this all goes, but I appreciate your enthusiasm."

"That's what I'm here for, babe, to get you to fall head over heels in love with me."

"I wish you luck. I'm a tough shell to crack."

"I've noticed," I say. "But no way in hell am I giving up."

"Good." She kisses my cheek and then rests her head against me again. "Were your parents writers?"

"No," I answer. "But Dad has always been an amazing story-teller. I think he could have been an author if he was afforded the luxury to do something with his talents. But back then, he was trying to make money, have a career, and follow along with what his buddies were doing. He went into software engineering, and it worked for him. He had a solid career, but on the weekends, when he was hanging with friends, he'd be the most entertaining of the group."

"That's who you get it from."

"Yup," I say. "Whereas my mom is more of the quiet one but will lay you down with an unexpected zinger. She's quiet and hardworking but also knows how to have a good time. Kind of like you."

"You believe I know how to have a good time?" she asks.

"Yeah, babe. I wouldn't be hanging out with you if you didn't."

"Wow," she says, making me laugh.

"I was going to say . . . yeah, you know how to have a good time, given what we did on the couch this morning, but I didn't want you to think that's the kind of good time my mom was having. The correlation felt off. But if we were to separate the two, I'd say your good time this morning shows just how much fun you can have."

She lifts up to look at me. "That's the first time I've ever done that position."

"Well, it was fucking hot. Did you like it?"

"A lot," she says.

"Good to know." I tug on a piece of her hair. "What else do you like?"

"Are you really going to ask about sex positions when we're staring at this beautiful lake?"

"Are the tiny waves lapping at the edge not reminding you of anything?"

She pushes up from me to look me in the eyes. "No. What would it remind me of?"

"The sound . . ." I drag out.

"The sound of what?"

I look her dead in the eyes. "Uh, the sound of your wet pussy?"

"Oh . . . my . . . God," she replies as I start laughing as she stares at me horrified. "What the hell is wrong with you?"

I laugh so hard I scare a pigeon. Wiping my eyes, I ask, "That doesn't sound familiar? Because it's bringing all kinds of memories back to my mind."

"You have serious issues, Wyatt," she says as she attempts to stand, but I pull her in close before she can get anywhere.

"Can't run away now, babe, we're married. That means you must stick with me through all of my insanity. Aren't you lucky?"

"Somehow, I'm thinking I'm not."

<hr/>

"AND YOU TOLD me all you could make in the kitchen is peanut butter and jelly," Aubree says as she sits on the counter, looking adorable in my sweatshirt.

I finish sprinkling some cheese on the noodles and sauce I placed in a baking pan and then wipe my fingers on a dish towel. "This is me trying to impress you as your new husband. If it tastes like shit, please forget I ever attempted this."

She chuckles as I place the baking pan in the oven and set a timer. "Well, I'm impressed so far. Smells good and looks good."

"Remember that when you're eating that." I spread her legs and move in right in front of her as I place my hands on her hips. "Did you like that I took my shirt off for you so you got a show while I was cooking?"

She rolls her eyes. "It was not necessary."

"But . . ." I encourage her to continue.

The corner of her lip tilts up. "But it was nice."

"That's what I thought. And even though I like this sweatshirt on you, maybe you can join me in the topless cooking show next time. Only fair."

"I thought this was a show for me, not for you."

I smooth my hands over her bare thighs since she's only wearing my sweatshirt and my sweatshirt alone, courtesy of my need to fuck her with my tongue the moment we got home. "It's a show for both of us."

She loops her arms around my neck and pulls me closer. "That's false advertising."

"Fine . . . consider it your tip for the meal I made you."

"But if it doesn't taste good, I won't tip you."

My face falls. "That's fucking rude."

She laughs such a hearty laugh that it brings a smile to my face.

I love seeing her like this so fucking much. The ease in her expressions, the ease she feels when touching and holding me. She's vocal and doesn't hold back but also very understanding and sweet. She's everything her childhood wasn't, and I love that about her because I know she could have easily followed in her father's footsteps. But she chose not to.

"Looks like you're doing some thinking," she says as she plays with the short strands of my hair.

"Yeah, just thinking about how amazing you are."

"Oh?" She wraps her legs around my waist. "Tell me more."

I lift her into my arms and bring her over to one of the oversized chairs in the living room where I sit us both down. I lean back against the cushion while she straddles my lap.

"Comfortable?" I ask her.

She nods. "Very."

"Good." I place my hands on her legs again, my thumbs running along her inner thighs. "I was thinking about how you had a hard childhood, and instead of letting it break you, you decided to make something of yourself. I find that incredibly sexy." My eyes meet hers. "And I know we haven't talked about it much, but what I do know is enough for me to know that you were faced with a decision to either sink or float, but you took the next step and soared out of the water."

She glances away, but I force her to look at me.

"It's nothing to shy away from, Aubree. Own it."

Her beautiful green eyes stare back at me. There's so much soul in them, so much life, I can't imagine anyone ever wanting to dull her spirit. It's criminal.

"I know," she says softly. "Just never really had anyone talk to me the way you do. I mean, Cassidy was always encouraging, and I know she loved me, Ryland and Hattie as well, but growing up, it was like we were all just trying to make it out of that house alive. We didn't have a chance to compliment or congratulate each other. And you just hand it over so easily."

"I'm not handing it over," I say. "I'm stating facts. I'm offering you my honest opinion. There's no sugarcoating over here. What you hear from me is truth, babe."

"Is that how your parents were when you were growing up?" she asks. "Encouraging, supportive?"

"Yes," I answer. "As well as my grandpa. I realize the kind of childhood I was blessed with. I think what I've learned from them has transferred over because my goal in life is to try to make people happy, whether through a joke or an escape from reality with my books. Anything to bring more joy into the world."

"Well, you're good at it," she says as her hands fall to my

chest. "I know I've been happier since you've stepped into Almond Bay."

I raise a brow. "Is that so? Even at the beginning?"

She shakes her head. "No, at the beginning, I wanted to wring your neck. But then somewhere along the way, I slowly loosened up and started to see you for the man you are. Kind and sweet and thoughtful. You took my thoughts, my feelings into consideration, and that's never happened before. Not even with my siblings, and I don't say that to slight them because we've been through so much. But with Amanda as a best friend, she didn't care about me. Matt, he brushed my idea of a beautiful life to the side and said it wasn't good enough. My father considered me his servant rather than his own flesh and blood." Her eyes connect with mine. "You're the first person in my life to want to know what I want." Her hands smooth up my chest as she leans forward. "You're special to me, Wyatt. You've made me feel like I matter. You've made me feel like I have something to offer this world."

I cup her cheek and bring her in closer. "Because you do matter, Aubree."

"Thank you," she says right before she closes the space between us and kisses me, soft and tender. Her hands barely grip my face before she leads her kisses over my jaw, down my neck, and then to my chest as she slides between my legs and kneels on the ground in front of me.

"Aubree . . ." I whisper as she reaches for the hem of my sweatpants and pulls them down, letting my cock spring forward. "Baby."

She moves her hair to the side and brings her sultry lips to the tip of my cock, where she runs her tongue around the head, circling it over and over, driving me crazy with desire.

Desire to have that mouth all over my length.

Desire to bring my cock to the back of her throat.

Desire to fuck her right here on the chair.

She sits back for a second to take off her sweatshirt, leaving her naked in front of me. My eyes immediately fall to her chest, where her nipples are hard. She's already turned on. I fucking love that about her. That going down on me will make her just as hot as me. She returns to my cock, where she grips the base and starts pumping while she sucks on the head with a force I don't think I was fucking ready for.

"Christ," I groan, my head falling back on the chair cushion. "So good—" She brings me back to her throat, sucking me all the way in, and my eyes roll to the back of my head. "Fucking hell," I whisper.

She pulls away, pumps me a few times, and then dips her mouth over my length again, to the point that she gags, and it's the best thing I've ever experienced. Fuck, I'm obsessed with that.

"Again," I say, helping her with her hair as it tries to get in her way.

She takes me to the back of her throat again, this time holding it for a few seconds. She swallows, gags, and pulls away.

"Fuck," I drag out. "Baby, that's so fucking good. Again."

She pumps my length, her thumbs working up and down a thick vein on the underside of my dick before she swirls her tongue over the head again and then brings me all the way to the back of her throat, gagging for a third time, and that's all I fucking need.

I pull her head away and stand from the chair. I pull her up off the floor and bend her over the arm of the chair, moving in behind her.

"I'm going to come quickly," I say as I kick her feet wide and spread her. I move my hand between her legs and find her wet pussy ready for me. "I fucking love how turned on you are. Such a good girl."

I position my cock at her entrance and thrust into her, bottoming out in one solid pulse.

"Oh my God," she yells, her back arching.

I lean over her, my chest to her back as I wrap my hand around her neck and pull her slightly back so she can hear the way she turns me on, my lips so close to her ear.

"This pussy has a chokehold on me," I whisper as my thumb runs up the column of her neck. "You make me so goddamn hard."

I start to pump into her, loving how she clenches around me with every thrust, knowing what I need. So I reach around to her front and grip her breast in my hand, rolling her nipple between my fingers.

"And these tits, Aubree. Fuck, they're so hot."

I thrust hard and pinch her nipple, causing her to let out a large moan.

"That's it, baby. I want to hear you."

I roll her nipple, making her squirm beneath me as I continue to pump into her, my own orgasm building.

"Ma-massage my . . . clit," she says, breathless.

I bring my other hand between her legs, find her soaking center, and start circling two fingers over the sensitive nub. Around and around, and with every circle, her inner walls spasm against my cock.

"Right there. Yes, Wyatt. Don't stop."

Needing to brace myself because I feel my orgasm on the very edge, I release her breast and grip her hip as I start to feverishly pound into her. My legs slap hers, my grunts become erratic, and my fingers work overtime on her clit.

"Yes, yes, Wyatt. Oh God . . . oh fuck . . ." Her body tenses.

Her breath goes still.

On a long yet loud moan, she comes on my cock, squeezing it so tight with her spasms that I pump two more times, then still as my balls tighten and I spill into her.

"Motherfucker," I cry out as I nearly black out from the pure pleasure striking through me.

Rolling.

Gripping.

Making me weak in the knees as I lean forward and use her for support.

I catch my breath and kiss her shoulder as I say, "Jesus, Aubree."

She swallows and lets out a deep breath. "Talk to yourself."

I chuckle and kiss her back again. "It's you, babe, you started this."

"And you finished it."

I pull out of her and then lift her into my arms and take her upstairs, straight to the bathroom, where I set her on the counter.

She squeaks and clings to me. "Cold," she says.

Chuckling, I reply, "Sorry."

Slowly, she lowers herself down, and when I know she's good, I step away and turn on the shower. When I turn to look at her, she lifts her brow and says, "What do you think you're doing?"

I shrug. "Trying to get you to shower with me."

"Isn't there food in the oven?"

"Oh shit," I say on a laugh. "You're right. Uh . . ." I look around, trying to figure out what to do.

"Rinse yourself off, and I'll listen for the food. But don't even try to coerce me into that shower with you."

I study her, waiting for her to change her mind, but when she doesn't, I say, "Fine, but you owe me a shower."

"We'll see about that," she replies, then leans in and presses a kiss to my lips.

I moan into her mouth, but she pushes me away. "Focus, Wyatt. I'm hungry, and I won't let you burn that dinner. I need to see just how good of a cook you are."

Smiling, I say, "Fine, but I'm having you for dessert."

"SO . . .?" I ask, watching her take another bite of my cheesy pasta noodles.

She glances up at me, her fork midway to her mouth as she says, "So what?"

"Uh, how do you like my dinner?"

She leans back in her chair and sets her fork down before placing her hands on her lap. "It's decent."

"Decent?" I nearly shout. "Aubree, you can't be serious. This is fucking delightful." I fork a noodle and pull it up toward my mouth, the mozzarella stretching with it. "Look at this. You don't get this kind of stretch just anywhere. This is formed from a master at work. Me being the master."

"You're going from I don't cook much to a master? That is quite the jump."

"Babe," I level with her. "Come on. This shit is good."

She grins and picks up her fork. "Yes, it's very good."

I smack the table and shout, "I knew it! Fuck, look at me being husband of the year."

"Wow," she says. "If this is what the standards for being a great husband are, they're pretty low."

"You might be right about that. Let's call it a stepping stone to becoming a great husband."

"Much better."

"Do you know what a stepping stone for you to becoming a great wife could be?" I ask.

Her eyes narrow. "I'm afraid to even ask. Knowing you, you're going to say something idiotic like blow jobs every night."

"Babe, that's just expected, the standard."

"In your dreams."

I laugh and push back from the table slightly. "I wasn't going to say that, but you know, if you want to make that a ritual, I'm all for it. Totally up to you." She rolls her eyes. "I was going to say sitting on my lap."

"What is it with you and using your body as my own personal seating device?"

I chuckle. "I like you on me. I like you near me. I like touching you. Feeling you. Is that such a crime?"

"When you put it that way, no," she says as she stands from her chair and brings her plate next to mine. Then she sits on my lap, and I wrap my arm around her waist and rest my chin on her shoulder. "Better?" she asks.

"Much. Such a good wife." I kiss her shoulder and sigh into her back, feeling fully content, like this is what it was supposed to be all along.

Me and her.

It feels so right. And if I have to address the elephant in my room, not hers, this connection I have with her feels significantly stronger than the one I had with Cadance. Looking back on that relationship, it almost seems like she was a stepping stone as well because without her leaving me the night before our wedding, I never would have felt the pressure to come to Almond Bay. I never would have sought out Aubree. I never would have reconnected with Ryland and Hattie and especially Mac.

I'm ashamed to say it, but it was hard to keep in touch when Clarke passed. It makes me wonder if that's the reason he made me part owner of the farm . . .

"Hey, Aubree?"

"Hmm?" She turns to look me in the eyes.

"Do you ever think about why Cassidy and Clarke left me part of the farm?"

She takes a sip of her drink quickly and then answers, "When I first found out, every day. I constantly thought about how it was such a huge inconvenience to me and didn't quite understand why they would do something like that."

"Do you have an understanding now?" I ask.

"I have a thought."

"What is it?" I ask.

"Well, this might sound a little morbid, but a part of me thinks they did it for this exact instance, where something happened to the both of them, and they wanted to keep us close together. I know they made the change after Mac was born. The lawyer told Ryland and me, so maybe it was their attempt to keep the families bonded."

"That's what I was thinking just now." My grip on her grows tighter as I say, "I'm ashamed to admit it, but I don't think I'd have stayed connected if it wasn't for the farm." I drag my hand over my face. "Jesus, I'm such an asshole."

"You're not," she says.

"No, I kind of am." I lean back in the chair, guilt swarming me. "Clarke and I were never that close. We were there for each other when we needed help, but we were very different. I was immersed in the world of fiction. I was enamored by crimes and murder and suspense, whereas he had a helping heart, one of pure gold, and wanted to spend his life serving as a humanitarian. I was proud of him, and he was proud of me, but that was as far as it went. I know when he got Cassidy pregnant, it was a kink in his plans. He grew slightly more distant after they moved in together, and I know it was because he struggled with his goals and responsibilities. I should have helped him. I should have been there for him more."

Aubree forces me to look her in the eyes when she says, "Trust me when I say this, Wyatt. Playing the would have, should have, could have game about a lost sibling will get you absolutely nowhere. I played it for months after we lost Cassidy. I still play it on occasion, and it's done nothing but made me increasingly more frustrated. You can't expect yourself to change the past with thoughts in the present. The best thing you can do to honor your brother is to do what you think he'd have wanted. If that means staying connected with the Rowleys, with Mac, then that's what you do."

"But it took my own selfishness to finally connect. Clarke never would have acted the way that I did."

"Probably not," Aubree says as she lifts my head and lightly runs her thumb over my cheek. "But it shouldn't matter how you got here. What matters is that you are here and you promised you would keep in touch, even after . . . well"—she grows quiet—"after all this ends."

And there it is, the shared elephant in the room.

Because we said this is for a year, but now that we're dating, what does that all really mean? Hell if I fucking know, and I'm pretty sure she has no clue either. We're both at a disadvantage and unsure of where to go from here. But I do know one thing. I like her and don't want to think about an end.

"Maybe it doesn't have to," I say.

"What do you mean?" she asks, looking confused.

I bring my hand to her thigh and gently rub my palm over

her soft skin. "Maybe we don't put a time limit on anything. Not on this marriage, not on this dating. I want us to be able to explore this, us freely without the pressure of anxiety of it ending in a year." I press my palm to her hip and hold her tight. "I like you, Aubree, a lot, and I want to give this a fair shot."

Her hand runs up my chest as she says, "I'd like that, Wyatt. A lot."

"Good," I say as I move in to kiss her neck, my hand sliding under her shirt. "Because I'm starting to grow addicted."

She spins on my lap and straddles me, letting me slide my hand all the way up to her breast while her head falls to the side, giving me full access to her neck.

Yup, fucking addicting.

Chapter Twenty-One

AUBREE

I don't think I've ever been happier.

Wait, I know I haven't.

I know for a fact that I have never been this happy. This care-free. This joyful.

I wake up with a smile on my face. I go to sleep with a satisfied smile on my face. I spend my days feeling like I matter, like I belong here, like I'm actually wanted and not an inconvenience.

And it's all because of Wyatt.

These past few days in Canoodle have been a dream.

We've walked around town every day, trying out different restaurants. Put a Wing On It was my favorite—their buffalo wings were heaven. We hiked some trails. We've made out in the middle of the woods, the rustling of branches and the tweeting birds mingling with our moaning. We even skinny-dipped into a lake on one of the trails for about two seconds before we both screamed from the frigid temperatures. We snuggled in the cabin in front of the fire while watching movies and drinking hot cocoa. We have fucked on nearly every surface of the cabin imaginable, sometimes twice. And at night, when he holds me, tucking me against his chest, I've felt safe and . . . loved.

I never want this to end.

I never want to lose this feeling.

This consuming, weightless, exuberant feeling.

But all good things must come to an end, hence why I'm zipping up my suitcase and rolling it to the stairs.

"Leave it up there," Wyatt shouts from down below. "I'll grab it, babe."

He's so thoughtful. Considerate.

I remember going on a trip with Matt one time, and he never offered to carry my luggage. Not that I need a man to help me, but the offer is nice.

I head down the stairs just as Wyatt starts coming up. We meet halfway, and he places his hand on my stomach. He leans in and kisses me. When I part my lips, he groans and leans me back against the stairwell wall. My arms loop around his neck, and I pull him closer as his hand smooths down my ass, gripping me tighter.

I deepen the kiss by letting my tongue tangle with his, getting lost in the sensation of just me and him.

"Fuck, baby," he says as one of his hands goes up the back of my shirt. "You're getting me hard."

To see if he's telling the truth, I move my hand to his jeans, where I'm greeted with a bulge. I smile against his lips, stroking him through the rough fabric.

"Aubree," he groans in frustration but doesn't stop me. "Babe, we don't have time."

But we do. I know we have time. I checked my phone. We have just the right amount of time.

I take his hand in mine and slip it down my leggings where I'm not wearing underwear.

"Fuck," he breathes heavily as he feels how wet I am already. He slips two fingers along my clit and then slides them inside me. "Jesus, Aubree. This clit wants me, doesn't it?"

"Badly," I say as I rock my hips over his hand. "Please, Wyatt."

He grunts and then says, "You better come quick." He spins me around and guides me down onto the stairs. He strips my leggings down to my knees, then I hear him unzip his jeans.

"You're playing with fire today, Aubree," he says as I hear him stroke himself. "But fuck, how could I say no." He props one foot up on the stair above the one he's standing on and then angles my ass in the air before he smacks it so hard that I yelp. Soothingly, he rubs his hand over where he spanked me and says, "You okay?"

Pleasure rips through me as I nod. "Again," I reply.

"That's my good girl," he says before spanking me again. I can feel my entire body convulse with pleasure from his hand.

"More," I say, and thankfully, he does it again.

And again.

And again.

Until I can feel my clit throbbing between my legs.

"Wyatt, inside me. Now."

His hand smooths over my backend before he props it up again. He spreads my legs just enough that I can still hold the stairs in a good position and brings the head of his cock to my entrance.

"My baby is so fucking turned on," he says as he enters me, one inch at a time. "Jesus Christ, this pussy." He sinks farther and farther until he can't go anymore.

And he stays like that for a few seconds, stretching me to the point that I feel like I wouldn't be able to take any more.

That's when he spanks me, startling me so much that I clench around his cock.

"Oh fuck," he drags out. "Fuck, Aubree. Baby." He grunts and takes a few deep breaths. "Christ, I'm going to come fast." And then he spanks me again, causing me to clench once more on a groan.

"Wyatt." I rest my head against the stairs, my entire body lit up, teetering, waiting for more.

"What, baby? What do you want?"

"For you to fuck me," I say, my body humming.

"Then hang on," he says as he thrusts so hard into me that my face nearly collides with the stairs, but it's just the right force that I need.

"Yes," I moan. "Just like that."

From the corner of my eye, I can see him gripping the stairwell as he starts to pump feverishly into me, his hips flying so fast. As if this is the first time we're ever having sex, and he can't get enough of it when, in reality, this is normal for him.

This need.

This drive.

This sense of complete loss of mind as he searches out both of our orgasms.

It turns me on.

It gets me hotter.

It builds me to the precipice as he pounds into me stroke after stroke until I can't hold on anymore.

"Oh my God, Wyatt, I'm there, please . . ."

He pulls out of me, and before I can gasp in displeasure, he brings his large body between my legs and spreads me only for his tongue to stroke at my clit. Fast flicks that cause everything around us to go black.

The pleasure is too much.

My orgasm too strong.

And I find myself screaming his name as I come all over his tongue, spasms shooting through me as he continues to lap at me until I can't take it anymore, and I squeeze my legs together.

Getting the hint, he pulls away and then brings his large cock up to my mouth. Our eyes connect as I open my mouth, and he dips himself inside, pushing his cock to the back of my throat.

"Fucking hell, Aubree. I want to hear you gag."

I grip his base, pump him hard, and then bring him to the back of my throat again, where I gag loudly.

"Yes, baby."

I do it again, letting him stay a touch longer this time.

"Oh fuck. Baby, I'm going to come." I pump him fast, bring him to the back of my throat, then run my tongue along the underside of his cock before sucking the tip hard. That's when he grips the banister and groans as he comes in my mouth.

I continue to suck until he's completely done, and he releases himself.

He leans against the stairwell wall, lets out a deep sigh, and then mutters, "Jesus fuck, that was intense."

I stand from the stairs, pull up my leggings, and kiss his neck. "But it was perfect."

I start to move away when he grips me and pulls me in for a kiss. "It's because you're perfect."

"SO . . . HOW WAS THE HONEYMOON?" Echo asks the moment Hattie, she, and I all take a seat at Rosa's Cantina. When they heard I was back in town, they both wanted to meet up for a meal, so I met them for lunch.

"I like how you get right to the point," Hattie says. "Because that's what I wanted to know too and was not looking forward to small talk."

I stare between the two of them, their eager faces making me chuckle. "Wow, you guys. Don't you think that's private?"

"No," they both say at the same time.

"Do you want me to tell you about what I did with Hayes last night to make you feel better?" Hattie asks. "It involved a garden hose."

"For the love of God, keep that to yourself." I cringe. I don't need to know about my little sister's sex life.

"You don't need to give us details," Echo says. "But you know, just an overall impression of your honeymoon would be fun to hear."

"Yes, and if you slip in details here and there, I won't be upset about it." Hattie practically bounces up and down on her chair.

Since we ordered our food before we sat down, we do have some time, so I lean back in my chair and say, "It was perfect. His cabin is everything I could have imagined when he talked about it. Secluded, picturesque, cozy. The town was so cute, and the people there were very kind. One of his friends actually just had a baby, so we visited with her and her husband. They were so sweet. We spent most of our time either hiking or you know . . . just hanging out."

Hattie places her hand on the table and says, "When you say hanging out, you mean having sex, right?"

"Honestly, Hattie." I roll my eyes.

"Well . . ." she says, not letting it go.

"Oh my God, yes. We enjoyed an immense amount of sex."

She claps her hands in glee. "Oh that's wonderful. And he satisfied you?"

My cheeks heat as I mumble, "Yes, very much."

"I knew it." Hattie jabs her finger into the table as if proving a point. "It's always the freaky ones who have the best sex, and given the kind of books Wyatt writes, I bet he has some amazing sex. Like . . . ooo, I bet he holds your neck when he fucks you."

How does she know that?

My cheeks flame even hotter, and she notices because she points at me. "Oh my God, I'm right, aren't I?"

I shift my silverware and say, "That's neither here nor there."

"Wow." She slow claps. "I don't think I'll ever look at Wyatt the same. Good for him. Wait, no, good for you." She pats my shoulder. "I'm happy for you. I love a good neck hold while being pounded into. Does Wyatt say things like he's going to slit his throat and use the blood to get himself off?"

"What?" I hiss. "No. Oh my God, Hattie, where are you getting that from?"

She shrugs. "Just . . . places."

"What the hell are you and Hayes doing?"

She scoffs. "Well, if you hadn't interrupted me while I was telling you about the garden hose, you would know."

I hold up my hand. "Please, spare me."

She shrugs again. "Your loss." Then she stands. "I have to go to the bathroom. Don't say anything too juicy while I'm gone."

When she's out of earshot, Echo turns toward me and asks, "So . . . how was it really?"

I lean in and whisper, "So freaking amazing, Echo. He told me he liked me, and I told him I liked him. We both want to see where this goes, and then it just felt effortless. Nothing was awkward. Everything was right. Like this is what we should have been doing this entire time. And oh my God, I like him so freaking much . . . like borderline feelings here."

Her eyes widen as she whispers, "Like . . . love?"

I nod and press my hands to my cheeks. "I can't believe I'm even saying that, but yeah, I think so. There's something different about him, Echo. And I know what you must be thinking—"

"I'm sure you don't," she says with a smile.

"You're not thinking this is insane?"

She shakes her head. "No, I'm thinking this is amazing." She presses her hand on top of mine. "You deserve happiness, Aubree, and you've found it."

I nod, feeling my emotions get the better of me. "Yeah, I did find it in the strangest of ways."

Echo laughs. "I wasn't going to say that, but now that you've put it out there, yes, it was a roundabout way to find someone to love, but I like the unconventional."

"I do too." I sigh and shake my head. "God, how life has changed so quickly. I never would have guessed this is where I'd be a few weeks ago, falling in love while married to a man who initially irritated me more than anyone else."

"Yes, I do remember you wanting to throw him off the side of the cliffs."

"Desperately." I laugh. "How was he able to change my mind so quickly?"

"Because he's a good guy, and you allowed yourself to recognize that."

I nod. "You're right. He's a very good guy. Besides my brother, he's the absolute best."

Just then, Hattie comes walking toward us, rubbing her hands together. "Did I miss anything good?"

I glance at Echo, who smiles. "Nope," I answer.

Hattie looks back and forth between us and huffs. "You totally talked about the sex, didn't you?" She shakes her head in disappointment. "Aubree, what kind of sisters are we if we can't share about our sex lives?"

"Normal ones," I answer. "Healthy, normal ones."

"So boring," she mutters, crossing her arms over her chest.

⸻

"HEY, YOU," Wyatt says as I walk into the farmhouse after taking a long, hot shower. When I returned to the farm after lunch, I decided to help Echo finish the bee house so she could expand her product line, but it wasn't easy. We got very sweaty and dirty, and I went straight into the shower, not bothering to check on Wyatt, who's been watching Mac this evening while Ryland attends meet the teacher night.

"Hey," I say as I walk up to him. Leaning into his chest, I stand on my toes and kiss him lightly on the lips. His arms wrap around me, and he holds me close, kissing me again.

"Missed you today," he says before giving me another kiss.

I smile against his mouth. "I missed you, too."

He pulls away just enough so I can catch his brows lifting in question. "You did? I must be really rubbing off on you if you're saying nice things like that."

I playfully pinch his side, which makes him chuckle. "I say nice things to you."

"That's right. This morning in the shower, you were telling me how big my cock was."

"Oh my God, Wyatt," I whisper before looking over my shoulder.

"She's up in her room, sleeping."

"Wait, what?" I ask. "Mac is already in bed?"

He nods. "Call me the Mac whisperer. After an early dinner

of peanut butter and jelly, my specialty, she kicked my ass in Twister, and then she was yawning a lot, so I asked if she wanted to go to bed, and she volunteered. So yeah, she's in bed."

"Did you lace her peanut butter and jelly with Benadryl?"

His hands slide up my back. "I'll never tell my secrets. But for the record and reassurance, no, I didn't drug her."

I chuckle. "Good to know."

"Are you hungry? I can make you a sandwich."

I shake my head. "Had a late lunch with Hattie and Echo. Not really hungry."

"Are you sure? I can whip one up real quick."

"Positive," I say as I take his hand and lead him over to the couch, where I pull him down next to me.

"Um, I think you know where you should be sitting," he says as he glances at his lap.

I chuckle and shake my head. "Not in my brother's house. I don't want him walking in thinking that we're dry humping on his couch."

"Are you afraid he doesn't know you've lost your virginity?"

"Oh my God, no, Wyatt," I say while he laughs. "I just don't want him walking in and seeing me straddling your lap."

"Hey, I just asked you to sit on my lap, not straddle. Huge difference. Although, given the voracious appetite you have for me, I can see where you have concerns. You can't control yourself around me. That's fair."

My expression falls to annoyance. "You are incredibly annoying. Do you know that?"

"Yes, you tell me almost every day." He leans in close and pops a kiss on the tip of my nose. "Now, how was your lunch with the gals?"

"The gals?" I ask.

He smirks. "Yup, the gals. Did you tell them about the stair sex? Because I still think about it. I told Laurel. I don't think she was impressed, more disturbed with the oversharing, but I had to tell someone. I've never fucked on stairs before."

"I didn't mention the stairs," I reply, deadpanned.

"Shame. Because that was hot, baby. Shame we don't have stairs in the guest house because I'd do a replay. Guess we'll just have to wait until we're down at the cabin again. Which brings me to a question I had for us."

"What's that?" I ask.

He takes my hand in his and entwines our fingers. "Not moving too fast, but just thought we should talk about this, given our current living situation. Do you think we should consider other housing?"

"What do you mean?" I ask just as Ryland comes in through the front door, wearing khaki shorts, a black polo, and his hair all done. It's sort of funny seeing him in his school gear when I'm so used to him being casual around the farm and out on the baseball field.

"Hey," he says as he takes his shoes off and puts them in the shoe bin. "Where's Mac?"

"Sleeping," Wyatt says. "She was really tired, said she wanted to go to bed, and then went to bed."

Ryland pauses and glances at me. "What the fuck, she really said that?"

"Yup," Wyatt answers with such pride.

"Why the hell does she not do that with us?" Ryland asks me. "She puts up such a fight every time she has to go to bed."

"Because she knows she can walk all over you," Wyatt says. "Not with me, her favorite."

"Oh fuck off," Ryland says as he takes a seat in the chair across from the couch. "And also, thanks for watching her."

"Not a problem," Wyatt answers. "She's so much fun."

"She is," Ryland says as he lets out a long breath.

"You hungry?" Wyatt asks. "I can make you a peanut butter and jelly."

Ryland waves his hand in dismissal. "No, they had food at school. I grabbed some stale-tasting pasta. I'm good." He looks back and forth between us and asks, "What were you two talking about? Seemed serious when I walked in."

"Housing," Wyatt replies before I can tell Ryland it's nothing.

"Oh yeah, I was thinking about that too," Ryland says as he sits up now and leans forward, resting his forearms on his thighs. "With you two married now, I was thinking that maybe the guest house isn't the best place for you." He drags his hand over his cheek. "I'm thinking about moving Mac and me closer into town."

"What?" I nearly shout. "You're going to take her out of her house?"

"I don't know," he says, looking truly pained and confused over the thought. "I want to be closer to town. The travel is hard, especially since the school is on the other side of town, and with baseball practices and some late nights, it would be easier to be closer. Then there's you two. What happens if or when you start a family of your own? You can't possibly both stay in the guest house forever. You need more space, you deserve more space, and you're not going to move when this is where you work."

"But this is Mac's home," I say. "Plus, we're still new. You never know what might happen."

"Uh, what?" Wyatt asks, making me think about my words. "Thinking about divorce already?"

"No," I say, realizing what I said. "I didn't mean it like that. I just . . ." I pause to take a deep breath before I say something else stupid. "We're in this for Mac. And if that means I share a guest house with my husband, then so be it. I want her to be comfortable."

"Don't you think she might be comfortable with a new start?" Ryland asks. "I've thought about this for a while, Aubree, before you two even got married. It feels like Mac is just stuck, you know? She's living her day-to-day, but I don't know if she's thriving. Sometimes I wonder if it's too sad for her to be here. She doesn't like going in my room. She told me it reminds her too much of her mom. She won't go near the tire swing that Cassidy pushed her on all the time. She hates going to The Almond Store. I think too much surrounds her, reminding her of what she lost. I don't want her to lose sight of Cassidy, but there's something to think about when it comes to how Mac lost her mom.

She watched her slowly get sicker and sicker every day. The most recent memories this house holds for Mac are of her mom passing. I don't think it's fair for her to have to live through that day in and day out."

I lean against Wyatt as he drapes his arm over my shoulders. "I guess I never thought about it that way. I just assumed this was the only house she's ever known so wouldn't she want to stay here, but yeah . . . you might be right. There are things she won't do that she used to do all the time."

Ryland nods. "And there's a Victorian house in town, across from the park on Bay Breeze Drive, that I've been looking at. Three bedrooms, two baths. Has a big backyard for a playhouse for Mac. It could be a fresh start for her, and we could move the things that bring Mac joy over to the new house. Things like the curtains and the pictures, some of the furniture." He shrugs. "I think she needs it. I know she seems happy, but when I put her to sleep, I can see the sadness in her eyes, and I think that's one of the reasons she gives me such a hard time when it comes to sleeping. I don't think she wants to fall into a dream state. I think she's always dreaming of Cassidy." Ryland gets choked up, which, in return, constricts my throat. When he looks up at me again, eyes watery, he says, "Will you take the farmhouse, make it your own, and maybe make it a fun place for Mac to be again?"

When he asks like that . . .

"Yes," I say, forgetting to even consult Wyatt. "Do you want to sell it to me?"

Ryland shakes his head. "I have plenty saved up from when I sold my house before moving here. I also have the life insurance policy from Cassidy and Clarke. There's plenty to support Mac. I just want to make sure that this house that Cassidy loved so much will be taken care of."

"It will," I promise him. "I will be sure to bring joy back into it."

"We promise," Wyatt says, feeling the energy of the room and making me fall for him that much more.

"Thank you." Ryland lets out a long breath. "Okay, fuck, that was heavy. I think I'm going to take a shower and get to bed. I'll let you know how the house situation goes. I want to take Mac there and make sure she likes it first, feel her out, and see what she says. But thanks for this conversation. It's been weighing on me."

"Of course," I say as I stand, and Wyatt stands as well. "Feel free to talk to us about anything. Don't let it sit there."

"I was waiting to get through the wedding. Don't worry, I can't hold that shit for too long. I need all the help I can get." He looks between the two of us. "Hope you guys had a nice time down at the cabin." He offers us a soft smile and takes off up the stairs.

I take that as our cue to leave as well, so we head out the front door and to the guest house, where Wyatt locks up, and we both get ready for bed in a comfortable silence. Occasionally, his hand runs over my back, along my hip, or across my shoulder blades. Light touches here and there to let me know he's still here with me.

Once we're settled, I slip into bed, he checks the door once more, and then slips in behind me. But now there is nothing tentative in the way he pulls me into his warm body.

"When are you going to stop putting the shirt on and come to bed naked?" he asks, his hand moving up my shirt.

"When you start going to bed naked," I reply as I turn toward him.

"Babe, say the word, and these boxer briefs are gone."

I smile softly and place my hand on his chest. "Hey, can we talk for a second?"

"You mean before I dive my tongue between your legs? I guess so."

My cheeks heat from the thought of it, but I remain focused. "About that conversation back there, I, uh, I didn't mean to make it sound like I didn't believe in us."

"You don't need to explain anything," he says.

"But I do," I say as my fingers dance over his short chest hair. "I'm still trying to shake some of the negativity I grew up with and come to terms with these overwhelming emotions between us. Unfortunately, I'm a creature of habit, so anything new in my life is sometimes hard to accept. I need you to know that I really like you, Wyatt. I want to share a house with you if you want to share one with me, and I believe in our bond."

"I appreciate that," he says softly. "I feel the same way, Aubree. So don't ever question that otherwise. I want to be with you, and if that means we're here in the guest house together, that's fine. If we move into the farmhouse, that's great too. I just want to be with you."

"Same," I say. "I want to be with you."

Because I'm falling for you.

Because I can't imagine what this world would be like now without you by my side.

Because you have brought color back into my life and air into my lungs, and I don't want to lose that.

"Good," he says as he pushes me to my back and drags my shirt up and over my head, only to toss it across the room. He brings his large body between my legs, spreads them, then kisses down my stomach, keeping his eyes on mine until he reaches my pussy. That's when he settles flat on the mattress, spreads me, and laps at my clit.

I sigh into the pillow, grateful for this man and this moment. For this change in my life.

This is all I need.

Him and me.

Just the two of us.

"YOU MISSED A SPOT," Wyatt says as we walk down the planked sidewalk of Almond Bay, hand in hand.

"What do you mean?" I ask.

He points at my neck. "Clear as day, a bite mark."

I clamp my hand over my neck. "Oh my God, seriously?"

He lets out a hearty laugh and shakes his head. "No, but could you look more ashamed?"

I narrow my eyes at him. "That's not funny, Wyatt. And I'm not ashamed. I'm just respectful. It's not nice to rub our sexual activities in other people's faces."

"Some might say it's actually recommended."

"No one says that."

He pulls me in close and kisses the top of my head. "I do. I think it's very much recommended. If you show off the bite marks, it accomplishes two things. Lets people know you're taken and shows them you are fully satisfied."

"Pretty sure the ring on my finger clues them in on me being taken. And the bite mark could possibly portray me as a harlot."

"Oh fuck that old rhetoric. A bite mark shows you're having a good fucking time with your brand-new husband."

I glance up at him and nearly sigh at the smirk he gives me.

This man.

How on earth did it come to this?

Where I'm sighing just from the sight of him?

Where I'm so beyond comfortable that I'd walk around with a bite mark from him?

Where I want nothing more than to stop work on the farm and just spend day in and day out hanging with him, joking with him? Where I know that moving into Cassidy's home would be like our own fresh and wonderful start.

It wasn't like that a few weeks ago, but he's instilled so much trust and comfort within me that it's changed my entire perspective on life.

"What are you thinking about?" he asks.

"What makes you think I'm thinking about anything?"

"You have this far-off look in your eyes like you're contemplating something. What is it?"

We head toward The Cliffs for some lunch and bear claws since Wyatt has been craving them. "Nothing," I answer.

"Really? You're going to hide from me after everything we've done to each other? Babe, it's okay to be exposed."

"Being naked in front of you is way different than showing you my raw emotions. One is easy, the other isn't."

"Feeling emotional over me?" he asks, but not in his normal teasing tone.

"Not emotional," I say. "Just . . ." I shrug as we reach The Cliffs, and he opens the door for me. "I don't know——"

"Wyatt, there you are."

Wyatt stops right in the doorway behind me as I look up to find a beautiful blonde standing in front of us. Curvy figure, stunning eyes, she's the complete opposite of me with her sleek hair and slender legs. Next to her is a short man with red hair and a snarly lip, a sneer that says he's ready to make someone's life hell.

"Cadance," Wyatt says, stunned. "What, uh . . . what are you and Wallace doing here?"

Wallace?

That's Wallace?

Wyatt's cousin?

They look nothing alike. Not even close. Somehow, Wyatt got the better genes.

I glance back at the woman, and that's when her name clicks. *Wait, Cadance, that's the girl Fallon was talking about?*

Wallace steps up and says, "Oh, just in town, heard you got married, which is so interesting since your engagement to Cadance just broke up."

Umm . . . what?

That can't be right. That's something Wyatt would have told me.

I'm about to ask him what's going on when Wyatt straightens up and says, "Not here." Then he steps out of the restaurant, and Wallace and Cadance follow. Confused and unsure of what to do, I follow as well until we reach the parking lot of The Cliffs, where Wyatt turns to face both Cadance and Wallace.

"Wyatt," I ask, feeling my voice shake. "What's going on?"

"You must be his new bride," Wallace says while holding out his hand. "I'm Wallace."

I look at his hand, then back up at Wallace. "Wyatt . . . what are they doing here?"

Wallace shoves his unshaken hand back in his pocket and says, "We're here to call bullshit on this marriage. Although, it seems like everyone we talk to happens to have a grand opinion of the thriller author, saying how much he's been in love with the town sweetheart." Wallace looks me up and down. "I don't fucking buy it, and from the stunned look on your face, I'm going to guess you had no idea what was happening."

"Wallace, leave her alone," Wyatt says.

Cadance takes that moment to step up to Wyatt and place her hand on his chest. My eyes narrow in on the touch, and I'm simultaneously ready to rip her away and throw up from the rapid emotions running through me.

"Wyatt, I know I hurt you, but marrying *her* . . . we all know it was a revenge marry. You can't possibly be serious about this."

Insult rips through me as I take a step back. What does she mean by "marrying her"? What's so wrong with me that the possibility of me marrying Wyatt seems so far-fetched?

Sure, I might not be as well put together as she is.

And my hair isn't as sleek.

My body isn't as curvy.

But . . . but . . .

My dad's voice pops into my head.

You will never amount to anything.

You're a waste of my time.

Could you do something with your hair? You look like a drowned rat.

I'll be shocked if anyone ever finds you attractive . . .

I bite down on the corner of my lip as I take a step back, my most personal insecurities taking hold of me as my lungs grow tight, my throat constricts, and my deepest hatred of myself rises.

"I am serious," Wyatt says, moving Cadance away and making eye contact with me. "Aubree, don't listen to them."

"Don't listen to them?" I ask as I take another step back. "Who should I listen to? You?"

"I wouldn't," Wallace says. "He's only using you to get what he wants. Did you even know he was set to marry Cadance two months ago? That the only reason he didn't was because Cadance didn't think she could trust him at the time."

"What?" Wyatt says, looking toward Cadance. "That's why you fucking left me?"

My stomach grows sick with anxiety and uncertainty.

"You were off and on the whole week," Cadance says. "Anytime I tried to talk to you about our marriage, about our future, about your past, you evaded me with answers that were never deep. Never to the point. You beat around the bush about everything. How could I trust you if I felt like I didn't even know you?"

And the truth in that feels so freaking real because that's what he's done to me. He's casually moved around real answers for me. He's skated on the surface, never giving me his full self, hence why I didn't know about Cadance. *Who he was fucking engaged to only two months ago. What the hell?* How did he think that *the past can stay in the past* when it's only been weeks since they separated?

He wants me to tell him about my emotions, about my past, but doesn't want to return with the same respect? Instead, I have to be confronted about it in town, making me feel so much worse than I could imagine.

"That's bullshit," he says, arguing with her. But why? Why is he arguing? Is it because he still has feelings for her? I mean, he has to, right? He was going to marry this woman two months ago.

Two freaking months.

That means . . . when he came to Almond Bay, he was fresh on heartbreak. He never showed it. Never spoke about it.

"I talked to you all the fucking time," Wyatt says. "I told you everything."

Well, at least he talked to someone.

"It was surface level, Wyatt."

"The fuck it was," he says, his anger something I've never seen before.

"Then why didn't you fight for me?" she asks, folding her arms over her chest.

"Because you left me the night before our wedding," he nearly shouts. "You said you weren't in love with me. You spoke nothing about trust. Why the hell am I going to chase someone who doesn't share the same feelings as me?"

So he was in love with her.

Maybe he still is.

From the anger on his face and the protruding veins in his neck, I'm going to guess that he's still in love, which makes me feel . . . stupid.

Incredibly dumb.

Incredibly stupid.

Incredibly naïve.

Here I am, falling for a man who is . . . as Wallace put it, using me. Sure, he's told me he likes me, and he's treated me so well, but in the grand scheme of things, that's what this entire situation has been, him using me, and I guess . . . me using him.

Feelings were never supposed to get involved, and I let them.

I let him take my heart.

I let him hold it carelessly in his hand.

And right now, as I stare at the man I love who is staring at the woman he loves . . . all I can think is how stupid I am for thinking this could be any more than what it actually is.

"I loved you, Wyatt. I was just scared."

Wyatt sifts his hand through his hair as he contemplates what he's probably going to do with all of this. Well, I'll make it easy on him because I never should have gotten involved in the first place. This whole idea was stupid.

So with a tear falling down my cheek, I turn away from them and head toward The Almond Store.

I'm nearly out of the parking lot when I hear Wyatt call out, "Aubree, wait."

But I don't. I keep moving forward. I need to get away from him, from this. Anything to hold my heart together by a thread.

I'm just about to cross the street when my hand is tugged back, and I spin toward Wyatt, right into his chest.

"Aubree, don't leave."

I push away just enough to look up at him. And as I stare into the eyes of the man I've found such comfort in, I almost feel like a piece of me is breaking apart. Because I never expected him to hurt me like this.

On a deep breath, I say, "Wyatt, I think it's best that you sort out your issues with her before you even think about speaking with me."

"Aubree, there's nothing to sort out."

I pull away from him and say, "There is. It's obvious in the way you reacted. Maybe if you told me about her, about your feelings, about your almost marriage, I would have a touch more understanding and empathy, but right now, I can't even look at you."

I try to walk away, but he grabs me again. "Aubree, they're doing this on purpose. They came here to manipulate the situation. We can't let them."

"We?" I ask, looking him dead in the eyes. "As far as I'm concerned, there's no we between us."

"Aubree, don't," he says, his eyes pleading. "Please don't walk away. Let me sort this out."

"Sort it out in your own time, without me." And with that, I snap away from him and jog across the street, right toward The Almond Store.

I don't bother to look back. I can't.

Not when I'm minutes from falling apart. Instead, I charge right into the store, the overhead bell ringing above me. Luckily, no one is in the store because when I make eye contact with Hattie, I burst into tears.

Chapter Twenty-Two

THE SIBLINGS

Hattie: *Meet me at the farmhouse immediately after school lets out. Hayes is grabbing Mac and taking her to our house. It's Aubree, she needs us.*

Ryland: *Wait . . . what? What's going on?*

Hattie: *I haven't been able to figure out much. She hasn't said anything. But she came into The Almond Store and burst into tears. She's up in the apartment, on the bed until I can have someone cover me at the store.*

Ryland: *Did something happen with Wyatt?*

Hattie: *That's my guess. I texted Ethel and asked her if she heard anything. She said there was some awkwardness at The Cliffs, but she doesn't know the whole story.*

Ryland: *If he fucking hurt her, he's a dead man.*

Hattie: *How could he hurt her, though? They just got married.*

Ryland: *I don't know, but he'll find out quickly not to mess with the Rowleys.*

Hattie: *Okay, before you get all heated, let's focus on Aubree first. We can't have you chasing down Wyatt. Not when you have a job that keeps you from being violent and a four-year-old depending on you.*

Ryland: *Then I'll have Hayes take care of it.*

Hattie: *Love that you think you can lean on him for that because he'd take care of it, but like I said, let's figure out what's going on first.*

Ryland: *I'll book it out of here once school is out. Was she really crying?*

Hattie: *Uncontrollably. I've never seen her like this. It's actually scaring me.*

Ryland: *Aubree doesn't cry. Have you seen Wyatt?*

Hattie: *I looked out the window but didn't see any trace of him. This was after I got Aubree settled upstairs, so he might have taken off.*

Ryland: *Should I text him?*

Hattie: *No. We need to hear from Aubree first.*

Ryland: *You're right.*

Hattie: *Try to keep your cool. I'll see you in a few.*

Ryland: *If he hurt her . . . he will never step foot in this town again.*

Hattie: *Agreed.*

Chapter Twenty-Three

WYATT

Fuck.

FUCK!

I push my hand through my hair as I slowly back away from the road, Aubree disappearing into The Almond Store. Do I go after her again?

Do I obey her wishes?

I'm so conflicted that I feel paralyzed.

Paralyzed in thought and paralyzed in movement.

I wasn't prepared for this, and I should have been. I should have known Wallace would come into town and try to fuck this up, and boy, did he do it in grand fashion. Never in a million years would I have guessed that he'd bring Cadance with him.

"You look like you care that she walked away," Wallace says. I turn to find him at the edge of the parking lot, arms crossed.

Something inside me flips as I charge toward him. Fear crosses his eyes right before I grip him by the shirt and push him up against my SUV.

"You motherfucker," I say. "You couldn't just let me be fucking happy, could you? You had to come over here and ruin it because you're so goddamn unhappy with your life." I slam him into the car again, causing him to wheeze.

"Wyatt, put him down," Cadance says, pulling on my shoulder.

I turn toward her, feeling the wrath of my anger unfold one layer at a time. "And you, coming over here trying to act like you left me because of me, not because of you. What kind of fucked up are you to try to mess with my head like that?"

"I'm not trying to—"

"The fuck you're not." I release Wallace as I turn toward her. "You told me you weren't in love with me. To my fucking face, you said it. If it was a trust issue, why would you say you didn't love me? Just to hurt me? Either way, I don't want to hear it. I don't even want to fucking see you. I've moved on."

"Oh please," Wallace says. "You and I both know the only reason you married that town bumpkin is because you want the cabin."

Town bumpkin?

The fuck did he say?

I pull back my fist, cocking it all the way back, and start to send it forward just as Cadance grips me, halting me from knocking the teeth right out of my cousin's mouth.

"Don't," she nearly yells. "He'll press charges, and you know it."

"Why the fuck do you care?" I ask her. "You don't care about me. If you did, you wouldn't have shown up here." I turn toward Wallace and say, "And call her that again, and you will find my fist down your fucking throat. Aubree is anything but a town bumpkin. She's my fucking wife . . . the woman I love."

"Oh fuck off," Wallace says. "You don't love her."

"I do," I say, standing taller. "And I don't need to prove that to anyone but her."

I turn away, but Cadance grabs me. "Wyatt, don't you think we should talk?"

"No," I say, looking her dead in the eyes. "I have nothing to say to you."

"You can't possibly walk away without at least talking to me."

"I can," I answer. "And I can't believe it's taken me this long to actually figure this shit out in my head." I turn toward her, knowing this is exactly how I feel, deep in my bones. "You did me a favor walking out on me," I say. "Because if you didn't do that, I very well might be in a loveless marriage right now. Because as much as I was devastated that night, I know now after meeting Aubree that what I felt for you doesn't even come close to what I feel for Aubree. I thought I knew what love was, but fuck was I wrong. So . . . thank you for that night, for crushing me, because I never would have known true happiness if it wasn't for you."

"Wyatt," she whispers, stunned and insulted.

But I don't give a fuck. What I said was true, and I'm not taking it back.

I turn toward Wallace and say, "Stay the fuck out of my marriage and away from me, or else I'm filing for a restraining order."

With that, I move away from them and jog across the street, right up to The Almond Store. I open the door just as Hattie appears from the back room. When her eyes meet mine, they narrow with hate.

Not surprised.

"Where is she, Hattie?"

Hattie folds her arms across her chest. "What did you do?"

"Please, Hattie, can I just talk to her?"

"You realize my sister doesn't cry, right? That's not something she does, so to see her in tears, it means you fucked up, and I want to know what you did."

"She's crying?" I ask, feeling so fucking sick to my stomach.

"Yes, she's crying. Now tell me what you did."

I let out a heavy sigh, trying to reason with the guard dog standing in my way. "Hattie, please let me just check on her and settle things with her. I appreciate you protecting her, but I need to talk to her myself."

Hattie purses her lips, thinking on it, then by the grace of

God, she says, "In the back, up the stairs to the apartment." I move toward the back, but she stops me before I can move past the door. "Ryland is aware you hurt her, and so is Hayes. Watch yourself, Wyatt."

And with that, she steps aside, and I move past her up the stairs to a closed door. I don't bother knocking. I just let myself into what looks like a small apartment with slanted ceilings and a queen bed pushed up against the wall. That's all I notice before my eyes land on Aubree, who is curled up on the bed, her back toward me.

My stomach plummets as I shut the door behind me.

"Aubree," I say quietly, and I watch her back go stiff.

In a sniffly voice, she says, "Go away, Wyatt."

Yeah, like that's going to fucking happen.

I move into the room and sit on the edge of the bed.

"I said leave, Wyatt." She sniffs, and it feels like everything in me shatters because I brought on those tears. I'm the one who hurt her when I told her I never would.

I'm supposed to be her rock, her comfort, and here I am, hurting her.

"Aubree, baby, please can we talk."

"A little too late, don't you think?"

Yeah, I deserve that.

And I know it will be really hard to break through to her, but I have to at least try.

"I'm sorry," I say.

She lifts up from the bed and scoots away from me. She pulls her knees into her chest and holds her legs tightly as she looks back at me. I'm met with red eyes, tear-stained cheeks and an expression of hurt.

It guts me.

"Why are you sorry?" she asks. "For hurting me? For not telling me the truth about Cadance? For lying? Or are you sorry that you got caught?"

"I'm sorry for hurting you," I say, wanting to reach out to her, but I know she won't allow it. "Back there, that was something you never should have been a part of."

"Why?" she asks. "Because you didn't want me to know?"

"No," I say. "You didn't need to find out like that."

"You're right. I didn't," she says. "I should have heard it from you. You should have told me about her when I asked. You should have told me more about you, but as I'm sitting here, staring at you, all I can think is . . . I don't know this man at all."

"Aubree, that's not true."

"It is true," she shouts, then scoots off the bed and stands. "I know nothing about you, nothing beneath the surface, nothing that I can't learn from your author bio. You haven't shared anything with me. I mean, Jesus, Wyatt, you were going to be married to someone else. Don't you think you should have shared that with me?"

"I was going to," I say in a panic. "I was just trying to find the right time."

"You mean you were trying to get over her first, right? Use me as a distraction to squash the hurt she caused. Meanwhile, I'm over here, falling in love with a man who can't even be honest with me when asked."

Falling in love?

She grips her forehead. "I mean, what the hell am I even doing? I've gotten so lost, so caught up in the fanfare of someone actually giving a shit about me that I lose all sense of myself?"

"Aubree—"

"No," she shouts, holding her hand up. "Don't. I don't want to hear anything from you. I should have known this was going to happen. I told myself to keep it together, not to fall under this enchanting spell you seem to put on people, but slowly, I got caught up in it as well, and that's my fault. I lost my composure, but that won't happen again." She wipes her tears and raises her chin. "I understand what this is, who we are together, and I understand the contract we signed. There will be nothing else between us other than what we signed up for. I should have never let it get this far. I see my mistake now."

She moves toward the door, but I stand from the bed, my heart tearing out of my chest with every step she takes away from me. "Aubree, please, just listen to me."

"No, Wyatt," she says, looking over my shoulder. "This is done . . . I'll see you back at the guest house."

And then she takes off, her stoic, empty persona pushing her loveable, soft exterior right out of the way. She's back to the woman she was when I first saw her.

And it's all my fucking fault.

AUBREE

"HOW LONG HAS SHE BEEN CRYING?" Ryland says as I lie against the couch, unable to control myself.

"Since we left The Almond Store," Hattie replies. "Wyatt was there and tried talking to her. I still don't know what's happening."

The floor creaks, and I hear Ryland approaching right before he sits beside me and places his hand on my knee.

"Hey Aubree, can we get you anything?"

I shake my head as more tears fall down my cheeks.

"Grab her tissues," Ryland says to Hattie.

Hattie is on it and has tissues to him in seconds. He takes one out and dabs at my face, which only makes me cry even more. We may have had a tough childhood, and we might not have been shown the kind of love every kid deserves, but somehow, we persevered and showed love to each other. That's exactly what Ryland is doing.

"When you're ready, we're here to listen," he says.

I take one of the tissues and dab at my eyes as well, realizing that if I'm going to make it through this next year, I'm going to need all the support I can get, which means telling them the truth.

While I was up in the apartment above The Almond Store, I

thought about what I was going to do with Wyatt and how I'd handle this. I could walk away and call everything off, but I know if that were the case, he'd hand over the land and consider me stubborn, but I'm not taking that for free. I'm earning it, even if it means saving up enough to buy it off him early. But I refuse to take it because he hurt me or he pities me. This means I'll be spending the next year with him, and I can only do that if my family surrounds me with support.

After a few deep breaths, I look up at Ryland and Hattie, who has moved an ottoman in close so we're all sitting in what feels like a triangle.

"Um, I have to tell you guys something."

"Okay," Ryland says.

"But I beg of you, please don't get mad."

Ryland's jaw clenches before he says, "Did Wyatt do something to you? Did he hurt you physically? Because I won't be able to remain calm about that."

I shake my head. "No, he's never harmed me. It's nothing like that."

Ryland only slightly relaxes as he nods his head.

"But I will say, I haven't been entirely truthful with you. Um . . ." I dab at my eyes again as guilt swarms me. "Wyatt and I . . . well, we married for convenience."

Hattie sits back while Ryland's brow creases in confusion. "What do you mean?" he asks.

"The week he initially came into town, well, it wasn't because we were secretly seeing each other. He actually came into town because he had a business proposal for me." I try to stop my hand from shaking as I continue telling the truth. "You see, he has this family cabin that means a lot to him, and the only way he'd get ownership of it was if he was married. He didn't want it going to his horrible cousin, Wallace, so he came to me and asked if I'd marry him."

"Why would he do that?" Hattie asks. "He barely knew you."

"He told me if I married him, he'd give me ownership of his half of the farm."

"What?" Ryland yells as he stands. "He fucking blackmailed you?"

"No," I say as Ryland's hand clenches at his side. I tug on him to sit back down, and thankfully, he does. "It was more of an agreement."

"Why did you go along with it?" Hattie asks, looking hurt.

"Because I felt desperate to do something right for Cassidy. To do something right for myself. I felt like I was drowning in uncertainty and lacking in confidence. I saw Amanda and Matt together, and well, it was a perfect storm of insecurity that made me say yes. And the more I got to know Wyatt, the more I realized that he was . . . well, he was the kind of guy who made me feel seen, and slowly, I started to fall for him." I bite my bottom lip. "I just wish I wasn't so naïve in those feelings."

"What do you mean?" Ryland asks. "Was he using you?"

I shake my head. "No, but I don't think he's fully over his ex-fiancée, who he was supposed to marry two months ago. I think that's probably why he came to me. That marriage didn't go through, so he struck up a deal." I dab at my eyes as a new wave of tears forms. "That's what I found out today. Here I am, falling for the man while he's holding in the kind of information that would have been good to know. He was holding back, and you should have seen the look on his face when he saw her. It was clear that there was still emotion there." I shake my head again. "I just feel foolish."

To my surprise, Hattie draws in closer and takes my hand in hers. "Do not feel foolish for letting your heart lead the way."

"Hattie, I fell for someone who I feel like I don't even know now. That is foolish."

"That's love," Hattie says softly. "And I know Ryland might not agree with me, but given the way we grew up, especially you, when you find comfort, you cling to it because our childhood was anything but comforting. I know when Hayes came into my life, it felt like this weight I've been carrying for so long was lifted, like I could share the burden of it. Is that how you felt with Wyatt?"

I nod as a tear slips down my cheek. "But it's stupid because it wasn't real."

"It was—"

"Why are you defending him?" Ryland says to Hattie. "He clearly used our sister, didn't tell her the whole truth, and made her fall for him. Why are you glorifying this?"

Hattie sits back, stunned by the harshness in his voice. "I wasn't glorifying it, Ryland. I was trying to help her see that what she was feeling wasn't foolish."

"But don't try to convince her that everything he did was right because it wasn't. He used her to his advantage. He wanted something, he had leverage with the land, and he used it. That's fucked up. No one treats my fucking sisters like that."

"His intentions might not have been right at the beginning, but I think toward the end, recently, they have been in favor of Aubree," Hattie says.

"Why do you think that?" Ryland asks.

"Because I know what love is," Hattie says while pointing at her chest and getting emotional over it. "I know what it means to give your heart to someone else, to depend on them to keep it safe. I'm not afraid to put myself out there like you are, Ryland."

"I'm not fucking afraid," he says.

"Says the guy who hasn't had a solid relationship since his high school sweetheart left him."

Ryland's eyes narrow on Hattie, and I can feel him ready to burst. "It's because I've had responsibilities," he says through clenched teeth. "Why do you think there was food on the table every night just before Dad died? It was because of me. Because I was working, because I was supporting this family. And the moment I had a chance to think about myself, Clarke died, which meant I was Cassidy's primary helper, Aubree a close second. I haven't had the fucking time in my life to even consider the kind of freedom to feel the way you have, Hattie. And don't get me wrong, I'm grateful you've found Hayes, but don't throw it in my face that you know what love is. If you grew up in my world, in my childhood, with Dad's fist being the only thing that kissed your face, you wouldn't be so prone to know what love is either."

"Ryland, I'm . . . I'm sorry," Hattie says as her eyes start to water.

"I know," he says while squeezing her hand. He then turns to me and lets out a deep sigh. "Fuck, Aubree, we lost sight of what's going on. I'm sorry."

I shake my head, looking between my two siblings. "Please don't apologize for wanting to protect me. I should have told you guys, but I didn't want you to change my mind. Hattie, I didn't want you to tell me that I shouldn't marry for anything but love, and Ryland, I didn't want you to try to help me buy the land from Wyatt somehow, which I knew you would have done. I wanted to do this myself, and it felt like this was the easiest way to do it because I've been so closed off." I press my lips together, trying to hold back another wave of tears. "I didn't think he'd wiggle his way into my life the way he did. I didn't think I'd find comfort in him, peace . . . protection. I didn't think I'd fall for him, yet I did."

"Does he know how you feel?"

"Yes," I say, wiping my tears. "And it's fine, I can—"

The front door to the farmhouse opens, and our eyes fall on Wyatt, standing in the doorway, looking distraught and disheveled.

Immediately, Ryland stands, but I grab his hand so he can't move forward. "What the fuck are you doing here?" Ryland nearly growls.

"I wanted to talk to Aubree." Respectively, Wyatt stands his ground, unmoving from the clear threat that is my brother.

"Talk to her about what? The deal you made with her? How you made her fall for you while you were in love with someone else?"

"You told them?" Wyatt asks, looking at me.

"Of course she fucking told us," Ryland says. "She should have told us from day one. Was that your idea as well? To lie to us?"

Wyatt stuffs his hands in his pockets but looks Ryland directly in the eye when he says, "I take full responsibility for everything. Yes, I told her not to tell you. I even threatened her if she did."

"You motherfucker," Ryland says as he starts to charge, but I grip him tightly. "Let me the fuck go, Aubree."

"No," I shout. "Ryland, stop. This won't make anything better."

"It sure as hell will make me feel a whole lot better."

"Let him punch me," Wyatt says. "I deserve it, and if it'll make him feel better, then let him do it."

"You heard him," Ryland says as he shakes free of my clutch and charges after Wyatt, who doesn't flinch, doesn't move. And before I can even catch up to Ryland, I see his fist cock back, only to fly forward and connect with Wyatt's face on a crunch.

A shrill scream tumbles past my lips as Wyatt falls to the floor, and Ryland starts to straddle him. That's when I jump on top of Ryland, and Hattie helps, pulling him away.

This is not the first time Ryland has raised a fist to one of the men in this family. He also got in a fight with Hayes as well. Ryland might not carry the same kind of fist our dad did once, but when he's protecting his loved ones, he sure knows how to use it.

"Stop, Ryland," I yell as I pull him away with Hattie's help. "Just stop."

Wyatt runs his hand under his nose, where it's bleeding, and looks Ryland in the eyes. "Feel better?"

"No." Ryland breathes heavily, ready to strike again. I can feel it. "You said you wouldn't fucking hurt her. You lied to my goddamn face."

"I didn't mean to hurt her," Wyatt says calmly. "I was trying to protect her when, in reality, I ended up hurting her."

"Protecting her? By forcing her to marry you?"

"He didn't force me," I say. "I willingly agreed to marry him."

"Because he dangled the farmland in front of you," Ryland

shouts, then turns his attention toward Wyatt. "What kind of man does that?"

"A desperate one," Wyatt says. "Pathetic one."

"Pathetic is more like it." Ryland stands taller. "Here's what's going to happen. You're going to get an annulment, you're going to give Aubree the title to the land, and then you're going to leave our fucking lives and never return."

"Ryland, no," I say, my voice growing stronger. "We're not going to take the land."

"Fine." Ryland moves toward the kitchen and digs into a drawer, where he pulls out a checkbook. "I have money. I'll buy it from you. Name your price."

"Ryland, that money is going toward a new house for you and Mac," I say. "You're not giving that up."

"Aubree, I'm not going to stand by and watch this fuckhead take advantage of you."

"He's not," I finally say, hating that I have to defend him. "I agreed fairly to work with him on this deal. I said I'd marry him so we both would win. And I'm holding true to my word. I'll stay married to him."

"You will?" Wyatt asks, looking confused.

"Yes," I say, finally looking at him and his bloody face. "We will stay married. We will put on a show because, if anything, I keep my word. But when it comes to you and me on a personal level, that's done." I turn to my brother and say, "Ryland, I expect you to be cordial around Wyatt. If anything, do it for Mac. He will be here for a year, so we'll have to figure out how to live with him being around." I now turn to Hattie, who looks like a deer in headlights, completely scared. "Hattie, this stays between us. This deal, it does not leave this room. I don't care how angry or upset you are. I want this land, and this is the only way I'll accept it. Understood?"

Hattie nods but doesn't say anything.

"As for you," I say to Wyatt. "I suggest you find a way to make this better with my brother because he's the one who protects Mac, and if you want any semblance of a relationship with your niece, then he's the one you'll have to speak with."

And with that, I head out of the farmhouse and straight to the guest house, where I take a long, hot shower. *Once again, I've let my guard down around a man who will never love me.*

But I refuse to be beaten down by this. I refuse to buckle.

I will pick myself up like I've done many times before, and I'll come out the other side stronger.

Like I've done many times before too.

<hr />

WYATT

THE DOOR SHUTS, and I'm left with Ryland and Hattie, who seem just as stunned and confused as I am. Hattie hands me a tissue, and grateful, I take it, wiping my nose and the blood that seems to still be dripping out of it.

They stare at me. I shift uncomfortably, and after a few moments of silence, Ryland says, "Do you have anything you want to fucking say?"

I really fucking do.

Looking Ryland dead in the eyes, I say, "I love your sister. I'm in love with her, and I will do anything to make this right. Anything."

Hattie takes a step forward. "You . . . you love her?"

"Yes," I say while wiping my nose. "And I wanted to tell her that, but well, I fucked everything up."

Ryland studies me for a moment, his eyes like lasers. After a few moments of dreadful silence, he finally says, "Take a seat. I'll grab you an ice pack."

Relief floods through me as I take a seat at the dining room table, Hattie following closely. She sits across from me, and so does Ryland as he tosses me the ice pack. Normally, I'd probably skip the ice, but fuck does Ryland have a strong right hook. My face is throbbing.

"Start from the beginning and don't lie. Whatever you say will be vital to how much or how little we help you," Ryland says.

"Understood, but I want you to know, I don't expect your help. I'm the one who messed up, so I'm the one who needs to fix this."

"I respect that. Now tell me, why did you think it would be smart to blackmail my sister into marrying you?"

I don't even correct him because if I want this to go right, I will need to take full responsibility for my actions. "My ex, Cadance, broke off our wedding the night before it was supposed to happen. I was nursing my wounds when I was reminded that the family cabin I was supposed to take ownership of would go to my cousin, Wallace, because he was the next in line to get married. He doesn't care about the cabin and would knock it down. That cabin, well, it means just as much to me as The Almond Store means to you, Hattie. Or the farm means to Aubree. I couldn't let it get into the wrong hands, so I stupidly came up with a plan. I knew Aubree would want the land, and I thought we could work out a deal."

"So you two didn't have contact before the week you first came into town?"

I shake my head. "The only other times I've seen or spoken to Aubree was when Clarke and Cassidy were still alive. I surprised her and offered up the deal. It wasn't until she ran into Amanda and Matt and their awful comments did she agree to go through with it. I know she did it to save face, and at one point, I tried to back out, but she was set on marrying me. And as we moved around town together, selling the idea of our relationship to everyone around us, I started to feel something for her on a different level. And those feelings grew with every moment I spent with her. Her strength and intelligence, her love for her family, her dedication to Cassidy's legacy, I fell hard for it all. Before I knew it, I was saying I do to someone I fell hard and quick for. And I was so fucking terrified that I'd lose her, that she wouldn't feel the same way, that I held back on anything that would scare her away since she was so skittish. Meaning I didn't tell her about Cadance. I know now how big of a mistake that was."

"When you got married, did she know about your feelings for her?"

I shake my head. "I told her when we were in the cabin. She confessed her feelings first, and I fell right in line, knowing it would be safe to tell her how I felt. I had plans to tell her about Cadance. I just wanted to find a time when it would work. I realize now that time would have been at the very beginning. But my stubborn ego got in the way, and I couldn't fathom telling her that I was left the night before my wedding."

Ryland nods as he sits back in his chair. "When did you tell her to drop out of the deal?"

"Early on," I say. "And I offered her an out many times. I'd offer her the out now if I knew she'd take it. I'd give her the land, I'd give up my fucking cabin, anything, and I mean anything, to just at least make this right."

Ryland slowly nods his head. "Good answer." He continues to study me. "I don't like what you did, but it seems Aubree was equally involved in the reason she married you. Regarding the rest, that seems to be between the two of you, but I will tell you that she doesn't trust easily, especially men. The fact that she trusted you enough to enter into some marriage deal tells me you've made an impression on her. Now it's up to you if that impression will be lasting."

"I knew you loved her," Hattie whispers. When her eyes meet mine, she adds, "And I knew she loved you. I could see it. She was so different. Lighter, happier. Like the weight of the world was no longer resting on her shoulders. Since you've gotten here, I've seen a shift in her behavior. She's smiled more. She's talked more. She's done things like the burlesque show that she wouldn't have done before. You've made an impact in her life, Wyatt, and I just need to say, if you're not serious about this, if you're not serious about her, then please walk away now. Don't hurt her any more than you already have. I know Cassidy would say the same thing. We want her to love and be happy. I think she could be happy with you, but only if you're in it for the long haul."

"I understand," I say. "And you have my word that I'm serious about this. I want her for the long haul. I want to be the man she trusts and loves. The one she can depend on other than her brother. I want to be the man who deserves her love back."

Hattie nods. "Then good luck. She's not going to give in easily."

"She's going to put up one hell of a fight. Good luck digging yourself out," Ryland says, leaning back in his chair. "Also, you owe me at least five nights of babysitting of my choosing. Mainly so I can see how serious you are at being in our lives, especially Mac's and Aubree's."

"Make it ten, then," I say.

Ryland leans over the table and holds out his hand. "Deal."

Chapter Twenty-Four

AUBREE

I stare at my reddened eyes in the mirror and shake my head. "What a stupid day," I mutter.

I'm all cried out. I'm emotionally spent. And all I want to do now after a long shower, some mindless scrolling through social media, and my dinner, which consisted of an apple, is go to bed.

Wyatt hasn't even bothered returning to the guest house, and for a moment, I was worried that perhaps Ryland forced him away, but then I dropped the thought because I shouldn't be worried about him. I should be furious, wishing he'd never come back to this guest house, but unfortunately, that's not how love works.

Because despite feeling heartbroken, I miss him. I hate that he did this to us. I hate that he didn't talk to me. I hate that he hid the truth, as if he was too ashamed to tell me anything. He knows so much about me. How did it happen that I skipped the part of getting to know him?

Exhausted, I finish brushing my teeth and then move into the bedroom just as Wyatt walks through the door. When our eyes meet, he gently smiles but doesn't say anything. I take in his already formed black eye and his fat lip. Ryland got him good.

Needing to ignore him, I move to my side of the bed, plug my phone in, and turn away from where I know he'll be sleeping. I meant what I said, I will earn this land, even if that means sleeping in the same bed as Wyatt for the next year. If I learned anything through the years of abuse from my father, it's how to persevere.

I hear him move around, getting ready for bed, but I keep my eyes shut, not wanting to look at him. After a few minutes, I hear him check the locks on the door and then the bed dips from the weight of his body. I expect him to move in close, but when he doesn't, I realize he's gotten the hint.

It's better off this way.

I curl into my pillow, let out a sigh, and try to focus on falling asleep, but with every passing second when his arm isn't wrapped around me, I realize this will be so much harder than I thought.

That's until he says, "I met her a few years ago in a coffee house." What is he talking about? "She was trying to sell her family's coffee, and I was writing. She spilled the coffee everywhere, and I helped her pick it up. I thought she was pretty, so I asked her out on a date. Our relationship was easy. There wasn't much substance to it now that I think about it, but at the time, I wasn't really aware what true love was."

He's talking about Cadance.

And what does he mean by not being aware at the time of what true love really is? Is he referring to the fact that he knows what it is now?

"I asked her to marry me, she said yes, and then it was wedding planning. I got lost in the mix of it all and had book deadlines. Now that I think about it, I didn't notice how much she was pulling away. The night before our wedding, she came to me and said she didn't love me anymore and didn't want to get married. I was devastated. But I think that devastation stemmed more from embarrassment than anything because as time went on, I started to realize that maybe I hadn't been in love with her like I thought."

He shifts on the bed but doesn't move closer to me.

"What made all of this glaringly obvious was when you came into my life. I quickly found out that the feelings I had for Cadance were nothing compared to the way I feel for you, Aubree. What I had with Cadance was surface level. What I feel for you rides so much deeper than anything I've ever felt. And I know you don't want to hear it, not after holding back things you should know about me, but I will spend every night for the next year showing you just how much you mean to me, how connected I am to you, and how much I love you."

I squeeze my eyes shut as my throat starts to tighten.

No, he did not just say that.

He did not just confess his love.

I . . . I've wondered, questioned, hoped that possibly he felt the same way, but now . . . now, it feels weird. Now, it doesn't feel real. It feels cheapened and less.

So I don't say anything. I stay silent, and I close my eyes.

One night down, over three hundred to go.

KEEPING my fuzzy socks on since it's a chilly night, I slip into bed while Wyatt is in the bathroom taking a shower. I spent the entire day out on the farm helping Parson and Echo, getting my hands dirty and trying to erase the feeling of last night.

It helped, up until the point that I had to have dinner with Ryland and the family. Wyatt was there, but he mainly interacted with Mac and played with her, which of course Mac was obsessed with. She dressed him up with horse ears, and together, they played with Chewy Charles and Chewy Chonda. He also helped put her to bed while I snuck out and showered. When he returned to the guest house, he smiled and went straight to the bathroom.

It's cordial but awkward.

I plug my phone in, and I turn away from Wyatt's side like I did last night just as he exits the bathroom. He locks up the guest house and then slips into bed.

He turns toward me, and I hold my breath, wondering if he will wrap his arm around me tonight, but he doesn't. Instead, he says, "There are some things I never told Cadance because I was ashamed to share them with her, just like I was ashamed to share things with you."

My body stiffens at the sound of his voice.

"My dad is a perfectionist. I love him very much and have a great relationship with him, but I also learned to suppress many of my misgivings to ensure I was doing the right thing in his mind. He wanted me to be a software engineer or a banker, something that offered stability. He didn't like that I wanted to write, but he supported it. It wasn't until I proved my worth with my pen that he accepted me for who I was. I'm not saying this to gather pity from you. I'm telling you this because I want you to know where I come from."

I wet my lips, listening intently.

"I think I put too much pressure on myself to look perfect on the outside when, in reality, it's the furthest thing from the truth. I've wanted to put on a show of no mistakes and shortcomings, so I'd never disappoint. That's carried on through my adult life. I don't want to disappoint the people around me, my friends, my publisher, my agent . . . my readers. And by suppressing who I truly am, I didn't allow myself to fully open up to you. I'm sorry, Aubree. You deserve so much better."

I understand what that feeling is like . . . to want to always be perfect and never show an ounce of weakness.

"So here is something not so perfect about me. I spent weeks on Laurel's couch after the wedding was cancelled, staring at the ceiling and wasting my life away. It wasn't until she forced me to take a shower did I start moving again. And when I took my clothes off to change, I singed the hairs in my nostrils from the putrid smell radiating from my armpits."

The smallest of smiles peeks past my lips.

It's very small, but it's there.

"The smell was so bad, I nearly passed out and cracked my head open on the sink. Luckily, I held it together enough to wash up. But I did leave a body imprint on her couch, one that's still there. I know now that depression wasn't from missing Cadance but from being imperfect." He moves an inch closer and lowers his voice. "But being imperfect is what makes us human, something I'm starting to accept. Good night, Aubree. I love you."

〔▭〕

I STEP out of the bathroom and find Wyatt sitting on the edge of the bed. I stayed later at the main house to work out some logistics with Hattie in The Almond Store and the chickens we have coming in soon.

When I got back to the guest house, Wyatt was already showered and ready for bed, so I took my time getting ready, thinking he'd fall asleep, but nope, he's been sitting on the edge of the bed this whole time, waiting for me. Not wanting to go around him, I enter the bed from the foot of it and then slide into the sheets from there.

He stands and checks the locks like every night before slipping under the covers, but like the other two nights, he moves another inch closer so I can feel his body heat.

We have yet to talk or interact other than his one-sided conversations at night, and when Hattie or even Echo ask me how it's going, I just tell them that we're living together but not talking. I don't miss the sad look on Hattie's face every time I tell her nothing's going on, but she's just like Cassidy, hoping for love for everyone.

When I close my eyes, pretending to fall asleep, he says, "You looked really pretty today. You look pretty every day, but I love when you wear overalls. I love when you have a bandanna tied up in your hair, and I love when you don't wear makeup. Your freckles pop through, and it's almost like I can truly see you unguarded. Today was one of those days when I was reminded, like a kick to the gut, just how beautiful you are."

My teeth fall on my top lip as I try not to let his words or the proximity of his body affect me. It feels like when he was trying to make me comfortable with his kisses all over again. Slowly and surely, he chipped away every night. And just like the kisses, I feel like it's working.

"I know I never told you about the first time I ever met you, and I don't know if you even remember it, but it was at Clarke and Cassidy's rehearsal. You wore this green dress that clung to your curves with this scoop neckline. You caught my eye immediately, and Clarke told me to keep to myself, that I was not to bother you, especially since you were younger than me. But that didn't stop me from stealing glances throughout the night. And at one point, you were leaning forward, talking to Cassidy at the table, and the neckline of your dress dipped. Fuck, did I take a good look at your cleavage. That night, it's all I fucking thought about, so when you showed up at the wedding wearing another low-cut dress, I nearly wept."

I can't hold back. I let out a small snort because how ridiculous.

"When I realized the dress had a high slit, I cried into my napkin." He scoots in another inch, and now it feels like there is but a mere centimeter between us. "I didn't know at the time that the crush I had for you would turn into a full-blown case of love, but here I am." His finger runs along my hip, and I still, my breath caught in my throat. "I knew there was something special about you back then. I wish I'd have approached you, asked you out, done something to make that connection with you because I think about all the things in life we could have experienced together. You could have held my hand when I found out Clarke died—one of the worst days of my life, a day I don't talk about much. We weren't that close, but that's what rocked me because we could have been if I'd put in more effort, one of the biggest regrets of my life. And when Cassidy passed, I could have been there for you, for the family, for Mac.

507

I know it's a would-have, could-have, should-have moment, but making a move on you back then would have been one of the smartest decisions I ever made. Good night, Aubree. I love you."

⊏⊐

HATTIE: *What do you think he's going to tell you tonight?*

I stare down at my phone as Wyatt is in the bathroom once again getting ready.

I had dinner with Hattie and Echo tonight, making it a girls' night, and I told them all about Wyatt and the things he's been saying to me at night. Of course Hattie was head over heels in love with the stories, while Echo took a more calming approach and asked me how I felt about it.

I told her it felt like he was wearing me down, making me forget why I was mad in the first place. She reminded me it was because he never opened up to me and that put things back into perspective, because now, it feels like he's an open book, like I can read him so clearly.

Aubree: *I don't know, but I'm worried.*

Hattie: *Why are you worried?*

Aubree: *Because I don't want him to say something to me that will break down my wall.*

Hattie: *A wall that's already cracked.*

Aubree: *Exactly.*

Hattie: *Would it be so bad if you did let down that wall, Aubree?*

Aubree: *Yes. I don't want to get hurt again.*

Hattie: *I can understand that, but a part of me thinks that you're not giving him the chance that he deserves.*

Aubree: *You think I should give him another chance?*

Hattie: *Absolutely. He didn't tell you the truth about his past. That's awful, and I get it, but he's telling you now. He's telling you he loves you. He's making the moves to be a part of your life, your forever life. Open up to him and give him the chance.*

Aubree: *And if he hurts me?*

Hattie: *He won't. From the conversation he had with Ryland and me, I can promise you, he won't.*

Wyatt takes that moment to exit the bathroom, freshly showered and looking so good in a pair of boxer briefs and nothing else. He checks the locks on the door, and when he turns to face me in bed and I'm not curled away from him, he smiles.

"Hey, you."

I press my lips together and quietly say, "Hey." Before he can respond or before I can take in his reaction, I turn away from him and plug my phone in. I rest my head on my pillow and curl my knees up toward my chest as he slides into bed. This time, he leaves no space between us as his hand lands on my hip.

"I was thinking about what I wanted to talk to you about tonight, and all that came to mind was our wedding day. I'm not sure we ever truly talked about it. We went from saying I do, to taking pictures, to dancing and eating, to straight to an airplane. We never reflected on the day. But I want to tell you"—his hand crawls up my hip to my side—"that was one of the happiest moments in my life because I felt you were my person that day. You became my person. It happened quickly, but every time I looked into your eyes, I felt like I was looking into the future. It felt like all my insecurities were washed away, all my thoughts on what love is were erased from my memory, and a new seed was planted."

His hand slides over my stomach, and I lean into his hold.

"Those days in the cabin, it was everything I could have asked for, Aubree. But I want so many more nights there with you. I want to take you there during the holidays, spend our anniversary there, take Mac down there and create memories with her, but most importantly, I need you to know this." His voice grows deeper as he says, "If I had to choose, if I had to give up the cabin to be with you, to gain back your trust, to earn your love, I'd do it without even thinking. I can always create new memories in a new cabin, but I can't replace you. I can't replicate this feeling I have when you're around me." His hold on me grows tighter as my breath shallows. He moves his lips closer to my ear, a mere whisper away. "You are what I care about. You are my end goal, Aubree. Only you."

I lean against him, to the point that when he tugs on my stomach, I roll to my back, and I'm staring up at him. His hand moves up to my face, where his thumb strokes my cheek before he tucks a piece of hair behind my ear.

"I love you, Aubree, so fucking much, and I plan on proving that to you every day. Not just with my words but with my actions." He leans in, and I give in, letting him take hold of my heart again. He brings his forehead to mine, and my heart bursts. My mind is made up. I don't think I can go another night without him wrapped around me, with me holding in these feelings I have for him.

"I . . . I love you, Wyatt," I say, finding my voice.

He lifts just enough to look me in the eyes. "Fuck, are you serious right now?"

The look of shock. The watery eyes, it's almost funny enough to smile. But I hold myself together as I nod.

"Very serious, Wyatt. I never stopped."

"Baby," he says, stroking my face. "Fuck, I'm so sorry. I'm sorry that you had to hear about my past from Cadance and Wallace and that you had to experience them at all. I should have protected you better, and I swear, moving forward, I'll do just that. Above anything else, you are my number one priority."

"You're mine too," I say as I touch his chest. "I . . . I just want you to be honest and open with me. I know there's still so much to learn, but when I ask you something, please tell me the truth."

"I will," he says. "I know that trying to protect you from the truth only hindered our relationship. I won't do it again. Please just tell me that we're okay, that we will be okay, that . . . that this marriage is still real."

I smile up at him and run my hand to the back of his neck. I look into the eyes of a man I never saw coming, and I realize that the farmland was the reason I married him, but I'll stay because of who he is as a man.

The loyalist.

The protector.

The lover.

The jokester.

The rock I've needed for so long.

"It's so real," I say just before he brings his lips to mine, and we kiss.

His lips control mine as they open, and our tongues meet. His hand drives up my shirt, removing it in an instant and leaving me naked in his arms. He lifts up for a breath and stares down at me, his eyes in total wonderment.

"Fuck me, I'm so lucky."

I pat his cheek. "You really are."

He throws his head back and laughs before he moves down my body and spreads my legs.

On the contrary, I think I'm the lucky one.

Epilogue

WYATT

"What do you think?" Ethel asks as she approaches me, wearing a green velvet kaftan with her hair done in an updo. "I think it came out beautifully, and have you seen the line outside?"

I take in the living room of the inn. Ethel transformed it into a miniature book signing with two other authors she had met along her journeys. She arranged everything. All I had to do was announce that I'd be signing at Five Six Seven Eight and show up.

Three tables are lined up side by side. She decorated them each in fall colors, which goes with the theme of the signing: Fall In Love With Books. There are orange, gold, and red leaf garland strung around the room, mums and pumpkins gathered together and stacked on hay bales and wagons throughout the inn. Cider donuts and warm apple cider are being served. She has prepared a set list for her to casually sing while people visit and we're signing books. Honestly, it's a really nice setup.

"You did a spectacular job," I say. "I'm really impressed, Ethel."

"Thank you," she says. "You're sitting in the middle. Let me go check on the girls and see if they're ready."

She takes off while I'm left in the living room by myself. Aubree and Hattie are showing up in a little bit. I know they're excited about the signing. Ryland and Hayes are taking Mac up to the redwoods for a fall hike, and the movers we hired are packing up the house as we speak.

We've spent the past few weeks helping Ryland figure out what he wants to sell, keep, and store for the big move. He ended up buying the Victorian house after he showed it to Mac, who was more than happy to move. We've actually never seen her happier, which has given Ryland an ounce of relief.

In the past few days, Aubree and I, along with Hattie, have spent some time turning Mac's room into a horse lover's paradise. We're talking a horse mural, horse bedding, and horse curtains. It's unlike anything I've ever seen, and we know she'll freak out.

I can't wait to show it to her.

On days that we haven't been helping Ryland, Aubree and I have settled into a level of comfort that is so real, like we should've been doing this all along. At night, we bring my computer on the bed, she curls into me, and we look at furniture, paint samples, and different ways to decorate the farmhouse and make it our own. We've talked about expanding the second floor and making a large main bedroom and adding a guest bedroom on the first floor for when Mac stays the night. It will take some time, but we want to make the house our forever home.

We've talked about kids and if she wants them, if I want them, and we both agreed that we're happy with helping with Mac, but Aubree doesn't feel—at the moment—that she is equipped to raise her own kid. She's still fighting demons from her childhood. I told her she's a wonderful aunt and the way she interacts with Mac is awe-inspiring. She'd be a great mom one day, but I don't want to push her. It's not a never-say-never situation. It's just a not-right-now situation, which I'm fine with.

As for Hattie, well, she's still waiting on that ring from Hayes.

At this point, I think he's just holding off because he truly wants to surprise her. I think he's waiting until she gives up all hope, and then he'll spring it on her. I know the minute he proposes, though, we'll be in full-on wedding mode.

Laurel and her girlfriend, Rhonda, broke up a few weeks ago but then recently got back together. Rhonda seems to really like Laurel, but Laurel is unhappy and is considering moving closer to Almond Bay and broke up with Rhonda because of that. Well, Rhonda came back and said she'd go anywhere Laurel went, so my best friend might be moving closer.

And for the cabin, Wallace tried to speak with the lawyer and call fraud on me, but the lawyer said as long as the marriage stands, Wallace can't do anything about it. We're celebrating Christmas in Canoodle this year with Ryland and Mac. It's going to be magical.

"Ah, there he is," a woman says from the side. I turn to find two women, standing side by side, one with thick-rimmed glasses and black hair, the other dressed in what I can only describe as classic Victorian garb with her hair piled on the top of her head.

"Hello," I say. "Can I help you?"

"You're W.J. Preston, are you not?"

"I am," I say to the woman with the glasses.

She stiffly holds out her hand and says, "Allow me to introduce myself and my comrade. My name is Keiko, and this is Victoria. I'm withholding last names for the purpose of security and well-being."

"Okay," I say, a chuckle on the tip of my tongue.

"We are avid and voracious readers. Victoria pens some sensational historical novels while some have reviewed them as being the real cat's meow."

"Keiko, please," Victoria says.

"This gentleman needs to understand he's in the presence of grandeur, a noblewoman of the written word."

"Well, I'm honored," I say, loving every second of this.

"You see, we accumulated friendship through the interwebs. I reside in the Windy City, and Victoria is a resident of Port Snow,

Maine. Through the written word, we found commonality and together have initiated the first installment of fan fiction based on your novel, *Don't Look In The Window*."

"Oh that's—"

"The ending was so ghastly abhorrent, we took it upon ourselves to make the wrong you did into a right."

Ehhh . . .

"It has now been written the way that the writing gods intended it," Victoria says, patting me on the shoulder.

"That's, uh, that's great," I say, trying not to be insulted. Sure, the ending of that book wasn't widely received by everyone, but is rewriting it in fan fiction necessary?

"We shall email you the eighty-five pages of corrections we've made as well as the alternate ending. We highly suggest you take a look at it and make adjustments."

"Keiko, Victoria, what are you doing? I told you not to talk to him." Rylee Ryan, famous romance author, walks up to us.

Keiko pushes her glasses up on her nose. "It was imperative he knew about the embarrassing attempt at a plot twist."

Rylee points behind her toward her table and says, "Go over there and keep your mouths closed, or else I'm never taking you to one of these again."

Heads turned down, Keiko and Victoria move toward the window.

I wave to them and say, "It was nice meeting you."

"Sorry about that," Rylee says. "I hope they didn't hurt your feelings."

I wave dismissively at her. "Nothing I haven't heard or read online before." I hold my hand out to her. "I'm Wyatt, you must be Rylee."

"That's me. How do you know Ethel?"

"Moved here. I married Aubree Rowley, who is part owner of The Almond Store."

"Oh my gosh, I love that store. It's like the California version of The Lobster Landing."

"What's that?" I ask.

"It's a shop in my town of Port Snow. Sells the best fudge."

"Here she is," Ethel says, guiding a very pregnant woman into the living room. "Wyatt, Rylee, this is Rosie Bloom, author of *The Virgin Romance Novelist*. Her movie is set to shoot next summer. I met her while I was in New York for an award. Lovely woman, this is her second child. Her husband, Henry, is back home with their first."

"Rosie," I say as I hold my hand out to her. "It's nice to meet you. When are you due?"

"A month and a half," she says. "But I wish today."

We chuckle as Rylee introduces herself. "I have triplets back home with my husband, but we adopted. I can't imagine how uncomfortable you must be."

"Triplets?" she asks. "I might take this raging sciatica over triplets."

"I'd be careful what you wish for," Rylee says.

"Let's get you seated," Ethel says, leading Rosie over to her table.

"Well, have a good signing," Rylee says before taking off as well.

"You too," I reply just as I catch Aubree walking through the door of the inn with Hattie next to her. Immediately, I feel at home as she walks up to me. I wrap my arm around her waist and pull her into my chest. "There's my girl," I say right before placing a kiss on her lips. I keep it short and sweet, but with a touch of tongue just so she knows what to expect later.

"Is everything all set?" She glances around.

"Yup," I say. "I actually met two readers already. They told me how they changed the ending of my book to suit a more popular plot twist better. Made me feel . . . magical."

She chuckles and pats me on the chest. "Good, you need someone to knock you down a peg or two."

"Babe, you do that all on your own."

"Doesn't hurt to have others participate as well." She stands on her toes and kisses me one last time, and I feel so goddamn lucky that this woman claims me as hers. That I found someone who understands me, appreciates me, leans on me. She's everything I could have asked for, and I've spent every day since we got back together showing her just how much I appreciate her.

I still look back on the day I was out on Laurel's deck, eating a cookie while she devised the plan for me to come to Almond Bay. At the time, I thought it was insane, but I was just desperate enough to follow through. And I'm so glad that I did because I couldn't imagine a day in my life without Aubree by my side.

A marriage of convenience.

Who knew such a book trope would become a reality?

And who knew that reality would turn into a dream.

I sure as hell didn't, but I'm so grateful she married me for land because now I get her hand for life.